THE KARMA CONSPIRACY

Robert Dresner

This book was printed in the United States of America, and
published by Virga Press, LLC.

To order additional copies of this book, please contact:
Virga Press, LLC
P.O. Box 4881
Boulder, CO 80304
www.robertdresner.com
www.virgapress.com

For all those who went,
and never returned.

"This is indeed India! The one sole country under the sun that is endowed with an imperishable interest for alien prince and alien peasant, for lettered and ignorant, wise and fool, rich and poor, bond and free, the one land that all men desire to see, and having seen once, by even a glimpse, would not give that glimpse for the shows of all the rest of the globe combined."

Mark Twain,
More Tramps Abroad

Preface

Following my graduation from college, I decided to travel through India. Perhaps I had read too many Hermann Hesse books—the author's influence on me was profound. I was very curious about life. I had pressing need to find myself, and to make sense of the afflictions of the world.

I had hoped that a journey to India might put things in perspective, if not provide some answers to the meaning of life. I suppose I was looking for God; I eventually left India thinking that God would have to find me.

I didn't fail to meet my objectives as much as I had exhausted myself in this remarkable process of self-discovery. Upon my return, I felt a deep and abiding impulse to share this experience with others, so I began to write this book in 1976—less than one year after I had returned from India. The memories were fresh. Though time was compressed, and certain events were crafted in the interest of story-telling, this account is essentially true.

I finished the first draft in 1980 and tried to find a publisher, but none were interested. I was told that the subject matter was already passé, and I was disheartened. But for the encouragement of several people, I would not have continually rewritten the manuscript every five years or so, for the past thirty years.

Pat Loud, my agent at that time, believed that *The Karma Conspiracy* was, among other things, a social document, a dramatic profile of a special time and place, and that it might prove valuable in twenty years. More than thirty years have passed, and I hope this is true.

Herb Gilbert, my mentor, was the Managing Editor at *Newsweek* (trade books). He also had a great deal of faith in me. If not for Herb, I doubt if I would have written another book. He told me to never stop writing, and this book is also dedicated to Herb's faith in me.

Vincent Ragone simply saw the future. When I told him that I had begun to write about my experiences in India, he said that I was recording them for a lot of other people who went to India and never came back, and for many others who would never go. He also told me that *The Karma Conspiracy* would be the first of many books. I guess I was flattered, but at that time, I could hardly imagine writing *The Astral Imperative* trilogy or *The Coming*.

I am truly humbled by the support I have received from so many others, especially Sue Richards and Sharon and Rudi Baumann, who were also there at the beginning, typing and editing the original manuscript.

I've written six novels in the past thirty years, yet the creative process remains a mystery to me. I sit in front of a computer, or a sheet of paper, and my characters speak for themselves. With a little help from my wonderful editing team, Arsen Kaskashian and Stephanie Walker, these characters create a cogent and entertaining story. I would also like to thank Grace Moreno for believing in me, Sita Sharan for her help with the glossary, John Ezell for his graphic design, Richard Abrams for his critical reviews, and Joel Broida for his keen eye and invaluable support..

Writing this novel was quite challenging, if only because it was my first. The original manuscript was 850 pages long. More than half has withered away over time, leaving the essence of the story behind. I adore this essence, which is the spirit that moved an entire generation to seek a better life, and I am privileged to share it with you.

Other books by Robert Dresner

THE ASTRAL IMPERATIVE
Vol. I The Dream
Vol. II The Machine
Vol. III ReGenesis

THE COMING
SATORI BLUES

THE KARMA CONSPIRACY

1

It was another time, another place. Another life it seemed, when heroes were born in their own minds, when people dared to be different, when difference was a virtue.

It was 1969. The battle of ages and ideas had already been joined, some left, some right; Max Rild opted for the transcendental. He was young and impetuous, only twenty-four years old, and he wanted to find God.

In India, Max thought, the land of his dreams.

It was a beautiful October morning in the Persian Desert. The sky was electric, so vast and bright and blue that it was nearly hypnotic. A long and wispy white cloud straddled the eastern horizon. A cool, steady breeze heralded the change of seasons. The earth was parched and desolate, a seemingly endless expanse of shifting sand, jagged rock and cracked, red clay.

Max was enchanted by the contrast between earth and sky, if not fatigued by the journey. He had been traveling over land for eight days: from Athens, to Istanbul, to Tehran. By the time he left the holy city of Mashhad, his logic had become lost in his weariness.

The old Mercedes bus screamed at every downshift, plunging ever more deeply into the vortex of listlessness. The filthy canvas

Glossary in back.

window shades snapped in the breeze as Max watched his mind unravel in the desert void.

There were camels and horses toiling in the early morning sun on the edge of town, then vultures picking at skeletons on the barren plain. There were men at work on the narrow two-lane road, filling cracks in the sand-swept asphalt, then no one in sight. There were rows of white-washed houses curling out of the city, then isolated earthen domes emerging from the desert floor.

Max read a book to pass the time until the incessant groan of the engine rattled his concentration. Tired of looking out the window at the hypnotic ebb and flow of the desert sands, he eventually became lost in thought, projecting himself into the future, sitting at the feet of a great master in India, then reflecting upon the distant past—his mind filling with incongruous images of people and things.

Such was the power of the desert; it sucked Max's mind like a vacuum until the bus stopped for morning prayer. Max watched in awe as his fellow passengers spread their ritual prayer rugs over the sand, faced Mecca, and paid homage to their desert Maker. It was at this singular moment, as the prayer rose up to the heavens, when Max's mind was stopped.

His body expanded to include the entire scene in front of him: the people, the prayer, the sand and the sky; for one fleeting moment, observer and observed merged and Max's self-identity was erased. He had, inadvertently, entered a stream of consciousness that few dared to imagine, and fewer still would ever experience. Whether by luck, by fate, or by the sheer force of will that drove him across the world, Max had already found what he was looking for.

But he was still so young and driven, and so greedy for life, that he could not appreciate the experience of a lifetime. Returning to his thoughts, he spent the remainder of the journey searching for the consciousness that had already escaped him.

*   *   *

Herat was a dusty old town with sand-blown streets, weather-beaten houses, horses tied to hitching posts, and a lot of surly looking men wearing dirty white pajami, with vests and frayed western sport jackets. Many were armed with shotguns. Others had six-guns strapped to their legs.

Max arrived at sunset, and as dusk receded into darkness, he prowled the small village square—from bus to bus, from one wooden stall to another—in search of an overnight ride to Kandahar and a decent meal. He was walking down a narrow street, immersed in thought, his eyes pinned to the ground, when he was nearly trampled by a mighty white stallion bearing a fierce-looking rider—a tall man wearing a thick, wool vest.

The horse neighed and reared up on its hind legs, backing Max against a mud wall. The rider, tightening his grip on the reigns, remained upright and unengaged. His eyes fixed ahead, he never looked at Max as he passed him on the evolutionary scale of machismo.

Max loved the grittiness of the place. He even thought about spending a few days in Herat, but was swept along by the momentum of his journey. Unable to find a ride, he eventually settled on a plate of stale rice and beans and the inevitability of taking an early morning bus.

He was fighting off a spoonful of flies when a small canvas-covered army truck stopped in front of the stall. He didn't see the tall brunette climb out of the back of the truck, but she noticed him. Not very tall, but dark and handsome, Max tended to attract the attention of women.

"You goin' to Kandahar?" she called out to him in a Texas drawl.

"If you are," Max said, smiling at his apparent good fortune.

The woman returned his smile and placed her hands on her curvaceous hips. She wasn't very pretty, but she was sexy: long legs, heavy breasts pressing against a tight, white t-shirt, and a round butt wrapped in a pair of faded blue jeans.

"We're leavin' in a few minutes," she said. "So if you're comin', you gotta be comin' now."

Max swallowed another spoonful of rice, shouldered his small bicycle pack, paid the driver, a middle-aged Afghani army officer, and followed the woman to the back of the truck. Once inside, Max saw two young soldiers sitting across the aisle from another young westerner.

"I'm Mary Beth," the boisterous brunette finally said. "An' this is my old man, Hans—he's German. An' these two dumb fuckers are Mohammed." She sat between Max and Hans.

The soldiers smiled, not comprehending the abuse.

Hans was tall, slender and stoic. He welcomed Max with a strong handshake and deferred to his girlfriend's crass behavior throughout the trip. She cursed and rambled and raged at everyone and everything that came to her vulgar mind. Worst of all, she continued to tempt and taunt the soldiers with her sexuality.

Their eyes never left her chest, and Max began to wonder if they would kill him and Hans in an effort to rape her. It was a sexually repressive society, these soldiers were heavily armed, and they were the law: How hard would it be for them to have their way with Mary Beth and drop them all in a few unmarked graves in the sand?

"Don't you think the boys have seen enough?" Max finally snapped, fearing the worst.

"You kiddin'? They ain't seen nothin' yet," Mary Beth retorted, locking her hands behind her head to reveal the fullness of her breasts.

"And this is okay with you?" Max challenged Hans.

Hans said. "She is okay if she can be free to do what she wants."

Free and dumb, Max thought, leaning back against the side of the truck, wishing he had stayed behind in Herat. He was staring out the back of the truck into a luminous cloud of sand, when they turned off the road and came to a sudden and frightful stop in the night.

Mary Beth fell silent. Hans froze. Max felt like running out of the truck, out of his mind, out of his body and into another life. All waited in a terrifying silence until the driver ordered them out.

All were greatly relieved to find a shack functioning as a restaurant on the side of the road.

"Here we eat," the officer said, escorting them to a large wobbly table near the front door.

The proprietor welcomed them, while his two teenage sons served tea and biscuits under the stars. Max had never seen so many stars.

"It's almost unreal," he said.

"Reality's what you make of it," Mary Beth said before turning her attention to the teenagers and titillating them.

"And she is always making the most of it," Hans added. The flickering light from a kerosene lamp at the center of the table cast shadows against the walls of the shack as he spoke. "We meet in Athens. I have no money and no woman. I want to see the world and Mary Beth tells me she can pay if I go with her to India. She is born again to follow the true path of Christ to India and to search for the lost tribe of Israel in Kashmir."

Max was surprised by the serious nature of their quest, but not unaware of the significance. Among other things, Max had read the Aquarian Gospel wherein Christ's life is marked by two holy pilgrimages to India before his crucifixion: to take teachings from various masters who prepared him for the rigors of the cross, and following his resurrection, when he returned to India to minister to the lost tribe of Israel in Kashmir.

Now staring at Mary Beth, Max was trying to fathom her crude and dangerous behavior in light of her sacred goal, when he noticed the poster nailed to the shack wall above her head.

"You know?" the officer began, tapping Max's shoulder.

"What?"

The officer pointed to the poster displaying a large dagger drawn into the bloody heart of a Star of David. Across the top, it read in English: **DEATH TO JEWS!**

The officer glared at Max before continuing. "You like Jew?" he bitterly asked.

Max was further stung by his contempt. While he fumbled for an answer, the officer translated the question to the proprietor and his sons.

Hans looked at Mary Beth; she looked at Max with concern. Religion was a far more deadly issue than sex in this part of the world.

"I like everyone," Max finally replied.

Though diplomatic, the response was insufficient and the tension mounted. Max squirmed in his chair while the officer translated his reply to his Muslim countrymen.

"You are Jew?" the officer pressed, his hand gripping the butt of his gun.

All eyes locked on Max.

2

The sun set over the Khyber Pass with grace and majesty. The sky turned pink. The jagged peaks turned gold. It was an odd and fleeting moment of beauty in view of a long and savage history as a "no man's land" and a vital link to unknown ravages and riches going east and west. A few great leaders, like Genghis Khan and Alexander the Great, had swept through Afghanistan. Lesser empires, like the British Raj, which was ruled by lesser men, were disemboweled at the mouth of the Pass that roared like a lion and writhed like a serpent between Afghanistan and Pakistan, between the rule of law and the impulsive nature of unruly men, between warriors and wanderers—and women in peril.

There was a trace of light on the ridge and a veil of darkness creeping over the valley as the wretched old bus came to a stop. Diane Appel followed the other passengers off the bus, thinking it was a brief respite from the long and arduous journey that had begun in Kabul earlier that morning.

She thought wrong: it was a hold-up. Kalib, a local bandit, and his group of men, encircled the passengers and had already robbed the bus driver before Diane realized what was going on.

"It is a bandit tax," Kalib said, approaching her. "All must pay something and no one will be hurt."

Diane's shock stymied her fear. Her humor belied her tension. "You take checks?"

Kalib laughed and told her not to worry. "From women and the poor, we take nothing. Such is the law of our village. We take only from the men what they can afford, a watch, a radio, a few Afghanis. We never take everything, only something."

Diane was momentarily relieved, if not charmed. "You mean like Robin Hood? You know Robin Hood?"

Kalib shrugged. "He was a great hero, Memsahib, but a very bad businessman. We are not so much like him because we keep everything for ourselves. That is why we are so rich."

Diane found it hard to believe. The bandits' weaponry may have been costly, but their appearance gave a poor impression. Dressed in dirty cotton pajami and rubber thongs, short black hair and thick black mustaches, the gang looked more like a hungry band of Mexican banditos than rich Princes of the Pass—except Kalib. He was the tallest and proudest of the lot. He had two ammunition belts crisscrossing his stout chest and two pearl-handled .45s strapped to his waist. And he was wearing a pair of new blue jeans.

"If you say so. If I ever see you again, you can take me to your palace," Diane said, turning to board the bus.

Kalib reached for her elbow and spun her around. "I am sorry to tell you this, Memsahib, but this bus does not leave."

"You mean you're taking the bus?"

Kalib smiled. "No, but tonight this bus will stay here. There is no driving in the Pass after four o'clock. It is too dark and dangerous."

Diane turned to the bus driver who confirmed Kalib's story. "No go," he said. "No night. Tomorrow go."

Diane was stunned and finally frightened. She was about to protest when she recalled the early morning delay. The bus, having broken down at the bottom of the Pass, was destined for an abrupt halt at the height of the Pass. It was after four o'clock and night was fast approaching. She was the only white woman on the bus.

Though dressed conservatively in an ankle-length peasant skirt and a loose cotton blouse buttoned to her neck, Diane was the only woman on the bus not fully concealed by a burka—and the sole focus of her fellow travelers' attention. Forty men stared at her as she took a measure of them: all curious, some lustful, none helpful. Two swarthy Pakistanis had already copped an "inadvertent" feel as she boarded the bus in Kabul. At the very least, she knew they would be trouble.

Diane was imagining the worst and trembling inside when another, smaller gang showed up at the bus and bid five hundred dollars for Diane. Kalib turned them away with the point of his gun before making his own offer to Diane. Her long, chestnut hair blowing in the breeze, her deep blue eyes filling with tears, Diane was trembling when Kalib spoke to her.

"It is not so safe for you to stay here in the night. But if you come with me to my village, you will not have a problem. I give you my word, Memsahib."

Diane found it hard to believe, but she was desperate. Whether out of instinct, stupidity or despair, she chose the lesser of two or more evils and followed Kalib down into the valley to his small village.

*　　　*　　　*

Perched on the edge of a treacherous cliff, the entire village consisted of several wooden shacks, a few dung huts and one old stone house. Sitting alone on the floor in a dark corner of a cold, stone room, Diane sipped a cup of hot tea and fought to maintain her composure. She was quietly terrified and began to regret her decision.

While she sulked in the dark, the bandits commanded the light at the center of the room. They ate goat and drank whiskey under the dim glare of a kerosene lamp. Kalib invited Diane to join them at the table, but she refused. The food was too greasy. The smell was nauseating. The men were intimidating. Now sick with fear and remorse, Diane wished that she were back in Kabul with her husband, David. He was a junkie, and she had enabled him to go to Afghanistan where drugs were plentiful, thinking that she would eventually wind up in India, the land of her dreams.

She had been thirteen years old, at home alone in The Bronx on a rainy Saturday afternoon, when she saw an old movie on television she would never forget: *The Razor's Edge*, based on the book by Somerset Maugham. It was a love story with an odd twist, about Larry Darrel, a young man born to wealth and privilege, who had forsaken these things, along with his ravishing fiancée, Isabelle, in an effort to find the meaning of life.

Being beautiful, Diane strongly identified with Isabelle, and she could not understand how Larry could leave her to go on such a whimsical quest. When Diane finally read the Somerset Maugham book in college, she began to understand that there was much more to true love than romance: there was a journey and the quest for self-knowledge.

Marrying David upon graduating college was a terrible mistake. Diane had a promising career as a metal sculptor when she fell in love with him, thinking that she could change him. In fact, she continued to enable him—until David tried to sell her for ten vials of morphine.

"All you have to do is take your clothes off and let the guy watch you while he jerks-off," David said.

Diane said she'd do it, then changed her mind; she was revolted by the idea and disgusted with her marriage. She waited until David was asleep before she left Kabul with half their money hoping to find a better life—now fearing for her life as Kalib and his men engaged in a rowdy game of midnight poker.

Diane tried to hide her face from them in a shadow, but her great beauty had already left a desirable impression. The long, thick, and wavy chestnut hair, the big blue eyes, the high cheekbones, the strong aquiline nose and thick lips: it was this odd combination of features that made her so desirable, and so vulnerable.

Time passed very slowly that night until a heated argument broke out at the table between Kalib and two of his men, and Diane was asked to settle it.

"They say I am a cheat," Kalib told Diane, standing over her in the dark.

"And you're not, right?"

Kalib clenched his fists. "It is not me who deals the cards," he snapped. "It is the will of Allah."

Diane cowered beneath his anger and said that she believed him.

But Kalib wanted more. He reached for her hand and said, "If you believe me, then you will show these non-believers that the will of Allah is with me tonight."

Kalib helped Diane to her feet and led her across the room to the table.

"Sit here in my seat and we will show them!" he declared.

Diane sat and stared at the combined show of riches on the table—rubies, diamonds, gold, and assorted currencies surpassing fifty thousand dollars—all piled in front of the players staring back at her.

Diane was astonished. "It's real, isn't it? You really are rich?"

Kalib shrugged. "All gifts are by the grace of Allah."

"I don't understand. Where did you get all this money? And these stones?"

Diane picked up a stunning ruby earring and studied it in the lamp light. The stone was unusually red and embedded in a white gold fleur de lis. She didn't know that these men were smugglers, whose business interests included drugs and weapons.

Kalib laughed and pointed across the table at his men. "From them I get everything. And now you will play for me and win more from them."

Diane lodged a weak protest before Kalib ordered one of his men to deal a hand of seven-card stud. Two minutes later, Diane had a pair of nines showing and nothing in the hole. She was facing a pair of jacks, a pair of kings, a probable rape, and possible death. While Kalib's men peered at their seventh and final "down" card, Diane looked up into Kalib's coal-black eyes and shuddered.

"You do not look at this last card. It is a card of faith!" Kalib declared. "It is the will of Allah."

Diane gripped the edge of the table in an effort to steady her nerve. "How much do I bet?"

"Everything," Kalib demanded. "You bet everything."

Diane burst into a cold sweat as she pushed more than ten thousand dollars in cash and jewels into the center of the table. She was on the verge of tears when she posed her last two fateful questions to Kalib: "What happens if I lose?"

Kalib twirled the edge of his mustache and responded evenly. "Allah can be merciful, but my men will want vengeance."

"What does that mean?"

"It means that you will dance for them."

Naked, she thought.

3

The mighty old behemoth hurled through the night, spewing smoke and steam in its terrific wake. The plains of northern India shook beneath the immense weight of the train. No matter how hard he tried, Shunya couldn't sleep, his mind racing the train to Mota Hari, a small town south of Nepal, where his good friend Delhi Dave had fallen on hard times. Among other things, Delhi Dave had been caught smuggling German auto parts across the Nepalese border into India and was sentenced to three years in a Mota Hari jail.

Shunya had been his partner in crime. He had put up the money for the auto parts and was responsible for bribing the proper Indian customs officials—who took the bribe and reneged on the deal. They busted Delhi Dave crossing the border the following morning.

In retrospect, Shunya realized that he had been better off selling hash, a much smaller commodity that did not compete with legitimate business and warrant such harsh punishment. In reality, Shunya couldn't wait to complete his mission of mercy and clear his conscience: get off at Patna, take a ferry across the Ganges River, catch the next train to Mota Hari, and purchase Dave's freedom.

Anxious, Shunya turned to a fellow passenger sharing the compartment with him—a fat Brahmin businessman, wrapped in a starched white dhoti, wearing an expensive Swiss watch—and asked for the time.

"Huh, ji," Shunya began in Hindi. "Kitneh bajeh hain?"

The Brahmin answered in perfect English. "It is near two o'clock in the morning. We will arrive in Patna in eighteen minutes only. It is scheduled."

Shunya stroked his long, red beard and sighed. He found it hard to believe; nothing and no one in India ever arrived on time. He began to think that the Brahmin was playing mind games, purposely confusing the young white sahib's sense of reality with unreal expectations. He was about to take issue with the Brahmin's intent when the man opened a papaya and offered to share it with him.

Shunya declined and smiled to himself. Having already spent more than two years in India, he still couldn't figure it out. The country defied logic and thrived on dichotomy. While Shunya took great pride in his own ability to reason, the greater irony escaped him: despite all the contradictions, Shunya thrived on India.

He loved India and was deeply concerned about the prospect of war with Pakistan. The mounting tension could be felt in Shunya's car. As the train sped through the night, tempers flared, arguments raged, lines were drawn. Following one particularly violent confrontation between a Hindu and a Muslim over a seat, the entire seating arrangement was changed to suit the political realities: the Hindu majority in front of the car, the Muslims in the back.

Shunya was undaunted. He kept his original seat and remained neutral. When asked for his point of view, he claimed Canadian citizenship and traveled in peace. He was tired of answering for the American government, whose policies were personally offensive and not popular in India. Given the nature of his mission, he was also loath to provoke a debate. He had 25,000 rupees in his jhola, enough money to buy Delhi Dave's freedom—he hoped—or tempt a robbery.

When the discussion in his compartment turned back to politics, Shunya wisely excused himself from conversation and headed toward the bathroom. The car was crowded, and as he picked his way over and through the tangle of humanity—clutching the jhola to his chest—he tripped over a "floating" crap game and fell onto a player sitting on the floor.

Shunya said he was sorry, and the player helped him to his feet.

"It is okay, sahib. Everything is okay," the player said.

Shunya thought so. The jhola remained intact and unopened. He felt the bulge of money through the cloth. He was nearing the bathroom when he thought he recognized the helpful player. Spinning around, he said, "I know you. I've seen you before, in Delhi, the other day?"

In particular, Shunya noted the young man's rotting, red mouth, the color and decay of his teeth indicating a predisposition for chewing betel nut.

"No, no, sahib. I come from Gaya today," the young man declared. "You can ask these people, my friends. All are from Gaya." His two friends smiled and nodded before he continued. "You will sit? You would like to play with us?"

Shunya declined and entered the bathroom, thinking this guy could not be trusted—his instinct having been honed on the streets and playgrounds of New York.

Before taking the name, Shunya, he was William James Rennet, was among the best point guards to come out of a New York City high school, the all-American kid with a crew-cut who married his high school sweetheart upon graduation and went to college on an athletic scholarship.

1962 was a good year. John Kennedy was President. The decade was filled with promise and propriety. Shunya imagined he would be a starter in college, as popular on campus as he was in high school. He wasn't prepared to warm a bench, or father a child, and was overcome by the unsettling conjunction of these events. His wife became pregnant during his freshman year in Gainesville, and he couldn't make the grades or the first team. The coach thought he was too small (five-foot-eight inches) and too "white."

Shunya dropped out of college the following year and returned to New York, where he lived in the shadow of his former greatness. Facing an era of tumultuous change and discovery, he was on the verge of becoming an anachronism. Shunya was a good husband and a good father, but he wasn't very happy and got swept up in the turmoil of the times. So he left his wife and daughter, and his country, in an effort to find himself.

He was thinking about his daughter when the train pulled into Patna at 3:00 a.m. By 3:10 he was racing the crowd to catch the last ferry across the river. An hour later he began the one-mile trek across the sand dunes to connect with the last train to Mota Hari, still clutching his jhola and schlepping a backpack filled with Alice Bailey books. He loved to read.

Unlike the train to Patna, the train to Mota Hari ran on narrow gauge tracks. It was very old, very slow, very small, and so crowded that a number of poorer passengers opted for seats on the roof. Shunya was pushing his way into a third-class car when a conductor reached for his arm.

"This is not for you, sahib," he said, leading Shunya away from the crowd. "Third class is for these poor people. You go first class, sahib. Only first class for you."

Shunya was flattered. He also figured the conductor was looking for a little baksheesh. But the conductor refused to accept his money.

"No, no, sahib. Please. Not for money. This I do for good karma."

*   *   *

The spiritual ass-kiss worked like a charm. Alone in a first class compartment, Shunya stretched out with an Alice Bailey book, *A Treatise on Cosmic Fire*, and forgot about the danger of carrying so much money. He fell asleep on page twenty-two, and was searching for God in a dream, when he was awakened by a knife at his throat.

4

It was no accident that Shunya, Diane and Max faced great danger on the same night. After all, they traveled the same perilous road to enlightenment, and they shared the same instinct for survival

Shunya wasn't about to let some knife-wielding Indian punk whip his Brooklyn ass and defeat his heroic effort to free Delhi Dave.

The young dice player, whom Shunya had recognized, held the knife at Shunya's throat. He had followed Shunya from Delhi, and he had paid the conductor a hundred rupees to set up the young sahib.

"Your money, sahib. You will give us your money," the dice player demanded, holding his knife at Shunya's throat. A second, shorter man stood behind him.

Shunya sat up, glared at the dice player's repulsive, rotting, red mouth, then removed the passport pouch that hung from his neck and gave it to him.

The dice player handed it to his backup man. Searching the pouch, the backup man found less than two hundred dollars along with several hundred rupees. The dice player was enraged; he pressed the point of the knife against Shunya's chin, drawing a trickle of blood. "I said all of it, sahib."

Shunya fought to keep his eyes away from his jhola. "It's all I got, motherfucker."

The player smiled, revealing the hideous interior of his mouth, then continued. "It is not all, sahib. I see how much you change in Delhi on the black market. You will give me all twenty-five thousand rupees in your jhola, or I will kill you with this knife."

Though frightened, Shunya's mounting rage eclipsed his fear. When the player finally reached for the bulging jhola, Shunya grabbed his wrist and punched him in the mouth.

The player fell back on the floor, unconscious, dripping blood and broken teeth.

Shunya grabbed the dropped knife and lunged at the backup man, who ran screaming down the aisle and leapt off the train.

*   *   *

"It was a lucky punch," he told Delhi Dave, arriving at the jail in Mota Hari later that same morning.

Delhi Dave laughed. "Wasn't no fuckin' luck, man. It was Brooklyn."

Shunya smiled and rubbed his aching fist.

Brooklyn formed the basis of their friendship, both having come from different Irish neighborhoods in the same borough. Both twenty-nine, their friendship was nonetheless unusual. While Shunya had spent much of his youth trying to better himself, Delhi Dave went looking for trouble. Rumor had it that Delhi Dave had ridden with the Hell's Angels before he beat a man to death in a Miami bar fight. He had also run guns to Fidel Castro in Cuba.

"Brooklyn or not, I was set-up and I didn't see it coming. The conductor had to be in on it," Shunya said.

"And my lawyer," Delhi Dave added. "He was the only other guy besides me who knew you were changing money in Delhi. An' he knew what you looked like—wit' that long, red beard anyone could-a-seen you comin' from a fuckin' mile. An' my lawyer's the one that told you to turn the dollars into rupees to make the pay off, an' he knew you would have to go to Delhi to the black market to get the best rate. The cocksucker," Delhi Dave spat between two broken front teeth, his beady, brown eyes bulging under the strain, his shaved head trembling with vengeance. Together with his flaring pug nose, Delhi Dave looked like a mad dog. "My lawyer did it an' I'm gonna make him pay for it."

With his life, Shunya thought, leaving the jail to arrange for Delhi Dave's release.

*   *   *

Diane survived the night through a measure of divine intervention. She couldn't imagine dancing naked for Kalib's men and not being taken by the force of their horny nature. She was so frightened, she could hardly stay in her seat, let alone play Kalib's cards.

Again, she looked up into Kalib's stone cold eyes and pleaded for mercy. "I can't," she agonized. "I can't."

"You can," Kalib declared. "The seventh card is God's will. It is the seventh heaven, which can only be obtained through an act of faith on earth. Believe me, Memsahib, it is the will of God who plays this game fro me. You are only the expression of His will," Kalib said.

Diane's right hand was shaking as she found the courage to turn over a third nine and take the pot.

"Dear God!" she exclaimed.

"The will of Allah," Kalib added, looking up to the wooden ceiling as if he were looking up to heaven.

Diane burst into tears and began to laugh, she was so bewildered by the remarkable turn of events.

Kalib waited for Diane to compose herself before presenting her with the ruby earrings she had admired. "For winning, and for the faith you have shown in my God," he said.

Diane was grateful and relieved, but she couldn't stop thinking about what might have happened to her if she hadn't won the hand. "I thought you'd hurt me," she said.

"Not in this house," Kalib declared, smiling upon her tearful victory. "Kalib does not punish his guests, or take orders from his men. They would not dare to hurt you. I played with you, Memsahib. It was only another game."

Diane was infuriated, but emotionally spent. She listened as Kalib explained.

"The Khyber Pass is not the Piccadilly Circus, Memsahib. There is not much for a man to do here. When the night comes to this little village, the mind is restless. There is no nightclub for dancing. There are no plays to watch, and nothing new to think. Everything is the same. In London it was different."

"You were in England?"

Kalib smiled. "Of course. For two years I studied at Oxford. It was my father's wish. But when he dies, I am to come back and oversee his business."

Diane was stunned. She looked around the cold stone room, at the poor condition of life, before continuing. "What business?"

Kalib widened his smile. "The tax business. Nothing and no one is coming through the Khyber Pass without payment."

Given the strategic location of the Pass, and looming prospect of war between Pakistan and India, the espionage business was particularly good. But Kalib didn't go into detail, and Diane didn't press the point.

True to his word, Kalib made no advance toward her and returned her to the waiting bus in the morning.

*   *   *

Max looked within himself for the answer to the fateful question: *Are you a Jew?* This posed a challenge of a biblical dimension. Does Max answer for the entire Old Testament? For the bastardization of Ishmael? For the politics of Israel? For his Jewish mother, or his Catholic father?

Max was lost in the terrifying vacancy that was his mind, fearing for his life; his eyes turning away from the scowling Afghani officer and looking out across the desert, searching for a clue in the night, when he came upon the Wisdom of Solomon.

"My mother is a Jew," Max declared. "My father is Catholic. And I am your brother."

The officer was momentarily stunned, and somewhat impressed. He translated Max's declaration to his countrymen, then raised his coffee cup and made a toast to life, liberty and the glory of Allah. The young, white sahib had balls.

Max also had the common sense to leave with the truck when Hans and Mary Beth chose to stay behind.

"To make a buck on my back," Mary Beth told Max with a wink.

Hans would pimp her. The proprietor and his sons would protect her. And the officer would send her johns.

Max was shocked by the arrangement. Brash though she was, Max could hardly imagine Mary Beth as a prostitute—plying her trade in such a primitive, Muslim country, no less. "I thought Mary Beth was born again to retrace the footsteps of Jesus."

"And we have told you that it is a path that requires money we do not have," Hans explained.

"That's one helluva way to make it—on her back," Max said.

"It is one hell of a life," Hans replied. "To be the Magdalene before the Mary."

"It's what you are that bothers me," Max shot back, before climbing into the back of the truck.

5

While Shunya headed to Nepal and Diane crossed Pakistan to India, Max pressed on to Kabul. He was determined to make it to India no matter what the danger. After all, he had been traveling this road for many years. Max was nineteen years old, still living in the Bronx, on the verge of flunking out of college, when he received a copy of *Siddhartha* from James, an old friend. "It's about God and growing up, and how much it hurts," James had said.

Max didn't know much about God, but he knew a great deal about sorrow. He had suffered quietly and deeply throughout much of his teens and always underperformed. A poor student, he had a genius IQ. He was nice enough and handsome enough to date almost any girl he liked, but was afraid to approach them. He was intrigued by the intelligence of others, but he never read a book. He was well liked in spite of his limitations, but he hated himself for no reason he could understand. He was at the bottom of despair, on the brink of suicide, when he finally read *Siddhartha*. The book saved his life and determined his fate. Upon finishing the story, Max decided to go to India.

*   *   *

Max spent one night in Kandahar before heading to Kabul, and he was continually surprised by the ruggedness of the Afghani people, the harshness of the environment and the colorfulness of the culture. The tribal women dressed in colorful halter tops and peasant dresses. The Muslim women were covered from head to foot by black burkas, seeing the world through cotton mesh veils, the world never seeing them. The men dressed in dirty white pajami, wearing colorful skull caps and white turbans. On cooler nights, they wrapped themselves in blankets.

The roads were severely pitted, the buses dilapidated, the air dry and dusty, the food so bad that Max could hardly eat. Few trees, little grass, the mountains were tall and barren. Time passed slowly on the bus, and the harshness of the journey wreaked havoc with Max's body. He was thoroughly exhausted by the time he arrived in Kabul.

Walking down the dusty streets past camels and horses and rickety old cars and rows of beggars, between cinder block buildings in various stages of rot and decay, he was struck by the unabated impoverishment and the appalling lack of greenery— but nonetheless enchanted with the place. It was so old and so primitive, yet so exotic to Max's weary eyes.

He was standing on a broken sidewalk in front of the Ansari Guest House when he met Hong Kong Rosie, a gorgeous young Chinese woman dressed in black silk.

"You are looking for a room here?" Rosie began, flashing a flirtatious smile.

Max said, "Yes."

"It is too bad, but there is no more rooms here, I think."

Max was about to reply when David Appel exited the guest house with his current roommate, a brooding young American with a black scraggly beard. David had kept a room in the guest house following Diane's departure.

"Is there a problem here?" David began. He was a tall, good-looking man with short blond hair and a spotty blond beard. His roommate walked ahead.

"No, No," Rosie said. "I think maybe he is too pretty to be a problem."

Max smiled and watched Rosie leave the premises with David. He was leering at her shapely figure when two other young Americans exited the guest house.

"Not bad, huh?" the shorter one said, following Max's eyes.

"Not bad at all," Max mused.

"She's a killer," the taller one added.

Max thought he was joking, and asked them where he could find a room.

The shorter one introduced himself as Carl said that he was welcome to stay with them.

*   *   *

Shunya had planned on returning to Delhi to get a much-needed visa extension, but he opted for a quick trip to Nepal to visit an old lama in Swayambhunath—a renowned Buddhist temple overlooking the Kathmandu Valley.

It was a beautiful evening. Dusk had just descended upon the valley and the moon was rising, shedding its white light on Mt Everest, as Shunya climbed the one hundred and eight steps to the holy old temple. Though Shunya had been to Nepal before, he never ceased to be amazed by the exotic scenery—and he never failed to think about his daughter: the greater the beauty, the greater his guilt.

He wished that she could see what he was seeing; he also knew that he could never fully explain his absence from her life. He was more than half-way up the steps to the temple, climbing with an increasingly heavy heart, when he was assailed by gang of silver monkeys. Eleven in all, Shunya counted as they surrounded him, bearing their teeth and screaming.

Surprised, but undeterred, he swung an arm at them and climbed two more steps before the monkeys tightened their circle around him, growing louder and angrier. At what? Shunya could not imagine.

Suddenly threatened, he began to look for a stick and tripped on a crack in a step. Falling steps backwards to the jeers of the monkeys, he hit his knee on the stone. Cursing the pain as he sat on a step, the monkeys pressed the attack, further tightening the circle around him, growing ever-louder and angrier.

Now thinking that they might be rabid, Shunya began to fear for his life. The great sahib, the white guy who journeyed to the East in search of darker man's God; Shunya, the Kshatriya in training, whose namesake reflected and defined the source of all energy, finally reached into his pocket for a weapon and discovered a handful of coconut candy.

Whether out of instinct or despair, he tossed the bounty to the gang, who took the loot and stopped the madness. The monkeys ran back into the night with his pride, and Shunya resumed his ever-humbling trek to the height of holiness: the one hundred and eight steps to the top of the world, each denoting a path to God. The problem was, Shunya wanted to take all roads at once, find all Gods and be all things to all people.

Now standing on the top rung of his world, Shunya looked down on the Kathmandu Valley and inhaled a vision of ten thousand flames glowing in the night, making dinner, making warmth, making prayer. The snow-white Himalayas towered above him under a waxing moon, making majesty.

Turning toward a huge Tibetan prayer wheel at the very top of Swayambhunath, Shunya wished his daughter could see the world through his eyes, and he prayed for her understanding and forgiveness.

Once inside the temple, he pressed his palms together and bowed to the magnificent gilded Buddha at the center of the room. There were hundreds of butter lamps flickering in his eyes when Shunya dropped to his knees and looked up into the jaws of a fire-breathing dragon, one of many wrathful guardians of the spirit world that adorned the temple ceiling.

He was dwelling on the dragon monster, imagining the talent and faith it took to paint it, when the old lama entered the room with his young disciple.

Shunya stood to greet the venerable old Tibetan master, pressed his palms together and bowed. "Tashi delek.," Shunya began. He had not seen the old lama in many months.

The lama and his disciple returned the greeting, bowed to the golden Buddha and left. Shunya followed them out of the temple. All sat facing each other at the top of the world, aglow in the moonlight, the disciple translating for his master.

"My master is pleased to see you again. He wishes to know where you have been all these months."

Shunya reflected upon his adventure to save Delhi Dave before answering. "Where I shouldn't have been."

The lama smiled, adjusted his orange robes, then lightly tugged on Shunya's red beard. "Netti, netti."

"Not this, not this," the disciple translated.

The lama continued, "The progression of consciousness is negative. Many roads are taken. Only one path arrives."

Shunya nodded. He understood. He was a road-weary traveler. The moon in his eyes, he began to question himself: *How many paths? How many lives?*

The lama responded to his thoughts. "How many stars?"

Shunya looked up into the night and sighed. "Too many."

"Like the Jew who wrestles with God, who takes many paths, who never arrives."

Shunya was stunned.

The lama and his disciple stood to leave. Their palms pressed together, they bowed out of Shunya's presence and disappeared into the night.

*   *   *

There were stars in the sky and tears in her eyes as the river of life flowed by in the holy city of Benares. Diane ached for birth, rebirth and renewal. Her long and luxuriant hair rustling in the evening breeze, Diane sat alone on a rock, on the shore of the Mother Ganges, grandmother of creation, healer of the sick and sorrowful, and cried out for love lost.

As the moon rose over the sacred river, joy and despair were indistinguishable for Diane. In a moment of exhilaration, she undressed in the darkness. Naked beneath the stars, she inhaled a whiff of death and took pause; there were bodies burning on the river's edge. Diane turned toward the distant flames and began to cry. Turning back to the river, she waded in, sinking ever-deeper into the water, swirling downward to nothingness.

She was drowning when two strong arms plucked her from the water and helped her ashore. "Are you crazy?" the young man began in an English accent, holding her trembling shoulders between his hands. "You're lucky I had my eye on you. I was sitting on the temple wall, playing my flute, when I saw that you were in trouble."

Diane coughed a few times before declaring, "I'm fine. I really am."

"Are you certain?" he pressed, clearing the wet hair from her face.

Of what? Diane didn't really know. It was her second day in India, her first night in Benares. She was bewildered, largely unaware that she had essentially attempted suicide.

The young man was awestruck by her naked beauty. He fought his straying eyes as he stumbled to introduce himself. "I'm Peter," he finally said.

"And I'm Diane, who's very lucky you had you're eye on me," she replied, looking up to his sparkling, brown eyes.

Only moments away from death, Diane was already flirting with life. Peter Harrington was a handsome, young Englishman, tall and thin with long, fine blond hair falling down below his bare shoulders. He was wearing a white lungi and a gold prayer shawl around his neck. When he smiled, Diane finally became aware of her nakedness and blushed.

"You'll have to excuse me," she said, reaching behind Peter for her black wraparound Tibetan dress, lying at the foot of the temple wall.

Peter turned toward the river as she slipped into the dress. "You don't swim very well, do you?" he asked, his eyes wandering over the river.

Diane tightened the sash around her waist. "I do, but I must have tripped."

"Into the water?"

Diane hesitated, then burst into tears. "I don't know," she sobbed. "I just hate my life; I hate myself."

Peter turned to Diane and gathered her in his arms, wondering what possessed her.

6

Dawn came with the ease of drawing a breath, the gray light spreading across the horizon, turning yellow, turning night into day. The streets of Benares were already bursting with passion and prayer, hundreds of thousands of souls paying homage to a thousand different gods and goddesses in ten different languages and a hundred different dialects on the banks of the Mother Ganges—her fluid bosom swelling with the multitudes cleansing their hearts and minds and bodies. The river Giver of Life made no distinctions, claimed no favorites and consumed all but one lonely old soul trapped in a young and unique body beautiful.

Diane watched from the deck of Peter's houseboat, wondering where she fit into the grand design of things she did not understand. She was glad to be alive, even if she didn't have a purpose. And she really liked Peter, though he was a tentative lover—still too self-conscious and inhibited to sate her wilder passions.

Peter was spiritual by nature and cavalier by birth. A twenty-seven-year-old Sanskrit scholar, he was an Englishman born to private schools and a higher calling than bedding a beautiful blonde. Within three days, Diane had already impaired his lofty visions and compromised his calling. He had been celibate for three years.

From across the deck, Peter studied Diane's sullen profile and began to regret his weakness for her beauty. He'd only known her for a very short time and had already fallen in love with her.

"Are you okay?" he began, walking up to her and leaning on the railing.

Diane forced a smile and said, "I'm alive, thanks to you. And I'll never forget you for that much."

"You mean you're leaving?"

Diane twirled her ruby earring with her thumb and forefinger. It was a nervous habit she had picked up upon receiving them from Kalib. "As if you want me to stay?" she challenged.

Peter studied her face and was again captivated by her beauty, He reached for her hand. "I want you to be well."

"If I only knew where to start," Diane sighed, looking down at the sparkling water. The boat gently swayed and creaked from age as she spoke.

"This river is the best place in the world to start," Peter declared. "It is the beginning of life."

Diane gazed across the water at the north shore and sighed: no boats, no buildings, and no people, the emptiness echoed her despair. "Not my life. If it wasn't for you, it would have killed me."

"Not *it*, Diane, you! It is the river that gives life and it is you who wanted to give it back."

"Then you want me to stay?"

"If you like."

"If I knew what I liked, I wouldn't hate myself so much," Diane said, before saying goodbye.

*   *   *

If not the oldest city on earth, Benares was among the most colorful and chaotic, a third-world wonder of devils and demons and dervishes, filled with saints and charlatans, beggars and beguilers. There were great yogis whose bodies radiated perfect bliss and naked sadhus covered with holy ash, their long penises dangling down to their knees, the cartilage ruptured by ritual initiation then stroked with ghee and stretched in rapture and in homage to the holy lingam of Lord Shiva, the mythic master of mayhem. The serpent, kundalini, coiled in the dark and forbidding corners of the Hindu soul, promised salvation to the holy faithful and damnation to the unbeliever.

The sprawling, convoluted skeins of streets and blind alleyways teased the imagination and continually boggled the mind. The stench of burning charcoal, body odor and stale urine combined with the burning incense and the wafts of petuli and jasmine to confuse the senses. The noise was deafening: people talking, dogs barking, monkeys screeching, camels spitting, cows chewing, tablas pounding, flutes singing, mothers screaming, children crying; Diane could hardly attend to her own thoughts as she meandered through the crowd.

First repulsed by the sight of a dying man lying in a pool of vomit, then charmed by the greeting of a young Tibetan Monk, Diane was telling herself to focus when she turned a narrow corner and tripped over a limbless beggar woman, begging to live another miserable day.

How could this poor creature want to live? Diane asked herself as she walked past a row of stores filled with huge barrels of spices, tall mounds of tropical fruits and thick bolts of fine silk. She was looking for a place to rest and have some chai when a shiny silver bangle caught her eye. "How much?" she asked.

The vendor said, "One hundred rupees, Memsahib."

Diane tossed her hair and smiled. She offered him twenty rupees.

The man laughed. She continued to flit and flirt and got it for thirty rupees. The woman was no idiot. She may not have appreciated the full value of life, but she knew the price of things and the value men placed on her beauty.

She liked being pretty; she also hated it. Most of all, she hated David, who had devalued her in Kabul. She couldn't stop thinking of him, and blaming him for hating herself—her mind stopping only to purchase two pairs of silver earrings at another stall.

"How about two bracelets for the price of one?" Diane asked.

The vendor hesitated, then agreed .Diane walked away wearing the jewelry, tossing her hair and swaying her butt in defiance of everything that was hallowed and holy in Benares to get what she wanted, which was the undivided attention of the known world.

Diane continued to sway and tease every man, woman, and child that crossed her path—many flattered, some offended and no one worth remembering—all day telling herself that no one was good enough to touch her where she hurts the most.

After a cheap dinner, she checked into a cheap hotel near the river and lay down beside all the jewelry and silk blouses and scarves she bought, and masturbated. She was reliving a rare erotic moment with David when she came and started crying.

*   *   *

Max was sick. The overland journey from Istanbul toward the land of his dreams had taken a hellish toll on his body. Max spent two weeks at the Ansari Guest House with Carl and Howard recovering from a mild case of jaundice, a moderate dysentery infection and a spot of pneumonia. He often thought about going home, but he didn't have enough money for a plane ticket, and he didn't want to admit defeat. After all, this was the same young man who, at the age of sixteen, considered suicide as a reasonable alternative to going through life without a higher purpose than fulfilling the will of the status quo.

Carl and Howard understood. Both expatriates, they had attended Harvard together before leaving the country under dubious circumstances.

"We couldn't go back if we wanted to," Carl said. "We're both wanted for the politically motivated bombing of a New York City bank."

"Really?" Max exclaimed.

Carl shrugged and said, "We didn't kill anyone, Max, if that's what you're thinking. In any case, we're just stuck here with Dean and Dennis, and we sell dope for a living—if you can call this living." Carl looked around the room, at the plaster peeling off the filthy walls.

Max followed Carl's eyes and sighed. He didn't ask about Dean and Dennis, who shared a room across the hall from them. All Ivy League, all tall and thin with short hair, all dressed in faded jeans, old chinos, and tattered wool sweaters. All wore loafers except Dennis, who preferred lizard skin cowboy boots.

They were apparently all out of step with the times and circumstances, but ignorance bred comfort, and friendship lent security. The nightly poker game in Carl and Howard's room—often attended by David Appel—marked time. And as the days passed, one being indistinguishable from the other, Max drifted in and out of consciousness and light-headed conversation about the coming harvest. Afghanistan did produce the best hash in the world, and Max's friends were desperate to find the money to finance the next big dope deal.

"The problem is finding an ass willing to foot the bill," Carl said, dealing the fifth and final card. The boys were playing stud poker.

"I don't get where an ass comes into this," Max said, swallowing another dose of penicillin. More than two weeks had passed since Max's arrival in Kabul, and he was finally feeling well enough to join the game.

"Because you haven't been here long enough to appreciate this particular cultural nuance, propagated by a lack of women for the taking," Howard said, conjuring a devilish smile before betting ten on a pair of tens.

"We get two hundred kilos of hash, the good stuff, the paddies with the mold, for nothing! On consignment. And all we have to do is let Mohammed fuck one of us in the ass—one time! He laid out the terms this afternoon and his preferences," Carl explained before raising the bet on an ace high.

This was the same infamous Mohammed who had offered David ten vials of morphine for an erotic view of his wife. Mohammed's extended family was knee-deep in smuggling drugs and running guns; they often used the Ansari Guest House as a front to make contact with young Westerners.

"We could make a hundred grand on this one—at least!" Howard added.

Dean and Dennis remained curiously silent. In fact, in the two weeks Max had known them, they hardly spoke at any length about anything meaningful.

Max said, "You can't be serious?"

Howard was about to reply when Mohammed entered the room and placed a cup of hot chai and two small cookies on the table next to Max.

"To make you feel better today," Mohammed said before leaving the room.

"Bet your ass we're serious," Carl said, brandishing a devilish smile. "You're his first choice."

Max was vacillating between shock and bewilderment when the boys burst out laughing. Later in the night, Max discovered that the offer was indeed credible, and that the deal would most likely depend on the procurement of someone else's butt.

"We'll find a strung-out French junkie somewhere, and pay 'em a few hundred dollars to turn the trick for us," David told Max over second cup of chai on the porch, later in the evening.

"You mean you're all in business together?"

"This time around maybe, but you never know with these guys—especially Dean and Dennis," David said, stroking his long, brown beard. The crew cut highlighted his bright brown eyes; he was a handsome man.

"You mean you can't trust them?"

"I mean no one and nothing in this town is what it seems. Its primitiveness belies its importance in world politics. If you ever took a good look at a map, you would see that Afghanistan nearly shares a border with five countries: Iran, Russia, Pakistan, India and China. And with Russia pressing the advantage to get a warm water port in the Persian Gulf, America is committed to stopping them at any cost—that's the up-card. The down card is the Mujahideen, the Afghani freedom fighters who are hell-bent on fighting against all western influence, and everyone in this town is looking to profit from the growing conflict: drugs make money and money buys guns. And I get high on the sly. It's just too bad the wife ran out on me—I could've made a fortune off her ass."

"Must've been a great ass," Max cracked.

"Fucking pain in the ass," David hissed before going inside.

Left alone to contemplate the reality of life on the road, Max was struck by its raw intensity and the odd collection of characters and conundrums. Though he enjoyed his new friends, he decided it was time to leave Kabul and press ahead to India, the Grand Master and Mother of all human dilemmas, where degradation ran rampant and the promise of bliss ran amuck, where mountains soared to the heavens and flat lands bleated in a trough of hellish depravity, where myth rivaled reality, and gods languished in praise, whose faithful died of neglect.

*   *   *

Left alone to contemplate the lama's challenge to "wrestle with God" and find one true path into the soul of creation, Shunya spent many frustrating hours in meditation inside the high temple. His thoughts vacillating between old friends and family and fleeting fame, he eventually recalled his flight to avoid prosecution in Israel. Shunya had stopped in Israel on his way to India, and was nearly apprehended for the crime of exporting Lebanese hash to America—which is why he couldn't return to America. He was on the Interpol watch list.

This recollection was most disconcerting. Unable to focus, he dropped five hundred micrograms of acid after midnight. He then proceeded to contemplate the lama's challenge as the molecular structure of the universe pulsated in front of his dilating eyes; ripples of orgasmic sensation washed over the lightness of his being, his thoughts swirling and gently swaying to the subtle rhythms of molecules in motion, within him and all around him. The painted temple walls and ceiling springing to life in his cosmic mind, Shunya consorted with myriad gods and goddesses.

His heart racing, anticipating the experience of God, it was well after three o'clock in the morning when Shunya finally discorporated and "flew" out of the temple, his astral body expanding to encompass the entire Kathmandu Valley below and several distant snowy peaks. Shunya was well on his way to Mount Everest when he looked up to the stars and opted for a trip through time—via the akashic record—to Jerusalem to witness the Crucifixion. He was nearing Golgotha when dawn broke over the valley: monkeys screaming, lamas praying, their long horns blaring as the light of Jesus filled Shunya with the miracle of life on earth.

*   *   *

In the heart of the valley below, Three-Finger Louie woke to another, harsher reality of life on the road. He tended to the needs of the broken people who had lost their way home. Some sick, some crazed and many too stoned to know the difference—all white, all poor, and all hopeless. Life hadn't been particularly kind to these people, but Louie made no judgments. He nourished the hungry and embraced the lonely.

Each morning Louie woke at dawn, stoked the fire, cooked breakfast and served the people who could no longer serve themselves. He was a tender-hearted man who was many things to many people: Guru, father, mother, brother, friend, idiot, charlatan, hustler, egomaniac. Now forty-two years old, Louie looked like a beatnik with his short black hair and neatly trimmed goatee. He talked like the street and acted like a saint.

Shunya liked his act and he paid for the show. He was coming down the valley when he passed Louie's porch full of lost souls and donated five hundred rupees to the cause. "Because I can afford it and you need it," Shunya said.

Louie was most grateful and invited Shunya to breakfast.

Shunya declined, telling Louie that he was on his way to see Sam Burke, an old friend who he had met upon his arrival in India. Shunya was nearing Sam's house when he heard the ruckus. He was about to knock on Sam's door when he stepped in a pool of thick, red blood.

7

"There are four noble truths. There is suffering. There is an origin for suffering. There is a cessation of suffering. And there is a path," Sayadaw said.

He was the meditation teacher Big Jane had talked about. Diane had met Big Jane shortly after arriving in New Delhi. Diane was staying at the Palace Heights Hotel in the heart of the city, still crying over the cheapness of her life. The door was ajar when Jane walked in, asking if she could help.

Diane said, "No," but Big Jane would not accept no for an answer. After all, these were sisters of the same painful journey—from man to man, from love to love—who traveled the world alone.

"I was married for two years in Portland," Jane explained over a cup of chai, sitting on the second floor patio overlooking Connaught Circus. She was a tall, shapely woman with short, black hair and round, brown eyes. "I grew up there and worked for the airlines to support my husband who was going for his Ph.D., until he left me for eight or ten of his nineteen-year-old students." Jane was twenty-seven, two years older than Diane. "So I quit my job and went back to school myself to study anthropology. Then I got an opportunity to go on an architectural dig in eastern Iran, in the desert, with two of my teachers.

After a few weeks on the dig they started playing a running game of chess to see who got the chance to fuck me first.

"I was really hurt, so angry. I'd worked so hard and nobody cared about anything that really mattered to me. They had no respect for me as a person or a woman. I cried so hard when I found out. Then I left; I borrowed their jeep one morning and never came back."

Diane was shocked. "You mean you stole their car and drove across Afghanistan and Pakistan alone?"

Jane forced a smile. "Sort of. I picked up guys along the way. You know, people on the road. I used them to protect me until I got to India. And I've been here ever since. I hated myself so much that I didn't want to go back to any place that reminded me of myself."

"And now?"

Jane reached for Diane's hand, looked into her sad, blue eyes and smiled. "It's taken awhile. I've been here almost a year, but now I think I'm learning to like myself."

Later in the day, as the sun set over the city, the tall one and the pretty one strolled against the flow of traffic around Connaught Circus. Jane told Diane about her experience with A.S. Sayadaw, the meditation teacher, and how the practice of Vipassana meditation saved her life.

Diane told Jane she wasn't sure if her life was worth saving. "But while I still have it, I should try and make the best of it—at least I'll know that I died trying."

*   *   *

Diane was thinking about Big Jane as she listened to Sayadaw outline the right Buddhist path to enlightenment. "Right Speech, right thought, right action, right livelihood. And it is through this practice of meditation and right behavior that righteous men and women are set free," Sayadaw said.

Max was sitting next to Diane. He had heard about the Vipassana meditation course from Narayan, a young California sadhu. They had met on the train to Bombay. Max was on his way to

Goa, to finish convalescing on the beach, when he changed his mind and headed to Alandi, a small town several hundred miles east of Bombay.

He wanted Diane; he resented Diane. He couldn't stop looking at her; he kept looking away. She was desirable, but desiring her wasn't spiritual. She hardly noticed him, a novice arrival on a vintage scene.

Max was still wearing blue jeans and a work shirt, while the mixed crowd of fifty-odd Westerners was dressed in silk and colorful cotton. All had longer stories to tell about their remarkable journeys to the East, and all could sit in meditation longer than Max—including Diane. Reduced and humbled by the comparison to his peers, Max turned away from Diane for the umpteenth time and paid close attention to the teaching:

"And so, by continuing to observe without judgment or analysis we refine the Observer. And through the constant practice of the Vipassana meditation we are opening our subconscious to our conscious mind and allowing it, those karmic impressions, to pass unobstructed from our lives," Sayadaw said.

He was stout man—somewhere in his early fifties, Max guessed—with short gray hair and a rich deep voice used with grace and precision to instruct men and women to engage in spiritual battles.

The tip of the nose posed as a metaphor for the point of the sword; it was here that the mind was focused, beginning with the practice of Anapana, a rudimentary exercise in concentration. Sayadaw explained, "By concentrating our attention on the sensations at the rim of our nostrils created by the passage of breaths, we sharpen our focus. And we can begin to observe our thoughts and feelings without interference or judgment." Sayadaw also urged his students to sit without moving or batting an eyelash for one hour, four times a day.

It was a lot to ask, and much more than Max or Diane had ever done for themselves.

*   *   *

The Dharamshala was a two-story, rectangular building. It had a dozen rooms, or cells, on each side of an open courtyard where meals were served, and where people quietly socialized on speaking days. Half the course progressed in silence, "in an attempt to further refine the practice," Sayadaw said. When not sitting in meditation, all students were expected to act accordingly with focus and equanimity.

At Sayadaw's suggestion, many students ate, walked, and washed very slowly, "to get in touch with the rhythm of life and the sensation of being," he said. "Observe the food, the color, the smell, the taste, the chewing, the path of digestion."

It was good food, prepared and served on banana leaves by course aides. Max ate slowly, while Diane ate as she pleased. She became so afraid of facing herself, she latched onto Paul, the first good looking man with the courage to court her and take her out to dinner in town on the eve of the first night of practice.

The formal introduction of Vipassana meditation, on the second night of the course, intensified the process and magnified Diane's fear.

"We begin by feeling the sensation at the crown of the head, then moving down to the neck, and the face, the forehead, your eyes, your nose, just feeling the sensations, being aware of them and not judging them, whether they are painful or pleasant, hot or cold, hard or soft, it does not matter."

It was a remarkable journey of feeling throughout Max's entire body, beginning at the crown of his head and ending at his tingling toes. Max thought it was easy until his right leg began to ache thirty minutes into the instruction, and he cursed the pain that challenged his will.

"Sensation, however painful or pleasant, is the finer nature of thought. Thought arises from sensation," Sayadaw said. "There is only a difference in the perception of these things and not their reality; how a person reacts to their thoughts and feelings in meditation within them is how they react to the thoughts and feelings of others in the outside world. All material objects, including the human body, are essentially the grosser nature of sensation vibrating at a slower rate. All existent things are vibrating: the rock, the fruit, the flower, the body, the endless chain of thought. It is only our perception of these things that sets them apart. This being true, we might say that karma is the difference we perceive between our self and every other person and thing in our universe.

"Vipassana meditation is the observation of our reactions to every level of being—physical, thoughtful, emotional and sensational—allowing the subconscious into the conscious, allowing sensation to become thought, allowing all things to pass in perfect equanimity."

Max was thoroughly enchanted by the teaching and the teacher. A wealthy Burmese businessman, Sayadaw had suffered from migraine headaches so severe that they drove him across the world in search of a cure. Finding no remedy, he was on the brink of suicide when he entered a meditation course in Burma similar to the one he was giving Max and Diane. It was the fourth day of the course, which Sayadaw was planning on leaving in disgust, when he merged with the pain in his head and experienced the unity of all things.

Diane was likewise impressed with the man and his teaching, but not convinced that Vipassana meditation could help her.

"I know I look pretty to other people, but I'm so ugly inside," she told Sayadaw on the third day of the course. She was on the verge of quitting the course and sought a private meeting with him in a moment of despair.

Sayadaw said, "It is not the beauty, and it is not the ugliness. The burden of one is the pain of the other."

"But knowing this doesn't change anything," Diane challenged. "I don't change. I'm afraid to change, and I can't stop crying."

"Then observe yourself crying."

"For what?" Diane agonized.

"For life," Sayadaw said, looking directly into her tearful eyes. "For the preservation of life there must be an observation of life. There must be a witness your life that does not identify itself as being pretty or ugly, that does not cry. It is not what you see; it is the act of seeing that is important. If it were not for our ignorance and our shame and our sorrow, we would not be needing meditation and we would not be practicing compassion. And it is this need and this practice that binds us and makes all men and women equal and necessary. The difference between you and I—your self and my self—is not a fact, it is a perception."

Diane found it hard to believe. She was about to leave the room when Sayadaw asked her to sit with him for a few minutes. It was in the darkness of her despair, her eyes closed, her mind racing, when Sayadaw shed a little light on her life. First a few, then many waves of sensations emanating from the lightness of his being washed over her, caressing her and awakening her, her entire body exploding in waves of sensation; now the tears flowed from joy.

*   *   *

Max remained alone in the meditative trenches, battling the pain in his legs with the sword in his mind—and not prevailing. After five days, Max could not sit for more than forty-five minutes without moving. The pain in his legs became so real, so constant, and so tough that it had begun to take on an identity of its own, apart from Max, inside of Max, hurting Max when he least expected it.

He was twenty minutes into meditation on the sixth night of the course, sweeping his body with sensation, observing his thoughts. He was imagining eating a slice of pizza in Angie's a restaurant in the old neighborhood, when the bastard pain attacked his right kneecap. Max felt like his knee was going to explode when the pain suddenly dissipated.

Deeper and darker into his subconscious, an animus temptress manifested, a dark woman with coal black eyes and raven black hair, who straddled his mind and turned into his mother. He wanted her; he was repulsed by the idea of having her and ran away from her.

Returning to the blankness of his mind, Max began to breath deeply and rhythmically—sweeping his body, sharpening his concentration at the tip of his nose before descending darker and deeper into his subconscious, into his childhood, into his lungs, listening to his heartbeat as he watched his thoughts, observing with perfect equanimity. Not quitting, not judging, not moving, no matter how much he wanted to sneeze or wheeze or itch or cough or ache, Max would not even flinch for forty minutes.

He was reveling in his fortitude when the pain attacked his left ankle at the beginning of the forty-first minute and finally bested him. The pain was so great after two more minutes that Max wanted to scream. His whole body began to shake when he finally moved and lost respect for himself.

"Meditation is not a war. It is not a battle to be won or lost," Sayadaw said, at the end of the hour.

Max wasn't convinced. As Sayadaw continued, Max recalled all he had studied and how many great texts and teachers talked about the destruction of the ego and the obliteration of self. These were violent, combative terms, war terms, and Vipassana meditation was a weapon that was not working too well for him, despite his great effort. Rather than admit defeat, he attempted to compensate for his many failures by impressing the teacher.

There were two community meditations each day, held in the meditation hall on the second floor of the Dharamshala, one sitting before breakfast and one before dinner. It was during these gatherings that Sayadaw would instruct the class. Afterward, there was always a small group of students who stayed behind to suck-up to the teacher under the guise of posing a question. On the seventh morning, Max posed a clever question to Sayadaw in an attempt to bolster his own self esteem.

"If thought is manifest from sensation, then we can assume that action, or behavior, is manifest from thought?" Sayadaw nodded, and Max continued. "Then who or what mechanism decides what sensations become conscious thoughts, and what thoughts translate into our actions?"

"Your karma," Sayadaw said.

"In other words, I have no real choice in anything I do or think or feel?"

"Perhaps not. Only to observe. You may choose to observe or not to observe. That is your free will."

"And I am asking who or what is making the choice." Sayadaw blinked and Max continued. "It can't be karma because karma is not an expression of free will, and it can't be the observer because the observer does not act."

Sayadaw fell silent for a moment and studied Max. It was a good question posed by a clever young mind intent upon deceiving itself.

"I cannot say what it is," Sayadaw eventually said. "But if you will continue to observe, you may discover that the very process of knowing is a probable cause for suffering. The great Gautama Buddha did not aspire to knowledge. He aspired to compassion through the cessation of all human suffering."

Sayadaw smiled and Max was humbled. He bowed his head and quietly retreated into himself while others came forward—some of whom were terminally ill and had more reason to cry than Diane and less time to indulge themselves than Max. In any event, however challenged, the practice remained the same, the unequivocal and unbiased observation of all thoughts and feelings—the mind watching the unending maturation and transformation of all these thoughts and images and feelings clamoring for attention, battling one another for prominence and possession of the thinker.

"Be me and be angry."

"Be me and be fear."

"Be me and be God."

"Be me and be at peace."

"Be me and be crazy . . . Be hungry . . . Be sleepy . . . Be sad . . . Be happy . . ."

Max and Diane had so many thoughts that couldn't even be still—despite Sayadaw's instruction..

*   *   *

The seventh and eighth nights of the meditation course were most intense. Each and every student was focused and no one was prepared to give an inch. The majority of the class had yet to sit for the requisite hour without moving. And if any one of these students could do it, the chances were they would do it on either of these nights.

On the seventh night Max posed a challenge to himself: remain still for the complete hour or be damned to mediocrity for the remainder of the course. As always, Sayadaw began the hour with a chant, his incredibly deep and mellifluous voice filling the hall, filling the soul, vibrating, echoing Max's challenge to himself, not to move until he heard Sayadaw's voice again at the end of the hour.

Max opened with a mindful blow job. He was getting it from an old girl friend, marveling at the joy she derived from pleasuring him, until he realized his higher calling—which was meditative observation. So he returned his attention to the tip of his nose, watching and feeling every part of the body, then sweeping the body en masse as waves of tiny sensations and pleasant feelings washed over him.

Twenty minutes into meditation, Max remembered Billy Cosco, the super's kid from across the street who went to fight the war that was still raging in Vietnam. Billy was a couple of years younger than Max and far more courageous. Max was in the pool hall. He was betting on himself in a game of three-cushion billiards, which he couldn't lose because he was the best young player the Bronx had seen in many years. Suddenly, a friend interrupted his hustle with the bad news: Billy Cosco had died in Vietnam, in battle, and had been posthumously awarded the Congressional Medal of Honor. He had jumped on a live enemy grenade, saving the lives of four other soldiers.

Max was trying to envision Billy's heroism on the field of battle when the pain attacked his left ankle again and muddled his mind. The pain was so great that Max cursed everything heinous and holy in the next ten minutes, but it would not stop. Then he tried to deceive it and distract it by employing sexually gratifying images, but nothing helped. The pain was searing, unforgiving, unyielding.

Fifty minutes into the meditation, Max began to tremble and sweat. His whole body shook from the pain. He tried every rhythmic breathing exercise he knew, but nothing helped.

Max was only five minutes away from victory, roiling in pain, afraid his ankle was about to snap, when he recalled an odd experience he'd had in Afghanistan, in the desert on the road to India.

There was thinking and there was a part of him that didn't think. "It" merely observed him thinking. It was the Witness, the innermost aspect of consciousness that made no judgments and had no vested interest in enhancing Max's life or preventing his death. "It" simply observed with perfect equanimity. "It" was what Sayadaw was trying to explain, this equanimous point of view that was the essence of being.

When Max finally made the telling connection, he stopped fighting the pain in his ankle and succumbed to it. The pain turned to sensation and began to ripple and expand until his whole body became engulfed in magnificent, intense waves of sensation. His mind floated around the mass of energy that was his deeply pained body. He envisioned a crystal palace, a luminous citadel at the center of his heart. He was on the verge of Samadhi, about to enter the cosmic palace of peace when Sayadaw began to chant, signifying the end of the meditation hour. The palace shattered into a million pieces of shimmering white light.

*   *   *

His experience in the desert connected to his experience with meditation, which connected to Max's first experience with an altered state of consciousness. It had been a cold winter night in New York. Max was home alone and depressed when he finally read *Siddhartha*. When the Ferryman enlightened the great Gautama Buddha, Max's kundalini was awakened. A hot wave of sensation raced up Max's spine and exploded at the top of his head, his whole body expanding, his ego dissolving, his mind floating out of his body. Max was way up in the night sky, hovering over the old neighborhood in his astral body, when a rush of white light knocked him unconscious. Waking in his body the following morning, Max's fear of life had turned into an insatiable curiosity about the world, which begot his journey to the East.

*   *   *

Diane didn't see any blinding white light, and she wasn't bathed in waves of sensation; she never left her body, but she was nonetheless reborn to another life. When she left the dharam-shala, she left Paul behind and sought a greater meaning to her life.

Diane was on her way to Bombay when she decided to visit the great Swami Puri, thinking she could learn even more at the feet of another wise man. But she had to wait and work with the women in the kitchen to prepare food for all the men who saw the great saint first.

After two days of waiting and working, Diane still hadn't seen the great man. Frustrated, she walked out of the kitchen on the third morning.

As always, Swami Puri was in the garden, surrounded by hundreds of men and several select women. Diane was standing at the crowd on the grass, beneath the shade of a tall banyan tree, when a middle-aged Indian man approached her.

"Very pretty. You are very pretty," he began.

Diane smiled and said, "Thank you."

"And I am thinking you should be with the women in the morning, to prepare the food for the men to eat."

"And I'm thinking that I've done enough and waited long enough to see Swami Puri."

"You mean that all the food is ready?"

"I mean that I'm ready to meet the Master."

The man was bewildered. He had not met anyone like Diane before. He was about reply when Diane pointed to several women at the front of the garden who were obviously welcome to stay.

"What about them?" she pressed.

"They are wonderful women who have done so much of God's work that they have earned God's grace."

"By serving men?"

"Exactly. It is through the service of men that women know God."

"Not my God," Diane snapped, before turning and leaving for Bombay.

8

Sam wasn't home. As Shunya later discovered, Sam had left Nepal for Bodh Gaya just days before the Durga Puja, the Hindu celebration of a significant manifestation of Kali, the goddess of death.

Durga was the goddess of fire, the lady riding the tiger of austerity who demanded a blood sacrifice from each and every holy Hindu soul in the Himalayas. Ages ago, they killed virgins to appease their God. These more civilized days featured the slaughter of water buffalo, sheep, goats, chickens and anything else that could double as a dinner entrée—which was a functional alternative to human sacrifice—but the scent and sight of so much blood tended to evoke the animal passion in the men who slaughtered them. Morning Prayer eventually turned into an orgy of misspent power, turning the streets of Kathmandu into rivers of blood-lust and cries of faith in the deity that drove them crazy.

Shunya had just stepped out of the pool of sacrificial blood in front of Sam's door, when an angry mob turned the corner chasing a man who had apparently absconded with a much prized goat's head. Crazy as the whole scene was, Shunya had seen it all before, and took the next train out of the country.

He had intended to go to Delhi to get a visa extension, but war with Pakistan, an American ally, was a moment away. So he decided to try his luck in Agra, and sit out the war in front of the Taj Mahal, unaware of its strategic significance, and nonetheless enchanted with its beauty.

The Taj Mahal glowed like a crown jewel of unearthly delights under the full moon, weaving fantasy and reality with its tragic history. It was a great Mogul king who had commissioned the Taj Mahal, and severed the hands of its creator upon its completion, making certain that nothing of its likeness and grandeur would ever be replicated.

It was the untimely death of his queen that had motivated him. She was interred in the Taj Mahal while her grieving king lost his throne to a more savage son. Several years later, following his death in a prison tower overlooking the splendor he had wrought, the king was interred for eternity beside his queen.

Shunya was filled with anticipation as he neared the main gate, but was met with disappointment: the looming prospect of war had closed the gates of the Taj Mahal to tourists and left Shunya out in the cool evening breeze.

But he would not be denied. Shunya was halfway down the western wall, skulking in the shadows of the rising moon when he was stopped by two men. *Cops*, Shunya thought—Officers from the Central Intelligence Division (CID.).

"Yes, you are looking for something?" the taller man began.

He was a highly educated Anglo-Indian, well-dressed in black knit trousers and a crisp white shirt, detailed with "military" epaulets and a monogram that Shunya could not read in the shadows.

"Something you have lost?" his partner added. He was shorter and darker, and similarly dressed.

"I was trying to sneak in," Shunya admitted. In these suspicious times, he figured that honesty was the best policy.

The men exchanged quizzical glances before betraying their own naïveté.

"Such a thing is possible?" the taller man challenged.

Shunya was perplexed. "You mean you don't know?"

"What? What is to know?" the other one pressed.

"You mean you're not police?"

No, they were tourists, who were likewise turned away from the main gate, they told Shunya. They claimed to work for Indian Airlines. One a navigator, the other a pilot, they had unscheduled layover in Delhi and had decided to visit the Taj Mahal. They were taking shortcut to their hotel when they ran into Shunya, who was greatly relieved and further surprised by their ingenuity.

Following ten minutes of small talk about people, places and things that they did not have in common, Shunya followed them further down the wall, beneath the light of the rising moon, to a small house. It was the home of the chowkidar, caretaker of the Taj Mahal, who could be bought with a little time-honored baksheesh. After all, the lineage of caretaking the great mausoleum, and making a little extra on the side, went back several hundred years.

"One hundred rupees only," Ramesh said, after haggling a deal with the chowkidar. He was the taller Anglo-Indian,.

"Altogether," Ashok added. He was shorter an stockier.

Shunya was delighted. For less than ten dollars, Shunya and his newfound friends gained entrance into the royal garden of earthly delights. The chowkidar served tea on a blanket in the grass. Ramesh chipped in with a small piece of hash, and Shunya provided the chemistry, a thousand micrograms of LSD, split four ways in an attempt to build a better union of the bizarre.

The chowkidar was a slight, bearded man in his early forties, dressed in old khakis and a skull cap. He was already high on the hash when he opted for the bigger trip to no place he had ever been before. Ramesh and Ashok were hard to figure. Though educated and well traveled, they both turned stupid on acid, both laughing at nothing in particular and rolling around in the grass.

Then there was Shunya, who belatedly realized that he might have made a slight error in judgment: the full moon ascending the night sky, so white and bright and radiant, like another-worldly pearl riding the crest of a black and beautiful galactic wave; the Taj Mahal turning whiter and brighter, playing tricks on the imagination of men like Shunya who thought it was a crown, and Ramesh who thought it was a boat, and Ashok who thought it was a rocket ship, and the chowkidar who thought it was about to collapse on top of him. LSD frightened him. Shunya was taking a piss at the wall when Ramesh and Ashok lit a small fire in the garden, and the chowkidar cried out for mercy.

Shunya was thoroughly bewildered. The party was turning crazy, the ground was getting shaky, and the sky was filling with color. Fireworks, Shunya thought, returning to the campfire to comfort the chowkidar—like no fireworks Shunya had ever seen before. The night sky bursting at the seams with a dazzling display of color, the ground trembling beneath their feet, Shunya began to think it was a cosmic prelude to the Second Coming. Dropping to his knees in awe, he expected Christ to spread his ever-loving arms across the sky.

The chowkidar, thinking it was the devil's work, ran screaming into the night, as Ramesh whipped out a set of high-powered binoculars to direct Ashok; he was using an expensive Japanese camera to photograph three Pakistani jets screaming overhead, using the radiant Taj Mahal as a beacon for a bombing run on the military airport in Agra.

It was war, and Shunya was caught in the middle of a surprise attack with two strange guys who might be Muslim spies working for the Pakistani enemy.

It was all so sudden and surreal that Shunya found it hard to comprehend. He was still on his knees, peaking on acid, beguiled by the loveliness of the lunacy, when three heavily armed, Indian soldiers burst through the main gate.

Ramesh and Ashok were the first to flee; Shunya ran a distant third. Sirens blared, bombs exploded, the ground quaked, and tracer bullets ripped the moonlight into a rainbow of terror.

And yet, despite the danger, Shunya loved every hallucinogenic, terror-filled moment of it: dodging soldiers and bullets and burning shells falling out of the broken sky, telling himself how wild and weird and wonderful it was to be so young and in love with a life exploding in his face.

*   *   *

Bombay was a big city thriving on the edge of a calamity. The newer and taller office buildings towered over the aging Tudor mansions and stately colonial buildings, vestiges of the British Raj, and all were in various stages of corrosion. The large and ornate windows sagged at the edges, crying streams of red rust into the very busy and dirty cobblestone streets.

The noise was deafening. The traffic was horrendous, going against all lights and logic. The sidewalks were crowded. The stores were packed with a mind-boggling assortment of hard wares and soft wares. Street vendors hustled the overflow of wares and people while the hordes of beggars lived off the scraps.

Diane was enchanted and bewildered by the passion and pace of the city. It was hard place to meditate, but she tried to maintain the practice nonetheless. She took a room at the Rex Hotel, and woke up at 4:30 each morning to sit.

The Rex was a popular dive by the bay—four dilapidated stories filled with young Westerners in various states of elation and despondency; the junkies slept in the back alley. Diane avoided the downside and had a lot of fun in town with friends she had made at the meditation course in Alandi.

Max took a room in the same hotel, and spent much of his time in Bombay checking his mail and waiting for money at Amex. In the entire week, Max had only seen Diane once, at Dipty's, a popular hole-in-the-wall dessert shop across the street from the Rex.

It was mid-afternoon. Diane was having a lassi with friends when Max entered and took a seat in back. They barely acknowledged each other. Max continued to resent her, but he couldn't take his eyes off of her. When Diane left the shop, Max's eyes followed her out the door and into the street.

Captivated by her beauty, he was still resentful of its power. He was still staring at Diane, musing over this conundrum, when his concentration was interrupted by a stranger. He was an oddly attractive, Anglo-Asian man, who had been standing at the small counter, talking with the owner of Dipty's.

"Do you know her?" the young stranger began.

"Who?"

"The girl, that one," the young Anglo-Asian said, pointing to Diane now crossing the street to the hotel.

"No, not really. I've seen her."

"Where? Where do you see her?" the man pressed.

The guy's sudden persistence and intensity made Max suspicious, and instinctively protective. "In my fucking dreams," he shot back.

The guy glared at Max for a moment, then left the shop. Max was tempted to follow and protect Diane from him, if necessary. He was about to leave his seat when the owner sat beside him and said, "There can be no problem with him if you do not involve yourself."

"You know him?"

The owner nodded and sighed, "I know enough to leave him alone, and there can be no problem with the woman if only because she does not have enough money for him to bother."

Max was bewildered. He pressed the owner to explain, but was met with a shrug and a sigh—and a free lassi.

Sometimes it was naiveté that saved Max from the harsher reality he sought to master; this time is was a bit of unsolicited advice from a stranger. In a city of so many millions living on the edge of despair, danger lurked around every corner. During the day the sidewalks of Bombay bustled with life. At night they filled with sorrow and pity.

More than a million people lived on the streets of Bombay, making many impassable after dark—as Max later discovered. He went out for dinner alone, to a small restaurant ten blocks from the hotel. He finished at eight and decided to take a longer walk back to his room. It was a beautiful evening, the tall palm trees swaying in the warm tropical breeze as Max weaved his way down unfamiliar streets, window shopping as he ate ice cream.

He had just turned down a quiet street when he tossed the near-empty cup to the curb and three beggars darted from the shadows, fighting one another for the rich sahib's garbage: there was one spoonful of ice cream left. Max was stunned by the mêlée, then accosted by four other beggars begging for money.

"Paisa, sahib . . . Paisa . . . Paisa," they cried out.

Max was reaching into his pocked for some spare change when he was surrounded by a third wave of beggars, grabbing at his arms and legs and tearing at his clothes as they pleaded with him for money. Finally frightened, Max pushed his way through the harrowing crowd and ran down the street, tripping over the bodies of many more beggars—some asleep, some sick and dying—until he reached his hotel.

Back in his room, Max took stock of himself: How could he turn down a dark street in the middle of a strange and foreboding city? How could he afford to go out to dinner when he had less than seventy dollars to his name.

*   *   *

Max had no answers. As the days in Bombay passed, he filled with despair. He had a thousand dollars in savings in New York, but he had trouble reaching his parents by phone from Bombay. Circuits were often busy or broken. Nearing the end of a long and frustrating week in the city, Max sold his watch, his Swiss army knife, his blue jeans and work shirt for eighty dollars, and headed for Udaipur, Rajasthan, where he would continue his meditation practice and conserve his money.

He was waiting for the train in Bombay Station, about to re-read a letter from his dear friend James Cohn, who was planning to make his own journey to the East, when he saw a group of beggars squatting at the end of the crowded platform and was reminded of his previous experience. He was wondering if he should give them anything when a remotely familiar voice interrupted his thoughts.

"It's hard to look at," Diane said, walking up to Max.

Max was momentarily stunned. "It doesn't get any easier."

"For her especially," Diane said, nodding in the direction of a young beggar girl sitting alone, her face covered with cruel scars, her arms severely twisted. "You know that someone probably did that to her when she was a child, maybe even her own parents, to make her look more pathetic. And they don't even get to keep a lot of the money because they have to pay off their bigger and stronger beggar bosses. A lot of these beggars are organized."

"How could you know that?" Max asked.

"Because I read about it, and I asked about it—especially about the second-class treatment of women in this country: how husbands mistreat their wives, enslaving them, battering them, and driving a lot of them to suicide."

Max finally looked into Diane's sparking blue eyes and said, "I don't understand what you're doing here, and why you're talking to me. Between the meditation class and staying in the same hotel all week, you barely acknowledged me."

"I guess I already had enough trouble," Diane explained. "I was being defensive, but I'm alone now, and I saw you and, well, I was wondering if you're going to Udaipur?"

Max said, "Yes, but . . ." His voice trailed off in belated bewilderment. He was standing so close to her, and she was so pretty. "We could sit together," he nervously added.

9

"I heard a lot about how beautiful it is in Rajasthan, and thought it would be a good place to practice the meditation," she told Max as their train pulled away from the station. "And I thought that traveling with you was better than traveling alone."

It was a simple explanation, but a step back from her admission of defensiveness. Max was confused—he thought Diane was attracted to him. He was also relieved. He was afraid that Diane might be too pretty for him and become too much of a distraction from his meditation if they became involved. So they kept the conversation light and friendly as their train headed north to Rajasthan, talking about the meditation course and about their experiences in India.

It would take twenty-four hours to reach Udaipur on a narrow gauge train, sharing a third class sleeper with four other people—all men and all inquisitive. And as the day progressed they wound up answering a lot of questions about their ages, their work, their families, their government, and their relationship.

Diane was courteous to a fault, but Max ran out of patience at nightfall. When asked about their "programs" in India for the fifth time, Max sarcastically replied, "We don't watch television."

"Exactly what is your mission?" they began again in earnest, unaware of how their formal use of the English language affected Max.

Max looked around the car and leaned forward. The four Indians leaned forward, expecting to hear a sacred truth.

"Our mission is Mars," Max whispered. "We're going to Mars."

The Indians were bewildered.

Diane was incensed by Max's behavior. "You're not as funny as you think," she heatedly whispered in Max's ear. "These people are trying to be nice, even if they are annoying."

At her insistence, Max apologized to their fellow passengers for his foolishness and explained how their choice of words and thrust of questions sounded unusual to him, too formal in some cases and too personal in others. The Indians were pleased by his explanation, but nonetheless curious about his relationship to Diane, continually asking them how it was possible for them to travel together if they weren't married.

"We're really just friends," Max kept telling them, but they found hard it to believe.

Nearing dinner, when they began to ask Diane if she was in love with Max, she excused herself from the conversation and went to use the bathroom at the back of the car.

She was standing in the aisle, waiting her turn, when an inquisitive woman approached her.

"This," the woman began, touching Diane's blue cotton blouse. "It is money?"

"What?" Diane was bewildered.

"What cost this?" the woman pressed.

"Too much for you," Diane snapped. She was offended.

When the woman touched a strand of Diane's shiny hair to see how it felt, as if the outrageous chestnut coloring would come off in her hands, Diane was inclined to push her hand away until she saw tears in the woman's eyes and reconsidered. She was about thirty years old, Diane guessed, wearing a bright green sari, a gold nose ring, and a red dot on her forehead, the bindi, denoting her married status.

"When I told her how much my blouse cost, she told me how much she paid for her sari," she told Max later in the evening, sitting side by side on the steps at the front of the car. "Which was gorgeous, and a lot more expensive than my blouse, and then she asked me a lot about America. She was very nice actually, but very unhappy in her marriage, I think. . . I also think you should know that I'm married, and that I left my husband in Kabul—to find myself. I was so lost."

Max was surprised. "I never got that impression," Max said, as they watched the world of earthly shadows and heavenly lights pass in the dark, the train spewing ash and smoke across the flat land.

"That I was married?"

Max nodded and leaned forward. He loved the feeling of the warm wind on his face. "You don't act like it."

"What's that supposed to mean?" Diane shot back.

"You do appear to be extremely flirtatious."

"Defensive. I told you it was defensive behavior, exactly opposite of what I was really feeling."

Now Max had a choice: he could accept her explanation and move on to another subject, or he could challenge it and test his own metal with such a pretty woman.

"You mean that you're really not attracted to me?" he challenged, looking back at her with a playful smile.

Diane avoided his gaze and deflected the question. "I also told you that I'm dedicated to the practice, Max, which supersedes all of my attractions."

"Then you are attracted to me?" Max pressed.

Several moments passed until Max turned away from her and she reached for his arm.

*   *   *

Arriving in the city the following morning, they rented a quaint little cottage on the edge of town and shared the only bed. On the first night, Diane had Max right where she wanted him, inside of her.

Diane had better lovers than Max, but no one kissed like he did and no one could rival the intensity of the orgasms he gave her. It was a maddening intensity, the way he pursed his lips around her clitoris and sucked it like a nipple until she came, screaming for relief.

It was almost too intense, almost unpleasant, but the intensity heightened the attraction. Diane couldn't get enough of him, and her desire eventually betrayed her despair. They were lying in bed, making love in the afternoon following a trip to the bazaar; Diane was on the verge of a peak experience when she burst into tears.

Max thought he had hurt her, but Diane told him it was her husband that hurt her. "He makes me cry, when I think of him," she sobbed, lying beside Max and looking up at the whitewashed ceiling.

"While you're in bed with me?" Max challenged, rolling onto his side and glaring at her profile. He was apparently hurt.

"What am I supposed to tell you, no, that I don't think about him? That I can control when I think about him."

"Then you must still be very much in love with him?"

"And if I said that I was, you would leave?" Diane asked, wiping tears from her eyes before turning onto her side and looking into his sad, brown eyes.

Max wanted to say yes, but he said, "No."

Diane read the conflict in his eyes and knew that she had already gained the upper hand in their relationship—and this pleased her. "It's not love, Max. It's attachment, resentment, hating him as much as I hate myself for marrying him. It was sex and drugs. It was losing myself in him when I should have been finding myself."

"But you're finding yourself now?"

"In another man's bed," she sighed.

"Then you want me to leave?"

Diane said, "No, I just need you to be nice and understanding. Given the choice, I'm not sure that I would have hooked up with you either, but I am a woman alone, and I was attracted to you from the first time I saw you at the meditation course; and then you showed up at the train station—it was serendipitous, I thought. I really was planning to come here alone and meditate, and when I saw you on the platform and began to talk to you, I began to think that it was fate that drew us together, that there was an intelligence to the coincidence."

"You're making it sound like an I Ching throw," Max cracked, turning onto his back.

"Sarcastic asshole," Diane spat, sitting up in bed and looking down at him. "As if I don't know what the I Ching is, or how to use it? Because I'm pretty, and I like nice things, you want to think I'm stupid and have pity on me, and fuck me as a favor to please yourself while you're telling yourself that you're doing it all for me? As if I never met a man that didn't want to fuck me for every reason but the right one—because they did love me.

"You think it's easy for me—for any woman—to come to India, to look for themselves, or God, for that matter? With no prescription for a woman to find God, because men wrote all the books and described all the divine-like paths to suite them?

"As if I never read the Tantric definition of this fucking crazy quest, where it says that the female is the mystery and the male is the process through which the female is apprehended? Meaning I'm supposed to just stand here and let every one of you fuck me over to get what you want at the divine end of things, and I get three kids, no life of my own, and cellulite.

"And I have to use men for protection just to get this far on my own, to fuck them and travel with them so no one else would fuck with me and hurt me in worse ways? To use my husband the way I did, to encourage him to go to Afghanistan to get high on cheap drugs so I could get to India, because I didn't have the balls to go it alone—especially overland. Then he tries to sell my ass for ten vials of morphine to some degenerate Muslim in Kabul to feed his habit? You think this makes me feel good inside?"

Max had no answers, but he did have some information to share with her. "I know your husband," he sighed. "I met David at the Ansari in Kabul right after you left. I was there for a while. I was sick. I played cards with him and . . ."

"Meaning that you're no better than I am—or him, for that matter—because you kept your mouth shut all this time, thinking that if you told me that you knew David that I wouldn't fuck you after all? So you just waited until now, until you got what you wanted, to fuck the pretty girl, and in a moment of unbridled honesty, you just had to tell me about David . . . Fucking user!"

Diane flew out of the bed, into the bathroom and slammed the door, leaving Max in a daze, trying to understand his relationship with her. To begin with, Diane was much more powerful than he thought, and much stronger and smarter than he had imagined. But she was so angry, and so terribly hurt.

She was also correct in her assessment of his motives. Had Max been more of a friend and less of a lover, he would have gotten to know her better before he slept with her. But she had goaded him and flirted with him; she had sized him up on the platform in Bombay and got him to satisfy her own desperate needs.

She thought about all this in the bathroom. In fact, Diane knew that she was stronger than Max—and a lot smarter. Looking at herself in the mirror as she fixed her hair, she knew that she could take him or leave him.

"And I know you meant to do the right thing," she said, exiting the bathroom and sitting on the edge of the bed. "I know that you do care about me in spite of everything, and I really do care about you, and I do believe that we were destined to meet for some reason. I also know I'm hard to be with right now, and I wouldn't blame you for leaving. . . "

When she began to cry again, Max sat up, took her in his arms and stroked her hair.

"I'm still so lost and confused. I made so many mistakes and there's so much going on. I'm trying so hard, but I'm still so bad," she sobbed.

Diane cried for the next three days—in bed, on the street, in the bazaar, in restaurants, before and after meditation—for no apparent reason and every reason imaginable. And she couldn't sleep very well, her mind filling with all kinds of odd and disconnected images from her childhood. The subconscious spilled into the conscious, as if the veil between them had been torn apart.

"It's the meditation," Max surmised, telling her to "keep watching, keep seeing; bear witness and know that you are not the images you see in your mind. You are not the tears that fall from your eyes. You are the energy, the intelligence who watches, who is aware without judgment—not good or bad."

Diane kept saying she understood, but she felt like she was going insane. "Like I'm being punished for who I am—even for being pretty," she agonized, as they walked across town to the bazaar one afternoon.

It was another perfectly sunny and temperate day in Udaipur. The old trucks and buses barreled down the road, kicking up clouds of dust in their wake; many students rode bicycles, weaving in and out of the slower foot traffic; the tribal women flaunted their primitive sensuality as they swayed through the crowd in their colorful halter-tops and peasant dresses, their heads bearing burdens to the marketplace.

The Indian women dressed in colorful saris, their husbands wore dhotis and kurtas. The teenage girls preferred blouses, the boys trended toward chinos and sport shirts, and pointy black shoes. And all of them looked at Diane, some smiling, many caterwauling.

The bazaar was tucked behind tall walls of an old red fort, built by the British to oversee the flow of people and commerce that stretched from Udaipur to Tehran. The old labyrinth of byways and alleyways were jammed with rotting wooden stalls, overflowing with rugs, fabrics, jewelry, and antiques, all available for a "special price" to the young sahib to please his beautiful "wife." After a few days in Udaipur, Max and Diane finally realized that it was easier to pass as husband and wife than to explain the moral chasm of boyfriend and girlfriend, anathema to many Indians.

After all, India was a sexually repressive society which followed a strict moral code. Unfortunately for Diane, this morality did not translate into good manners. The staring and the badgering intensified in the bazaar, and a few men made it a point to "bump" into her. It was annoying to the point of becoming demeaning.

"Everywhere I go, every fucking minute of my life," she agonized. "There's always one man, or ten men, who won't leave me alone."

"You keep saying that, but it might serve you to consider the alternative."

"Which is?"

"Being unattractive."

Diane drew a deep breath, sighed, and squeezed his hand.

Nearing the end of the day, they finally stumbled upon the Lake Palace, a summer respite of a late and great Mogul king that was built at the center of a clear man made lake in the heart of the city. Its delicate tile and stonework were living testaments to the artistic genius of the Mogul Empire, and a sorry indictment of the British Raj. They had stolen the inlaid gems off the walls before vacating India, thereby robbing the rooms of color. The sun once passed through these jewels, creating red rooms from rubies and purple rooms from amethysts. Still beautiful in spite of the cultural rape, the Palace served to distract Diane until it closed and the sun began to set.

Sitting on the shore, they watched the lake and the barren hills reflect the sky, turning red and gold and violet.

"It is so beautiful here," Max said.

"Just perfect," Diane said.

Max reached for her hand and looked into her eyes. They were about to kiss when they realized that they were not alone. They had been quietly surrounded by a large family of silver monkeys, sitting arm in arm, shoulder to shoulder, head to head, watching the sunset over the miracle of creation. Not so different from Max and Diane.

And not so troubled.

10

It was nearly twenty-five hundred years before the arrival of Max and Diane and Shunya to Bodh Gaya, when Gautama Buddha sat beneath the famed Bodhi tree and made the Great Resolve, to experience the absolute perfection of being, or die trying.

He lived, and spent his entire life deeply and truly loving each and every sentient being in the world without screwing any one of them—which was a hard act to follow.

The little village of Bodh Gaya was located on the edge of a very large and dry flood plain, with few trees, lots of dust, and the usual over-planted, under-rotated, green fields encircling it.

The Mahabodhi Temple stood at the heart of the village. It was a tall stone stupa, soaring a hundred and eighty feet into winter-blue sky, overlooking the renowned Bodhi tree, and framed by a sunken grotto of flowers and stone sculptures denoting the many gods and goddesses Lord Buddha did not believe in.

The temple was a Hinayana monument to the dream of perfection on a Buddhist path of enlightenment. The Tibetans lived in tents inside the predominantly Hindu village, while the peasant farmers fashioned their homes out of dung on the edge of town. Across the road from the Mahabodhi Stupa stood a long row of shacks and stalls and tents erected to service the ever-changing international community of rich pilgrims; the streets were invariably lined with beggars.

True to the spirit of the place, Sam Burke opted for a small room in the Gandhi Ashram, a single-story L-shaped building located in a small clearing behind the row of shacks and stalls. A Canadian national, he had been in India for several years already, traveling north in the summer to the Himalayas and south in the winter—watching his mind, always watching his mind.

He was taking his afternoon walk along the dry river bed when he saw his good friend Shunya sitting in meditation beneath a big, old banyan tree. He approached quietly and waited several minutes before Shunya opened his eyes.

"Go anywhere interesting?" Sam began, suppressing a smile. He hadn't seen Shunya in several months.

Shunya stroked his red beard before replying. "Kathmandu, among other places, looking for you."

"That's a bit linear," Sam cracked.

Shunya laughed, realizing that Sam was questioning his meditation experience. "As if there is a substantive difference between our inner and outer realities?"

"In the short run, maybe. In the long run, I can imagine that it's all the same—assuming home is where your heart is."

"Then why go anywhere?" Shunya asked.

"My point exactly," Sam declared. "I can learn as much about myself on a short walk as you can traversing the entire continent."

"But you wouldn't be having so much fun. I have to tell you about the Taj Mahal."

Sam lit a bidi and smoked while Shunya explained. "The chowkidar is crying. The Anglo-Indians are laughing. And the soldiers are coming through the front gate. I'm running from the soldiers and away from those two clowns, Ramesh and Ashok, because I'm no longer sure whose side these two guys are on. Then I make it out onto the street and this taxicab pulls up to me and the driver says, 'Taxi, sahib?' Of course I needed a fucking taxi! One more minute on the street and they'd have locked me up and thrown away the key, especially with my history smuggling dope out of Israel."

Sam hadn't laughed so hard since the last time he had seen Shunya. He was about to question Shunya further when Max and Diane walked by, arguing about their relationship.

"Because you want something doesn't mean its right, or good for me," Max was saying.

"Because you're selfish doesn't mean I'm needy or greedy," Diane was saying.

Sam said, "She might be the most beautiful woman I've ever seen."

Shunya said, "I'm surprised you noticed."

"I practice equanimity, not stupidity. I try to see things as they are, and that woman is stunning from any perspective."

"And my practice is derived from my own experience. Listening to them argue reminds me why I haven't been with a woman in the last three years, since I left my wife."

Both watched Max and Diane disappear into the distant trees before continuing.

"Are you taking the Sayadaw course?" Sam began again.

"I suppose. I could use the focus, and the rest. I probably covered three or four thousand miles last week: Delhi, Nepal, Agra, back to Delhi to Bodh Gaya."

"And nothing's changed?" Sam challenged.

"Meaning I could have done nothing, been nowhere, and turned out like you," Shunya shot back.

Sam took a long drag on his bidi and exhaled. "Karma is the difference we perceive between ourselves and others. Movement is an illusion. No matter what you think, what you say or what you do, the observer will always have more real power, more of an enduring positive effect on the world than the actor."

Shunya studied Sam for an extended moment before replying. Sam was short man, about five-foot-five, with crew cut brown hair, small brown eyes and a modest black beard. He would not stand out in a crowd of three, but he had a razor sharp mind that never failed to amaze Shunya.

"One way or another, there's still no substitute for peak experience," Shunya said, reaching into his pocket for two hits of Owsley acid.

*   *   *

Max and Diane spent three weeks in Udaipur before heading to Bodh Gaya, where their budding relationship was sorely tested.

It was an early winter morning. They had rented a room in a The Government Guest House on the edge of town house, a two story, white-washed building with remarkable clean rooms. Max was dressing to leave, to meditate in the Mahabodhi temple, when Diane confronted him about the deteriorating nature of their relationship.

"You hardly talk to me, except when we argue, which is a lot lately. And when we make love, I have your body, but your mind is elsewhere. I can feel it." she said, sitting up in bed, her thick and wavy chestnut hair shining in a ray of sunlight.

Max looked out the window, at the Bodhi temple rising in the distance, and sighed, "It's just hard for me to focus right now."

"Because you came to India to find God and I'm getting in the way," Diane shot back. "Because I'm not spiritual enough, or exotic enough to understand you—because I'm just another Jewish girl from the Bronx."

Max wanted to say "yes" because that's how he really felt, but he chose to deflect the question. "You're welcome to come with me. We could sit together."

"Or we could stay here and you could make love to me like it really matters."

Max was torn. He wanted her; he wanted God; he didn't think he could have both. "I just need to be alone sometimes. Can't you understand that?"

"Then go fuck yourself and stop using me," Diane spat.

Max studied Diane for a moment—her hair reflecting the sunlight, falling down below her bare chest, her fierce blue eyes swelling with defiance—and was filled with an odd combination of lust and rage.

Diane read the passion in his widening, brown eyes and baited him: "If you only had the courage."

"For what?"

"To do what you want with me."

"As in wrapping my hands around your neck and shutting your mouth for good," Max said, flashing a sardonic smile.

Diane dismissed him with a shrug, and Max was infuriated. He grabbed a colorful, silk scarf off the nightstand, sprang onto the bed behind Diane, and wrapped the scarf around her throat. "You like this, don't you?" he hissed.

"I'd love it if you knew where to put it," Diane shot back.

So Max accepted the challenge and took her from behind, intensifying her orgasm by choking off her oxygen at the precise climatic moment, satisfying her and punishing himself.

*   *   *

Max was not proud of his prowess in bed that morning. Good as it felt at the moment of orgasm, he left the room filled with guilt, thinking he was a better man than that. Consequently, he spent much of the afternoon alone, sitting beside the great Mahabodhi Temple, beneath the holy old Bodhi tree, contemplating the irony of his life: how far he had traveled in an effort to become a better man; how badly he felt about himself for ravaging Diane; how much he loved her; and how he knew it was time to leave her.

Tears were streaming down Max's cheeks when the Monk Master of Anapana meditation, one of the foremost scholars of Hinayana Buddhism in the world, approached him. He had been observing Max from a distance.

"It appears you are not feeling very well?" the monk began, his orange robe shining brightly in Max's surprised, tear-filled eyes.

"Not well at all," Max sighed, looking away from the Master Monk's soft, brown eyes and clearing the tears from his face.

"I can sit with you?" the monk asked.

Max said, "Of course."

He didn't have to know the Master Monk's impressive credentials to recognize his stature. The Master Monk was a slight man with a shaved head and wire-rimmed glasses. Somewhere in his late forties, Max guessed, with a sharp, hooked nose and bony cheeks. He was the first Buddhist monk Max had ever met. The only monk in Bodh Gaya who wasn't Tibetan, who wasn't sitting in meditation or walking around the stupa repeating mantras, or using the prayer boards—some devotees did as many as ten thousand prostrations each day in deference to their lord Buddha.

"So it seems that you have come a long way to find out that you are still at the beginning?" the Master Monk began, cutting right to the chase.

Max was one of the hundreds, if not thousands, of young Westerners who had come to Bodh Gaya, but he was now among the very few who could sit so still for so long. Max wasn't aware that he had been sitting in meditation for nearly two hours. "Thinking, mostly," Max said.

"And the rest of the time, when you weren't thinking?"

"I don't know. But this wouldn't be the first time I lost my mind."

The Master Monk smiled. He liked Max's self-deprecating humor. "If you could lose it without wanting it back, it may be the best thing that ever happened to you."

"I can't wait."

"Your life is so bad?"

"No, not really. But it's been really difficult since I met this woman," Max finally admitted. It wasn't so easy for him to talk about such worldly things to such an other-worldly man.

The Master Monk nodded. "Today it is a woman, tomorrow it is money, or a child, or a disease you will have, or a great store of knowledge. All is common to this life and all are attachments. And all have the potential to create great joy and great discomfort."

"And all are to be observed with perfect equanimity?"

"Ideally, perhaps, but not realistically. As we both know, it is much easier to observe our thoughts than our actions. Because thought leads to more thought and, in itself, creates very little karma. Most often, it is our behavior that creates real problems for ourselves and others."

"But some thoughts do serve as a prelude to our actions?"

"Of course, and all thoughts are rooted in sensation and impulse—which are in turn rooted in karma, the activities of past lives."

The Master Monk was brilliant, and far more engaging than Sayadaw. Talking to him made it easy for Max to forget Diane. The next question Max posed, however similar to his naïve attempt to impress Sayadaw, was born of genuine interest.

"I understand, intellectually at least, the distinctions you are making between thoughts and actions and impulses and karma. But I don't understand who is making those distinctions—who is it that decides what is acted out in the world and what remains in the realm of thought?"

The Master Monk smiled, adjusted his wire rim glasses, and looked directly into Max's eyes. "Who is it that asks the question?"

Max didn't know. The Master Monk's question was so unexpected, so simple and stunning that it stopped Max's mind. His thoughts erased in the blink of an eye, Max's body-mind expanded to include everything that was around him—the trees, the grass, the sky, the birds and the monk—then contracted to a peaceful and quiet mind. The expansion and contraction happened so rapidly Max thought it was an illusion, or a hallucination.

The monk said, "If you wish to stay with us longer in the mind of India, I will write you a letter to take to the authorities in Gaya who will extend your visa as often as you wish. I think you may do very well here."

Again, there were tears in Max's eyes as he pressed his palms together and bowed to the master of the moment.

11

The Burmese Vihara was located on the side of a dirt road, at the entrance to the village. It was old and lush, the stone walls covered with vines, the grounds covered with grass and flowers. There was a vegetable garden in back. A row of tiny meditation huts lined one side of the garden. A huge tent had been erected on the opposite side of the garden to accommodate the overflow crowd of men who had come to take the ten-day course with Sayadaw, who traveled all over India teaching meditation. The women stayed in the main three-story building. The community meditation hall was on the top floor.

Max was directed to the tent upon arriving in the Vihara. Diane went to look for Big Jane in the main building, hoping she had signed up for the course She was thrilled to find Jane in the meditation hall.

"Getting a head start?" Diane began, waiting on the patio for twenty minutes until Jane exited the hall.

"Not on you," Jane said, reaching to embrace her. "I knew you would be here if you took the course in Alandi."

"It was the best thing I ever did for myself, even if I still feel bad about myself."

"Why so bad?"

Diane shrugged. "I just don't like myself very much, and I still don't know why. And I still can't find a relationship that's healthy and fulfilling."

Diane went on to characterize her relationship with Max as they walked downstairs. "He wants to leave me, but he doesn't have the balls," Diane concluded, pointing out Max in a crowd before they exited the Vihara.

"He's cute."

Diane conjured a wicked smile. "He's also arrogant, because I have the balls in this relationship—even if I don't show them. Anyway, we decided to put off the decision about our relationship until after the course."

The meditation course would not begin until evening, so Jane and Diane decided to take a walk a long the dry riverbed, past tall palms, old banyan trees, gnarly bushes and green fields, and a tired water buffalo pulling a plow.

"You may not feel different, Diane, but you are different. You look different to me," Big Jane said.

"I still cry every day, but . . . I'm here taking another meditation course, which is a lot better than having nowhere to go. And Sayadaw was very helpful when I spoke to him in Alandi."

Jane was about to reply when Sam walked by. He exchanged greetings with her before disappearing in the bushes. "He's a pretty interesting guy, so is his friend Shunya, the guy with the long, red beard. Gary introduced me to them over breakfast this morning."

"Gary?"

Jane smile and sighed, "I also met a guy, a good guy this time, maybe the best guy I ever met. And he's seriously devoted to the practice. He pays me to practice, ten rupees for every hour I sit."

"What does he get out of it?"

"Laid!"

Their laughter rolled down the riverbed.

*   *   *

The course began in the early evening with Sayadaw telling the parable of the mustard seed.

"A woman came to Lord Buddha in great sorrow after burying her dead child and pleaded with him to bring her child back to life. Lord Buddha agreed if the woman brought him a mustard seed from a house in the village that had not experienced the death of a loved one. The woman ran off to the village, thinking it would be a very easy task. But upon knocking on the door of every household, she could not find one family that had not suffered the loss of a loved one. Finally, she returned to the great Gautama Buddha, realizing that sorrow and death were common to every life, and took refuge in the dharma."

It was a simple story that got right to the point of the journey to the East, to find refuge from an increasingly unstable and dispassionate world.

Max was humbled by the story and was moved to do something nice for Diane. They were sitting alone in a quiet corner of the Vihara, discussing their meditation experience, when Max reached into his jhola and handed her a copy *Siddhartha*.

"It says things a lot better than I can about the meaning of our lives. It's an old copy that I got a long time ago from my friend James in New York."

Diane was pleased, but not deeply moved.

"Given the choice, I'd rather get a piece of jewelry," she told Jane later in the evening. "Which is something Max doesn't get."

*   *   *

Max slept near Shunya in the tent; he sat close to him in the meditation hall from time to time, and he repeatedly saw him in the courtyard, but he didn't meet Shunya until the fifth night of the course.

Both had gone to bed early. Max was becoming increasingly discontented with the course. The tent was too crowded, the food wasn't very good, the morning line at the one and only water pump was much too long, bathing proved difficult, and the meditation hall overflowed out onto the second floor patio. Plus, Max had a sour stomach.

After several hours of tossing and turning and running outside to heave, Max finally fell asleep near midnight. Bill Viletitski, who slept next to him in the tent, woke him at four-thirty in the morning, thinking he was doing Max a service.

"Time to meditate," Bill whispered, adjusting his thick, horn-rimmed glasses. He was the course nerd, the guy who did everything right for himself and got on the wrong side of everyone else in the process.

Max said, "I'd rather sleep."

Bill said, "Meditation is better."

"For you maybe, but not for me. And I know what's good for me right now."

"That's assuming you know yourself."

Max was infuriated. He reached up, grabbed Bill by the collar and hissed, "You little cocksucker. You ever wake me again and you'll know your own fucking death!"

Bill trembled and ran out of the tent in fear.

Shunya, who was sleeping next to Bill, overheard their argument and ran out of the tent after Bill.

Max became nauseated and left the tent to vomit. He was nearing a tree at the side of the tent when he saw Shunya rolling in the grass—crying, Max thought, until he walked over to Shunya and saw how hard he was laughing.

*   *   *

Max withdrew from the meditation course the following day and took a room at the guest house, where he had stayed with Diane. Shunya had likewise withdrawn from the course, owing to the poor living conditions, and moved into the Gandhi ashram, next door to Sam. He was having chai with Sam, at a chai shop across the street from the Mahabodhi Temple, when Max walked by and Shunya waved him over.

"This is the guy I was telling you about, the one who threatened Bill last night," Shunya told Sam.

"Which is why I left the course," Max explained, taking a seat across the table. "Because I couldn't deal with anything anymore: the living conditions, my stomach, and the girlfriend—I can't deal with her either."

"Which reminds me—your girlfriend gave me this," Shunya said, reaching into his jhola, producing Max's copy of *Siddhartha*. "She came to the tent looking for you, but you had already gone."

"Did she read it?" Max asked.

"She said she did, before she went to sleep."

"Did she like it?"

"She didn't say, but she didn't sound too happy."

Max drew a deep breath and sighed, "What else is new?"

Shunya handed the book to Max and smiled. "Can I ask where you got this book?"

"In New York, from my friend James."

Shunya widened his smile. "Did you ever notice the inscription in the back of the book?"

"Oh, yeah," Max said, before opening the book and reading the inscription aloud. "W.R. to James. At the something of life?' I could never make out that one word."

"Buzzer," Shunya said. "W.R. to James at the buzzer of life. As in time-clock, as in basketball, meaning to score in the clutch at the buzzer. Before I was Shunya, I was W.R., Willie Rennett."

Max was momentarily bewildered, then jumped to his feet and exclaimed, "The point guard from Brooklyn!"

Shunya explained, "I got the book from Tim Leary in Millbrook. That's where I met James. I gave it to him after I read it."

*   *   *

"Amazing connection, isn't it?" Max asked Diane.

Amazing or not, Diane didn't care. She hadn't seen Max in three days, since he left the course, and went looking for him at the Mahabodhi Temple. It was late in the afternoon when she found him inside the temple, sitting in front of an imposing gilded statue of Lord Buddha. They spoke outside in the sunken garden, under the shade of the Bodhi tree.

"You said that you were going to come back and sit in on the evening meditations with me," Diane began.

"I know, but I really got sick. My stomach is so screwed up. The only sitting I've been doing is on the toilet."

Diane glared at him before continuing, "That's not what I hear."

Max met her glare and pressed the issue. "What, Diane? What do you hear?"

"About how you spend most of your time hanging out in the Tibetan restaurant and the chai shops with your new friends, Shunya, and that Sam guy."

"Bullshit! A few times, maybe. I've got to try and eat something."

Diane was about to reply when Paul passed by and flashed a flirtatious smile—handsome Paul, the same Paul who had courted Diane at the Alandi course.

"That guy doesn't give up, does he?" Max added.

"Why, do you think he should?"

Max wanted to say no and walk away from Diane for the last time, but he said yes.

*　　　*　　　*

Arthur, the Atman, as he liked to be called, was a great soul trapped in a sick and dying body, the result of an obscure but deadly disease that drained the fluids from his bone joints and left him stiff as a board, incapable of moving his crew-cut head more than a few degrees in any direction. And yet, though paralyzed, he crossed the world in a Volkswagen camper driven by hired hands in an attempt to realize his full spiritual potential.

Before becoming the Atman, Arthur was a Hollywood gopher, running errands for so many rich and famous celebrities for so long that the aura of celebrity had rubbed off on him. Even now, facing death, his thin, rigid body covered in the orange robes of a monk, the Atman was a formidable force of life for Max to reckon with.

Max met him the morning after he spoke with Diane. He was leaving the Mahabodhi temple with Shunya when he saw the master monk kneeling beside the Atman, and approached them.

Following an inquiry into Max's welfare, the master monk introduced him. "This is Arthur," the monk said.

"The Atman," Arthur added, incapable of shaking Max's extended hand. Two Indian boy servants had carried him down the stairs on a prostration board into the sunken garden.

"I was hoping to see you again before I left Bodh Gaya. I wanted to thank you for the experience of stopping my mind," Max said to the monk.

The monk was bewildered. "I wasn't aware of this experience."

"Toward the end of our conversation, my mind stopped and expanded. My whole body expanded for a split second, a microsecond. And I understood from this experience what you were trying to tell me in words, at least, that's what I thought."

The master monk said, "Even if I was unaware, I am nonetheless pleased, and I am hopeful that you will remain in India and continue your studies."

Max said he would, and the master monk renewed his offer to get Max a much-coveted visa extension before leaving. "To prepare for his Holiness," the monk said. He was referring to the Dalai Lama, who was due in Bodh Gaya at the end of the month.

Max watched him walk away, then turned to the Atman and said, "That *was* really strange."

"Your experience or the monk's lack of awareness of it?"

"Both, I guess, but . . ."

Max fell silent and looked to the Atman for help. His prominent hooked nose, sunken cheeks and bony brows lent him the look of death, but his brilliant, brown eyes offered defiance, and he spoke with the wisdom of the ages.

"You know the Jains?" the Atman pressed.

Max nodded. He saw a few of them in Bombay, all dressed in white, their mouths covered with gauze for fear of breathing in and killing an airborne microbe.

"You know Lord Mahavir?"

"The Jain Buddha," Max said, describing the symbol of perfect Jain enlightenment.

"Do you also know that Lord Mahavir's closest disciple was his dearest friend, who had bestowed enlightenment upon dozens of beings without ever being enlightened himself? Lord Buddha, too. His closest disciple, his cousin Ananda, also enlightened dozens of beings without entering nirvana—until his Lord Buddha died."

Max asked, "How was that possible?"

"Consciousness knows itself. It doesn't know personality. It is not a possession. It expands and contracts. You don't."

Just then, the Atman's two servants arrived and picked up his prostration board.

"Where are you going?"

"To die."

"Now?"

"Soon enough, but dying is not the worst."

"Then what is?"

"Living. Living without love, and never knowing."

"What?"

"Yourself," the Atman said, before saying goodbye.

12

Max had lied to Diane. Though sickly, he had been spending a lot of time with Shunya and Sam. The next day,
he found a basketball court at a parochial school, just north of the little village of Bodh Gaya. Shunya found an old leather basketball in the town of Gaya, and the game was on: six guys playing three-on-three basketball, twelve thousand miles from home, in the middle of nowhere, playing like they had never left the schoolyard—cows and oxen and water buffaloes lumbering by, peasants and beggars and teachers and students watching the young white sahibs play a black man's game in a brown man's country. In any event, the focus was still on winning. Playing with Shunya, Max couldn't lose and wouldn't relent until a rush of cramps and nausea forced him off the court.

Later in the day, after basketball, Shunya tracked down a small ball of opium and gave it to Max. "To kill the pain and deaden the brain," he said.

Max took the "bitter pill," went numb in all the right places, and joined Shunya for dinner in a large Tibetan tent, housing the best restaurant in town within its filthy canvas walls. Max was stoned stupid, eating a vegetable dumpling and licking his fingers when Diane entered the tent with Paul.

Max glared at Diane. She forced a smile and followed Paul to a table at the back of the tent, where they joined Big Jane and her boyfriend Gary for dinner.

"Fuck is that about?" Max began.

"Looks like a date to me," Shunya said.

Max was angry, bewildered, hurt, sick and tired. Then the cramps returned, and Max ran out of the tent to wretch. He was leaning against a tree, rubbing the knot in his solar plexus, fighting to keep the food down when Diane walked over to check up on him.

"You really are sick," she began.

"Obviously," Max sarcastically replied.

Diane said goodnight. She left the restaurant without Paul, and was on her way back to the Vihara when she ran into her husband, David, who was waiting for her in front of the Vihara.

*   *   *

"I've been looking for you for a month," David said, parting from an awkward embrace.

Diane said, "And I've been in hiding, meditating mostly." She was shaken, but pretended otherwise.

"With your boyfriend. I know you have a boyfriend. I know Max. I met him in Kabul."

Diane nodded. "He told me, but . . ."

"What?"

"Do we really have to do this now, David?" Diane asked, looking up at the stars. It was another beautiful night in North India, crystal clear, about fifty-five degrees without a trace of wind.

David said, "Yes, we have to do this now—if only because you're my wife. You owe me that much."

"And you owe me money, David. I left Kabul with a thousand; I left you three at least, maybe four."

"You mean that I have to pay for the pleasure of talking to you after you walked out on me?"

"A few hundred would help."

David reached into his passport poach and produced two hundred dollar bills.

Diane hesitated, then snatched the money out of his hand. "It's a start," she said, before turning away from him and entering the Vihara.

*   *   *

"So David shows up at my door, and starts screaming and yelling about our friendship in Kabul, and how I betrayed it by fucking his wife," Max told Shunya the following morning. They had met in front of a chai shop across from the Mahabodhi Temple. "I told him that I didn't know Diane was his wife until I was already involved with her, thinking I could take the edge off of things. Then he asks me if I want to split a vial of morphine with him. Then I go looking for Diane at the Vihara and find out that she left town early this morning—no goodbye, no note, nothing."

"What about that Paul guy? Did she go with him?"

"No, the prick's still around. It's hard to know what to think except that she must have been really scared. She's still attached to the David in some intensely negative way. I mean I feel really bad—she could have left me a note or something. I tried to talk to Jane about it and all she said was that Diane needed to go and take care of herself."

"She didn't tell you where Diane went?"

"No, but I have to admit that I'm also a bit relieved. I'm not sure that we made for a very good couple. She was so needy and I am a bit wrapped up in my own little quest. Diane was right when she said that I didn't come to India to find a neurotic Jewish girl from the next neighborhood, even if she was beautiful."

Shunya was about to reply when Sam walked by with Bill Velititsky. "Talk about an odd couple," Max added.

Shunya said, "You ain't seen nothing yet."

Sayadaw's meditation courses, having achieved a great deal of popularity in India during the past year, attracted all kinds of people. This second course in the Burmese Vihara included one famous American actress, one European descended from royalty, two renowned rock musicians, four junkies trying to kick, an IRA terrorist on the lam, eight Jewish kids from New York running the "grace race" in an attempt to win their souls before they lost their minds to the time-honored tradition of "Nu, Harold, be a doctor and forget all this meshugass," two climbers who recently ascended Mount Everest, a seventeen-year-old Norwegian "boy" who had sailed from England to Bombay alone on a fourteen-foot sailboat, two people who were on the verge of taking formal vows to Buddhist monk-hood, one person working for Interpol, one representative of the CIA, and Bill Viletitski, the nerd, from Rockford, Illinois, who had quietly lost his mind near the end of the first meditation course, and who manifested his insanity in the middle of the second course when he got naked and refused to dress until he got laid.

Big Jane was inclined to oblige him with an act of mercy, but her boyfriend, Gary, talked her out of it.

Bill wouldn't talk to Sayadaw, and his presence was tolerated until several women began to fear him. Consequently, Sayadaw finally had naked Bill removed to Sam's room in the Gandhi ashram, at the suggestion of the master monk.

"Because you may be having a cultural understanding of this young man's problem that we lack," the master monk told Sam, dropping Bill off at his room in the Gandhi Ashram one sunny afternoon.

Bill went willingly, thinking he might get laid. Sam humored him until nightfall, when the temperature dropped below forty and naked Bill reached for a blanket, and Sam pulled it out of his hands.

"If you want to be naked, be naked," Sam said.

Bill said, "But I'm cold."

"That's tough. And if you don't like it in my room, you can spend the night outside and beg someone else for a blanket."

"I'm not a beggar."

"For attention, you are."

That relatively quick and simple exchange was all it took to get Bill dressed and focused.

"He wasn't beyond reason because he wasn't beyond pride," Sam told Max and Shunya over a cup of chai after returning Bill to the Ashram, obviously proud of his quick psychological fix. "I challenged him where it hurt the most. He could play the fool, but when it came down to it, his pride wouldn't let him play the beggar. I just hope he was worth the effort."

"Because he could relapse?" Max asked.

"No, because he could leave. For every person that stays in India beyond a year, a thousand go home in a few months. They want to stay, but they can't handle the sickness, or the poverty, or the stress created by being so far away from home. And they miss the point of being here, because their fear kills the spirit of adventure and self discovery. Because they don't have the courage to endure it and see who and what is behind it, they never get to see the deeper truth of themselves. You know all those fire-eating dragons and fierce deities in Chinese and Tibetan mythology?"

Max nodded and Sam continued. "On a journey to India, which is a metaphor for all internal processes of self discovery, disease functions as a dragon of the material world. It is the fear of disease and instability and, ultimately, death, that sends all these people home before they really want to go."

Toward that end, Max's two new friends spent the next couple of weeks teaching him the basics of survival in the East: what to eat and where to sleep, how to use the black market, what trains to take, what medication to take, what and who to avoid.

"Including women, especially the one you were with," Sam concluded.

"Why her?"

"Because I can feel her pain through yours. And two people who are so out of touch with themselves couldn't possibly know the meaning of love."

The truth hurt, though it was easier to avoid after David left town to look for Diane.

*   *   *

Puri was a large town south of Calcutta, located on the shore of the Sea of Bengal. Diane had heard that it was a beautiful place, filled with palm trees, tropical fruits and sandy beaches. Arriving in Puri in the early evening, four days after she left Bodh Gaya, Diane found a clean room in a small hotel on the beach. She had a nice fish dinner and spent the rest of the evening in meditation in her room. Her plan was simple: to become strong enough and centered enough to deal with her husband and her boyfriend, to transcend both entanglements by the time she left Puri, and embark upon a righteous life independent of these men.

The following morning, she squeezed into a bikini and went for a swim. She was drying off, lying on a towel in the sun, when she opened her eyes and found a small crowd of teens gaping at her ample cleavage. A larger crowd of adults jeered at her from a distance. She was the only westerner on the beach and the only woman wearing a bathing suit.

As Diane belatedly discovered, Puri was a religious town, the site of the Jagannath Temple, one the holiest shrines in India. So she packed the bikini away, braided her hair, wore long cotton dresses and returned to the practice of meditation exclusively—at least six hours a day, every day, in an effort to duplicate the schedule of the course she had vacated.

Try though she did, Diane found no peace, her thoughts constantly vacillating between anger and guilt: She hated David for driving her out of Bodh Gaya; she hated herself for lacking the courage to stay—always thinking that the meditation would help, always hurting in spite of the effort.

Not unlike Max and many other novices of meditation, Diane was inclined to think that meditation produced peace of mind, not knowing that different meditative techniques yielded different results.

"Peace of mind may come from the practice of Vipasanna meditation," Sayadaw had said. "But knowing oneself by the practice of observing oneself can be very difficult at times, and not peaceful at all."

In fact, Diane's Puri experience proved increasingly difficult: the loneliness often compounding the intensity of the practice, spending day after day within her mind, watching her mind, feeling the heartache of a broken marriage and a lost boyfriend, dwelling beside a small crowd of beggars and lepers that lived in back of her hotel, interacting with a sexually repressed culture that glorified the repression of all women.

She often thought of writing Max and apologizing for her quick exit, but she had nothing good to say about herself and nothing new to report after ten long and uneventful days. And she began to regret taking money from David, which she had used to escape from him. She was walking toward the beach, weaving between houses and palm trees, berating herself for taking the money, when she fell down a well filled with enough water to drown her.

Her head hitting the wall as she fell, Diane heard a loud buzzing in her ears; her mind filling with a rush of remarkably bright colors and shapes before she passed out. Regaining consciousness under water, she floated to the surface, coughing water and phlegm, gasping for breath.

The stench was nauseating. The standing water had collected filth and bacteria for the past five months, since the end of the rainy season. A rat nipped at her badly bruised shoulder as she swallowed another mouthful of brackish poison and vomited. Her arms flailing, fighting to get a grip on her life, she went down for a second and third time, thinking she was dead.

13

Apart from a surge of curious young Westerners, the much anticipated arrival of the Dalai Lama in Bodh Gaya attracted a great many Tibetans, some having walked hundreds of miles to receive their leader's blessing, one having prostrated himself every inch of the way from Kathmandu. Such was the zeal and loyalty of this ancient root race to their origins, facing ruthless decimation by the Chinese.

Shunya had been planning to attend this special puja all winter, but his visa expired and he needed an extension. "And business calls," he told Sam.

They were sitting on Sam's favorite bench at the entrance to the Tibetan Temple. They had spent more than an hour sitting together inside the temple, which reminded Shunya of Swayambunath. The ceiling was painted with wrathful deities, and the walls were inlaid with gold and adorned with antique Tonka paintings, all paying homage to an imposing gold Buddha at the front and center of the meditation hall.

"If you would only learn to profit from the experience," Sam said, lighting a bidi.

"And how would I do that?" Shunya snapped. He didn't appreciate the critical inference.

"By making less and seeing more of yourself in the process. Every deal you do is the next best deal, and no deal is ever enough."

"Then you shouldn't take the money," Shunya shot back.

Now it was Sam's turn to squirm. Without Shunya's timely and greatly appreciated stipends, Sam would not find it so easy to watch his mind. Sam took another drag on his bidi and exhaled, "Point well taken."

"As it should be—because I know how to make money, I should make money. Because you know how to sit with yourself and learn from yourself, you should sit and learn. Because Bill Viletitski doesn't know how to be with himself in a dignified way, he learns it from you. Everyone is engaged in the process of fulfilling each other's purpose, which is the natural order of things. And I have decided to entertain a higher purpose this time around, which requires more money."

"Which is?"

"To build a school for occult studies and comparative religion in Nepal, a place where people can come from all over the world, regardless of inclination or denomination, and learn from each other. I figure it'll take fifty grand to get it off the ground, and the only way I can make that kind of money is with hash oil."

Sam was stunned by the magnitude of Shunya's calling and the high degree of risk it would entail. The last big deal in Israel nearly destroyed his life, when he attempted to smuggle hash into America. He had concealed several kilos of it in an assortment of small furnishings and musical instruments, and shipped it to three different friends in New York. All of whom were arrested and subsequently fingered Shunya to save themselves from jail.

As a result, Shunya couldn't go back to America without going to jail, and he had barely escaped capture in Israel—begetting the journey further east, to India, to escape prosecution, and the desire to do greater things by beating the odds already stacked against him.

It was this peculiar dichotomy of idiot peril and humane purpose that raised the third eye of holy powers like Swami Puri. Shunya spent less than a month in the Swami's ashram following his arrival in India, and was offered the cherished position of valet and chauffeur—which Shunya rejected in favor of the adventure of a lifetime on the road to uncertainty.

The old Tibetan lama presented a second remarkable opportunity for Shunya to take formal teachings from a great master. He, too, had offered Shunya the exalted position of first disciple. Though tempted and flattered, Shunya interpreted the second offer as a confirmation of the first offer, both being divine signs of the good karma he had already accrued on his own merit, following his own path.

*   *   *

Max visited the Atman on two occasions, but he didn't stay very long. The Atman was dying slowly and painfully, and he only had one thing to say to Max, which he often repeated: "Don't waste your life thinking about how things could be or should be. And don't lie to yourself in the process."

It was a good counsel, but Max couldn't stop thinking about Diane, and he began to visit the post office twice a day hoping to find a letter from her.

"I never should have let her go," he told Big Jane one morning, walking past the Mahabodhi Temple. He had sought her out to talk about Diane.

"As if you had a choice in the matter?" Jane challenged.

"I could have loved her more," Max said, stopping in front of the temple entrance.

"You had your chances."

"I suppose, but I wouldn't mind having another. I think about her so much. If you can just tell me where she went?"

"I can't and I won't. I won't break my promise to her. Besides, I think Diane's had enough men in her life trying to help her and hurt her. It's time she found her own way."

Max nodded and sighed, "Diane said you were tough."

"Tough-minded maybe, but not hard-hearted. I have no doubt that you did your best for Diane, and I do believe she appreciated your efforts. But you can't have her see the world through your eyes, you can't be conscious for two people, and you can't really imagine how the world looks through her eyes, the eyes of a woman. She read *Siddhartha*, the book you gave her. She loved the story, but she also thought it lacked something, which was the point of view of a woman seeking perfection. In fact, if I know Diane, she would have been happier with a romantic evening walk down the river bed with you.

"That's what she thought she needed, more from you and less of her husband, which is why she left him in the first place. On the other hand, maybe it's just as well that you didn't fulfill that need for her, because she'd still be here, focused on you and not herself, and arguing with her husband. I just think that it was about time she confronted the inevitability of her own loneliness."

"I understand that, but I still think she could have said goodbye."

Jane was about to reply when an old beggar reached for her elbow; Jane gave him a few paisa before Max clued her into the bigger picture as they continued their walk.

"It was nice of you to give, but it's a bad habit to get into because that beggar and every other beggar in town works for the chai walas across the street. And they only get to keep half of what you give them."

"Then feeling half good about myself is still better than doing nothing for these people and feeling no good."

It was a hard point to argue. As a result, Max spent the remainder of the day meditating inside the Mahabodhi Temple, contemplating his great good fortune—having already met so many remarkable people, having seen so many wonders—and he was still at the beginning of his journey.

In the early evening, as the full moon rose over the Mahabodhi Stupa, he saw a thousand and eight butter lamps flicker beneath the Bodhi tree, turning the holy old grotto into a garden of unearthly delights. Several hundred Tibetan monks wrapped in burgundy and saffron robes, wearing coral and turquoise charms to ward off the evil and invite higher spirits, sat perfectly still in homage to the Great Resolve and chanted to the lord of the moon and the stars: conch horns blaring, bells clanging, the eerie sound of a hollowed out thigh bone, salvaged from the body of a late great Lama, lilting then wilting in the evening breeze as the Dalai Lama took his seat on the throne of magic and mystery and began the Great Puja.

Max was sitting on top of the stairs—watching in awe as the procession of devotees and admirers sought the blessing of His Holiness, each presenting him with a colorful silk scarf—telling himself to remember every remarkable detail.

*   *   *

Calcutta was anathema to God and man. The diseased and disabled occupying every crevice of the city, every corner, every sidewalk, every gutter, every alleyway, every thought. Rats stole food from beggars, battling the homeless for a slice of life on the crowded streets overflowing with millions of people and tongas and taxis and rickshaws and buses and trucks, fighting each other and the stinking air for every precious bit of space, going every direction at once, together drowning in an endless perversion of life and no liberty and no happiness.

The bent palm trees and decaying colonial buildings and broken cobblestone streets denoted a punishing British history and a chaotic political reality, communists fighting socialists and capitalists for a piece of the ever-diminishing rancid pie. There were remnants of the Raj, the dithering old men dressed in khaki, wearing pith helmets to protect their weathered brains, and the old women dressed in matronly white, unsoiled and unmoved by the march of time.

Diane was nonetheless glad to be there, grateful to be alive. She had gone down for the third and last time when she was plucked from the well by two young men who saved her life and gave it meaning. For the first time in a long time, Diane realized that her life had value: she thought she had been saved for a reason, and she began to think that she should return home to America and start all over again. She could go back to school and get another degree, or pursue her dream of becoming a sculptor. She didn't want to stay in India and tempt fate again.

She left for Calcutta the following morning with less than twenty dollars in her pocket, thinking she would call home and get the money for a plane ticket.

David convinced her to stay. He ran into Diane in Calcutta at the Salvation Army Hotel, a popular flop house for young Westerners.

"I was on my way to Puri looking for you," he explained.

She was crestfallen, thinking Jane must have betrayed her confidence. "She must have told you."

David said, "No. She didn't even tell your boyfriend, Max. But I spoke to a lot of people at the course, and I figured it had to be Puri because you expressed so much interest in the place."

"I love Max," Diane declared.

David shrugged and stroked his long, blond beard. "But you feared me more than you loved him, or else you wouldn't have run away so fast."

"And you take pride in that?"

"I take power because I have the money you need, and because you're still my wife. If you want a plane ticket to America, I'll buy you a plane ticket. If you want to stay in India, I own your sweet ass."

"Junkie fuck," Diane spat before leaving the hotel in a rage.

She never hated a person more than she hated David, but old habits were hard to break, and Diane wanted to remain in India more than anything. "So I'll sell my ass to you, for a hundred a night, payable each and every night," Diane told David, returning to the hotel at dusk.

David said, "You get five hundred a week, at the end of each and every week."

And the deal was done, sweetened with a daily visit to a local opium den because David insisted, and because Diane needed to kill the pain. Besides, she loved opium, and shopping for clothes and jewelry, and eating in better restaurants.

As much as she hated David, Diane hated herself even more. In fact, she was still addicted to the hate, which proved a far more powerful aphrodisiac than meditation. By the end of the first week in Calcutta, she began to believe that she was still in love with David. Nearing the end of their second week together, they were making plans to spend the summer together in Nepal—until Diane was forced to confront herself. Again.

It was a sunny Tuesday afternoon when Diane ran into Peter Harrington at the Amex office. She was stoned on dope—having chased the dragon around the hotel room with David all morning—when she turned and recognized him.

"Remember me?" she began, smiling flirtatiously and looking up into Peter's clear blue eyes. He was taller than she remembered.

"Of course," Peter stammered. "Diane, if I remember correctly?"

"As if I was so easy to forget," Diane pressed, peripherally aware of the woman standing in back of Peter.

Peter was about to reply when the woman stepped forward and introduced herself. "Ute," she said rather forcefully, extending her hand.

She was German, a pretty brunette—in her early forties, Diane guessed—and obviously connected to Peter.

"So that's how it is," Diane said.

Ute forced a smile and declared, "He is with me," before kissing Peter on the cheek and telling him that she would meet him outside.

"A bit possessive, I would say," Diane noted.

"Yes, she is, but she has also been very good for me—as you were, because you were the first woman I was with in many years, and my experience with you made it possible for me to be with her."

"It's the least I could've done," Diane sighed.

Peter reached for Diane's hand, looked into her hazy blue eyes and sadly said, "But I still think that you can do much better for yourself."

Diane could hardly argue the point, and sadly watched Peter leave. Stoned on dope, and filling with guilt and self-hatred, she eventually left Amex and wandered through the streets of

Calcutta in a daze, tears falling from her eyes as she confronted the cheapness of her life: men groping her and jeering at her as she careened from one crowded bazaar to another. Passing hordes of beggars living beside open sewers filled with rats, Diane stopped to witness the existence of one particular beggar, so deformed that Diane was unsure of its species.

It's head bashed in—no nose, one eye, no ears, a hole in the face for a mouth—the chest plate was so twisted that it was difficult to tell the front from the back of it; the arms and legs were so deformed, protruding from so many odd places in the torso it was hard to tell if "it" was truly human. Yet it begged to live another day.

Diane was still crying when she arrived at the train station, leaving all her possessions behind in the hotel, vowing to change the direction of her own life or die trying.

14

Nearing the end of winter, the change in weather heralded a change in plans. Max thought about going to Calcutta to pick up much-need money from home, but decided to retrieve the money from an Amex office in Delhi, where he would meet up with Shunya.

Bill Velititsky decided to spend the spring hot season in the Himalayas, so he took the same train as Max and proceeded to talk about the dharma. After three hours of this inanity, Max was finally moved to ask Bill how he found his way to India. After all, Bill hardly fit the mold of a world traveled seeker.

"I met this guy, Narayan, in California," Bill began. "He was a sadhu and he told me about this kid guru, Swami-ji who was visiting America. So I went to see the guru and I gave him all of my money, about five thousand dollars, to take me back to India with him. Then when I got here a couple of months ago, I realized that I made a big mistake . . . Then I heard about the Sayadaw course . . . Then I met Sam . . ."

It was a very long and tedious story on a scheduled sixteen-hour ride to Delhi that took twenty-nine hours and a small piece of Max's mind. First the train was held up outside of Gaya by several hundred radicalized and politicized peasants waving red flags and real hammers and sickles. Then the mail car was seized by a band of dacoits, highway robbers who boarded the train outside of Benares and robbed the mail car in the middle of the night. The following morning, the train hit a water buffalo.

All this on a train so crowded that many people rode on the roofs of the cars while Max and Bill rode on the filthy floor. Max had failed to secure a third class sleeper, and suffered the consequences of a third class life in a third class country in chaos: the air stinking from that all-to-familiar mix of charcoal, sweat, and stale urine; people talking throughout the night and periodically arguing over a lost seat; a lack of patience and one old beggar who took up too much precious space and was eventually tossed off the moving train into the night. Each episode was punctuated by another footnote in the life of Bill.

*   *   *

New Delhi reminded Max of Long Island: the tree-lined streets and private houses and garden apartments that dotted the suburbs, the colonial two-story shopping mall that ringed Connaught Circle in the heart of the city, and the new high-rise office buildings that dotted the horizon. While the construction might have been a bit shoddy, the overall effect was distinctly western—with a few holy old cows and tongas thrown into the frenetic mix of cars, and people basking in the afterglow of a short war and a quick victory over Pakistan.

Old Delhi was over-wrought, over-populated, dirty and dilapidated. The buildings were covered with rust and soot, and the streets were filled with people battling one another for space and air.

As Shunya had suggested, Max avoided the old and clung to the new, taking a room at the ever-popular Palace Heights Hotel before touring Connaught Circle.

Max was eating ice cream, drooling over the memory of much better stuff he used to get at Zito's Bakery on Arthur Avenue in the Bronx, when he ran into Shunya and Delhi Dave in front of the ice cream parlor. They had been out on the town all afternoon looking to buy papers on the black market. Shunya needed a visa and Delhi Dave needed a new passport.

"Cocksuckers wanted another fuckin' grand for that," Delhi Dave was telling Shunya when they met Max. "That stuff taste as good as it looks?" he asked Max, following introductions.

"It ain't Zito's," Max snapped.

"On Arthur Avenue?"

"Where else?"

"You know Joe Sick, the fuck from Arthur Avenue who used to ride his big fuckin' Harley naked on the Concourse?"

"I heard of him." Max said

"Yeah, well, I grew up wit'im an' the Fordham Baldies. You know the Fordham Baldies?"

Max knew; he was in grade school when he heard the harrowing stories about the gang who terrorized the Bronx during the fifties with zip guns and gravity knives. "You were the guys who beat up a teacher at Roosevelt High School and shaved his head, weren't you?"

Delhi Dave widened his smile. He was proud of his murky past. "Cut'im up pretty good, too. But I tell ya, the best thing I remember about the Bronx were the Dvorak sisters. You know 'em?"

Of course Max knew them. The most beautiful blond junkie twins in the history of the Bronx, they destroyed their looks and their lives using dope and gang-banging around the Bronx.

"They grew up in my building," Max said.

"An' I fucked 'em both, you believe that?" Delhi Dave declared.

Max didn't believe him, but said he did, and their nostalgic conversation stretched until midnight, repeatedly punctuated by Dave's relationship to the Dvorak sisters, and to Fast Freddy Fein, a Bronx friend who had run guns to Castro with Delhi Dave. Max knew Freddy by reputation. He was an older Jewish intellectual who had taken an active role in the Columbia riots.

"We worked outta Miami," Delhi Dave added.

"Where Dave's wanted for manslaughter," Shunya told Max the following morning, over chai on the patio of the Palace Height Hotel.

"And you're his friend?"

"Like you are, Max. It was one of those things."

"What things?"

"Business," Shunya finally admitted.

After all, the drug business was in the habit of making strange bedfellows.

*   *   *

The next morning, following another unsuccessful attempt at buying papers on the black market, Delhi Dave ran out of patience with the process and came up with a better idea: steal two American passports and trade them in for one common-wealth Australian passport, requiring no visa.

He did this by the end of the day. Dave also told Shunya that he had a great idea for making more money than he could ever steal in India. "In Kashmir, wit' this guy Mohammed. One of my best friends in the world. An' he's sittin' on some of the best shit in the world."

"Shit" meaning "hash." "Best deal" meaning Shunya would have to finance it. "But not all of it, because we'll take Moham-med in as a partner," Delhi Dave said.

Shunya wasn't impressed until Delhi Dave put an ingenious spin on the deal.

"The beauty of this is the shit never leaves the country," Delhi Dave explained. "All I gotta do is run it down to Bombay an' sell it to guys who want to smuggle it out of the country, who don't want to make the trip to Kashmir or Afghanistan an' fuck with all these Mohammads. We just bring the shit down there to 'em and make 'em pay a decent price for it. You know, like an eighty-dollar kilo of Kashmiri we sell for two-twenty in Bombay. An' they can still get a grand or two for it in America or in Europe for taking the bigger an' everyone's copasetic."

"It's a stroke of marketing genius," Shunya told Max later in the evening. "To create a market where there is none."

Max was impressed, if not curious. "You mean Delhi Dave figured this out all by himself?"

"You can't imagine how much of Delhi Dave's New York street talk is an act, to appear stupid in an attempt to gain the edge on you and everyone else he meets, who thinks they're so much smarter."

As Max found out on the train to Dehra Dune the following morning, Delhi Dave had spent a lot of time in a lot of jails reading a lot of books.

"Historical biographies, philosophy, an' religion, which is the most ingenious scam in the fucking world, to make money of promises that never deliver in this life, so you promise 'em all another life, an' start countin' the coins," Delhi Dave said. "An' they use the money to build the biggest house on the block because it's the nature of people to look up and kiss bigger ass because it makes 'em feel bigger. The more guilty you feel, the more you pay, an' the more ass you kiss. An' once they got you apologizing for being born, they own your ass."

"So, you don't believe in God?" Max asked, after Delhi Dave whipped his ass in a game of chess for the third time.

"In other words, I don't kiss ass."

"Sounds very Buddhist to me," Shunya concluded.

"If I hadda be," Delhi Dave said. "In the meantime, I'd rather be rich an' let 'em all kiss my ass."

Shunya gave Delhi Dave two thousand dollars when they arrived in Dehra Dune.

"Which leaves me with less than a thousand," Shunya said.

Delhi Dave said, "Not to worry, 'cause if I can't make it in Bombay, I got somethin' even better cookin' wit' these college guys I know in Kabul."

15

Dehra Dune was a small bourgeois town, due north of Delhi, nestled in the Himalayan foothills. Its many fine homes served as second dwellings for wealthy businessmen and politicians; its police station harbored at least one corrupt official, who was in the habit of selling visa extensions to desperate people.

Shunya had luck in Delhi. "Because of the times and the politics, there isn't much sympathy for Americans in the Capital, but this is the 'burbs, and there's a Colonel Singh here who's supposed to be more of a capitalist, from what I gather."

With the help of the master monk in Bodh Gaya, and ten dollars, Max had received his visa extension from a Colonel Singh in Gaya. "Can't be the same guy," he said.

It wasn't. But there were dozens, if not hundreds, of Colonel Singhs in India—Singh being the last name of all Sikhs, many of whom were predisposed towards commerce and military service. Throughout history, it was the Punjab, the Sikh homeland in India, that formed the backbone of the Indian economy and army. All Sikhs had small knives tucked into their turbans, a symbol as dear to them as a Christian holy cross, and all wore beards. The Sikhs formed a powerful and distinct racial identity within the larger race of the Indian brotherhood.

After spending three long and tedious days in a cheap Dehra Dune guest house, Shunya had finally run out of patience with this Colonel Singh.

"The bastard was supposed to give me a six-month extension for a hundred dollars. Now he's talking three months for two hundred—maybe!" Shunya ranted, returning to the guest house after spending another six hours in Colonel Singh's office.

"Then maybe we should try another bastard in another town," Max said.

"As if they would be cheaper by the dozen? You don't get it because you haven't been in India long enough to appreciate the mentality of a poor colored person getting one over on the rich white sahib. But it's easy to figure if you look back at history, at the British who oppressed these people for so long, and left them with an inferiority complex that a lifetime can't erase. Between now and then, we suffer the consequences—like when a white man asks a question and an Indian answers it with wrong information rather than no information at all because they don't want to look stupid. Or they fuck with you on purpose sometimes because they can, like when you try and find out what platform a certain train is leaving from and each person you ask tells you a different platform—including the conductor—and they watch you run your ass off from platform to platform, hoping you get it wrong!"

"Assuming it's all true, it's hard to believe anyone in this country can become enlightened," Max sighed.

"It is hard to believe, but I'm becoming convinced that it's in the numbers. You have a billion people living here so you have to figure that the odds are four times greater to find more wisdom here than in America, where there's about two hundred and fifty million people. Add in all the poverty and so many millions of people without jobs with a lot of time on their hands, walking around and asking about the meaning of life, and the odds are that someone's going to come up with an answer. Fortunately for us, one of those guys just arrived in this town."

Max followed Shunya across town the following morning to meet Shiva Swami. Max had never met a real Indian guru before, and many of his preconceived notions were immediately shattered: the private house where the gathering was held was huge, and many of the disciples were apparently wealthy. The Indian women were dressed in gold braided saris, and their husbands wore designer business suits or white dhotis and expensive Italian leather shoes; many of the young westerners looked disheveled and impoverished by comparison.

"It's not what I expected," Max said, sitting cross-legged on the white tiled floor beside Shunya. The living room was cavernous, holding more than two hundred people.

"Me either," Shunya said. "Because Shiva Swami supposedly lived in caves most of his life, doing penance for the world, enduring dozens of snake bites and scorpion stings—a California sadhu friend told me about it."

Max was about to reply when the roomful of disciples burst into devotional song: chanting to the melody of a harmonium for the greater glory of guru and God, then dancing out of time and tune, spinning out of control and slamming into the nearest wall. Max was reminded of a documentary he had once seen on Pentecostal Holy Rollers in America, and was struck by the similarity.

Shunya said, "Its shakti-pat gone amuck. Either the energy is weird or the disciples aren't evolved enough to accommodate it."

Max was bewildered He was processing Shunya's analysis when Shiva Swami finally entered the room and focused the energy. Max didn't see the holiness, but he was impressed with the great guru's appearance. Bare-chested, wearing a red lingotti, his matted black hair reached the floor, and his palms had grown together as a result of spending so many years in prayer.

The guru sat cross-legged on a tiger skin covering a wooden platform. A young American dressed in a blue blazer stood beside him, enumerating the great guru's accomplishments.

The scene was bizarre, even by Shunya's experienced standards; none of the disciples seemed to reflect the majesty of their master. And the master did not appear to connect very well with his disciples. He smiled, but he did not speak.

When the young American finished speaking, the scene broke up into chatty little groups. Max was nearly out the door when Shunya grabbed him from behind and told him not to leave without paying his respects to the Guru.

Grudgingly, out of curiosity, Max took Shunya's advice. He crossed the room, pressed his palms together and bowed to the guru, his head barely touching the swami's knee.

Shiva Swami smiled and said (through an interpreter), "Look with your heart and not with your mind."

When Max looked up into the Swami's large black eyes, he was stunned by their depth.

"Eyes like I've never seen before," he told Shunya, following him out of the room and into the garden. "They were so deeply pained and so filled with compassion—like they were crying without tears. And I saw all those ugly scars on his body where he was bitten by snakes and scorpions, and his palms were grown together. I saw the connective tissue! How is that possible? How can someone like him be represented by so many people like them?" Max asked, looking around at the crowd of mundane disciples now milling around the garden.

Shunya was about to reply when Peter and Ute approached them. They had been sitting at the back of the room with several other young Westerners.

"We need a place to change money. Do you know if there is a place here in Dehra Dune to change money?" Ute began, without introducing herself.

"Not that I know of," Max replied, stung by her sudden intensity.

"What about you? Do you know where we can change money?" she pressed Shunya.

Shunya said "no" and Ute walked away with Peter.

"Nice lady," Max cracked.

"Interesting guy," Shunya sarcastically added.

Max was watching them disappear into the crowd when Narayan walked up to Shunya and embraced him. He was a tall California sadhu, with long, blonde dreadlocks and three white strips painted across his forehead, denoting his loyalty to Shiva.

"Been a long time, my friend," Narayan began, parting from the embrace. He had also been sitting in the back of the room.

"Too long," Shunya was about to say, when Max excitedly interceded, "I know you! You're the guy that told me to take the Sayadaw course."

"You're also the guy who told me to see Shiva Swami, if I had the chance," Shunya added, raising his eyebrows.

Narayan smiled self-consciously and shrugged. "I heard that he was an extraordinary guy, but, it *was* a little strange in there—even for me."

"A little?" Shunya challenged.

Narayan looked around the garden and widened his smile. "I guess we could say that God does move in some very strange ways. Nothing about these disciples paired with that guru makes sense to me either. Then again, this *is* India."

Narayan pressed his palms together, turned and bowed to the house, as if he were bowing to the guru, then said goodbye to Max and Shunya before leaving the grounds.

"Interesting guy," Max said.

"Remarkable guy! Left a wealthy family and came here when he was only sixteen, and he's already one of the leading western authorities on the Hindu culture and religion. He's also lived in caves and spent years studying."

"What?"

"The paradoxes—what else?"

16

Max never heard from Diane. He didn't even know if she was still in India. Though he didn't talk about her, he continued to think about her.

Shunya rarely discussed or displayed his feelings about anyone. He alluded to his daughter on several occasions, but he never spoke about how much he missed her, and how much her letters tore at his heart, all of them ending with the same question: *When is Daddy coming home?*

Each time he told her, "maybe next year," unable to tell her that he could not come back until his New York lawyer said it was okay. Such was the nature of the crime and punishment Shunya had exacted upon himself. Would his daughter ever understand? Would she forgive him? Would she even recognize him?

Having secured a six month visa extension in Dehra Dune for two hundred and fifty dollars, Shunya and Max decided to go to Almora to visit Sam. They took a train to Raniket, then rented a car to take them as far as Nainital, a popular Indian resort.

As their car climbed higher and higher into the mountains, Shunya wished his daughter could see the world through his wide eyes: all the tall trees and colorful wildflowers that lined the ever-curling road to Nainital, and the dramatic perspective view of the earth, arching into the distant horizon on a hot summer day as the cool mountain air blew across his face.

Nainital was a small town tucked into the evergreen mountains, its many hotels and guest houses built into the hillside overlooking a long and languid lake. A former British resort, Nainital was now the favorite of India's burgeoning bourgeoisie. Loud, pushy, and opinionated, Shunya despised the whole lot.

Max reserved his harsh judgment for the disciples of the renowned Kenchi Baba, many of whom were staying at the Evelyn Hotel.

"Baba said this . . . Baba said that . . . Baba didn't eat today . . . Baba smiled at me . . . Baba read my mind . . . Baba saw my dreams . . . Baba . . . Baba . . . Baba."

They talked about their guru over every meal, down every hallway, in every room, their wide eyes sparkling with the blessed joy stemming from their master; always smiling and annoying Max.

Shunya found them endearing, if not enviable. "To be so in love and have so much faith in a perfect master," he told Max as they walked through the woods the following morning. They had spent the night in Nainital.

"Assuming the master *is* perfect," Max declared.

"Not necessarily," Shunya replied, as they neared the top of a steep hill.

Max found it hard to believe until he recalled a conversation he'd had with the Atman about Lord Buddha and Lord Mahavira, whose closest disciples enlightened many aspirants before they achieved perfection.

Reaching the top of the hill, Max hoped to see the fabled snow-capped mountaintops glittering in the distance, but was sorely disappointed; the entire range was immersed in clouds. Down below, Shunya pointed to the Kenchi Baba summer ashram nestled in a thicket of evergreens.

Shunya had hoped to see the great man and was disappointed that he didn't. "Because Baba's not seeing anyone this week., his disciples told me."

Max said, "He'll see me."

Shunya laughed. "Of all people," he sarcastically replied.

When Shunya turned to leave, Max headed down the hill. When the ashram gatekeeper told Max to leave, Max asked him to speak to the Baba in charge.

*   *   *

Before he was Kenchi Baba, he was a sadhu—one of millions of wandering holy men without a home or a recognizable name—until he stopped a train with his mind. Legend said that Kenchi Baba was a young ascetic when he was denied passage on a train. The British Raj was still in power at the time, and it was not inclined to give a poor sadhu a free ride.

Miffed by the indignity, the young sadhu sat on the platform and sharpened his mind; by an extraordinary act of will nullified the power of a locomotive, holding the train in the station until he was granted free passage—and the legend was born.

Whether out of instinct or dumb luck, Max was invited into the ashram and granted a private audience with the perfect master.

He expected to see a dignified old man swathed in white; he found a short and stout old man, wrapped in a colorful wool blanket, sitting cross-legged on a wooden platform in the shade of a tall tree. Baba had a small, bald head, round dark eyes, large floppy ears and a toothless smile. Hardly divine, Max thought, but eminently likeable.

"Baba asks why you have come to India," the interpreter began.

Max hesitated. He was nervous, now thinking he might indeed be in the presence of a man who knew God, the creator of all the grass and trees around him, and the mountains and the sun and the sky.

"To find God," Max finally said.

The old Baba laughed. "Now Baba asks why you have come to see him?"

"To see if he's real, if he knows God."

Kenchi Baba laughed louder this time and explained through his interpreter. "Baba says that he is as real as you are thinking, as real as the grass and trees and the mountains and the sky. The sun too! He also says that God is knowing you, and when you can accept that, you will know God."

Max was stunned. Kenchi Baba had apparently read his mind.

"Baba wants to know if you will give him a gift. He wants your necklace."

Max had heard that Kenchi Baba often asked for things his disciples highly valued. Max loved the Tibetan mala he had purchased in Bodh Gaya, studded with turquoise and coral, and was reluctant to part with it. "No," Max stammered. "Not yet, not until I'm sure of who he is."

Kenchi Baba laughed so hard that he began to rock back and forth on his haunches. "Then Baba says you will come back tomorrow morning, and we will discuss the value of things and people, and your interest in knowing God."

*   *   *

Shunya was flummoxed by the odd turn of events that put Max in a much-coveted private audience with one of the greatest living saints in India. And he was stung by Max's arrogance—or was it ignorance? To travel so far and endure so much, to be so graced and spurn the opportunity on a whim.

Max did not return to the Kenchi Baba ashram the following morning as requested. "Because it didn't mean that much to me," Max said, as their bus left Nainital for Almora.

Shunya could hardly believe his ears. "And you say the guy read your mind and you weren't even interested enough to find out how and why?"

Max said, "Not really interested because I would never become a disciple. Beacuse it's not my way, bowing down and kissing ass every day, and singing songs about a God I don't believe in or understand."

"Then why'd you try and see him in the first place?"

"To see if I could."

"Is that also why you came to India, to see if you could?"

Max was searching for an answer when his mind came to a screeching halt: all of a sudden, Max was unsure of why he had come to India, and his ears began to ring.

"Are you okay?" Shunya asked.

"I don't know," Max stumbled, looking out the window at the tall trees climbing the mountainside.

And just like that, in a moment of uncertainty, Max was plunged into an existential dilemma. As the bus wound its way up and through the narrow canyon roads to Almora, Max recalled that stellar moment in college when he was reading *Siddhartha* and experienced the ascent of the Kundalini force. Then he recalled his experience with higher consciousness in Iranian the desert, and his subsequent experience with expanded awareness at the Sayadaw course, and when he was speaking to the master monk in Bodha Gaya.

It was these experiences that drove him to India and sustained him. And yet, Max had this peculiar feeling that his inner journey was already at an end—which was a very strange and unnerving revelation, suddenly feeling like he was going through the motions of seeking, and not really seeking anything at all. After all, he could have returned to Kenchi Baba's ashram, if only for the experience of being in the coveted presence of a great guru. Bewildered, the ringing in Max's ears grew louder as the bus continued its ascent.

"Are you sure you're okay?" Shunya reiterated several minutes later.

"No, I'm not sure, Max sighed. "I always wanted to come to India, and now that I'm here, I suddenly feel like I don't have to be here anymore. You asked me that one simple question, about why I came to India, and it imploded within me: My thoughts are scrambled, and my ears are ringing, and I just don't have any answers. Just like that, you ask a simple question and my whole life is suddenly turned upside down, and I don't know why."

"The guru moves in strange ways," Shunya said.

"What's that supposed to mean?"

"These teachers we meet, good, bad and indifferent, are very powerful people that often reflect things about ourselves that are hard to fathom—whether you believe it or not. You met the master, you left the master. I asked a question and, all of a sudden, the meaning of your life comes into question. Is this coincidence, or is at all connected to your own becoming in some fateful way. Time will tell. In the meantime, your job is to be aware of the pieces even if you can't see where you fit into the whole puzzle. The fact is that you are still in India, and you're still on the move, going somewhere you haven't been before."

*   *   *

Almora was a small, rustic town perched on a thousand-foot cliff, due south of Tibet and just west of Nepal. The seven-hour bus ride from Nainital straddled many higher and precipitous cliffs until it ended in the heart of the Kumoan hills, where Jim Corbett, the great white hunter, had stalked man-eating lions and leopards at the request of the British Raj.

Arriving in the town late in the afternoon, Max and Shunya were at once exhilarated and exhausted. The air was very thin. The view was breathtaking: clouds clung to the tree tops below, darker clouds swirled overhead, a thick shaft of sunlight illuminated a distant hillside as two rainbows crisscrossed the western sky. Max had never seen anything like it.

"It's so beautiful and so unusual, it's almost unreal," Max said.

Shunya smiled and said, "You ain't seen nothing yet."

So they took a room in a local flop house, and headed out of town and up to the fabled ridge early the following morning. The steep and twisted dirt road was lined with weather-beaten wooden houses, stone and dung huts and frayed canvas tents.

The two walked slowly and deliberately uphill past an occasional army jeep, an uneven flow of old work horses and mangy dogs, and a mix of weather-beaten people, many Indians, a few Nepalis and several Tibetans.

"Long before partition, Almora belonged to Nepal," Shunya explained as they passed an odd row of well-kept summer cottages built by the Raj.

Max was about to question Shunya about the vestiges of British rule that permeated India when they rounded a curve and passed the entrance to an army post. Max was surprised. He couldn't imagine its purpose.

"To defend the border against China," Shunya said. "Beautiful as it is, this is a very paranoid neighborhood."

It was after nine o'clock when they stopped at the Chota Bazaar to catch a second breath and have a cup of chai. The ridge where Sam lived was still two long miles away, and the last leg of their trek was the most punishing: the incline was steeper, the road turned muddy, and Shunya's back was beginning to ache because his backpack was filled with his collection of esoteric books, this month featuring *The Dawn of the Magicians* and *The Theory of Celestial Influence.*

After chai, Shunya led the way through a grove of evergreens to the top of the ridge, cursing the burden of knowledge in his backpack.

His feet full of mud, his right shoulder burning from the pressure of an abrasive leather strap, his legs aching, Max said, "This better be worth it," as they emerged from the trees onto a flat clearing, known as Epworth Estate.

"You tell me," Shunya said, pointing to the sky over Max's shoulder.

When Max turned and saw the mighty white Himalayas towering above him, the OM sound filled his ears and forced him to his knees at the foot of Nanda Devi, one of the highest mountain peaks in the world. It was so tall and so grand, the snow so white, the sky so blue, the sun so bright, the mountain seemed so close that Max felt like he could reach out across the green valley below and touch it and every other mountaintop that stretched as far as his wide eyes could see—from Nepal in the east to Kashmir in the west, and back into Tibet. The view was so spectacular and so overwhelming that it brought tears to Max's eyes.

"It's almost like being inside of a dream," Max said.

"In the mind of God," Shunya whispered, sinking to his knees in awe and reverence.

Max was counting his blessings when Sam emerged from the woods at the other side of the clearing with Diane at his side.

17

Diane knew that Max was coming to Almora and she wasn't happy about it. Shunya had written Sam about their travel plans. She wanted to be alone with her new man, Sam, and not reminded of her past. She was also nervous and terribly self-conscious, rubbing her shaved head with one hand as she approached Max. In deference to the delicacy of the situation, Shunya and Sam retreated to a bench on the front porch of the large brownstone house at the back of Epworth Estate.

Max was shocked. He hardly knew what to say, or even where to begin.

"I didn't plan any of this," Diane began, parting from an awkward embrace. "I want you to believe me. I also want to explain."

They sat on a flat rock at the edge of the clearing, overlooking the valley below, and Diane continued. "I just couldn't deal with things any more, so I went to Puri to meditate on my life, and I fell down a well. I was dying, drowning, and I was saved... Then I went to Calcutta and I ran into David and revisited the cheapness of my life. .... I became so filled with hate that I ran away from him a second time. I hated myself so much that I couldn't even stand the sight of myself anymore, so I went back to Bodh

Gaya and shaved my head. I also ate every damned thing I pleased and gained ten pounds.

"I spent more than a month in Bodh Gaya, much of the time alone in meditation inside the Burmese Vihara, until it became too hot to remain on the plains. Then I came here to visit Jane and her boyfriend Gary in Bincer. It's a small village ten miles further up the ridge, closer to China. Then I met Sam. I was trekking back to the town of Almora, thinking I would take another meditation course in Dalhousie, when I walked by Sam's house on Snowview Estate. It's a little white bungalow about a mile down the ridge from here. I was just walking by. He was sitting on the porch, and he asked if I'd like a cup of chai. I said yes, and I never left."

Though understanding, Max was nonetheless stung by the odd flow of events, which left the most beautiful woman he had ever known with a new and dear friend he respected, in the most beautiful place he had ever seen.

"I'm not the same woman," Diane added, as if she were reading Max's mind.

She was a better woman, Max thought. Not as beautiful, but still pretty enough to make his heart ache—and daring enough to earn his respect. Now wanting her more than ever, he realized that he would never have her again.

"Different or not, you are in love with Sam," Max bitterly declared.

"I'm in love with the spirit that moves him to help me become a better person."

"Meaning I didn't?"

"Meaning you wanted to fuck me, like every other man did. And when I couldn't give any more of myself than sex, you left me. Sam takes me as I am."

"Without sex?"

"Without judgment," Diane angrily concluded, before walking away into the jungle, leaving Max in a brokenhearted daze.

Sam had witnessed the scene and joined Max on the rock in an effort to explain himself and mollify the pain. "It was an act of conscious suffering on her part, returning to Bodh Gaya and shaving her head, and I became a part of her process when she arrived here. I didn't look for her, Max, and she wasn't looking for me. It just happened, and I would have told you we were together if there was time. In any case, I'm not the better man, I'm the next man. As far as she's come, she still has a long way to go with herself. We all do."

When Sam extended his hand, Max shook it and said, "Then maybe the next man will be the best thing for her."

18

The ridge wrapped around the mountainside like a colorful exotic ribbon, through thickets of tall trees, fields of tall grasses and colorful wildflowers, and rows of trimmed hedges and prickly rose bushes. Parakeets and magpies sang in the trees, and kites rode the wind over the valley below. Leopards roamed the ridge at night making monkeys scream, and lions hunted the valley below during the day, making villagers beware. Everyone feared the cobra and the black viper. Almora looked like a country forest, but it was really a jungle.

Jim Corbett, the great white hunter of man-eating beasts, had lived in Epworth Estate, in the same apartment that Max had rented for the summer. Sam encouraged him to stay against Diane's wishes, because Max continued to reminded her of her past.

Bill Viletitski lived next door, much to Max's dismay. Bill had showed up in Almora a week after Max and Shunya arrived, looking for Sam.

Diane also resented Bill because he took up so much of Sam's time, often spending entire afternoons at Snowview. After all, Sam was her man now, the best and wisest man Diane had ever known. He asked little and gave a lot in his own special and measured way: He was sexual, but not affectionate, compassionate, but not indulgent; he was always turning Diane inwards, telling her to watch her mind and look into her heart for the source of her resentment.

*   *   *

Max loved Almora, despite the challenges of having Diane living with another man a mile away, and Bill living next door at Epworth Estate. The big brownstone with the brown tin roof was divided into four apartments: two larger apartments in the front and two smaller ones in back. Bill lived in the back; Max lived in front. He had a huge living room, a big back bedroom, an enclosed side porch where he slept, and a small kitchen; the rooms furnished with four twin beds, six wicker chairs, two rocking chairs, one wicker sofa and a large coffee table—all for the equivalent of twenty-two dollars a month.

The entire ridge was divided into country estates, beginning with Epworth and stretching northeast to Snowview and beyond, each estate separated by a thicket of jungle. Epworth was built for an English lord at the turn of the twentieth century, according to Swami Buddhananda, and was turned into a sanitarium following the lord's death.

Buddhananda was a fat and jolly sixty-five-year-old Englishman with the bright red face and orange robes. He was addicted to morphine and occupied one of several small cottages that comprised Snowview Estate. He was also fond of baking muffins and biscuits between rushes and nods.

Ramesh Harris lived in the big house. A tall and handsome Anglo-Indian in his late thirties, he was rumored to have murdered his first European wife for her money. He was now living with a middle-aged Belgian woman whose death was rumored to be imminent. "Poison, this time," Buddhananda told Sam and Diane over an afternoon tea.

Sunyata lived alone in the main house at the center of Kalimot Estate. Eighty-eight years old with a hunched back, the old man made the eight-mile round trip into town every single day for the past twenty years, through rain, sleet, snow and heat, using a cane for added balance and protection against snakes and dacoits.

Originally from Denmark, Sunyata journeyed to the East as a young man, and gained the distinction of being Prime Minister Nehru's gardener before taking his vows. Also a Buddhist monk, Sunyata wore the burgundy robes of a different order from Swami Buddhananda's. He ate one meal a day, consisting of a single bowl of rice and two chapatis, and was not in the habit of speaking to strangers.

Peter and Ute lived in a modest stone house down the road. Diane had seen Ute in town on several occasions, but made no effort to befriend her, or visit with Peter.

An ever-changing community of Euro-trash occupied a third house on the estate. Reputed junkies, they often took the back path into town, where the dacoits often did their dirtiest, if not deadliest work.

"Black" Michael lived in small, red bungalow due west of Kalimot. A graying, self-defrocked Anglican priest who had reportedly spent much of life serving the untouchables in a leper colony in South India, he dressed only in black and served the Tantric god of the Hindus. He was a stern looking man, with a hard-angled face and beady black eyes that did not engage others.

Lastly, there was the world-renowned Lama Govinda, the German-Tibetan priest whose book, *The Way of the White Clouds*, chronicled his experiences during his many years of study in Tibet. He lived in a large country house, overseeing a huge meadow of wildflowers.

Max and Shunya walked several miles to visit with Lama Govinda at the end of their second week in Almora, but he wasn't home. Disappointed, they sat on the edge of an old whitewashed stupa and peered into the far reaches of Tibet. Row upon row of snow-capped mountains teased their imaginations as two bolts of lightning streaked across the darkening eastern sky. Then a rainbow sprang from behind Mount Kailash to the north, and the clouds hovering over the valley turned aquamarine.

Max was searching himself for the words to describe the beauty, when Shunya noticed a plaque attached to the stupa. It read: *E. Evans-Wentz.* The stupa was a memoriam to the man who had introduced *The Tibetan Book of the Dead* to the world. Enthralled by the view and humbled by the memorial, Shunya quoted the Great Invocation:

"From the point of light within the mind of God, let light stream forth into the minds of men. Let light descend on Earth.

From the point of love within the heart of God, let love stream forth into the hearts of men.

May Christ return to Earth.

From the center, where the will of God is known, let purpose guide the little wills of men—the purpose, which the Masters know and serve.

From the center, which we call the race of men, let the Plan of Love work out. And may it seal the door where evil dwells.

Let Light and Love and Power restore the Plan on Earth."

*   *   *

While Shunya prayed, Sam and Diane served tea and biscuits to Helen Doyle on their front porch. Another quirk of life in Almora, Helen lived in an old Victorian just beneath the ridge, behind the Chota Bazaar. She was a tall, slender, Irish-American, whose husband worked for the Swiss legation, she said. No one had ever seen her husband. She claimed to be sixty-years old, but looked seventy, owing to the deep creases in her skin. With her long, gray hair wrapped in a bun at the back of her head and her thin, hooked nose and boney old body, she was bird-like, almost vulturine in appearance. She drank a cup of her own urine every day—"to stay young and healthy," she said—and she loved to gossip.

"You know, of course, that Buddhananda claims to have angina, which is why he takes those god-awful drugs all the time . . . And Lama Govinda's wife is a terribly bitchy woman, like the wife of Socrates was said to be, an embarrassment in public . . . And Black Michael does seem a bit too popular among the young boys in town . . . Ramesh definitely murdered his last wife. No way she could have fallen off that cliff by herself . . . Sunyata must be a lot closer to a hundred than ninety, the old fool doesn't remember his name half the time, and some people think he's so wise . . . And, of course, you must know that none of us have spoken very much during the last ten years. We used to meet for tea now and then, but now we barely acknowledge each other, which is just as well . . . But at least we have character," Helen proudly declared. "Hardly ordinary."

Reaching into her colorful jhola, she produced a faded article from the *Times of India* entitled, *CRANK'S RIDGE*, which characterized Almora as a home for eccentrics in India since the turn of the twentieth century.

Sam and Diane were about to read the article when Max and Shunya arrived and discovered that Lama Govinda was teaching in Europe.

"He's been gone nearly six months now," Helen explained, following introductions.

Max was reading the article aloud when Colonel Singh showed up on Sam and Diane's porch. "Hoping to meet with our new guests," he said, smiling at Max and Shunya.

He was an unusually muscular man for an Indian, with a thick, black mustache and piercing black eyes—somewhere in his early forties, Shunya guessed, studying his profile as he spoke.

"It is my job to meet you, to know who is here with us. It is also my pleasure," he explained, looking directly at Max. "You are the one who is paying the rent at Epworth, I believe."

"Until the fall," Max said, before introducing himself and Shunya.

"And your papers are in order?"

"Back at the house. I'll go get them if you like." Max was about to stand and leave.

"No, no, please. Please remain seated," Colonel Singh insisted. "If you are telling me the visa is good, then it is good enough for me."

"They're both good," Max said, nodding in Shunya's direction.

Shunya wasn't too comfortable with Colonel Singh, due to the nature of his hashish business and because this Mr. Singh was almost too nice and slick.

"Here I have grown up," Colonel Singh said, as if he were answering Shunya's thoughts. "And here I will stay and maintain the peace and harmony."

"It's still so beautiful here, isn't it? Even if we are a bit strange," Helen added, pointing to the article in Max's hand.

"Not so strange for me because I am getting to know everyone as I do every year," Colonel Singh replied, looking across the valley at the panorama of snow-covered mountains. "I am just having tea with Peter and Ute."

"I know Peter," Diane offered. "I met him in Benares." She offered Colonel Singh a cup of tea, but he refused.

"A nice young man, I think," Colonel Singh said. "And I am thinking his girlfriend, Ute, is also very nice. I see her many times in the town talking to many people. But those other people I am not seeing so much in town?"

"You mean the Europeans staying at Kalimot?" Sam asked the Colonel.

"Yes."

Sam took a long toke on a bidi, looked Colonel Singh directly in the eyes and exhaled, "None of us have anything to do with any of them, and we have nothing in common with them. All of us have spent the entire winter in Bodh Gaya studying meditation. We hardly ever see them."

Colonel Singh smiled and apologized for the dubious inference. "Your integrity is not in question here. As I said, it is only my job to inquire. I am not meaning to offend any of you."

"I'm not offended," Diane said, smiling warmly. "And you must know that you are always welcome here."

"And I refuse to overstay my welcome," Helen said. "Besides, I have another engagement at my house."

When the Colonel offered to escort her down the ridge, Helen gushed, "Such a handsome man. This is my lucky day."

"Lucky and quite safe with me, under the circumstances," Colonel Singh replied.

"Is there a problem?" Diane inquired, nervously twirling her ever-present ruby earring.

"Not in Almora, at least not yet. But there is a man-eater that is attacking villages in the valley, and there have been some problems with dacoits in Bageshwar and Jageshwar."

"Oh my," Helen exclaimed, before saying goodbye and leaving with Colonel Singh.

"What's a dacoit?" Max asked, as they disappeared into the jungle.

"Highway robbers," Sam explained. "They kill for Kali."

19

Sam and Diane's house was modest compared to Max's apartment, just a small, white bungalow with a white picket fence. The front and back lawns were filled with wildflowers. Diane wanted to clear a space to grow roses from seeds given to her by Swami Buddhananda, but Sam discouraged her, telling her that there were too many poisonous snakes in the area.

Buddhananda told her not to worry; he hadn't seen a cobra in more than a year. So Diane disregarded Sam's advice and cleared a little space on the front lawn, at the entrance to the house, and spent the next six weeks marveling at her roses, and at the symmetry of her life: waking at dawn, making breakfast, shopping in the Chota Bazaar, walking along the ridge, meditating—avoiding Max and Bill.

"I don't think I've ever been so happy," she told Sam. It was near eight in the morning. Neither had slept very well owing to a monstrous thunderstorm that struck the ridge in the middle of the night. Sam was dressing; Diane was lying in bed. "In fact, I didn't think I could be this happy; I didn't think I was worth it because of how I lived, how indulgent I was, all the bad thoughts I had. I still don't know all the reasons why I hated myself so much, but at least I can be with myself now without punishing myself so much . . . I mean I still have bad thoughts, but . . . I mean I don't exactly love myself, but . . . At last I have some breathing room in my head for better thoughts."

Sam forced a smile and casually stroked his short, black beard; his eyes riveted on the giant snake slithering up the stucco wall behind Diane's head, thinking one sudden move would be the death of her.

Diane continued unaware. "And a lot of it is because of you. I owe you so much, but . . . it doesn't excuse you from your own shortcomings. You could be more affectionate, even if you just held my hand sometimes when we're walking. And you don't always have to turn me back to myself every time I complain about something, telling me to watch myself . . . I mean, we're in a relationship, we could share more . . . You're not right all the time about everything. I know you have problems. You're not perfect. You could talk to me about your problems. And I'm not so sure that we shouldn't be discussing our differences as much as we observe them."

The head of the snake, a King cobra more than eighteen feet long, was less than ten inches from Diane's head, stopping and starting as it slowly ascended the wall—toward the open window above the bed, Sam hoped.

"I already told you that you were my best teacher," Sam said as casually as he could, fighting to maintain his composure. "Even if I don't admit to it sometimes, I learn a great deal about myself from you."

Diane finally noticed the beads of sweat gathering on his forehead, and the riveted intensity in his straining brown eyes.

Are you okay, she asked, about to sit up.

Sam gestured for her to stop and continued speaking softly. "In one minute, I'll be okay, but you have to listen to me very carefully and not move one inch—not one inch!"

Diane froze as the snake continued to climb the wall behind her.

Sam continued definitively, the pitch and cadence of his speech not wavering—"You're going to be okay . . . . You're going to be okay . . . Just a few more seconds,"—until the head of the snake disappeared out one corner of the window. "Now, without looking back, slowly roll off the bed to your right onto the floor and come to me."

Her heart pounding, her ears ringing, Diane rolled out of bed and crawled toward Sam. Standing beside him and trembling, she watched the long body of the snake slither up the wall and out of there lives.

"It must've come in out of the rain," Sam said, holding her as tightly as he could.

"From hell, I think, because I still have too many bad thoughts," Diane sobbed.

"From God, I believe," Sam concluded, "Because the cobra is the manifestation of the Lord on earth."

*   *   *

Snowview had snakes. Epworth had ghosts. Despite the exotic and pacific beauty of the place, Max and Shunya did not have one good night's sleep at Epworth since their arrival. Both slept in the back bedroom on hemp beds, on top of their sleeping bags, often waking in the middle of the night from nightmares, fearing for their lives.

On the eve of their third week in Almora, Shunya was visited by a particularly odd and violent dream on the night of the storm. He was walking up the side of a mountain when an old sadhu with a short, natty beard beckoned him into a cave. Shunya hesitated, then stepped forward and noticed a deep, bloodless gash on the old sadhu's neck. The closer Shunya came, the deeper the gash. When it began to ooze blood, Shunya began to scream, realizing it was in his own neck.

Max woke, thinking he was dreaming the scream—until he saw Shunya sitting up in bed.

Both frightened, they returned to the living room and sat in front of the fireplace. Their faces turned red in the smoldering firelight as they drank chai, the wind whipping through the trees while the leopards prowled the dark, and the monkeys ran shrieking for safety. Shunya was describing the blood gushing from his neck when something pounced on the tin roof, moving from the back of the house to the front. Max ran to look out the front window and saw a fleeting shadow cross the front lawn.

"A leopard?" Shunya asked.

"More like a man without a head," Max said, trembling with fear.

Shunya interpreted the dream as a sign to leave Almora. Besides, he had an appointment with Delhi Dave in Delhi.

Max was tempted to join him, especially after they ran into Helen Doyle in the Chota Bazaar the following morning. When Max told her about the headless man he had seen, she told him about the ghost of the old chowkidar.

"He was decapitated in a car accident in the Chota Bazaar. A British officer was driving. It was a long time ago. Way back in the thirties, I think. And they say that the chowkidar came come back to haunt the house that he had served, which was Epworth."

"Who are 'they'?" Max asked.

"Us," Helen said. "All of us who've been living here for so long. We tend to avoid the place, especially after dark, which is why it's always for rent."

"And you don't tell anyone?" Shunya asked.

"And ruin all the fun?" Helen replied, smiling before turning to leave.

Shunya turned to Max and said, "I'm leaving tomorrow."

*   *   *

Shunya woke before dawn, planning to take the first bus out of Almora, but was sidetracked by a bad stomach. Max offered him a handful of Flagyl, a very powerful antibiotic often prescribed for dysentery, but the drug never agreed with him—besides, Shunya had a better idea.

"It's called Shanka Prakshalana," Shunya declared, showing Max an old yoga text. "A yoga kriya that is guaranteed to kill everything that ever lived in your intestinal tract, from top to bottom—and we could do it together."

Max had heard about the kriya, and he had thought about doing it himself on several occasions, but he lacked conviction.

"It might be especially good for you, considering how sick you were. And now that you're okay, this would be like icing on the cake—just clean all this out once for all and start again."

Max agreed, partly because he thought it would be good for him and also because he felt that Shunya didn't want to perform this task alone. Besides, it sounded easy enough to drink a little salt water, and do a little hatha yoga between drinks until nature called.

With a smile on his face, yoga text in hand, one bucket of salt water and two brass cups, Max followed Shunya out of the kitchen at sunrise, to a small clearing at the edge of a very steep hill at the back of the house, where they would perform the sacred ritual cleansing. The first five cycles of drinking and yoga exercises went without a hitch; the next five cycles went awry.

Shunya said, "I feel really bloated and heavy, like I'm about to explode."

Max looked at Shunya's distended stomach, forced a smile and said, "Me too. By the way, how many glasses of water are we supposed to drink; how many cycles?"

Shunya hadn't read that far so he waddled over to the yoga text and read it, replying, "Only seven glasses."

Max rolled his eyes. They had already drunk ten glasses of water, and had performed the requisite four hatha yoga asanas, four times each.

Shunya said, "We already came this far, and I can't see how more of this would hurt."

Max said, "Might as well go to the bitter end."

So they made a pact, to drink and exercise until they shit or exploded. By the fifteenth cycle, they were very nearly delirious: barely able to stand, often bumping into each other and holding onto nearby bushes for support, their stomachs now protruding way over their bare feet.

Max said, "Maybe we should stop."

"And go where and do what? Go back in the house and wait until we shit all over your living room?" Shunya said.

Max said, "We can't just stand around like this."

They couldn't even sit, their stomachs were so bloated and painful. But they pressed on, moaning and groaning, whining and whimpering, cursing God and each other until the nineteenth cycle when Shunya said, "I feel nauseous."

When Shunya began to vomit, Max began to shit. Standing at the far edge of the small clearing, at the crest of the steep hill, both sickly and dizzy, they bumped into each other again and fell down the hill, vomiting and shitting all over themselves.

*   *   *

Shunya left for New Delhi the following morning, hoping to conclude his business with Delhi Dave in a hurry—it was so hot on the plains. But Shunya should have known better, nothing ever went smoothly with Delhi Dave. After waiting for four days in the punishing spring heat—nearing 120 in the shade—Shunya received a telegram from Delhi Dave: *Meet me Bombay, Oberoi Sheraton. Good news*—meaning Delhi Dave had gone ahead and made this first deal without him.

Elated, Shunya caught the next train to Bombay. He fell asleep in his first class sleeper counting on his profits to make ever-bigger deals to fund his dream of creating a school for occult studies in Nepal.

The following morning, as the sun rose over the plains of India, Shunya was having tea in the club car when he noted a headline in the *Times of India*: *GURU KILLS SON IN ACT OF FAITH*. It was the story of Moti-Lal, a great local guru from Lucknow who, in an effort to impress his following with his power over life and death, killed his youngest son. He tied the boy to a railroad track, waited until a passing train severed him in half, then proceeded to chant over the boy's body parts in an effort to join them together in a demonstration of faith.

Shunya was nearing the end of the article, wondering why Moti-Lal didn't experiment on a mangy dog first, when his train was suddenly derailed on the edge of Tent City, an impoverished suburb of Bombay that compared with the worst ghettos in Calcutta. No one was hurt, since the train had already slowed down as it approached the heart of the city, but everyone on board was summarily dismissed and dumped into the streets of unmitigated squalor and despair.

So the young white sahib was forced to fend for himself and find his way out of ten square miles of rotten wood, rusted metal, piles of cow shit, open sewers, and thousands of filthy canvas tents housing millions of people who fought rats for a breath of stinking air in the grueling early morning heat.

Was it just bad luck or a bad omen? Shunya wondered as he searched for a taxi in the pitiful streets, acutely aware of his India experience. With his mind on bigger things and better places, his feet were invariably stuck in shit, piss, puss and vomit.

20

Max spent most of the next six weeks alone with the ghost of the Chowkidar, afraid of the dark. Each night, as the embers smoldered in the living room fireplace, Max retreated to the small, enclosed porch at the side of the house where he slept reasonably well. Protected from the jungle by a thin screen, he checked his room for cobras each and every night before entering the porch—at Sam and Diane's urging—and read himself to sleep by the light of a kerosene lamp.

Within days of Shunya's departure, Bill left Almora to take a month-long Sayadaw course, and Max found a small library in the attic containing the entire collected works of Mark Twain, Rudyard Kipling, and Sir Arthur Conan Doyle. He especially liked to read about Sherlock Holmes while leopards and dacoits and ghosts stalked the dark.

He often woke at dawn, serenaded by a flock of parakeets nesting in a nearby tree. After bathing out of a bucket of water, he did a little yoga, meditated for a half hour, had a cup of chai, a bit of curd and a bowl of cereal.

After breakfast, Max went to fetch water—a mile trek down a narrow path on the side of a very steep mountain—from a lovely little waterfall that was often attended by a family of silver monkeys. After the first week, Max began to wave and say hello to the monkeys; by the end of the second week, they began to wave back and chatter when he passed—even smile, Max thought.

Returning to Epworth, he cleaned the house and went shopping in town or at the Chota Bazaar, which was often a frustrating experience. The selection of fruits and vegetables often proved quite limited, one week featuring okra, the next week beets; one week papayas, the next week oranges. The problem was that Max hated okra and beets; as a result, he became deft in the creative use of Indian spices to veil their taste.

These shopping excursions also provided Max with an opportunity to meet with the other westerners who lived on the ridge, but no one was particularly friendly, grudgingly saying hello or avoiding eye contact with Max altogether. He rarely encountered Peter, and when he saw Ute, she was often in the company of locals, sitting in a chai shop or a restaurant engaged in discussion.

He saw her exchange money with a fat Sikh on one occasion, and assumed that it was a black market transaction. In any event, as a result of these trips, Max also began to learn conversational Hindi, which was a source of great pride to him.

Since the temperature reached into the eighties by noon, Max often had a light lunch comprised of fruit and a bowl of rice pudding. The afternoons passed very slowly: napping, writing letters, cleaning the rice and dhal for dinner, watching the weather, and watching his mind. Hardly a day passed when Max didn't recall his existential conversation with Shunya, when Shunya asked him why he had come to India.

Max still had no answers, and no desire to meet another teacher or take another teaching. He often told himself that he remained in India because it was pretty, and because he had nowhere else to go. But he wasn't unhappy or disillusioned, and he was looking forward to seeing his friend James who had written him from Greece, telling him that he was on his way to India.

Max only thought about Diane when he was lonely, or after running into her in the bazaar, when the subject of their murky past relationship was discussed, one invariably blaming the other for love lost. Diane thought Max should have made a greater effort to find her in Puri; after all, David had found her. Max told her it wasn't his job to save her from herself.

"Which is why I'm with Sam," she declared. "Simply because he loves me more than you did, and because he's less involved with himself and more interested in me."

Diane never alluded to the growing problems she was having with Sam, and Max refused to admit his attraction to her. Diane looked ravishing in short hair and she lost seven pounds.

Sam made it a point to visit Max every week, sometimes for lunch or a game of chess, other times to go shopping with him in the bazaar. Always a gentleman, Sam was inclined to play down his relationship with Diane, telling Max, "She still isn't easy to be with, and she still has a long way to go with herself," as if the pleasure of loving her rivaled the labor of it.

Max appreciated Sam's friendship, but as time passed, he began to feel that Sam was acting more like a guru and less of a friend, as if he had no problems of his own. Sam would never admit to a weakness or even a mistake, which was something that also irked Diane.

*   *   *

"Because Sam thinks more than he feels," Diane told Big Jane. "I don't want a guru, I want a boyfriend. I never wanted *per*fection. I want *a*ffection."

It was late in the afternoon, the beginning of June, when Sam and Diane visited with Jane and Gary in Bincer, a small village at the far end of the ridge with a grander view of the strange and forbidden mountains of Tibet. Sam and Gary were gathering firewood in the jungle behind the house, postulating the existence of yetis in the unexplored valleys of Tibet, while Diane and Jane cleaned rice and dhal on the front porch.

"I imagined that you would be very much in love with Sam by now," Big Jane said.

Diane said, "I could be, if he would let me. But he's so cerebral, and he's such a private person. If I have a problem with him or anything else, he tells me to observe it. If I express a feeling, he doesn't respond to it. He doesn't react, like it's a weakness for him to display his feelings. And it's getting to the point where I'm feeling as alone with him as I was without him."

"What about Max? Do you speak to him?"

"Once in a while, but I can't talk about any of this to him, because it'll just serve to justify his own feelings about Sam—which are similar to mine. He never says it, but I can feel it."

"Are you still in love with him?"

"With Max, no. In retrospect, I'm not sure that I ever was. He was just there at the train station in Bombay when I hooked up with him, and I got used to him, and the sex was good. But the timing wasn't great—I was so fucked up back then."

"But you're better with Sam?"

Diane looked out at the snow-covered peaks, drew a deep breath and sighed, "Definitely better, but I still don't like the idea that I have to be with a man to feel better about myself."

"You mean that you would leave him?"

"I think about it—a lot lately—but the truth is that I don't really want to be alone again. What am I supposed to do, run back to Bodh Gaya, and sit on my ass for another month until another guy comes a long? The truth is that I like being with a man, I like being in love—if Sam would just let me in, let me come closer, I could be very happy with him."

Jane smiled and playfully rubbed Diane's head. "Spoken like a true woman: You don't want a man, but you do want a man, as if you do need one of them to complete yourself. And the only problem we have is overcoming the impression of our needs and conflicts as a sign of weakness or neurosis—if only because men wrote most of the books on the subject matter.

"In terms of my experience with men, I think a lot of them would be even happier if they could just talk about sports and God and fuck themselves—American men especially. Gary vacillates between extraordinary passion and celibacy on a regular basis. One week the sex is great, the next month he hardly notices me—as if loving me is an affront to his grander process of becoming. He gets wrapped up in his meditations and his esoteric studies, and starts talking about enlightenment and perfection as if I'm standing in the way because I have breasts and it's a sin to suck on them and lick my pussy, as if God never had a womb and never birthed all of this in a moment of extraordinary passion," Jane said, with a grand sweep of her hand, highlighting the magnificent view of the Himalayas before continuing. "But I'm working on him, Diane. I keep on reminding him that, as a woman, I am one half of the reason he is here. I remind him that I have equal value, and I won't let him shame me into thinking less of myself because I want more of him. In fact, I told him that I won't even consider having his child if I don't get more—without asking for it.

"You mean that you want a child?"

Jane looked into Diane's wide blue eyes and smiled. "As much as Gary wants God, and I get the feeling that if things did work out with us and we did have children, he would find divinity in our own creation."

"So you think that I should continue to confront Sam?"

"Definitely. And tell him that you're watching yourself confronting him, which is your idea of meditation."

*   *   *

After spending six weeks alone in Almora, Max grew tired of his daily routine, and this morning promised to be no different from any other morning at Epworth: waking at dawn, practicing a little yoga, meditating for a half-hour, making breakfast, and rereading two letters he had received earlier in the week—one from his parents, and a second one from James Cohn.

He was sitting in a rocking chair on the shady side of the house, reading a *Time Magazine* article profiling the kill ratio in Vietnam, when Shunya turned the corner.

"It's about time!" Max exclaimed, standing to embrace him. He hadn't heard from Shunya since he left Almora.

"Time is money," Shunya cracked. He had made more than five thousand dollars on his deal with Delhi Dave, which was much more than he had expected.

Max was about to reply when James Cohn turned the corner of the house and added to Max's sudden joy. He was stunned, thinking James was still on his way to India, forgetting that letters often take four or five weeks to traverse the world.

"I was in Nainital the past two weeks with Kenchi Baba," James explained, parting from their long embrace.

Max was beaming, standing between his oldest and newest best friends. "It's like a dream come true," he said, unaware of the magnitude of his good fortune until he followed them around the corner and saw all of the people that had gathered in front of his house.

Narayan greeted him with a hug and introduced his best friend, Sadhu Mani. Then Shunya introduced Max to White Mike, standing at the far edge of the front lawn. He was a striking young Englishman with long blonde hair, who was talking to Pierre, a young Frenchman, and Maya Nightingale.

Her long and straight raven black hair blowing in the breeze, her lithe body swaying ever so gently as they spoke, Max was immediately smitten and distracted from the significance of this sudden and auspicious gathering of the tribe at Epworth.

Dr. Prakash Chandra sat at the far end of the porch. He was talking with Bill and several disciples of Kenchi Baba who had left their guru to take teachings from the Doctor.

Shunya explained, "I'm coming back from Bombay, and I run into Narayan and Mani in Delhi, and they start telling me about this homeopathic doctor who lives in Sonepat, an industrial suburb of Delhi—an ugly fucking place. They're telling me that this doctor might be the greatest teacher of all. So I go with them to meet the guy out of curiosity, and the guy's teaching blows my mind—so I invited him to Almora, and we picked up all these other people along the way."

The Doctor was tall and thin, with a high, shining forehead, wavy black hair, and a short, graying beard. Dressed in white pajami and a white silk kurta, he looked like a modern day saint and spoke like an Oxford gentleman.

Following introductions, Max was overwhelmed by the charismatic presence of the man. "It's like sitting in the presence of

Sayadaw," he told James, his eyes riveted on Maya, stretching her legs on the front lawn and making mudras with her long arms.

James followed Max's eyes towards Maya and said, "I saw her in Nainital at the Evelyn Hotel and at Kenchi Baba's ashram—she's hard to miss—and I asked about her. She's a dancer of some kind from San Francisco. I also heard she's not so pretty inside, so I'd be mindful if I were you."

About Max's height with sandy brown hair, James' soft blue eyes were a lot sharper than Max's. He was streetwise and he had a reputation as a lady's man, but Max was already smitten. He couldn't take his eyes off the woman.

*   *   *

"Human mind holds nothing. Its true state is emptiness. Thought maintains the world as we know it. It is the source of all conflict, all sorrow. Without thought there would be no war. And if we proceed to inquire further, if we take a closer look, we see that thought, in itself, is sorrow. It is at once the cause and effect of all our difficulty for living a harmonious life. To put an end to violence, we must put an end to thought activity. Not by squashing our minds by repeating endless mantras, or by charming our minds to sleep by singing hours of bahjan each day, or by sublimating mind activity into body emotion, such as doing yoga each day—and certainly not by allowing our minds to be mesmerized by some great siddha. Psychic powers will not quiet our minds. They will drain them or deceive them. No, these are all modes of conditioning of one sort or another—one being no better than another, none of which can lead us to freedom," the Doctor said.

It was early evening when the Doctor began to speak at Epworth, the living room filled with young Westerners eager to learn, including Sam and Diane, who had returned from Bincer the day before.

The Doctor sat on a pillow, on the seat of a tall wicker chair, all hearts and minds focused on every word.

"Enlightenment is dynamic. It changes from moment to moment. It is the movement between the ego state and the non-ego state. What is described in the Vedas a thousand years ago is no longer. What Buddha had experienced in Nirvana is also no longer. What was impossible then may be possible now, if only we inquire with an open heart and mind free from the concepts of history," the Doctor concluded before taking questions.

Max figured there had to be dozens of questions for this man, but no one spoke. Some people were bewildered, while others were intimidated. The man spoke with certainty and eloquence; he was enthusiastic and precise—and revolutionary, Max thought, marveling over the Doctor's definition of enlightenment, which seemed eminently practical and attainable.

Diane didn't know what to think. Sam was suspicious by nature, if not defensive. He thought he had heard it all before. Shunya was in the kitchen preparing dinner with Narayan.

Following a long minute of reflective silence, James posed a question. "Doctor, can you elaborate on what you mean when you say that enlightenment is the movement between the ego and the non-ego state?"

"Yes, of course. The ego is the 'I'. It is thought—desire. It is manifest when the subject and object fail to merge. On the other hand, the non-ego state comes into being when the mind activity comes to a complete halt and subject and object are merged. There is no distinction between the experience and the person having this experience. And it is this non-ego state that is so often confused with enlightenment. The experience of it is so intense—whether it is the experience of the Christian Holy Spirit, or the Hindu experience of the Kundalini—that it completely overcomes the individual, and they begin to define themselves and the remainder of their lives on the basis of this one experience. But if we can observe, if we can take a careful look at it, we will see that even this blissful state of being is subject to change and deterioration. The ego will reemerge. It will try to capture this divine state for eternity and sell it to the world.

"The inquiry into this process, the very observation of this process taking place, the conscious movement from one experience to another, whether it is from ego to ego or ego to non-ego, is what we might call our enlightenment. In this state of observation, thought may or may not be active. Perception is a momentary thing—God one moment, ego the next moment. Enlightenment, if it is anything, is a continuous process of education, of observation. It has no end . . . Is there another question?"

White Mike was sitting in a half lotus position near the Doctor's feet, reflecting on his experience with Sayadaw and Vipasanna meditation. Only eighteen years old, he had already spent a year in India. "I've been practicing meditation for eight months, and it sounds very similar to your teaching," White Mike declared.

"Except for the rules," the Doctor said. "Though helpful and insightful in the short run, in the longer run, these techniques will destroy the natural state of being. The use of any system or technique dulls the mind. It trains it to be one way and thus renders it tranquil, but not free and spontaneous. And that is our choice, whether we want to have freedom or slavery for ourselves. Whether we want to inquire intelligently, spontaneously with our awareness, into the state of things as they are—be it the mind or a tree or a sunset—or whether we wish to be calm at any price. Calmness we can have. We can repeat mantras and the like to calm ourselves, or we can meditate according to certain rules.

"Each of these things will quiet the mind, but these practices will never free the mind. I say again, freedom is spontaneous. It is an uncultivated state of being. If we inquire into our mind, we see that it is busy, restless, like a child babbling on incoherently. We can spank the child to make him behave or we can give him some candy to quiet him. But will we know his problem? Will we be able to appreciate once and for all the cause of his discontent?

"Of course not. How can we know it without knowing the child? How can we know without observing him as he is and seeing quite clearly the cause for his restless behavior? And how can we be sure that every child responds to the same treatment? It is this way with our mind."

Bill was about to ask the next question when Shunya emerged from the kitchen with a huge bowl of rice and vegetables.

"Remarkable teaching," Max said, serving Diane. He was very excited, as if his spirit were suddenly awakened.

"From a man's point of view," she replied.

Diane was miffed by the Doctor's use of the metaphorical male child to illustrate the unruliness of the mind; she thought he could have employed the feminine gender to make his point with her.

21

It was a desperate time when some children died on the battle field for no good reason, and other children took drugs and killed themselves. And yet, it was a great time to be alive and bear witness to the changing of the gods. After all, it was the Age of Aquarius. There was a full moon in the heart of the Himalayas when the tribe poured out of Max's home after dinner, onto the front lawn, to celebrate the miracle of new beginnings and the coming of the high Doctor.

Tablas beating, cymbals ringing, guitars strumming, flutes singing, and Maya dancing—her arms and legs moving effortlessly and gracefully across the front lawn in the white light.

"She's incredible," Max said to Diane.

"Really beautiful," Diane added, careful to hide her envy.

Max was careful to hide his attraction to Maya, recalling the conflict of interest he had experienced with Diane in Bodh Gaya, pursuing love in the face of wisdom.

*   *   *

The teaching continued in Max's living room the following morning after breakfast. Ever the gentleman, the Doctor picked up where he left off last evening, taking Bill's question first:

"I tried to listen very carefully to what you said yesterday, but I still don't understand what the point is."

"No kidding," Max muttered, creating a ripple of laughter in the room.

The Doctor shot him a stern glance before answering Bill's question. "The point, if any, is silent mind. It comes about spontaneously, by simply looking at something clearly, or by posing the proper question to oneself. Both are unconditioned modes of awareness resulting in a tremendous transformation of consciousness. An explosion takes place. A silent explosion, or shall we say implosion, of awareness comes about of itself, and from that point on we can look clearly into the depths of any problem or conflict. Sometimes this silence has been confused with various stages of enlightenment. Many wonderful things can happen in this state. Repeating mantras can bring it about. Various yoga exercises and meditations can do it also. But all of these things bring it about at the sacrifice of your intelligence. You may have the experience, but you will not have understanding. And without understanding there is no true discovery—no true enlightenment.

"My God, let us forget about what happened two thousand years ago, or two hundred years ago, or last year or even yesterday! Please, just see the world as it is now. Look at yourself in this very moment. Human responsibility cannot be manufactured from doctrine or historical record. It cannot be written on a scrap of paper, or spoken as a sacred word, or revealed in tribal ritual. It is an act of spontaneous inquiry into the moment, at all the violence within us and around us, resulting in a clear perspective on our conditioned knowledge, drawn from a history of violence, fought over the boundaries of nations and freedoms and the names of our many gods. And if we have the courage and the patience to see this clearly, we will set ourselves free."

The Doctor sat erect in a lotus position on a cushioned chair at the front of the large room, his handsome face shining in the morning sunlight, his wavy black hair rustling in the breeze passing through an open window. He continued seamlessly:

"How do we know that we need a guru to show us God? How do we know that we must do ten or twenty years of spiritual sadhana or a lifetime of work before we gain entrance into Samadhi or heaven or nirvana? Because someone told you? Because you read it in a book somewhere? Why not inquire about it yourself? Maybe it would only take you two years or two days or two months. Maybe the rules have changed over the last few hundred years. How would we know without inquiring?

"Please understand me. No, better still, understand yourselves. The world is sick. It is an extremely violent place. It is on the verge of destroying itself. Time is short. We can all see that. We know that we must work hard to avoid annihilation. We may not have the luxury of a whole lifetime to wait for the guru's grace or to search for the truth at our own leisure. We must take more responsibility unto ourselves.

"The advent of greater crisis and conflict in human evolution necessarily implies the availability of a greater consciousness to meet the challenge, a descending force of awareness as opposed to the age-old kundalini, which may rise with great effort and instruction by the guru, but will never take you beyond the experience of the collective subconscious, or beyond what is already known.

"The experience of kundalini is still in the realm of self projection, where the subject and object do merge, but never evolve. It is a static consciousness able to recreate familiar documented experience—not a new and dynamic descending force for change, which is the result of the human evolutionary process, and which is now available to the silent and open mind, created by the simple and unfettered inquiry into the human condition."

Max and James and Shunya looked up to the ceiling, half expecting nirvana to descend upon them at that very moment.

When Diane looked at Sam, he shrugged and said he was leaving. He wasn't impressed.

*   *   *

The Doctor took questions for more than an hour, many answers often paraphrasing previous answers, the repetitiveness sharpening the focus of the group mind and building intensity. Afterward, as the day progressed, many more people arrived at Epworth to hear the Doctor—including Helen Doyle and Colonel Singh. As a result, Max spent much of the day shopping in the Chota Bazaar with Shunya, and preparing for dinner, unaware that Sam had returned to Snowview alone.

"He said it was because he was already aware of this teaching, but I think it was because he feels threatened," Diane admitted to Max at the end of the day.

She had been sitting on a flat rock on the front lawn speaking with White Mike, Narayan and Sadhu Mani when Max joined them after cutting vegetables in the kitchen. Within moments, as if on cue, the boys peeled away, leaving Max and Diane alone.

The western sky was clear and blue. The northern and eastern skies were filling with storm clouds. A long and jagged bolt of lightning lit up Nanda Devi.

"I'm surprised you would be telling me this," Max replied.

"And why is that?" Diane wondered, marveling at the ever-changing sky. She was wearing a black, sleeveless wrap-around Tibetan dress—and so beautiful, Max thought, studying her profile.

"Because you hold him in such high esteem," Max said. "And because you've never been critical of him before."

"True, but I'm changing, even if he isn't."

Max could hardly suppress a smile, thinking he was somehow vindicated. Though he remained grateful for Sam's friendship, he continued to question his wisdom.

Diane was miffed by the smile and drove the larger point home. "It's not only him. It's you, too, Max," she added. "All of you: Sam knows, Shunya knows, you know, and now the high and mighty Doctor knows even more. But no women ever seem to enter into the equation of knowing. And I'm beginning to believe that it's an issue of control, men controlling their own minds so they don't feel too much—as if feeling, which is a state of being that is often ascribed to women, is somehow tainted.

But I'm starting to believe that a lot of men don't know the value of feeling, so they denigrate emotion and opt for mind control under the guise of enlightenment. Now this Doctor comes along and displays a great deal of wisdom with no apparent feelings, and all of a sudden Sam becomes intimidated and slinks away thinking he knows less. Meanwhile, no one ever discusses the value of feelings—as if feeling anything is a precursor to knowing nothing."

"Not exactly. I remind you of the bhakti path of devotion, which might be the oldest and grandest tradition in the world," Max said.

"Prescribed by men, like Kenchi Baba and Swami Puri, who are still in the business of telling me and everyone else how to feel about truth and God."

"You mean the Doctor is no better than them?"

"I mean he's no different, telling everyone about this new revolutionary path of enlightenment, all this bullshit about silent mind, which is nothing new to me because he's just another man telling a lot of other men and women how to see the world. And as good as it sounds, I think it would be a lot better one day when humanity finally experiences the other half of the equation, when women learn to express how they think and how they feel on the subject of enlightenment."

Thinking back on all the spiritual books he had read, Max could hardly argue the excellent point. "You might be right," he said. "I would be very curious to meet a wise woman and hear what she had to say about all this."

"Then maybe you can start paying more attention to some of the women you do know. We might not be enlightened—we may never get there—but we are on our own path, which is new and different; we are half the equation of life and, at the very least, we may have something to add to your manly journey," Diane said, before standing to leave.

Max watched her walk away, filled with wonder. Diane had changed a great deal since they met, and she was still so pretty. He was happy for her and sad for himself: Diane was the kind of woman he had always wanted, but she was returning home to another man. Watching her walk away, he was wondering if he would have a second chance with Diane, when Maya approached. She had been watching them from the front porch.

"We traveled together for awhile. Then we split up, and she met Sam and . . . well . . . She's quite a woman, actually."

"Too much for you?"

"Too little back then, maybe too much now: It's hard to say. But having her for a little while was better than not having her at all," Max sighed.

"You mean you're still in love with her?"

Max looked into Maya's round, black eyes, felt his attraction to her, and seized the moment. "The situation changes, but my feelings about people don't really change that much. I imagine that I'll always feel something for Diane, but that wouldn't preclude me from being attracted to someone else—like you."

Maya smiled and said, "I like your answer."

"And I love how you dance, how you move with so much ease and grace."

Maya rolled up the edges of her red peasant dress, revealing three wicked scars on her knees. "I got as far as a tryout with the San Francisco Ballet. Then I needed surgery, and more surgery, and now I dance for the fun of it."

Fun was the key word. Max wanted to have fun. He had spent so much time alone in Almora, and Maya was so pretty and talented. As the day passed into night, and massive streaks of heat lightening lit up the northern sky, he thought less about Diane and more about Maya.

*   *   *

More than thirty people gathered at Epworth to hear the Doctor speak, Indians as well as young Westerners, and Max was amazed at how quickly the word had spread about the emergence of this new teacher.

Shunya said, "We told everyone we met along the way—from Delhi to Nainital." He also told Max to expect even more people.

The talk began after dinner. Rain was pattering on the roof. There was an occasional flash of lightning and a roll of thunder which added a bit of drama to the event. There were two large pots of chai simmering on the fireplace, and the living room was dotted with kerosene lamps. The shadows of many people flickered across the walls and ceiling as the Doctor began, inquiring into the nature of things as they are:

"And not as we would like them to be. There is only one way to kill the truth—organize it. Organize it and it will certainly die. Once people form a hierarchy of events and positions and label it, the truth will certainly disappear. We need only look at the beauty of Christ's life and compare it with the perverse reality of the Catholic Church. Only the name lives, the spirit dies. There are many powerful and evil forces in the universe waiting to destroy that which is real and beautiful among men. By forming an organization or a religion, or calling this silent energy by name, we are necessarily inviting difficulty and chaos into our lives. This energy, this explosive silence, is personal and spontaneous, changing in quality, texture, and range from moment to moment in the same manner that human relationships change. It is always in flux."

The atmosphere was at once relaxed and focused, almost meditative—everyone in the living room hanging on every one of the Doctor's words. He spoke without interruption for twenty minutes until he accepted a question from White Mike.

"You've been telling us about this silent energy, this silent mind, but I'm not sure I've had the experience yet. I do feel quite relaxed; your voice is soothing and your words are challenging, but I was wondering how we can experience the full measure of this silent energy?"

"Through trial and error," the Doctor said. "By learning how to pose the proper questions to our own intellect or to the intellects of others; there is no other way and no better way. The intellect is a thinking mind. It is thought. It is calculated intelligence—conditioning. To silence it, all we need do is toss it back upon itself. To ask a question of it that cannot be examined or explained. Intellect cannot see itself or beyond itself. It therefore quite naturally comes to a spontaneous halt when confronted with its own limitations. A tremendous transformation then occurs."

"Can you give us an example?" White Mike asked.

"Why?" the Doctor snapped.

The question stung; White Mike was befuddled. "Because you said you would explain."

"To whom?"

"To us. To me. I was interested and . . ."

"What is your interest?" the Doctor pressed.

"In learning about myself."

"Then you can show it to me?"

"What?" White Mike was confused.

"Yourself. Show it to me. Your body is here, is that yourself?"

"No, not all of it. A part of it."

"Then where is the rest of it?"

"Inside."

"Inside your body?"

"No, no. It is more than that."

"More of what?"

"I don't know."

"Please take a look. We will wait. I am very serious."

White Mike hesitated, then closed his eyes for several moments before replying. "I see thoughts, I feel my body, but I can't see my deeper self. That's why I asked you to explain. That's why I came to India."

"Have you seen yourself in India, your truer and deeper nature that is connected to the essence of all things and beings?"

"I've learned—I've been practicing Vipassana—I watch, I observe, but I can't say I've seen."

"Then you don't know where your self is, or what it is?"

"No, I don't think so."

"Then how can I give you an example of your true self, if you are not capable of seeing it?"

White Mike was tongue-tied. The Doctor's skillful use of dialectical reasoning, combined with a great deal of insight, had stopped his mind and silenced the entire room. Several minutes passed until the Doctor spoke again.

"How do you feel?" the Doctor began again, in softer voice.

White Mike said, "Quiet. Alert and very calm. Observant—like I'm in a deep meditation with my eyes open, and I'm obviously speaking."

The Doctor smiled. "This is good, but do not try to understand this experience, just go with it, be with it and observe. . . . Now close your eyes again. Everyone, please close your eyes."

Everyone in the room complied. After several minutes, the Doctor continued questioning White Mike.

"Now tell me what you are experiencing. Do you have thoughts?"

"Some," White Mike said.

"Are they deep or troubling thoughts?"

"No."

"Do they pass through your mind easily?"

"Yes."

"Like fluffy clouds, shall we say, on a clear and tranquil afternoon?"

"Yes, that's it, like there is space between them, like my mind is floating among them."

"And you feel fine?"

"Yes, very fine. Still very relaxed. Very quiet."

"And alert?"

"Yes, very."

"Then I've answered your initial question by introducing you to this silence, halting your intellectual function by simply posing the right question. In this relaxed state, in this quiet, we may first begin to view our true selves. Simple isn't it? No mantras, no yoga, no meditation, no ten year wait. From this silence you can watch your whole mind unfold and see your true nature. Observing what is within and without is the key to all real intelligence. It is the beginning of enlightenment."

*   *   *

"It was instant Vipasanna, instant awareness, instant silence," Max told Shunya and James much later in the evening. The three were sitting together on the front porch while many others prepared for sleep. "I felt like a heavenly body orbiting a brilliant star in the depths of space without end, and I never posed one question to him. I was just riveted by the intensity of their dialogue, and when the Doctor posed that one pertinent question to White Mike, about seeing himself, it stopped my mind."

"Instant Zen," Shunya declared as the rain continued to fall. "Like a master asking a disciple what the sound of one hand clapping is. I've been watching him do this for a week with larger and larger groups. He's so skillful, so brilliant."

"The most remarkable experience I ever had," James said. "Now I'm thinking I should spend more time with the Doctor and less with Kenchi Baba. What about you, Max?"

Max was about to reply when a leopard darted across the front lawn.

22

There were a lot of snakes in Almora, and leopards hunting the ridge at night, and man-eating tigers roaming the valley below, and monkeys running for their lives, and dacoits. And there was a generation of western young seekers and dreamers who went there in search of something miraculous, who would not shrink from the dangers and the challenges to better themselves and the world closing in on them.

"Even if you don't agree with the Doctor's teaching, you have to be impressed with the willingness and interest so many people have in bettering themselves," Diane said.

"Maybe too interested and too willing, if you ask me," Sam said, lighting a bidi.

"How could you be the judge of that?" Diane challenged.

They were sitting on the front porch of their house, having fruit salad, curd, and chai for breakfast. It was another beautiful morning in Almora following a long night of rain; hardly a cloud in the sky, the snow covered mountaintops were shining in the brilliant sunlight.

Sam took a second, longer toke on his bidi and exhaled, "Only because it's apparent to me that everyone's in such a hurry to learn, and the Doctor is in such a hurry to teach, telling everyone that Armageddon is a moment a way. Because of that, everyone wants to believe that enlightenment is likewise a moment a way, whipping everyone into a frenzy."

"Meaning you don't believe that?"

"Meaning it's besides the point of hearing it from someone else. Most of us came to India looking for something new and different, hoping to change ourselves and make a better world, and we're all so desperate for change that we're inclined to reach for the next best thing—or teaching—without taking a closer look. The Doctor has been here two days and people are already proclaiming his enlightenment, which is ridiculousness born of despair—as if he's the first teacher to use Socratic dialogue as a means toward self-knowledge . . . Do you really think that this is the first experience humanity has had with what he calls 'silent mind'? And because he calls it a descending force, something new and different, does that mean it is descending and that it is so much different?

"I sit on this porch every day and watch my own mind, and the world passing by, and I experience this silence on a regular basis with no desire to teach anyone—or be taught—and because I won't go along with the crowd at Epworth, I have you telling me I'm jealous . . . Well, I'm not jealous, Diane, and I'm not in such a big hurry to lose myself in someone else's perception of the world."

"The problem is, you won't lose yourself in anyone," Diane shot back. "Whether it's another teacher or another teaching or another person. You tell me you love me, but you don't act like you're in love; you won't ever hold my hand—even when we're alone. I also have issues with this Doctor. I also I think he might be just another man telling other people how to live, and not that much different from you, for that matter.

"And now you're probably getting ready to tell me that I shouldn't be in such a hurry, and that my desire for affection is an expression of weakness, that I should simply observe it until I don't crave affection, meaning I should become more like you and less than myself. But I won't. I owe you a lot, Sam, and I've learned a lot since we met—you've been so helpful and loving in your own way—but I want more. I deserve more."

Diane stood to remove the dishes from the table when Shun-ya appeared at their front gate with the Doctor.

"Bad timing?" Shunya began, instantly surmising the situation.

"On the contrary," Sam said, standing to greet the Doctor. "We were just discussing the nature of relationships—ours and others."

Diane welcomed the Doctor before going into the house to prepare a cup of tea for him.

"We missed you last night at Epworth," the Doctor began, sitting across the table from Sam. Shunya sat between them.

"It was raining, and to be perfectly honest, I wasn't drawn to the scene; neither was Diane, for her own reasons."

Shunya smiled and said, "You missed a pretty good show."

"I suppose that's one way to look at it, but I have all I want right here," Sam said, looking directly into the Doctor's sparkling brown eyes."

"So I've heard," the Doctor said. "And this visit is not meant to convince you otherwise. Shunya suggested a walk, and we were passing your house, and you were kind enough to invite us for a visit."

The conversation flowed effortlessly for more than twenty minutes, the subjects ranging from international politics to the rumored presence of dacoits combing the ridge for victims.

"We saw a leopard last night—me, and James, and Max—went right by us on the lawn."

Sam was surprised. "Out in the open? In the rain? I thought they favored trees and underbrush."

"I thought so too," Shunya said. "But there it was."

"Thank God for the unusual," the Doctor said, sipping his tea.

"You mean you believe in God?" Diane asked.

The Doctor said, "To the extent that someone must have been responsible for all this. To my mind, there is no doubt that life is a miracle. I just don't think that we need to build a monument to it."

"You would have made a good Jew by your avoidance of graven images," Diane cracked.

"In a previous life, no doubt."

"Then you believe in reincarnation?"

"To the extent that energy, or consciousness, has the inexorable ability to recreate itself in many forms—nothing dies, everything changes."

Diane and Sam were both surprised.

Sam said, "After listening to you the other night, I would hardly expect you to be sympathetic with such high concepts."

"Reincarnation is karma, and karma is history. I don't deny history; I deny the ability of history to correct itself. I also believe in God. Where there is life, there is God. There is no life apart from God, but I do not believe that God is static. And as God changes, we must change by inquiring into the nature of His creation with an open mind and an open heart. Curiosity, I believe, is a sign of the divine."

"Can you imagine God as a woman?" Diane asked.

The doctor flashed a wide smile and said, "I will take what comes—today masculine, tomorrow feminine. But as a condition of my manhood, I must see the world through a man's eyes."

"Then you're not enlightened?" Sam challenged.

The Doctor widened his smile and said, "I have moments of special experience, which are connected to other moments that are rather ordinary, and it is the relationship of these moments, the ebb and flow of these events, ordinary and extraordinary, that bear truth."

"Are you married?" Diane asked.

The Doctor's smile faded. "Still," he sighed.

"You mean you're not happily married?" Diane pressed.

"No, and it is this relationship that served as a catalyst for curiosity about the nature of things. I am a homeopath, and a surgeon. I ran for office once to become a member of our parliament. I was always interested in changing things for the better, and in the process, many things became worse. Maybe I wasn't as good of a husband as I thought; maybe I wasn't home enough to see the changes in my own wife. In any case, it was the pain of this relationship that drove me to the depths of despair some years ago.

"I wanted to die from the pain and shame of it, and no amount of prayer and traditional practice would help. I can never forget riding in a taxi from Delhi, and I was experiencing so much mental anguish and heartache that I asked the driver to pull over beside a small pond. And it was there, sitting on the edge of the pond, thinking about killing myself again, when I finally saw the truth. I just sat with the pain, and watched and watched and watched, until I found myself at rest in the center of the universe—finally at peace.

"In fact, my wife was my best teacher. Nevertheless, I still have painful memories from time to time. I still have the body of a man, and the thoughts and desires of a man. I'm still curious and still inquiring into the nature of things. It just reached a point of critical mass one day, this desire to share my experience with others, and help them see the truth of themselves. In fact, it is my belief that the deeper nature of truth, of the divine, can only be experienced in relationship. If you can't share what you have, I am inclined to believe that it is hardly worth having."

*   *   *

Maya was an odd beauty: small black eyes, long thin nose, pouting red lips, pale white skin, and raven black hair. The sum of these unremarkable features was nonetheless astonishing.

"My father was gypsy," she told Max as they strolled into the town of Almora to shop for dinner. "My mother was Russian."

"And you're stunning," Max declared. He was so happy and confident, flirting with this beautiful woman while the Doctor resided at his house—he hardly thought about Diane or reflected on his lack of passion for the quest.

Over lunch, Max discovered that Maya had been married twice already, and she was only twenty-five years old.

"Once when I was eighteen, because I had to, and the second time because I wanted to, but he didn't want much to do with the baby," Maya explained. She had a six-year-old boy who was being raised by her parents in California.

*   *   *

Max was surprised, but undeterred. "If for no other reason than to be with her to feel better about myself after losing Diane to Sam," he told James, returning to Epworth with bags full of fruits and vegetables.

James told him that he understood. "No doubt Maya's pretty enough, but I also told you to be mindful about her because I get the feeling that this kind of a woman will always take more than she gives and leave you spinning."

"Dancing," Max cracked. "She can leave me dancing." He was feeling so good about himself and the burgeoning scene at Epworth that he couldn't imagine a painful end.

It was getting late in the afternoon when Max walked around the house and counted forty-one people for dinner, including Sam and Diane, and Helen Doyle—who was again escorted by Colonel Singh, keeping a casual, but ever-sharp eye on the presence of so many foreigners in his town. Much to Diane's surprise, Peter showed up with his German girlfriend, Ute. Diane had invited Jane and Gary, who were unavailable.

Max was about to begin final preparations for dinner when White Mike told him that they were running out of water. It was Bill's job to oversee the chore today, to retrieve water from the waterfall, and Max became enraged when he found three empty buckets in the kitchen. He was further enraged when he exited the house and found Bill standing around back sipping lemonade.

"You were supposed to get the water," Max heatedly began, pointing a finger in his face as he walked up to him.

"I will. I'm planning on it," Bill said, as the Doctor emerged from the kitchen behind Max.

"When? In the middle of the fucking night? You little fucking twerp, you bring that water now or you won't eat tonight, you won't listen to the Doctor, and you won't have a silent mind."

Bill looked over Max's shoulder and widened his smile. "We'll see."

"See what?" Max asked, turning around.

Bill departed smiling, leaving Max to face the embarrassing consequences—he thought.

"There is some problem here?" the Doctor began sternly.

"Not really, nothing unusual," Max stammered. I, ah, I didn't mean to . . . I'm sorry I was . . . but . . ."

The Doctor nodded, "I think I understand. We had a boy like Bill in my high school class. It was very difficult, most irritating."

"What did you do about it?" Max asked, anticipating a pearl of wisdom.

The Doctor said, "We beat the shit out of him."

Max laughed so hard, he had to lean against the house to maintain his balance.

"But we know better now, don't we, Max?" the Doctor added, unable to suppress a smile.

"You mean I should try harder," Max said.

"Or not try so hard at all. Bill will be Bill no matter who you are—until he can see himself clearly."

*   *   *

In view of the traditional high moral tone of most spiritual teachings, the Doctor's perspective continued to challenge tradition. When asked about the practice of homosexuality by Pierre, the apparently gay, young Frenchman who had arrived in Almora with Maya, the Doctor made no distinctions.

"If a man can love another man with all his heart and soul, then what is the problem? I say there is no problem. The object of our love is not any more important—perhaps it is even less important—than the expression of our love. The practice of sex in these relationships may or may not be necessary. In this process of inquiry, we must begin to see who we are now and where we are now in life, whether we are asexual, heterosexual, or homosexual. If a change in these relationships is necessary, it will be revealed to our powers of observation and perception. Again, I must caution you, that in order for us to understand who we are, we must begin with who we are, and not with who we would like to be."

"What if we are unsure of our sexuality?" Pierre asked.

"Uncertainty is often an expression of conflict. Where there is conflict, there is no room for transformation. And if we act out of conflict, we are acting out of ignorance and the result is often harmful to ourselves and to others."

Peter posed a follow-up question. "In other words, are you saying that it is better to be celibate than sexual if you are unsure of your sexuality?"

"If you like, but I am not telling you what you should like. This is your choice, your process of discovery. I am merely voicing an opinion that is based upon my experience. Your experience may be different. If we are here to learn, if our lives are an experiment in living, we will all make mistakes. I am only saying something that you have all heard many times before, which is that we may learn from our mistakes. So, perhaps one day you will find yourself in conflict and you will act out this conflict and you will see what prevails, whether your actions are resulting in a good and positive experience for yourself and others, or whether they have caused unnecessary pain and discomfort in your life and the lives of others. But if you have the strength and fortitude to sit quietly and observe your conflict without acting it out, you may become enlightened."

The Doctor smiled at Max before taking another question, this time from Helen Doyle. The curious Colonel Singh sat next to her.

"Although I have been living in India for more years than I'd like to remember, and have been exposed to the Hindu and Muslim faiths, I am still a practicing Christian, and I am wondering where you stand on God."

"Hopefully nowhere, Ms. Doyle. I would hope that He is standing above me."

"Are you saying that you believe in God?"

"Where there is life, there is God. There is no life apart from God. The essential nature of being is blessed."

"Then you believe in the Divinity of Jesus Christ?"

"Yes, I believe in the divinity of all souls."

"Then you don't believe that He can be our path to salvation."

"Not the only path, but a blessed path nonetheless. I am only asking you to observe the journey, to become aware of the scenery on your way to heaven and see if it can't be quickened, and to not fear a question of faith, and to not cling to a preconceived notion of God, or ascribe to someone else's notion of God.

"The fact is, we are here, and I am only asking that we bear witness to our own presence—nothing more. The single most important thing in our life is our experience with it, how we interact with our thoughts and feelings and each other, and our ability to observe this interaction. For most of us it is the pain of simply being here in this life that governs our interactions; whether it is a childhood rejection that was beyond our control or a poor choice that was made in our adulthood, whether it is something that was forced upon us, or something we have brought upon ourselves. It may even be the karmic impressions we are born with, if we believe in the existence of past lives. Whatever our beliefs, whatever the process, we find ourselves here together on this night, in this house, because we have experienced some degree of discomfort in our lives. To some degree we are all in a measure of pain. Is this not so?"

Maya Nightingale, who was sitting next to Diane, raised her hand and asked, "What if you're not in pain?"

"Who is not in pain?" the Doctor challenged.

"I'm not." Maya declared. "I feel pretty good, actually. I just came to India to study dance, and I'm really happy I'm here. I feel really good about myself, probably for the first time in a long time. I feel whole and healed."

"Then you are not connecting with the sorrow of others?"

"You mean because other people suffer, I have to suffer?"

The Doctor surveyed the room before looking directly into Maya's eyes and replying. "You were born Christian?"

Maya said, "Yes."

"And despite all the changes in your life, and what we have discussed here tonight, I ask you if you still believe in the divinity of Jesus Christ?"

Maya said, "Yes."

"Then I remind you that your Christ died a broken person. In fact, He died for you."

Maya was stung, and a familiar silence descended upon the room.

The Doctor waited several minutes before continuing. "We are all fragments of the whole experience of mankind. What we are seeing within ourselves, in our silence, is also taking place in the world: Good thoughts, bad thoughts; good people, bad people; a cancer of the bladder or a polluted lake or a beautiful sunset that connects with an inner feeling of grace. Meditation is the observation of these pieces within and outside ourselves. It is the observation of the subtle and gross interplay of these pieces that may lead to our so-called enlightenment. And it is by no accident that it is our pain that more often connects us to the pain of others—which is the beginning of compassion, which in turn is the foundation of joy.

"It is your hearts touching my thoughts in silence, your pain touching my pain in silence; your joy connecting with my joy in silence. It is at that moment that something happens. A transformation takes place and all is silent and all is one. True joy is shared experience; being healed implies the healing of others. To become whole and wholesome, we must be connected in becoming whole and connected to the least of us and the best of us.

"Enlightenment, among other things, is the highest expression of humility. Whether it is asking your God why He has forsaken you, or whether it is the Lord Buddha, who walked with his head slightly bent toward the ground in all the years following his experience with nirvana, humbled by the experience of his own enlightenment."

23

Sex, morality, enlightenment, history—there was no subject off limits in the discussions with the Doctor. As the evening discussion progressed, Sam was particularly struck by the Doctor's references to Buddha and Christ.

"You said that our history, what's in our past, doesn't matter," Sam began. "And I've heard you say that the existence of gods and goddesses are projections. And you've also said that the experience of great saints like Buddha and Christ means little in terms of our own experiences with higher consciousness, so I wonder why you continue to reference their life experiences as examples in your teaching?"

The Doctor surveyed the room and stroked his short, graying beard before explaining. "Because we have to begin somewhere, and we have to meet people where they are and not where we would like them to be. And to do that, we must find a common point of reference. To that extent, the experiences of these great men are important. While I don't believe that their experiences can be duplicated—as I have said, enlightenment is dynamic and ever changing—they can be instructive. In time, however, it may be to our benefit to discard this instruction and pursue our own enlightenment. After all, if you take a close look at your experience with life, with the learning curve, you will note that the progression of all consciousness is negative. Perhaps you are familiar with the expression, *netti netti?*"

"Not this, not this," Sam interpreted.

"Exactly. Essentially what it means is that in our quest for truth or wisdom—or God—we try many things and eventually discard them when they are no longer valid or helpful. Perhaps it is true that learning about our history is or was necessary at some point in our development, and also learning about our gods and goddesses and great saints of all ages and cultures. But there must be a point in the evolution of the human consciousness when an individual or a group of individuals must take a leap into the unknown, into the great silence, in an effort to propagate the evolutionary scale of awareness.

"As I've said before, with the world teetering on the brink of a nuclear holocaust and facing a crisis owing to increased population and diminishing natural resources, and the realistic possibility of several kinds of environmental disasters on a mass scale, it is necessary to experience a greater consciousness to confront these great crises.

"I think it was Gurdjieff, the great Russian mystic, who compared the evolutionary scale of consciousness to the traditional western music scale, including two half notes and five full notes. The first half note is fulfilled by the will of God; the second half note, is necessarily fulfilled by the will of man. This act of will that Gurdjieff talks about is a collective expression of human consciousness that is necessary to transform a deadly crisis into a lively leap in the evolutionary gap.

"Please understand, life as we know it is not self-perpetuating. If one person cam commit suicide, an entire species may likewise end its own life. Nowhere is it written, so to speak, that this earth must or will survive. And to understand this much we need intellect, we need metaphor, we need science and theory. Most of all, we need common sense and a profound interest in what is possible. We require the experience of consciousness, which is facilitated by a silent mind, to meet these challenges."

The Doctor closed his eyes and receded into himself for one hour. During this time, many people opened their eyes in meditation and thought they saw a halo of white light gathering at the back of the Doctor's head, which is the stuff legends are made of.

*   *   *

After dinner the tribe split up into smaller groups, some playing music on the front lawn, most talking about the Doctor, marveling at his insight, wondering if he was, in fact, the New World Teacher.

Diane and Peter found a wicker bench on a side porch where they could talk quietly. They hadn't seen each other since their brief encounter at Amex in Calcutta. Diane felt she owed him an explanation, her behavior was so embarrassing.

"I was so stoned when I saw you, I didn't know who I was or what I was saying," Diane said.

"And you know now?" Peter challenged.

Diane was miffed by his directness and his utter lack of friendliness, thinking that he was using his suppler mind to squelch hers—for reasons she could not imagine. "Know what?" she snapped back.

"Who you are."

"Why, is that important to you?" Diane shot back.

Peter hesitated and stumbled. "Not so important."

"Then if who I am is not so important to you, why do you care if it is important to me?"

Peter was stunned by the quickness of Diane's mind and was momentarily silenced. This was not the same suicidal floozy he had met on the bank of the Ganges. He fidgeted, first stroking his long, blond pony tail, then scratching his chin before replying, "I guess you've changed a bit."

The acknowledgment meant a great deal to Diane, and made her smile. "Not bad, huh?"

"You're not bad at all," Peter said, reaching to embrace her under Ute's watchful eyes. She just happened to be standing nearby and waited until they parted from their embrace before approaching.

"Oh, hi," Diane began. "We met in Calcutta. Remember?"

"I did not forget," Ute coldly replied, standing beside Peter as if she were claiming her territory. "So you like this Doctor?"

"To some extent—I still don't know if I like his attitude towards women."

Ute smiled and said, "I was thinking that, too."

Peter was out; Ute was in. She sat on the other side of Diane and monopolized the remainder of the conversation.

The most remarkable discussion was taking place in front of the fireplace in Max's living room, where Sadhu Mani was taking questions about the Doctor's teaching and translating answers, seamlessly, in several languages. He was fluent in English, Spanish, Italian, French, German and Hindi. Born Manuel Enrico De La Vega, Mani was the son of Castellón aristocracy; his mother and father both served in the Spanish diplomatic service in Chile. He was only seventeen when he arrived in India and met Narayan.

"We have been traveling together for years, learning Hindi, studying Sanskrit, and meeting all kinds of teachers wherever we can find them, in the middle of the cities, or in mountain caves. "I heard about the Doctor from a learned Indian friend who was passing through Delhi," he said. "The man had taken sick and was referred to Dr. Chandra in Sonepat. He was unaware of the Doctor's higher calling to teach, but after spending several days with the Doctor, my friend realized that he was in the presence of a master. Then he met me and described his experience with silent mind. Always curious, I took a train to Sonepat the next day and spent a week with the Doctor. Then I introduced him to Narayan."

"But you're a sadhu, deeply immersed in a traditional Hindu path, wearing the sign of Shiva on your forehead; how is it you can find common interest with the Doctor?" Erik asked. He was a young German.

"Easily. Shiva has many arms. God has many paths. And in my studies and meditations, I have discovered strength in the diversity of teachings—learning more or less from different teachers espousing different paths, each shedding greater light on my path. And if my traditional path cannot stand the challenge of the revolutionary ideas, then I will walk another one. In all my experience with the Doctor, he has never required me to give up my belief in the Trimurti. He has only asked me to take a look at it from an objective perspective, to be open-minded: Brahma one moment, Vishnu the next, then Shiva, and not necessarily in that order. It is the interaction of these forces in nature that I am observing: the birth and death and presence of all things and beings and ideas, clarified as a result of my experience with the Doctor."

"But the Doctor continually reminds us about the limitations of organized religion," a young Italian woman said.

"So you've been reminded, and I've been reminded. He said religion was limited, he didn't say it was false or unworthy. I am still a practicing yogi, refining my health through the practices of hatha yoga and kriya yoga, refining my mind through the practice of jnana yoga; I still chant to the lords of the universe and spend a great deal of time living in caves refining the ritual arts. But the most important thing of all, I still ask questions. I will not accept anything on face value."

Max had heard about the intellectual prowess of Sadhu Mani, but watching him in action, speaking so eloquently about so many complex subjects to so many different people in so many languages, was simply astounding.

In fact, the whole experience at Epworth was turning into a marvel of unexpected delights for Max, who had thought that his quest was over.

*   *   *

The following morning was unusually hot, the sun spreading out behind the clouds like a fluorescent white paste. The summer monsoon season was approaching and plans were being made. Mani and Narayan were going to sneak across the border to Tibet. Shunya was heading back to Delhi. "On business," he told Max. James had planned to return to the Kenchi Baba ashram, but was now thinking about studying with the Doctor in Sonepat.

Max imagined that he could live with Maya at Epworth—against James' advice.

"She doesn't feel enough and she doesn't care enough," James reiterated over a cup of chai. Both were sitting at a small table around the side of the house. "She revealed as much when she questioned the Doctor."

Max was about to reply when Diane emerged from the kitchen, and James waved her over—against Max's wishes.

"Tell him about her," James said to Diane, pointing at Maya, who was doing her morning yoga on the front lawn.

"As a woman, I can be jealous of her; as a man, I would be attracted to her; as a friend, I would tell you that she reminds me of who I used to be—which is too self-involved—and I wouldn't encourage you to become involved with her."

Max understood, but he couldn't help himself. In a very short time, he had become enchanted with her. He couldn't stop thinking about Maya and wanting her. As planned, he kept his date with her to shop for dinner in town—against the cautionary advice of his friends.

As they descended the ridge, past the Chota Bazaar and the army post into the heart of town, Max tried to push his friend's advice out of his mind and focus on Maya, aware that they were moving ever-closer to their first kiss—if not their first night in bed. But he kept the conversation light, and he kept his distance. He wanted her to come to him, to make the first distinctly romantic move, thinking that he would be in a much stronger position to deal with her if she were as challenging as his friends had indicated.

But nothing happened. Maya met Max where he was, in a spell of amorous uncertainty, which only served to intensify his desire for her. After shopping, they returned the house, helped with dinner and sat next to each other in front of the Doctor.

"And what is it we will explore tonight?" the Doctor began, sitting in a familiar lotus position on chair in the center of Max's living room.

"Ego," Max blurted out, hoping to disguise his lack of confidence with a display of hubris. "You said that enlightenment includes both the ego and non-ego state. You said that they are in flux. You said that even the most highly conscious human being is not beyond manifesting ego. And I am curious to know if that person's manifestation of ego has the same negative effect on the universe as my manifestation of ego?"

"Ego is not positive or negative, Max. Does that answer your question?"

Max was reduced and embarrassed, thinking a longer answer might have reflected better on him.

Erik, the young German, posed the next question: "I spoke with Mani last night and he said that you are not against the practice of religion and . . ."

"I am not for it or against it, young man."

"But you are not religious."

"Not in the traditional sense, running off to the temple to make sacrifices to the gods, or paying a Brahmin priest to perform puja for me. But I can feel the presence of God in my life when I step outside of this house and witness the miracle of creation, and I am humbled by the experience."

James asked the next question: "I was just wondering if you would comment on the guru-disciple relationship. I think it's pretty obvious that many of us are still enchanted with it, in spite of what you have said."

"Essentially, there is nothing wrong or bad about the guru-disciple relationship. But what has happened over the years is that it has been corrupted and misused. Ritual has come to take the place of spontaneous inquiry. The guru, rather than functioning as guide, has come to function as an authority. A true guru encourages inquiry and independence on every level, for he knows that the greatest guru of all is life."

After several minutes of reflective silence, Shunya posed a question to the Doctor.

"Do you find any value at all in the study of the occult or the experience of psychic phenomena?"

"Of course. These phenomena are also a part of the life experience. They, too, must be observed."

"But not cultivated?"

"They may be, with the understanding that they are not an end in themselves, and with the knowledge that they may be entrapping. Understanding all aspects of the human psyche can be very helpful, as long as we understand its limitations, and our own limitations."

"Can you comment on our limitations? I'm not sure what they are."

"Are you pleased with your life?"

"Not entirely, or else I wouldn't be trying to understand it."

"Which is why you have traveled across half the world, to gain this understanding."

"Obviously."

"Then maybe you can tell us about your life in America, what you left behind that challenged your understanding?"

Shunya was unexpectedly shaken. He hardly expected to be discussing his private life in public.

"We are waiting," the Doctor pressed.

"My wife and my daughter," Shunya reluctantly replied. "I left my wife and my daughter."

"And you don't understand why?"

Every fiber of Shunya's being resisted an answer. He was berating himself for opening this dialogue when the Doctor pressed the issue again.

"We are still waiting."

"I can't say," Shunya finally said.

"Perhaps because this is a subject that embarrasses you?" the Doctor asked.

The challenge made Shunya tremble inside. "Sometimes," he sighed.

"Because you are so filled with guilt that you have emotionally murdered two lives to find one god who will forgive you?"

Shunya was devastated and quieted by shame. The silence that descended upon the room this time was unlike anything previously experienced with the Doctor—most disconcerting and thoroughly unexpected; all felt sorry for Shunya until Maya dared come to his rescue. "How can you be so cruel?" she blurted out.

"How can you be so deceived?" the Doctor shot back. "As if Shunya didn't ask for this? As if you aren't asking for it now?"

"What am I asking for?"

"The truth, Maya, no matter how much it hurts, or else you shouldn't be here. You should return to your own child in America and come to his defense when he needs you."

24

The tribe was aghast, all wondering how the high Doctor could hit so low.

"Because he's testing us," Max said

"Because we asked for it," James said.

"Because he's not so high and enlightened as you people think," Diane said.

Several of Shunya's friends had met on the front porch later in the evening to discuss the incident.

James said, "He was high enough and smart enough to set us up for the fall, and Shunya fell furthest."

"Because Shunya's the strongest," Sam declared. "And because he can handle the worst of it."

"The worst of what?" Diane asked.

"Himself," Sam said. "As revolutionary as the Doctor claims to be, he fulfilled the role of traditional Guru tonight. It was classic—textbook—the disciple approaching the guru with his head in his hands and the guru kicking it over the goal line."

"It's not a game," Diane snapped. "This isn't about winning and losing; it's about learning and caring. Sayadaw would never treat people like that."

"Different teacher, different teaching," James said.

"You mean you people still like the guy?" Diane challenged.

Sam said, "I don't dislike him."

"I know you don't like him," Diane said to Max. "You can't possibly like him after what he said to Maya. He was even harder on her than Shunya—simply brutal."

Max drew a deep breath and sighed, "I'm not feeling too good about any of this at the moment, but I guess I'm still willing to see if there isn't some transcendent point behind all this."

"I've seen enough for now," Diane said before walking away.

*   *   *

The following morning was reminiscent of early spring weather: vibrant blue sky, the snow-covered Himalayas sparkling in the sunshine, stretching the imagination to infinity. The tribe had gathered for breakfast in Max's living room; the Doctor appeared at the end of the meal to explain.

"To begin with, you all must know that it gives me no pleasure to see pain in this life. And it is not an easy thing to engage the sorrow of those you love. I have a tremendous amount of respect and affection for Shunya and for Maya, for all of you who have risked so much to come so far to learn the truth of themselves—which may be pleasurable, but is often painful. The journey to self is not easy, and it is often the source of great discomfort, requiring tremendous courage and patience and faith.

"During these past few days, we have entered onto a path of understanding, and to the best of my ability I have tried to guide you on this road to discovery. And please know that while I may serve as guide, I also serve as student. I am a new teacher who has much to learn from his students, and I am eminently capable of making a mistake. I am not of European descent, and I can imagine that there are certain cultural boundaries to overcome.

"In retrospect, I may come to understand that my conduct toward the end of last evening may have been a mistake. At this moment, I am not inclined to think so." Turning to Shunya, he continued, "My point is this: if you have chosen to suffer the loss of family in your quest for a greater love, you must be willing to embrace the greater pain of it, however public or private. There is no shame in suffering ourselves inasmuch as it is an expression of our humility, which is the cornerstone of community."

Turning to Maya, he added, "And if we wish to celebrate the miracle of life, let us not forget the pain of life, the death of our many selves, which connects us to the losses of others. After all, life is not a game; consequently this teaching is not to be taken lightly. If it cannot stand by itself in the light of day, if we cannot stand to be seen as we are, neither the teaching nor our effort is worthy of consideration in the grander scheme of things.

"Lastly, I would like to express my gratitude to all of you for sharing your lives with me these past few days. From nothing we have evolved a sense of community and intensity which is necessary for transformation to silent mind, which is the beginning of our own true enlightenment. I will be leaving in the afternoon and will not forget the kindness you have shown me."

The Doctor pressed his palms together and bowed to the tribe; the tribe returned the salutation, Shunya bowing lowest.

25

"I did ask for it," Shunya told Max and Sam before leaving for Delhi the next day. "I left my family and my country to find the truth and the truth hurts—a lot more now that the Doctor confronted me with it—because I still haven't found enough here to pay off the karma I owe back there."

To that end, Shunya thought he needed more money to hire a better lawyer who could expedite his return to America. He also thought that building a school for esoteric studies would be the perfect vehicle to spread the Doctor's teaching. So he headed to Delhi for another prearranged meeting with Delhi Dave, and discovered that Delhi Dave was still in Kashmir working on a bigger deal. *Come Srinagar now,* Delhi Dave's message read.

Shunya was not happy—Kashmir was long way from Delhi—until he remembered the upcoming trek to Amarnath cave, this year in July. It was a legendary Hindu pilgrimage Shunya had always wanted to make. Now thinking he could combine business with a show of faith, Shunya bought a plane ticket to Kashmir and spent the evening sitting on the patio of the Palace Heights Hotel with Rich Tom.

Rich Tom had just returned from Kathmandu. He was a tall, dark and lonely guy; a hulking figure with a thick, black beard, who was born to a wealthy New England family, and looking for adventure at any price. Shunya had met him in passing in Kathmandu several times before, but had never engaged him in conversation until that night over a cup of chai.

"So you're on your way to Kashmir," Tom said.

"To make the trek to Amarnath," Shunya said.

"I've thought about that, but that pilgrimage doesn't start for several weeks."

"I'm also visiting friends."

"I heard Delhi Dave's up there," Tom said, much to Shunya's chagrin.

Shunya said, "I wouldn't know." He didn't want anyone knowing his business.

Tom smiled and said, "I saw him in Bombay a little while ago, before I went to Nepal, and he told me he was going to Kashmir."

Shunya shrugged. "He does get around."

"He also sells some pretty damn good hash, but I got a better deal on hash oil—if you're interested."

Shunya forced a smile and sighed, "I didn't know you were in the business."

"For the action, not the money—I have plenty of money and I think everyone knows that by now."

As big as the Asian sub-continent was, the western community was still small enough to accommodate one degree of separation in the smuggling business—and Tom seemed nice enough, and he had been on the scene for awhile.

"What kind of action are you looking for?" Shunya asked, always looking for a better deal.

"Hash oil, like I said. The quality is remarkable. There's going to be a great supply at harvest time, and the price will be right—about a hundred-and-seventy dollars a kilo in Kathmandu right now, less next month when the harvest comes in. The product is perfectly malleable and containable. I put up the money, you put up the means."

"What kind of money are you talking about?"

"Ten thousand; we can split a hundred thousand in profit—if you have the balls."

Shunya had the balls, he had the dreams, he believed in the intelligence of coincidence, and he liked Rich Tom. But he was also suspicious of the nature of the business. "Why me? And why now?" Shunya pressed.

"Because I know about you; I've seen you with the old lama. I know you're serious about your practice. And whether you know it or not, a lot of people know you and think highly of you. I also saw your picture in *Newsweek* last year, sitting in front of a stupa in Kathmandu, talking about the Dharma to some other young people. I was still in America, and seeing that picture was another thing that motivated me to make the journey. I always wanted to meet you, but I didn't really know how, and now that we have met, I want to help. I heard about that school for esoteric studies you want to build."

Shunya was alternately stunned and flattered, and though modest by nature, he was acutely aware of his charismatic personality. People had always looked up to him on the basketball court, and they continued looking up to him in the grace race, still gravitating toward him. He always thought the best of them—as if he owed them something for believing in him. So he promised Rich Tom that they would meet again and talk business when he returned from Kashmir.

*   *   *

James returned to Nainital. "To spend more time with Kenchi Baba and see how it feels at the ashram compared to what I experienced with the Doctor," he said.

As planned, Mani and Narayan went to find magic and mystery in Tibet. Within three days, more than thirty people left Almora, leaving Max to spend more time with Maya.

"And the more time I spend with her, the greater the attraction and the greater the conflict I have about being with her," Max told Diane.

Max and Diane had drawn much closer since the Doctor arrived in Almora, often preparing food together in the kitchen and debating his teachings. Despite their checkered history, they began to share a casual ease even when talking about relationships: Diane complained about Sam's lack of affection, and Max expressed his misgivings about Maya.

Diane was sympathetic, though hypersensitive to the subject. "So you want to know God more than she does, which makes her unworthy of your affection," Diane concluded after listening to Max's critical appraisal of Maya.

It was a rainy morning, both carrying umbrellas as they were walking down to the Chota Bazaar through a thin layer of fog. Max needed kerosene; Diane needed a break from Sam. They had argued all morning, Sam telling Diane that her need for affection and affirmation was a crutch, Diane telling Sam that she required more man and less guru.

Max said, "It's not about God; it's about awareness, a desire to learn and explore. And from what I gather, Maya doesn't have much of an interest. In fact, she doesn't seem to feel very deeply about anything—as if she's in a perpetual state of denial. Even those challenges from the Doctor, which were brutal, hardly rattled her. She was shaken for a few minutes, then nothing. She didn't even have an interest in discussing it, not a word about her kid. She wasn't even critical of the Doctor. It's so weird. Meanwhile, she dances like an angel with such feeling and intensity, like she's intoxicated with life."

"She must be great in bed."

"I wouldn't know," Max sighed.

"You mean you haven't slept with her?"

"I want to. It's all I think about, but I'm afraid to, to feel any more than I do because I'm so unsure of her."

"Unsure of yourself, it seems. Did you ever think that she might need someone to embrace her, to make her feel comfortable about expressing her feelings?"

"I thought you said that Maya wasn't good for me; you and James both told me that."

"She may not be, but at this point I'm willing to reconsider. Look at how I was when I met you. By the time I met Sam, I was doing a lot better, but I was still remarkably fucked up, and he accepted me the way I was, and it was helpful."

"Meaning I wasn't helpful?"

Diane drew a deep breath and sighed, "We've been through this so many times already, and it seems to be the one point that we can't resolve—what I needed and what you gave when we were together. But now I see things more clearly. You did try, Max. I know you tried, which is why I don't hold it against you so much anymore.

"The odd thing is that I still wound up with the same problem with Sam: like I'm less of a human being because I want to get laid three times a week, and I need a little affection from time to time, and acknowledgment. But all I get from him is how I should be watching myself more closely rather than asking more of him. And now he's telling me that I'm obsessing because I talk about it so much, as if talking about the Ramayana or the Vedas, or the Buddhist Sutras is more important. In the mind of a man maybe, but I'm just not buying into that bullshit anymore. If God didn't make women to get fucked, he wouldn't have created humanity—as if sitting in meditation for nine months is a higher calling than having a child. Bullshit, bullshit and more bullshit!"

"So you think I should sleep with Maya?"

"I think you should be fearless."

*   *   *

There were nine people left at Epworth, including Maya, White Mike, Pierre, and Erik. Tall and lanky with a blond ponytail, Erik often wore two large turquoise earrings. He also spent a lot of time with Maya. At times, Max wished he would leave Almora with her, thereby resolving the issue by proxy; at other times, Max was fiercely jealous of him.

Three days had passed since Max spoke to Diane. It was late in the evening and Max was lying in bed on the side porch, separated from the jungle by a thin wire screen. He was reading an old *Newsweek* by the light of a kerosene lamp, when Maya walked in and lay beside him, telling him how much she loved him, how much she wanted him.

Max was surprised and pleased, feeling her warm body pressed against his, telling her how much he wanted her, looking into her eyes; the soft amber light cast shadows on the walls as the leopards prowled the underbrush for prey and the night hawks cruised the ever-darkening sky.

Max kissed her forehead, her eyelids, her cheeks and the corners of her mouth as Maya stroked herself, whimpering then gasping for breath as Max caressed her stiffening nipples and placed his hand on top of hers.

Moments later, Max turned to roll on top of her when Maya said, "No, I want you behind me, inside me where it hurts the most."

So Max fucked her in the ass—first gently, then wildly—and Maya began to moan and groan and squeal. When she began to scream, Max thought she was in too much pain; he was about to pull out when she begged for more.

When Max reached around her thin waist and down between her legs, she moved his hand away and began to stroke herself crying out, "Love me, hurt me; love me, hurt me!"

Max grabbed her butt cheeks with both hands and squeezed until she cried out to God for mercy and came close to heaven.

*   *   *

Max spent six days sleeping with Maya, hurting her as he made love to her. "Which is how she likes it," he told Diane during a stroll down to the Chota Bazaar on another foggy morning, both holding colorful umbrellas to deflect the intermittent drizzle.

"Meaning you don't like it?"

"I did like it at first—at least I didn't mind it—but now I've begun to question it because the sex is getting a lot rougher and she's more demanding. She's just so wrapped up in herself, especially in bed. The woman just can't stop playing with herself and licking her fingers. It's like she can't get enough of herself. Like the other night, I'm inside of her and she's telling me how she's putting her finger up her ass so she can feel me inside of her."

Diane fought to suppress a sinful little smile. "It's not my style, but it does sound a bit erotic."

"Erotic and complicated; it's just never easy and simple. There's always a twist to everything and everything always reverts back to her. It's not like I'm sitting on the front porch reading a book and she shows up with a hot cup of chai out of the kindness of her heart. She doesn't do the small things."

"You mean she doesn't really love you?"

"She says she does, but . . . well, she also has this tendency to disappear for hours at a time—with Pierre mostly, but lately with Erik, the German guy."

"And you're jealous?"

"At times," Max sighed. "Because I've developed an odd attachment to her. I don't think I am in love with her, but I'm always wanting her when I'm not having her. I'm afraid to lose her, but I really don't think she's good for me. I didn't come to India for this. I know it sounds like the same conflict I had about being with you, but it's not. It's qualitatively different. You did want to better yourself and learn more about yourself; Maya doesn't and it's the lack of curiosity that bothers me, and I can't imagine how I can find a way to compensate for that."

Diane twirled her umbrella and smiled and said, "I guess you're growing up in spite of yourself, aren't you Max?"

Max was momentarily bewildered, unsure if Diane was complimenting him or deriding him. "If you mean that I'm changing, I can accept that."

"It's that, Max, and it's more than that," she said, looking into his wide eyes.

When Max looked into Diane's soft, blue eyes, he finally realized that she still cared about him. He stroked her hair; she stroked his arm. Their lips were about to meet when Bill Velititsky emerged from the fog with a shit-eating grin on his face.

26

Kashmir was among the most beautiful and chaotic places in the world. The snow-covered Himalayas towering above, the high, lazy white clouds hovering over the intensely green valley below, Kashmir looked more like a mythological kingdom than a disorderly Muslim state thriving on the edge of perpetual rebellion against its Hindu keeper. Shunya's taxi passed several armored vehicles and troop carriers on its way into Srinagar.

Dhal Lake stood at the heart of Srinagar Valley, reflecting the ever changing sky and the sparkling mountaintops. As the taxi sped around the water, passing row upon row of ornate houseboats and hydroponic gardens, Shunya marveled at Delhi Dave's choice of residence. Kashmir produced some of the best hash in the world, and the underlying instability did pose a plethora of possibilities: many people could be bought, and many things could be smuggled in and out of the country amid the added pursuits of spying and gun running.

Shunya had also heard that the food was quite good, and was looking forward to a scrumptious lamb dinner on Delhi Dave's houseboat when his taxi stopped midway around the lake in front of a crowded market. Shunya was about to get out of the car, thinking Delhi Dave must be waiting for him—after all, Delhi

Dave had the driver meet him at the airport—when Isaac, the driver, turned and said, "Ten dollars American."

"For what?" Shunya asked.

"For Dave. He say you pay."

"No fucking way," Shunya shot back, knowing the price was too high, and knowing he was being hustled.

"No Dave," Isaac said, exiting the car.

Shunya got out of the car to argue the point. "To begin with, knowing Dave, I know he already paid you, or someone you work for, and there's no fucking way you're getting paid twice."

"No money, no Dave," Isaac reiterated, repositioning his red, Muslim skull cap and defiantly crossing his arms over his chest.

"I'll pay five dollars," Shunya said, suddenly aware of the crowd their argument was drawing.

"You pay eight," Isaac demanded, rubbing his fingers together.

Shunya said, "Six. I pay six, no more."

"Seven dollars American," Isaac retorted. "It is very dangerous, sahib, you know."

"I know Delhi Dave," Shunya sighed, agreeing to the price.

So Isaac circled the lake again, past many more rows of houseboats—varying in size and shapes, from whitewashed shacks on a raft to opulent and colorful floating palaces—frequented by tourists from around the world and serviced by an unending stream of rowboats selling anything under the sun: from groceries to jewelry, carpets, clothes, and information.

When Shunya's taxi finally came to a stop, Isaac declared, "Dave is there," pointing to a row of large and opulent houseboats moored in the center of the lake.

Shunya said, "Where?"

"The red one," Isaac said, still pointing at the largest and flashiest houseboat in the row.

Shunya found it hard to believe, thinking Delhi Dave would have chosen something with a lower profile. "Now what?" Shunya asked, getting out of the car and reaching into his pocket for the seven dollars—he always carried a hundred in cash.

"Now you pay water taxi," Isaac declared, reaching for the money.

Shunya pulled back, asking, "And where will I find that?"

"It is coming for you right now," Isaac said, pointing to a small rowboat that had just emerged from between two houseboats. "He is Abraham, my cousin, who has the boat."

The rowboat docked, the cousins exchanged salutations in Kashmiri, and Isaac turned to Shunya and said, "Only two more dollars for the boat."

Shunya said, "No fucking way, I paid enough."

Isaac told this to Abraham and a dispute over charges broke out between the three of them in two languages. Within five minutes, there were seven Kashmiri surrounding the taxi, debating the fairness of costs and the division of payments.

Shunya, caught between the arguing and the haggling, finally exploded screaming, "Shut the fuck up!"

The debate stopped long enough for the crowd to ply Shunya for more business, asking him if he needed to see a doctor or a dentist, or wanted to buy a pair of leather shoes, or a necklace for his wife, or a carpet for his living room in America.

Shunya was lying across the hood of the taxi, his face in the sun, his mind turning to mush, when he sat up and finally agreed to pay Abraham two dollars for the use of the water taxi. It was an exorbitant rate, but nothing involving Delhi Dave ever came cheap or easy.

"Nice view," Shunya said, climbing onto Dave's houseboat. "And I love the low profile," he sarcastically added.

"As if it fuckin' matters," Dave said. "As if they don't know every fucking white man who ever set foot in this fucking place."

"Then why do you come here?"

"Because I can afford it now, an' for as long as I pay, my ass is covered by the Kashmiri assholes and the Indian mother fuckers, an' there's a shit-load of money that can be made between 'em," Delhi Dave said, reaching for a pair of high-powered binoculars. After focusing them on the shoreline, he handed them to Shunya, telling him to survey the smaller houseboats on the shoreline.

"Just move left until you see someone lookin' back at you on the back of a big, white boat."

Shunya looked until he saw someone looking back at him and asked, "Who's that?"

"One of the Mohammeds. He's Mohammed, the cousin who owns this boat and that one. Then we got Mohammed the uncle, who's the Magistrate of Srinagar, then we got Mohammed the rug dealer who's runnin' guns and hash on the side, then we got Mohammed the slow-witted cousin who services the boats and runs messages between everyone, an' Isaac and Abraham who do all kinds of shit, like fucking wit' you and each other—I saw it all wit' the binoculars; it was hysterical—and we got my man Mohammed in Phalgam who's into everything and everyone an' runs the scene beyond the scene.

"Him I know for years; he's the guy that gets us the hash, an' now he's tellin' me we got a shot at an even bigger deal wit' the Afghani hash, the patties, the shit wit' the mold, which has gotta be the best shit in the world. An' the deal goes down like this: they front us all kinds of shit, Kashmiri an' Afghani for nothin' an' we sell it anywhere in the world for whatever we can get an' they get half—no questions asked."

"How much shit can we get?" Shunya asked, stroking his long, red beard.

"As much as we can handle—tons, even, if we can handle it."

"And why is that? Why's everyone so generous?"

"'Cause they need the money to buy guns, far as I can see."

"To fight who?"

Dave shrugged and scratched his clean-shaven head. "Whoever's in their fuckin' way: the Russians in Afghanistan, the Chinese on the border, the Indians here—who gives a fuck what these people do wit' their end?"

Outrageous as it sounded, Shunya wasn't too surprised. After all, Delhi Dave had a history of running guns to Fidel Castro in Cuba.

"Wit' Fast Freddy Fein from the Bronx," Delhi Dave reminded him. "An' I know we can move a bunch of shit through 'im. I already talked to 'im about it. Meanwhile, I can get rich an' you can build that school you want for those lily white fucking morons who come here thinkin' God lives in the middle of this shit-fuckin' mess."

It sounded like a good deal to Shunya; it also sounded a bit too easy, and there was also a higher moral question, funding a conflict he might not believe in. "I got to think about it."

"Yeah, well, just think big."

*   *   *

As much as Diane appreciated the influx of new people at Epworth she was inclined to favor the local color, often having afternoon tea with Helen Doyle and Jennifer Williamson Harris (wife of the rumored murderer, Ramesh Harris), and Swami Buddhananda. Her attempts to befriend Sunyata and Black Michael were fruitless.

Sunyata did say hello on occasion, but he wouldn't engage in conversation. Black Michael wouldn't say anything. He despised the presence of all young Westerners on the ridge in general. In particular, he hated the flourishing scene at Epworth. When Diane chanced to meet him on her way to Buddhananda's one afternoon, he returned her friendly smile with a scowl.

As usual, Diane showed up at the old Swami's house with a handful of wildflowers that she had picked along the way. Much to her surprise, she found Maya sitting in his living room sipping a snifter of Hennessy VSOP; the two had become fast friends, having met on the ridge shortly after Maya's arrival in Almora.

Buddhananda filled another snifter for Diane and raised his glass for a toast. "To youth and beauty, and the Buddhist sutras that comfort their passing."

"To friendship," Maya replied, tapping Buddhananda's glass before turning to Diane and widening her smile.

"To all good things and people," Diane added, tapping Maya's glass.

All sipped their brandy in the old Swami's living room as a light rain continued to fall on the jungle and set an historic mood.

The dated wicker furnishings and slowly turning ceiling fan reflected earlier colonial times.

Diane looked at the front door and said, "I'm half-expecting Ronald Coleman to walk in and join us."

"Clark Gable," Maya said. "I loved him in *Mogambo*."

"How about Tyrone Power in *The Razor's Edge*?"

"I'll drink to that," Maya said, finishing her second glass.

"Me, too," Buddhananda added, before proposing another toast. "To the great adventure of loving and living in the past," he declared.

After filling their glasses again—a little fuller this time—the chubby old swami gave the women a peek into his swashbuckling past, which included several photographs of him as a much thinner man in uniform serving the British Raj in Kashmir.

"I was a Master Sergeant in charge of military supplies and hardware—you know, small field cannons and the like, running around the countryside putting down rebellions and hunting dacoits in the dark. I suppose it was all rather romantic.

"I was stationed in Burma during the war when my wife died, the old bitch—a stroke, they said. We had a small cottage in Dehra Dune. We never got on very well. I think she wanted me to be an officer. Anyway, I didn't think I would miss her at all. But I did, terribly. I was very lonely and I suppose I did drink too much, and I became very angry with the Christian God for making my life so miserable.

"Then one day when I was somewhat sober, a Buddhist monk came to my door begging for food. I was very nasty to him and I said, 'Why don't you get a job?' And he said, 'I have a job.' And I said, 'Exactly what is it that you do?' And he said, 'I allow people to give me things so that they may feel better about themselves.'

"I said, 'If everyone worked to support themselves, like all good Christians do, we would not be needing the likes of you.' And he said, 'Yes, that is true. But it will be a very lonely world without the practice of compassion.' When I looked around at my empty house, I became a Buddhist right then and there."

It was an engrossing story, which served as a prelude for Maya and Diane to tell the story of their lives as they finished a third and forth snifter of brandy, both spending much of their time talking about their over-bearing mothers and the bad men they married; Maya never spoke about her son.

Still tipsy after two cups of coffee, the women bid goodbye to the old Swami as a ray of sunshine peeked through the clouds. As the women walked side by side through the jungle, a light drizzle falling on their shoulders, Diane thought about Max; it was easy for her to see how he had fallen for Maya.

She was so playful and so perfectly charming—and so pretty, Diane thought as they continued down the narrow path, their arms and shoulders rubbing against each other as the clouds parted and the sun lit the mighty Himalayas for the first time in days. Diane was pointing to a rainbow, springing from behind Nanda Devi, when Maya was drawn to a lone blue lotus growing in a small pond that had been created by the seasonal rainfall.

"My God, it's beautiful!" Maya exclaimed.

Diane followed her to the edge of the water and sank to her knees beside her. While Maya focused on the extraordinary beauty and color of the flower, Diane studied her profile: her long, slender hands caressing the flower, her wet blouse clinging to the curvature of her body, her raven black hair falling around her shoulders, her long and slender silver earrings glittering in the sunlight, she was a vision of uncommon beauty.

Diane was attracted to her; she even thought about making love to her. Then she thought about Sam and Max, and realized that she would risk too much friendship for too little pleasure.

"Sometimes being beautiful just isn't enough," Diane sighed.

Maya said, "I don't understand."

Diane said, "I wish I could explain."

Maya was about to pose another question when Diane stood to leave. Pressing her palms together, she backed out of Maya's life.

27

Procuring a visa extension in India was never easy for an American. With the United States favoring the Pakistani dictatorship due to its role in brokering better relations with China, many young Americans, like Shunya, had to make costly efforts to remain in the country, while others, like Max, had to take long and inconvenient trips.

Max left for Gaya to procure a much needed visa extension just a few days after Diane's interlude with Maya. Neither woman discussed the incident with Max, and Max had no reason to believe that anything had changed in his relationship with Maya.

"I still give and she still takes," Max told Diane before leaving.

Diane said, "Then you should take care of yourself before she takes too much out of you."

Max appreciated Diane's concern and figured he would finally address the issue when he returned to Almora.

The three-day journey to Gaya required two buses, two trains and a whole lot of patience. It was very humid, and everything seemed to move a little slower during monsoon season.

It was pouring rain when Max finally arrived in Gaya Station at one thirty in the morning—too wet and too late to go looking for a room, so Max wound up spending the night on the train station floor with several dozen other less fortunate people, thinking he had something in common with them, blinded to the disparity by the dark.

When dawn broke, reality produced a dead body at Max's feet. It was an ugly old leper who had simply rotted to death in the middle of the night and reminded Max of the gap between the young white sahib and the poorer and darker souls who sojourned through the shadows of relentless squalor and sorrow.

Not only was Max incapable of identifying with it, he couldn't stand the smell of it. In this life, Max knew that he could never be that poor, or that tragically sick, and wind up that unceremoniously dead; and that his journey to the East was a luxury born of noble sentiments and rich choices; and that these poor bastards had no choice and no inclination to look for a god that had apparently deserted them.

After breakfast, Max headed over to the police station to procure a visa extension from Colonel Singh. Armed with a letter of introduction from the master monk, which Max had wisely saved for such an occasion, Max figured to be one step ahead of this particular Singh who had already granted one visa extension to him in the winter. He could not imagine a problem until he arrived at the visa office and discovered that this particular Colonel Singh had died.

"He has had a heart attack only three weeks ago," the new Colonel Singh explained.

All Singh's being equal to the task of extending Max's visa, Max produced the master monk's letter of introduction and politely asked for an extension.

The Colonel smiled and accepted the letter and said, "You will please return tomorrow. Today I am so busy."

Given the gentle curve life had thrown him, Max decided to take advantage of the time and visit Bodh Gaya. He looked forward to seeing the master monk and Arthur, the Atman, and was again met with bad news: the Atman had also died and the master monk was visiting the Dalai Lama in Manali.

Sad but undaunted, Max decided to spend the day meditating in the Mahabodhi Stupa, but he had trouble sitting still for more than a half hour at a time; his legs ached from a lack of daily practice and his mind conjured all kinds of goodbye dramas involving Maya. In a moment of clarity, during the train ride to Gaya, Max had decided to leave her.

He had dinner at the Tibetan Tent and took a long and lonely walk along the formerly dry and cracked river bed, which was now overflowing from the monsoon rains. The sun setting, the clouds turning pink, a gentle breeze carried a rather remarkable Gershwin melody to Max's ears:

Summertime, and the livin's easy.
Fish are jumpin' and the cotton's high
Your daddy's rich
And your mama's good lookin' . . .

The voice was extraordinary—strong, raspy and colorful—sounding very much like Janis Joplin's version of the song, Max thought. Max was singing along in his mind, marveling at the power and beauty of the voice, when he turned a bend in the river and saw the singer. It was a young, stocky, white girl with a shaved head, wearing the burgundy robes of a Tibetan monk, who was belting out the blues while washing a load of dirty laundry in the river.

"That was incredible," Max began, waiting until the end of the song before approaching the woman.

Mary Beth looked up at him and smiled. "Glad you liked it, Max."

Max was shocked. The last time he saw Mary Beth she was making money on her back in Afghanistan!

Mary Beth explained as the sun set and the sky turned red and the full moon rose behind the gathering clouds. "My daddy wasn't rich and my mama wasn't good looking. My life wasn't worth shit and I hated myself. I sold myself because I couldn't own up to who I was, which was a kid with a broken heart, who couldn't put all the pieces together. Fuck, man, I couldn't even find the pieces.

"I was dying inside, using guys to screw me because I didn't even have the courage to screw myself. I wanted to die, man. My whole life's been a death trip until I got here somehow and saw the truth. I was lying here by the river, about six months ago, and

I'd been drinking some local poison that tasted like gasoline or something. And I'm feeling sorry for myself and crying over horror of my life."

"I thought you and Hans were following the trail blazed by Jesus in the Aquarian Gospel?"

"I thought so too, but . . . dreams die easy with me, and Hans didn't really give a shit, so I eventually went my own way and wound up here, half-drunk and half-dead, waking up by the river bed. It was getting late and I was thinking that I was better off dead. I was at the end of my rope when I see these two Indian guys carrying this other white guy down to the river on a stretcher over there." Mary Beth pointed to the bend in the river before continuing, "And I walk over there because I got nothing better to do with myself, and I see this real skinny guy lying on the stretcher, and he's stiff as a fucking board, and he tells me he's dying. And I said something like, 'Good for you, man.'

"And he says, 'You think dying is so good?'

"And I said something like, 'It's better than living like me.'

"And he said something that changed my life forever. He said, 'If your life isn't worth living, you wouldn'' be crying about it.'

"Then I started to wonder what was worth living for. And I talked to this master monk, and he said something like, 'If you can't find a reason to live for yourself, you can live for other people.' So I became a monk and I do things for other people like washing their laundry and stuff. And I started feeling better about myself. I really love doing the laundry. It's like by me cleaning things, I'm cleaning myself somehow, and I don't walk around feeling so dirty inside, and I'm also helping other people in the process. Most of all, I found a place I can call home."

Max embraced her before kissing her forehead and saying goodbye.

Early the following morning, just before sunrise, Max returned to the Mahabodhi Stupa, to the sunken garden and knelt before the Atman's ashes and thanked him for Mary Beth's life.

*   *   *

Shunya woke to a perfect morning: the lake reflecting the mountains and reflecting his peace of mind. Following yoga and meditation in his room, he ordered breakfast on deck. Sitting astern as the sun rose over the vale of Kashmir, he was about to butter a perfectly toasted bagel, when Delhi Dave arrived and saw that familiar faraway look in Shunya's sparkling blue eyes.

"You goin' somewhere?" Delhi Dave began, taking a seat opposite Shunya. Mohammed, the slow-witted cousin, served coffee.

"I've been here two weeks already and I think God's calling me to a higher purpose," Shunya said, looking over Delhi Dave's shoulder at the shimmering, snow-capped mountaintops and pointing to Mt. Amarnath, the phallic home of Lord Shiva.

"So you mean you ain't down wit' the deal?"

"Maybe not. It may be too big for me, and I'm not really down with the spying and gun running thing, making money for people to buy weapons. Anyway, I told you about that Rich Tom guy with the oil, and that's sounding better to me the more I think about it. And I can bring you in on that one too if you want."

"Yeah well . . . We can talk about that another time. In the meantime, while you're praying to Shiva's dick, I'm headin' over to Kabul to see some college guys, and meet this other guy Kalib who runs the scene in the Khyber Pass. He's like a tribal chief or somethin' an' my man Mohammed says he's got the best shit in the world."

*   *   *

For the sum of three hundred rupees, Max procured another visa extension in Gaya and returned to Almora a week later, stopping again in Nainital to visit with James, who had fallen for a good-looking redhead from Canada.

"I got Kenchi Baba in my heart, the Doctor on my mind, and the girl on my dick," James told Max. "I'm really happy and really confused.

Max convinced James to return to Almora with him. "Where you can relax and reason things out without any pressure.

James agreed and the two old friends arrived at Epworth one hot and hazy morning to a slew of bad news: Maya had left Almora with Erik, the German, White Mike said—which put Max through some very odd and intense emotional changes, especially after reading the note Maya left behind: *Dearest Max, You were gone when the change came, but I will always love you in the sameness we shared.*

He was glad she was gone; he was angry at her running out on him—with another man, no less. He could hardly imagine her in bed with Erik, he was so attached to her. Bewildered, relieved, hurt, enraged, Max was fuming over a cup of chai on the front porch when Diane showed up in tears and told him that David had died of an overdose in a Delhi hotel room.

"The American embassy contacted me through Colonel Singh, who just left my house," she said. "And now I have to go to Delhi with Sam to identify the body and have it cremated. I also have to call and tell his mother, who might drop dead of a heart attack herself when she hears the news. And it's so hard on me, not because I loved David so much—I didn't—but because he died so young without having a chance to change his life, and mostly because I didn't have the strength to help him make the change. I could have tried harder," she sobbed, falling into Max's arms.

"And you might have died trying if you had stayed with him any longer," Max concluded.

"That's what Sam said, that David was still a lot stronger than me at the time."

"How did the embassy know where to find you?" Max asked.

"That was another thing that was so sad. It seems David had known where I was for a while. I think they found a letter addressed to me in Almora in his room. I guess I'll know more about it when I get there. We're leaving tomorrow with Jane and Gary."

*   *   *

Pahalgam was a very small town located in the heart of a long and narrow green valley, the mountains soaring above twenty thousand feet on all sides. It was also the home to Mohammed, Delhi Dave's good friend and partner.

"The guy's like a fuckin' brother to me. He's beautiful," Delhi Dave reiterated before Shunya left Srinagar.

But the bus to Pahalgam was three hours late, and it was raining heavily when Shunya arrived in town. The following morning Shunya rose before dawn and joined more than ten thousand pilgrims on the twenty-six mile trek to Amarnath—including many wealthy Brahmins, too fat to walk, who were consequently hauled up the mountainside on the backs of peasant bearers.

The bulk of the crowd was comprised of middle class merchants and clerks, who bullied their sadly subservient wives when they weren't comparing their new wristwatches, or listening to Indian movie music on their tape recorders.

The pilgrimage progressed in three stages. From Pahalgam, through the woods and past several lush green valleys, to Chandanwari, a tiny respite whose sole existent purpose was to service the annual pilgrimage to Amarnath.

This first stage was long and tiring, but very beautiful; it ended moonlight and prayer—and a cloud of hashish. Each valley had a harvest, and every pilgrimage attracted a throng of gaffers and entrepreneurs looking to make a quick rupee on the crowd, from fetching water to providing a quick and easy hash high. And while the bourgeoisie tended to look down upon the use of drugs in their home town, they tended to be a bit more liberal—if not indulgent—on the road to salvation. Campfires burned throughout the night and many chillums were passed among the affluent faithful.

Higher up on the mountainside, above the din of the crowd, on top of a great waterfall, Shunya sat with holier men smoking better dope. There were more than one thousand sadhus from a dozen different sects who spearheaded the trek, their nearly naked and painted bodies pointing the way to redemption through prayer and religious song.

Shunya hardly slept, he was so excited and taken by the spirit that moved so many people so high in the sky.

*   *   *

Dawn broke above the clouds where Shunya had spent the night. By sunrise, the pilgrimage stretched out and spiraled up the mountainside like a huge serpent, writhing slowly above the tree line to Sheshnag. The second day seemed longer, the path was steeper. The view was increasingly barren but nonetheless beautiful. Like walking on the moon, Shunya often thought, trekking past huge flat rocks and fields of tundra, and up through a second layer of clouds: watching hawks and falcons and kites ride the wind over the lush green valleys and meadows below, watching the clouds gather and part, watching the sun peek through, watching the rain make the rainbows, watching it snow, watching the lightning and cowering beneath the thunder of the mountain gods.

The second night at Sheshnag was much colder and other-worldly, but Shunya didn't feel a thing, he was so far removed from earthly considerations. He had one tab of acid left which he shared with three sadhus—one of whom spoke English and translated. Together, they paid homage to Lord Vishnu. It was just after sunset when the acid combined with the legend to manifest the profile of Lord Vishnu, the preserver of life, from an odd juxtaposition of shadows and light and mountain peaks.

The moon was so bright, the landscape so barren, the heavens so close at hand that Shunya touched them with his mind and spent the entire night in the realm of the spirits.

"The place in the heart where man and God meet," the English-speaking sadhu said. He was a younger man with hair down below his knees, wearing only a loincloth to protect himself from the elements, which he experienced as energy. His face painted, his bare body covered with holy ash, he spent much of the night with Shunya pointing out the stars, which to his hallucinogenic mind, told the story of the Ramayana in the form of ever-changing constellations.

It was a wonder-filled night that dwarfed the experience of the following day. The morning trek was short and uneventful. Within hours, Shunya reached the wide mouth of the Amarnath cave and followed a long line of faithful inside to witness the manifestation of Lord Shiva on earth.

The ice lingam was reputedly tied to the phases of the moon, often waxing in the summer months. Nearly three feet wide and more than four feet tall on this holy afternoon, it rose like an erection from the floor of the cave and mesmerized the crowd: some praying, some singing, some dancing, some making mudras, a few bouncing off the cave walls from the shakti-pat that they could not process. Offerings were made, flowers were laid, incense was burned and Brahman priests were hired for special pujas—all this to worship the Lingam of the Lord whose faithful continued to repress their own sexuality.

Shunya found the paradox even more intriguing than the holiness of the shrine; once again, the journey was far more enticing than the arrival.

28

Tibet harbored some of the greatest mysteries on earth; consequently, it generated the wildest fantasies in the minds of men. James Hilton wrote about it in *Lost Horizon*, the best selling 1933 novel that postulated the existence of a utopian society in the Valley of the Blue Moon. Legends persisted about the existence of the yeti, who roamed the high tundra and uninhabited distant valleys of Tibet. Rumors still circulated about great yogis, lighter than air, who could run a hundred miles an hour, and high lamas who could dematerialize at will, and reincarnate in other lives and dimensions.

Reality was another, more tragic story of a country under siege by its Chinese neighbor. Narayan and Mani were determined to discover the mysteries before the realities set in, so they decided to sneak across the border in the middle of the night and were summarily arrested and jailed for two weeks.

It was another rainy day in Almora when Narayan and Mani limped into Epworth, beaten to a pulp by their Indian jailers.

"For what?" James asked.

"For spying," Mani said, wiping a mix of dried blood and sweat from his face with the filthy end of his prayer shawl.

"For who?" White Mike asked.

"For the Chinese and the CIA. The Indian border guards caught us, but they couldn't make up their minds whose side we were on, so they beat us until we proved to them that we were sadhus."

"How'd you do that?" Max asked.

"By sitting in mediation for two hours at a time without moving," Narayan said.

"And by drinking a cup of our own urine every day," Mani added. He got the idea from a conversation he'd had with Helen Doyle at Epworth.

After resting for two days, Mani and Narayan left for Benares, undeterred, and still on a quest for the miraculous.

"To see this old swami who's supposed to be the guardian of an ancient Sanskrit text. And if it has your name in it, he can read your past lives!" Narayan said.

"It would seem that surviving this life is hard enough," Max cracked before saying goodbye.

Mani said, "That is true, but what is truer still is the progression of civilization and modernization, and the real probability that all these teachers, and teachings, and cultures that are still tied to the past may be lost forever. As important as it is for some of us to find God in this life, it is also important that we preserve and protect the many paths to Divinity that have been discovered and developed over so many thousands of years. That's why we tried to go to Tibet, to see what we could see and meet with who we could find. And it's also why we're going to Benares to see this old swami—because someone has to do it, and because we are honored to do it."

*   *   *

Diane was lying in bed beside Sam in their room in the Palace Heights Hotel when she fell into a bad dream. She was fast asleep in David's parents' house in Queens when it caught fire. Terrified, she ran screaming from the house into the street looking for David. Then she smelled something horrid, like burning flesh, and she heard someone else scream. David, she thought, waking with a start and that awful smell in her mind.

The following day, she witnessed the cremation of David's body in a field outside Delhi, placed high on a stack of wood. The smell reminded her of the dream.

"I felt like I was dying inside when his body was burning, as if I were burning in reality. It was even worse than the dream I had," she told Big Jane, who had attended the cremation with Gary—both chanting as the body burned and Diane wept.

It was early evening. They were sitting on the second floor patio of the hotel beneath a large umbrella, watching the traffic circle Connaught Circus as it continued to drizzle.

"Karma, Diane. It was your karma burning and now you are free," Jane said.

"To some extent, but I still feel so bad for him because he never had another chance."

"On the contrary, David was in Bodh Gaya, and he had every chance in the world to renew his life—and you can't blame yourself for his bad choices."

Diane was about to reply when Sam and Gary joined them at the table. Gary was a big man, six foot three, with short blond hair and a huge blond beard; he wasn't very good looking, but he was nonetheless imposing. He had come to India on a university grant to study sadhu culture.

"Feeling better?" Gary began, sitting next to Jane, across the table from Diane.

"Not better or worse," Diane said. "Just different I suppose— like I lost something and I can't find it."

"In time, you'll stop looking. In the meantime, you can lean on us," Gary said, reaching for her hand.

Sam lit a bidi and said, "It's not about leaning; it's all about looking."

Diane turned to Sam and said, "Don't you ever stop?"

"What?"

"Looking, learning, leaning; who gives a fuck?" Diane shot back. "Every thing's a fucking teaching with you, and nothing is ever spontaneous. I just burnt my no good junkie husband and all of a sudden I feel like I need a drink and I know that you're going to have a problem with that—as if it's a sign of weakness."

"I didn't say that."

"Then you will go out with me tonight?"

"I will go, Diane, and I'll watch myself drinking."

*   *   *

Time passed slowly in Almora, especially for Max, who couldn't stop thinking of Maya. Losing her hurt even more than losing Diane, and Max couldn't figure out why until White Mike told him over a game of chess.

It was another drizzly afternoon on the ridge, the sky turning ever-darker and more ominous as the day progressed. James was sitting inside, rubbing hash into perfectly round balls. He had spent the past two days below the ridge on a farm with White Mike, culling the resin from a field of wild marijuana plants.

Max was sitting at a small table on the front porch playing chess with White Mike, losing as usual. After all, White Mike was the better player. He had also become a very dear friend. He had an unfailing dry sense of British humor and required little attention—unlike Bill Velititsky, who had sustained his unfailing ability to show up at the wrong place at the wrong time and say the wrong thing.

"Losing again, huh?" Bill said to Max before asking to borrow a cup of flour. Turning to White Mike he added, "Because he can't think clearly."

"And you can?" Max snapped.

"Clear enough to see through you."

"What's that supposed to mean?" Max shot back.

Bill adjusted his ever-present, horn rimmed glasses before replying. "Maya. It's hard to make the right move after you make the wrong move. I knew she was wrong for you, but I was afraid to tell you."

"And you think telling me this now is the right move?" Max was so enraged, he wanted to spring off his chair and grab Bill by the throat.

"To the extent that I feel bad for you," Bill sadly replied.

Max was stunned by the unexpected display of compassion. "The flour's in the pantry, take what you want. There's also some rice pudding." Turning attention back to the board, Max continued, speaking to White Mike. "That might the first genuinely nice thing he ever said to me—even if it was ass-backwards. I just wish I knew why it hurts so much, even more than Diane."

"Because Diane really cares for you and Maya never did," White Mike surmised.

"I'm not sure I cared for Maya that much either, to be perfectly honest. It was the wanting, it wasn't the loving."

"Then it seems like you wanted too much."

Max was further stunned by White Mike's insight. To Max's knowledge, White Mike was still a virgin. "Seems like I'm the only idiot in town," Max cracked before making the right chess move and putting White Mike's queen in check.

White Mike studied the board, and resigned by toppling his king. "Well done, Max!"

Max was swelling with pride when a bolt of lightning hit the roof, and a crash of thunder rattled the enter house.

The boys were scared. It was the beginning of the worst storm any of them had ever seen; wave after wave of ear-splitting thunder followed by streaks of jagged lightning struck the ridge. The sky turned dark as night as the wind felled trees in the distance and threatened to tear the roof off their house.

More than a storm, it seemed like an act of vengeance. Perhaps Nanda Devi had suffered a broken heart and was shedding her immortal rage on all lesser beings that lived below her expectations. Or some god had fallen from grace and in homage to his passing the mountains and the sky came together in a staggering eulogy of fury and agony. Or maybe it was the ghost of the old chowkidar manifest in the form of a wrathful deity. It was hard for the smaller minds of men to know, but with each thundering flash the gods and goddesses of the spirit world stood naked and dared humanity to look upon them.

Four hours later, when all the madness and mayhem had passed, a sadder truth was revealed. Max was sitting in front of the fireplace with White Mike and Bill when Ute entered the living room and told them that Peter had been shot in the back.

"Last night," she sobbed, standing in front of the fireplace, soaked and shaken from the storm. "These three men broke in and robbed us . . . And they punched me and they threw me down on the floor . . . and they began to rape me . . . then Peter tried to help and they shot him in the back."

"Where is Peter now?" Max asked.

"In town, in the hospital, where I come from just now. I ran to Black Michael for help, and he gets the Colonel Singh and we go to the hospital. But no one is helping now and he is lying down there alone in the hospital and he is dying. "

"What about Black Michael? Where's he?" Max asked.

"I don't know. I don't know," Ute cried out before bursting into hysterics.

All took turns comforting her, but no one could get the whole story from her, she had been so terribly violated, and broken-hearted, and battered from the storm.

Max thought she needed time to rest and compose herself, but Ute wouldn't hear of it. "He's alone. He's so alone," she repeated. "He can't be alone anymore. I can't. I can't . . . I can't anymore."

So Max escorted her back to the hospital as the clouds parted, alternately comforting her and trying to get the whole story. "Are you sure you're okay?" he asked for the third time, holding an umbrella in hand and his other arm around her shoulders.

"Yes. I think yes, maybe."

"Did you see a doctor?"

"No."

"Are you sure Peter is dying?"

"Yes, I think so."

"What happened to the guys who shot him?"

"I don't know."

"Did you recognize them?"

"I don't know. I don't think so."

"What about Colonel Singh? You say he came to your house and drove you to the hospital."

"Yes."

"But he didn't offer to drive you back up the ridge in this weather?"

"No, I don't know. Maybe he is looking for the offenders."

Every question begged another question until Ute pleaded for understanding. "I cannot think so well so soon. I am feeling too much about so many things. Later, maybe I will think better later," she agonized. She was still in shock.

Max understood and responded compassionately until they reached the hospital. When she expressed sadness, he addressed her sadness. When she cried, he consoled her. When she thought Peter would live, he encouraged her to believe so. When she said Peter was dying, Max sympathized with her.

When she spoke of the crime, Max listened carefully and did not challenge her recollection of events, which changed each time she told the story. She had originally said that three Indians had broken into the house; now she claimed that four Indians had broken into her house. Near midnight, she had said, then she said it was nearer to three in the morning. She claimed that they were drunk, then she said they were high on drugs.

Although Max ascribed the conflicting details to her state of shock, he could not help thinking about one strange event he had witnessed in the town of Almora several weeks ago, when he went shopping with Maya. He saw Ute sitting outside a restaurant with two Indian boys and a fat Sikh who took money from her.

The hospital was a small, whitewashed building, dirty inside and out, grossly under-staffed and ill-prepared to treat a white sahib with a gunshot wound. Peter lay on his back alone and unattended, dying a horrible death at the back of a small ward. He was in shock, having lost a great deal of blood to a bullet that entered his back and lodged near his heart. Alternately convulsing, and gasping for breath, he rambled incoherently. He looked much worse than Max had anticipated.

"Where are all the doctors and nurses?" Max began.

Ute didn't know.

"Why is he in so much pain? Did they give him anything for his pain?"

Ute didn't know.

Max was about to pose another question when he realized that Peter wasn't even hooked up to an IV. "This is outrageous," he declared, before running out of the ward to look for doctors and answers.

Which were brutally simple: "I cannot operate to save his life because I do not have the experience. And I cannot provide him with pain medicine and allow a merciful death because my hands are tied," the doctor on duty explained.

"By who?" Max challenged.

The doctor hesitated, then stumbled, "It is something criminal that has happened, and your friend is a foreigner. It is not some infectious disease, and I cannot be responsible here for any-thing."

"In other words, there's a white man dying in a dark man's hospital," Max sneered.

"It is not what I am saying."

"But it is what's happening."

"Even so, this a small town and a very small hospital. We are poor and I cannot act on my own."

"And you won't tell me who speaks for you?"

"I cannot say, first it is one person then another, and that is all I will say."

"And you won't let me speak to one of them?"

The doctor hung his head and trembled, he was so scared.

Afraid of Colonel Singh, Max finally realized. He had to be behind all this, but Max had no way of finding him in the dark, and Peter needed immediate help.

"Do you believe in God?" Max asked the doctor.

The doctor said, "Yes, of course."

"Then I am asking you to help my friend in the name your God," Max implored, his voice straining with emotion as he pressed his palms together in supplication. "I am begging you in the name of all that is holy to at least relieve his pain."

29

While Max fought for Peter's life, Colonel Singh visited Epworth, asking a lot questions. As always, his good manners belied a dubious agenda.

"So, you are not sleeping at this hour?" the Colonel began. It was after 10 p.m.

"Ute was here," James sighed. "We know all about it, about Peter."

"All?"

When their eyes met and James realized he had to be very careful with this particular Singh. "As much as Ute told us. She was in pretty bad shape."

"And you are?"

"James Cohn. I was here when the Doctor was here. I'll get my papers."

"No, no, it is not necessary. This is not an interrogation. And you are familiar to me, all of you."

White Mike and Bill were flanking James.

Always an English gentleman, White Mike invited Colonel Singh to have a cup of chai with them, and the colonel graciously accepted his invitation. "I have had the chai in this house before, when your Doctor was here, and I was very impressed."

Sitting in front of the fireplace, the Colonel began again. "And where is the other fellow who is living here, Max, I believe? Where is he tonight?"

"At the hospital with Ute," James said, knowing all too well that Colonel Singh knew exactly where Max was. This cop was not the first cop James had dealt with. He was street smart and hoped that Bill and White Mike would follow his lead.

"They have been friends for some time, Ute and Max?"

"Not to my knowledge. Max hardly knew her. She just showed up here in desperation. She was hysterical. This whole thing has been a pretty big shock to all of us."

Which was true. Not one of them had ever heard of a Westerner who had died a violent death in India.

The colonel turned his attention to Bill. "You have told your friends at Snowview?"

"They're still in Delhi with the body, but you must know that?"

"I only know what I am told, and I am forced to ask these questions. You can tell me if Sam and Diane have known Peter and Ute?"

Bill said, "Diane met Peter in Benares, when she first came to India. They went out."

James and White Mike glared at Bill, enraged at his stupidity.

"Went out where?" Colonel Singh pressed, missing the romantic inference.

"Around the city, to the ghats and the temples. I think he taught her meditation," Bill added, realizing his mistake.

The Colonel sipped his chai and twirled his mustache before turning his attention to White Mike. "You are knowing Ute and Peter?"

"Not really. I only saw them when they came to hear the Doctor speak."

"And you have been living in this house with Max?"

"For a while."

"And you have seen Peter and Ute in the town shopping sometimes?"

White Mike smiled and shrugged his shoulders, making himself look as young and dumb as possible. "I guess," he said.

James was exceedingly pleased with White Mike's performance. Instinct continued to tell James to give this Colonel as little as possible until they knew the whole story. After all, Peter and Ute could have been involved in drug deal gone awry, which could reflect suspiciously on all Westerners on the ridge.

Colonel Singh smiled and turned his attention to James. "This chai is very good. You are using alachi seeds?"

"Alachi, cinnamon and licorice, and one drop of vanilla extract."

"The vanilla is something new to me. I will have to try it." The Colonel took another sip of chai before continuing. "So, you have spent much time in our town?"

"No, not really. When the Doctor was here at Epworth."

"And you have come back?"

"With Max, a few days ago. I've been spending most of my time with Kenchi Baba outside Nainital."

"He is your guru?"

"Yes, but I'm becoming more interested in the Doctor since I met him."

"Max must be a very good friend to the Doctor, to have invited him here for so many days?"

James took the bait without getting hooked. "Max is his student. But a lot of the people who came here to listen to the Doctor showed up on their own accord—through word-of-mouth."

"I think Ute was also very interested in this Doctor. She seemed very attentive the night I was here."

James refused to comment and was becoming increasingly uncomfortable with the thrust of Colonel Sing's inquiry. Assuming a bunch of murderous Indian locals were responsible for the attack, as Ute said, why was Colonel Singh so interested in many of the Westerners?

Whether out of frustration or simple inquisitiveness, the Colonel finally got to the dark heart of the matter. "You know that there is more than one thousand American dollars in cash and as much as twenty thousand rupees that has been stolen from Peter and Ute?"

James was genuinely surprised, which was a point in his favor. "That is a lot of money."

"You know why Peter and Ute would keep so much money in cash?"

James shook his head. "I can't even imagine. And like I said before, I hardly know them. None of us really do."

The Colonel looked to White Mike and Bill, and both agreed with James, who was growing tired of the game and took the offensive. "If the people who shot Peter were Indian, why are you suspecting so many Westerners?"

"Because everyone is a suspect until somebody is caught," the Colonel sharply replied.

James drew a deep breath and sighed, "I'm sorry, Colonel. I didn't mean to question your sincerity or your integrity. We're still in a bit of shock."

The Colonel nodded and smiled, genuinely this time, and ran his hands through his hair. "This is a terrible thing that has happened. It could be locals. It could be dacoits from the north. It could be anyone because the woman does not give a good description of the perpetrators, and she does not give a good reason for having so much money in the house."

James said, "I don't know anything about the money, but I do know the woman was beaten and raped. That's what she told us, and I can't imagine why she would lie."

The Colonel drew a deep breath and sighed, "It is a very long night for all of us, I think. And there is still much to do. Perhaps you need a ride into town, to the hospital?"

James refused the ride and explained. "Max is taking care of the hospital. We are taking care of the house. And I'm sure the police will take care of the criminals."

James thought he had done a pretty good job of deflecting the Colonel's curiosity, but he could not imagine the dark depths from which it sprang.

* * *

Peter died at dawn.

It was a long and painful and harrowing death—for no good reason Max could imagine. Peter was not given as much as an aspirin, let alone a shot of morphine to kill the pain. The god that had spoken through Max did not reach the devil that possessed the doctor in Almora. He adamantly refused to treat Peter under any circumstances, for any reason. In despair, Max called doctors and hospitals in Nainital, and the British High Commission in Delhi. But nothing could be done to save Peter's life or alleviate his suffering.

Max spent much of the night at Peter's bedside with Ute, holding his hand and wiping sweat from his brow and blood from the corners of his mouth. The pain was so great it often ripped through Peter like a jagged knife, his long and lanky body convulsing from its intensity. He suffered beyond reason, beyond necessity, beyond help—until Ute proposed a mercy killing.

"You could do it," she told Max. It was after three in the morning. They were taking a much needed break on the hospital veranda. It was the night of the dark moon, still clear and brisk after the storm—as good a night as any to die, Max thought.

"If he could talk, Peter would ask you to do it," Ute added, tears streaming down her face.

Therein lay the conundrum for Max: he wanted to end Peter's life, but Max ultimately refused to do it unless Peter returned to consciousness and asked him. He was also disturbed by the details of Ute's story that continued to change throughout the night. She had said she was beaten for not telling them where the money was, then she was raped repeatedly by all of them, then by two of them, before Peter was shot, then after Peter was shot.

She said that she had never seen any of them before, then she said that one of them was "familiar" to her. She said they all dressed western, then she said one or two might have been wearing kurtas or white pajami and "looked like dacoits." When Max asked her why they kept so much cash in the house, she didn't answer and changed the subject. When he asked her a second time, she began to cry.

She was still crying when Colonel Singh finally showed up at the hospital, expressing his deep regret before asking Ute about the junkies living in another house on Kalimot.

"I went to them first for help, before I went to Black Michael. And they didn't care for anything, to help me or Peter. I think they must get very scared when I tell them what has happened to us."

"You are certain that they never came to your house for any reason, before or after the crime?" Colonel Singh asked.

Ute said, "No."

Colonel Singh found it hard to believe and asked Max what he thought.

"About what?" Max asked.

"About anything that has happened. You must tell me what you know."

Max said, "I only know what she tells me."

Colonel Singh had heard all it before and did not believe it. "There is more. There must be more," he said, before turning to leave.

Max followed him down the hallway, grabbed his shoulder and spun him around. "That's it? You have nothing more to say? You can't be of any help?"

The Colonel said, "What kind of help?"

"For Peter, you mean you can't even tell the doctor to give him medication for his pain?"

Colonel said, "No. I have no authority."

"Then who does?"

Colonel Singh shook his head, looked down at the floor, then directly in Max's eyes and sighed, "No one, because I am afraid no one wants to take this responsibility. The doctor answers to higher doctors and administrators, and I answer to my superiors and, in the end, you will have to answer for yourself."

"What's that's supposed to mean?" Max asked.

"Time will tell," the Colonel said, before promising to speak to his superiors again, and promising to return in an hour.

But he never returned and never helped. Peter died in agony with Max and Ute at his side.

*   *   *

Out of respect for the dead and the broken hearted, Max again retreated to the hospital veranda. Ute eventually found him sitting cross-legged and chanting to Lord Shiva as the sun rose over the Himalayas. She waited until an appropriate pause in the melody before approaching him. "I'm so sorry," she began, fighting back tears.

"For what?" Max wondered.

"For getting you involved with all this," she said.

Max said. "This is life. You didn't do anything."

When Ute burst into tears, Max embraced her. He waited until Ute calmed down before posing a necessary question. "What are you going to do with Peter's body?"

Ute didn't know. "I will talk to Colonel Singh," she said. "He will know, I think."

Max didn't know what to think or who to trust.

*   *   *

James, White Mike, and Bill were up all night at Epworth, drinking chai, playing chess, and trying to analyze the crime. They were each on their third cup of chai when Max finally returned at sunrise and told them how Peter died.

All were aghast and enraged—especially at Colonel Singh.

"The prick came here after you left," James said. "He was looking for something or someone to hang this thing on. I don't think he bought Ute's story."

"Neither do I," Max sighed. "Not entirely."

With Max's added input, the boys spent much of the day trying to unravel the mystery behind Peter's death, entertaining all kinds of theories and paranoid possibilities—including Colonel Singh's complicity in the crime. Perhaps the most unusual thing about this case was the criminal use of a gun. Few crimes in India were perpetrated with a gun because they were so expensive and hard to find.

"Unless you were a military cop like Colonel Singh," James surmised. "He could have put some guys up to the job and provided them with a gun, and maybe something went wrong."

Max said, "I find that hard to believe. But the one thing that I can't help thinking about is when I was shopping in town with Maya, and I saw her sitting outside a restaurant with some kids, exchanging money with a fat Sikh."

White Mike was about to reply when Ute knocked at the door. Taking a seat in front of the fireplace, she finally answered Max's curiosity.

She said, "The money was for the hash we buy from the farmers in the valley and send to Germany. It is also to pay for a school for music in the town. It was Peter' idea to buy a building near the restaurant from the Sikh people, who I pay every month. The boys I use to help me shop in the bazaar, and also to do chores around the house. Peter gave them music lessons, too, sometimes. We also changed money with the Sikhs sometimes, a lot of money the last time, and I think these Sikhs are behind this."

It all made sense to Max. He was ashamed of himself and sorry he had second guessed her, and Ute preyed on his guilt, she was so desperate. "There is no one who will help with Peter's body, and I need help to dispose of it" she agonized.

"Where is it now?"

"It is taken to an autopsy. It is not what I want, but Colonel Singh said it must be so."

"Then what?"

"Then there is nothing. I have no idea what to do, and no one will help." Try as Ute did, no one in town would touch the body—not a Hindu, or a Sikh, or Colonel Singh. "And I am afraid that they will just push the body over a cliff and leave it in the jungle for the beasts."

*   *   *

In despair, Max waited until the following morning before turning to Swami Buddhananda for guidance. "We just can't let him rot," Max said. "It was bad enough the way he died."

Buddhananda said, "I can't say I'm surprised. Murder is not the sort of thing to have as a companion in a small village."

"Except Peter is not the murderer, he's the victim," Max declared.

"Obviously, but he's not the only one. In a situation like this, mistakes can beget mistakes."

"I don't understand. The woman was raped and the guy was murdered. It's only a simple matter of disposing of the body."

"From your point of view, but there is nothing little or simple about the murder of a white man by a dark man in India. In a case like this, we are all likely to suffer the consequences in one way or another owing to the inferences that will be drawn: some Indians claiming that it was a crime of passion fueled by drugs—they blame the white sahibs for bringing their decadency with them—while others are simply frightened away by the whole mess. I cannot overstress the racial and cultural undertones involved in all this.

"As you well know, violence is not uncommon in India—beggars kill each other for food, parents kill children they can't afford to raise, husbands kill prearranged wives they don't like. Indians kill each other over a variety of reasons—but they rarely, if ever, kill a white person. A white tourist walking alone in India, in its worst neighborhoods, may be robbed at knife point, or beaten in the act of robbery, raped even, but not killed. Such a crime, perpetrated against a white in the heart of a big city would make headlines. In a town like Almora, it makes people afraid—terribly afraid—and most suspicious."

Max thanked Buddhananda for his time and a shot of brandy, but he refused to heed Buddhananda's advice. Now filled with righteous indignation, Max returned to Epworth and told Ute and the boys that no one can be expected to help, and that it would be up to them to dispose of the body.

While Ute went looking for Colonel Singh, to plead for his help one last time, the boys returned to town to retrieve the body from the coroner's office.

The autopsy was performed and the body was wrapped in a gauze bandage from head to foot. The boys felt a bit queasy at the sight of the body, but they were not deterred. For the price of ten rupees, they rented a stretcher and carried Peter's dead weight out of the coroner's office on their slim shoulders.

In life, Peter weighed only about one hundred and seventy pounds. In death, he weighed a ton and attracted a lot of unwanted attention—the townspeople stopping, and staring, and pointing as the boys carried the body through the center of town.

At the far edge of town, they took a rest in the shade, beneath a small grove of tall and leafy hemp plants. It was an unusually sunny day—already too hot to bear the burden. Ute never showed up and the boys realized that they needed a plan of their own.

James said, "There's got to be a burning ghat around here somewhere."

White Mike said, "No doubt, but if no one will tell us where it is, it's a moot point."

Max said, "Then we'll carry him all the way to the ridge and bury him behind Epworth somewhere, say a few words, do a little chanting, and call it a life."

All agreed, and all sprang to their feet with renewed enthusiasm. They were about to hoist dead Peter onto their lively shoulders when Black Michael appeared around the bend screaming, "You stupid fools; you stupid misguided fools! What do you think you're doing?"

"Burying the dead," Max said. He was surprised to see Michael, but not intimidated by his bellowing voice, or his black robes, or his salty Tantric reputation. As far as Max was concerned, Black Michael was just another guy who was standing in the way of the right path.

Michael's face flushed red. An ugly vein popped out of the side of his neck as he continued to shout, "And where do you think you will bury him?"

"As if it's any of your fucking business," Max shot back.

Michael's lips began to tremble. Gritting his teeth in an effort to contain his emotion, he hissed, "You little twit, I think you've done enough already."

"Which is a hell of a lot more than you did, Michael. Where the fuck were you last night? I didn't see you at the hospital. Or maybe you were just too busy praying to your little Tantric god to concern yourself with the pains and problems of the rest of us."

"Okay, I'll tell you where I was," Michael snapped. "I was busy trying to save your menial little life!"

"What??"

"You stupid, stupid young fool," Michael screeched, his voice breaking under the strain. Lowering his voice, he continued harshly, "Do you know who killed Peter?"

"I know what Ute said."

"Well young man, at this very moment I happen to know what Colonel Singh and everybody else in this town is saying. He thinks it was a conspiracy between you and Ute to hire those thugs to get Peter out of the way, so you two could live happily ever after. He never believed a word she said. But you better believe me when I tell you that it is you who is suspected of Peter's murder!"

30

Returning from Kashmir, Shunya planned on heading up to Almora until he received a telegram from Rich Tom at the Amex office in Delhi, urging him to come to Nepal: *Weather is great. Business is good. Come soon.*

So Shunya took the next plane to Kathmandu, hoping to combine business with pleasure. He loved Nepal, especially in the fall. The monsoon season was nearing an end when he arrived in Kathmandu Valley, and the view was spectacular: the snow-white jagged peaks rising above the green valley into a crystal blue sky, the air crisp and cool at night. The streets were filled with Tibetan monks, Hindu priests, tourists, mountain climbers, deadbeats, and drug dealers. It was harvest time in the Himalayas, and the Valley was filling up with hash.

"The best time of the year to make a deal," Shunya said.

Rich Tom said, "I put up the money and you take the risk, or we can go partners on the money, if you like, and we can find someone else to take the risk."

They were sitting in Aunt Jane's pie shop, having coffee and a piece of New York cheese cake—which was surprisingly good. It was a funky old store, a staple in the cultural mélange that defined Kathmandu. Three-Finger Louie was holding court in a far corner of the room, answering questions about his life and inquiring into the welfare of others who were less fortunate.

Shunya stroked his long, red beard and said, "I need all the money I can get, so I would be willing to take the risk—assuming I can return to America. I already have a call into a lawyer in New York, and I won't decide anything until I hear from him. In the meantime, I'll hang around the valley, take in the view, and meditate."

Rich Tom said, "I'd like to learn meditation."

Shunya was surprised. "You mean you've been here all this time and never learned?"

Tom shrugged. "I didn't come here to learn. I came to get away and have a good time, but no place seems far enough and, well . . . I've done some yoga, which is a form of meditation, I guess, but . . .

"You could take a Sayadaw course. You've heard of Sayadaw?"

"I have, but the idea of sitting with all those people never appealed to me. But you could teach me."

Shunya was flattered, though somewhat befuddled by the quality of Rich Tom's life. Sipping his coffee, he took a closer look at the man: curly brown hair, bushy eyebrows, round brown eyes, wire-rim glasses and thin lips. Shunya's attention finally centered on the long and deep creases in Tom's forehead, indicating a lot of wear and tear on this young man's brain.

"I get migraines," Rich Tom added, as if he were answering Shunya's thoughts.

"Then you should definitely learn how to meditate."

"And you'll teach me?" Tom pressed.

Shunya drew breath and sighed, "I can try, but I would recommend someone else, a homeopathic doctor who lives in a town outside of Delhi. He's new and different, and accessible. In fact, I can highly recommend him to you."

"You mean I look that bad?"

"I mean you look that needy, as we all do from time to time, or else we wouldn't be here."

"I can't really argue with that. After all, I am here. But the truth is, it's the neediness of other people that bothers me—them knowing I have money, and so many of them always needing money."

"You didn't have to tell them what you have; you didn't have to tell me. I don't need to go into business with you to be a friend."

Therein lay the crux of the problem with Rich Tom: he loved money more than he loved people. "I guess I like the power," he reluctantly admitted, flashing a coy smile. "Knowing I do have something that a lot of other people want. But I guess I get lonely sometimes because I don't connect with them in any other way, and I suppose I should. But the idea of meditating never attracted me, because it always struck me as another lonesome pursuit."

"You must have some friends?"

"I know a lot of people, and there are a lot of people who think they're my friend, but . . . I'm not blaming them. It's me. I'm just so wrapped up in myself most of the time. And, like I said, I don't need the money, but I do like the action. And I always wanted to meet you."

Overall, Shunya was struck by Tom's honesty and candor. He liked the guy, and he decided to go into business with him instead of Delhi Dave, who posed a higher risk factor and greater moral challenge. "But we can't talk here," Shunya said, looking around the crowded pie shop.

"You know of a better place?" Tom asked.

Shunya said, "No, and that's the one problem I have with this town. It gets too crowded, and there's no place to go except here and a few grungy old chai shops, and the *Yak and the Yeti* for dinner."

"Then we should open a place of our own with some of our profits," Rich Tom declared.

And the idea for opening *The Eclipse* was hatched.

*   *   *

Max had to think fast and act quickly. Michael told him there was a burning ghat in a meadow just outside of town, and in an uncharacteristic gesture of kindness, Michael offered to make the arrangements.

While the boys oversaw the cremation of the body—without Ute, who never showed—Max returned to Epworth to consider his options. He didn't trust Colonel Singh, and imagined he could be arrested at any moment on a whim. In fact, he didn't trust Ute. The discrepancies in her story continued to turn over in his mind—she had an answer for everything, but nothing seemed to fit well enough to suit Max, who was now bearing the brunt of suspicion for the crime.

"All things considered, you have to leave town—fast—before she turns on you somehow," James said, returning with Bill and White Mike at the end of the day, following the cremation.

Under the pressing circumstances, Max found it hard to argue the point. So he waited until three in the morning to slip down the ridge with a flashlight, and out of town, where he flagged down the six o'clock bus on the road to Nainital.

He caught the last bus to Raniket, slept on a bench in the train station, took the morning train to Delhi, and reached the Doctor's house in Sonepat by noon the following day, thinking he had outwitted the twisted and possibly sinister Colonel Singh. If not the safest place to be, Sonepat was the wisest place to be, and the Doctor was happy to see him.

Max spent the first three nights in the Doctor's house, sleeping on the crowded living room floor with nine other Westerners He passed the days sitting alone at the back of the room listening to the Doctor's teachings. He had never met any of these people before, most of them having recently arrived in India by plane. These were "good" white kids from affluent, suburban neighborhoods in Europe and America. Max was a seasoned veteran compared to them, and now a murder suspect.

The Doctor's old stucco ranch house was modest by middle class Indian standards: a few small bedrooms, an office, an examination room and a moderately sized living room. The furniture was adequate; the space wasn't. The Doctor was a practicing homeopath whose patients were forced to sit among his new students. His two young teenage boys, though unsure of their father's new role as teacher, were entertained and intrigued by his western students. The wife was another, darker story. She remained in the back of the house, out of sight.

"We are living together only for the practical necessity of raising our children. Beyond that we have no functional relationship as husband and wife," the Doctor told Max during an early morning walk on the edge of town, four days after Max's unheralded arrival in Sonepat. "I tell you this in confidence. I have also spoken of this to several of your friends in Almora—also out of necessity to make a point."

"I'm flattered by your willingness to take me into your confidence, Doctor, but why me? Why now?"

"Because if I share an intimacy regarding my life, I am hopeful you will tell me what it is that has so upset your life."

Max drew a deep breath and sighed, "It's that obvious?"

"Painfully so, my dear Max."

"Which is the result too many bad choices," Max confessed. "Beginning with Maya, who I fell in love with against my better judgment, and ending with Peter, who was murdered."

The Doctor was not surprised to hear about Max's relationship with Maya, but he was stunned and saddened by news of Peter's death.

"And you blame yourself for both of these things?"

"More or less, because I should have known better. I saw the end at the beginning of my relationship with Maya; I knew it wouldn't last, but I got involved anyway, and I allowed the inevitable to take place, which was her leaving with another man, and me suffering the consequences; I grew very attached to her in a short amount of time. The Peter thing was much different, only because I couldn't expect to see it coming—him being killed—but I should have seen the complications resulting from my involvement in the situation at the end. Buddhananda warned me. In any event, I didn't act wisely in either case."

"So you engaged in a process of punishing yourself for acting less like a man and more of a fool?" the Doctor concluded.

"Exactly."

Max was about to elaborate when the Doctor suggested a cup of chai, and Max followed him to a small chai shop across the dusty road. Taking their seats, Max looked out across the dreary edge of town at a large chemical plant in the distance, and at the farmers working in a nearby field; it was very green, but not very productive land, dotted with of shacks and stalls. It was a sunny day, but not very pretty.

The Doctor waited until their chai was served before beginning again. "To not know something can be a very good thing, as in the case with Maya. And to give more than you are asked can be a wonderful thing, like you have done for Peter. You know Mother Teresa?" Max nodded and the Doctor continued, "A disciple of hers, a rich Brahman, once asked her how he can know God, and she said that if he would give until it hurts and give again until the pain is unbearable, and give more of himself after that and more still, he can know God. The problem is not in the giving of yourself, Max, it is in the wanting something in return."

"I really didn't want to fall in love with Maya. It didn't start out that way. I just wanted to have some fun and kill a little time."

"Then we can see that how things begin is often how they end. Killing begets killing, however emotional or physical."

"Following that train of logic, I guess I would have to say that suspicion begot suspicion following Peter's death. Ute was unclear and Colonel Singh was untrustworthy. I got caught in the squeeze and wound up being a suspect in the murder."

"Are you guilty of this crime?"

"No."

"Then why do you still feel so guilty?"

"Because I should have known better," Max reiterated.

The Doctor sipped his chai before posing his final question. "And if you knew more, would you have given less of yourself to this lonely and dying young man?"

Max drew another deep breath and sighed, "No. Despite what you said, and despite what I know now, I would have done the same thing. There was no way I was going to let this guy die alone, and let his body rot."

The Doctor smiled and nodded. He was obviously pleased with Max's answer. "So now we can see that knowing something may not be as important as loving someone. And as we have said before, we must try and meet people where they are, Max, like the new people who are staying in my house, and not where we would like them to be. Every meeting of the mind poses a risk, and every meeting of the heart poses a threat. I remind you again that your Christ was killed for loving too much. It is not how much you know, Max. It is how much you give in spite of the knowing—how much you love in spite of the risk. That is the path of the Kshatriya , the noble warriors of the spirit. You are not a fool, Max. You are a young man straddling the razor's edge of life, seeing where you fit on the battle of being and becoming—always watching and engaging, and in doing so, sharpening the sword of wisdom."

*   *   *

Shunya figured that he would open *The Eclipse* in the winter, after they had successfully cashed in on their first drug deal. Tom saw no reason to wait and immediately put up five thousand dollars. Within a week they found a small building for rent near the center of town, and began to design *The Eclipse* with the help of Patrick the Poet, a third partner.

"It can't miss," Shunya told Patrick, an old Irish friend who spent the last three years living in Kathmandu. "Tom's got the money, you know all the right people, and I know how to pay them off."

After all, they did need a Nepali name on the lease, and a Nepali to buy the beer for them, and another Nepali to tell every other Nepali in power that Shunya was a great guy with deep pockets—Rich Tom's pockets, of course. He also put up the money for the two kilos of hash oil that Shunya had woven into the border of a colorful, four by six foot Tibetan rug.

After phoning his lawyer in New York and discovering that he was finally out of legal jeopardy, Shunya had intended to take the rug back with him to New York—until Tom talked him out of it.

"We can mail this rug, and two others, to my sister, Carol, in Manhattan. I've been promising to send her something nice for months. It's a low risk proposition because hash oil is a relatively new product with an odor that's easy to disguise. All you have to do is show up at her house, pick up the loaded rug, and sell the contents."

It sounded awfully good to Shunya, almost too good to be true. Within six weeks of his arrival in Nepal, he had found a new business partner and was on the verge of opening *The Eclipse*; he had also acquired the blessing of Lord Shiva, and was graced by the presence of the old Tibetan lama.

It was a sunny morning in Kathmandu Valley. Shunya had been up all night on acid. He was sitting in meditation on the side of the hill near the top of Swayambunath when Lord Shiva manifested in front of him in the form of a king cobra! His eyes closed, his legs locked in a half lotus position, his body molecules having merged with the subtle ethers, his mind was floating in space when Shunya sensed a disruption in the energy field and opened his eyes.

The snake, less than two feet in front of him, had spread its hood and was poised to strike when it met Shuny"s gaze.

Shunya was horrified. Thinking he might be hallucinating, Shunya closed his eyes and prayed to all gods to dispel the illusion. Opening his eyes again, he saw the snake and began to chant to Lord Shiva, guardian of the spirit word. He was preparing himself for a painful death when the snake recoiled and slithered down the hill.

Now thinking he had been blessed by a manifestation of Lord Shiva, Shunya climbed to the top of the holy hill to give thanks. He was standing at the temple entrance when he saw the old Tibetan lama, with his English-speaking disciple, looking out over the Kathmandu Valley.

"My master is pleased to see you," the disciple began. "He remembers his last conversation with you, and he asks if you have still been wrestling with God?"

"With Lord Shiva, this time," Shunya said.

"You mean the snake?" the old lama replied through his disciple, who continued to translate.

"You mean you saw it?" Shunya was surprised.

"Through your eyes, which can be a deception to you, who does not see himself," the old lama said.

Shunya was momentarily flustered. So many things had been going so well that he assumed his vision of success must be true. "What is it that I do not see?"

"The Jew."

Now Shunya was totally bewildered until he recalled the context of their last conversation. "Who wrestles with God, who takes many paths, who never arrives," Shunya recalled aloud, as if he were reciting a mantra.

The lama leaned on his cane and explained. "It is the Jew who is chosen by God to wander the world of samsara, to show us the folly of attachment to the world of things. It is for Israel that they live, and it is for Israel they will die without knowing that the Israel they seek is not a place, but a state of being in the heart of a God that they have forsaken. When you will know yourself as the spirit, and not as the place you seek, you will know who you really are."

Once again, the lama had befuddled young Shunya, who was reduced to an inaudible mumble. The lama was so old and frail, his face so dark and creased, his nose so prominent, his body so thin that he was virtually lost in the folds of his burgundy robes.

In an odd and fleeting magical moment, upon looking down into his ancient brown eyes, Shunya "fell" into their depths and saw Moses in the desert, his arms spread out to embrace the tribe of Israel. Then he saw Abraham emerge from a cave and look up to the sky and ask God, *Why?*

Then Shunya saw nothing. The lama and his disciple had already departed, having disappeared into the crowd of holy faithful at the front of the temple. Left alone to contemplate the meaning of the lama's teaching, Shunya missed the point and prepared to meet his destiny in New York.

*   *   *

Sam and Diane wound up spending three weeks in Delhi, and another week in Nainital. Both were shocked by the news of Peter's death when they returned to Almora—especially Diane.

"He did save my life," she told Sam.

Sam knew the story, how Peter had pulled her out of the Ganges, and was very suspicious of the details surrounding Peter's death. Having already spent three years in India, Sam had never heard of an Indian shooting a white man.

Dope deal, it had to be," he told Buddhananda. "And someone must have put these people up to it."

Sam had hoped to speak to the boys at Epworth, but all of them had disappeared from the ridge several days after Max's slick exit. So he and Diane visited Swami Buddhananda looking for answers.

"It might have been drugs," Buddhananda said, serving chai on the front porch. "Where there's money involved, there can always be crime—but I'm also troubled by the use of a gun. In all the years I've been in India, I've never heard of such a thing. The rape is something else that doesn't sit well with me—in a big city like Delhi, maybe, but it is also unlikely to happen here. I just can't emphasize enough the cultural nuances that would prohibit such a thing, especially here in a remote region like Almora, where the old class distinctions and religious traditions are still upheld—even the rape of an Indian girl by an Indian man would be most unusual.

"What I'm saying, what I told Max before he got involved in all this, is that this crime has crossed many lines. I also think that this is the reason behind Colonel Singh's behavior, which was most unhelpful and ungracious by any standards. Then he tried to blame it all on Max, thereby exonerating all Indian involvement. I get the feeling that he must have been very scared by all this—something went awry, something most unusual."

"What about Ute, have you spoken with her?" Diane asked.

"No, not a word. But I have seen her walking with Michael, who was quite helpful after all."

"You mean they were friendly?" Diane asked.

"No, not that I recall. But I have to say that Michael might be the only one who derives any benefit from all this—getting these young Westerners to leave the ridge. There's no one left here besides Ute at Kalimot, and you two."

Diane was about to pose another question when Colonel Singh emerged from the brush.

"I have just left your house," he began, looking down at Sam and Diane as he stepped onto the porch.

"There's a problem?" Sam asked.

"No problem. I was just visiting. I heard you have just returned from Delhi—such a bad thing, all these deaths from all these drugs—first your husband and now Peter."

"And you really think that Max had something to with it?" Diane asked.

"Who said this?" Colonel Singh snapped, locking eyes with Buddhananda.

"Not me," Buddhananda declared.

"Then who?" Colonel Singh pressed, looking directly at Diane.

"Black Michael, from what I gather," Sam said. "He told Max that you suspected him of killing Peter."

"So Max tells you this? You've seen Max in Delhi?" The Colonel demanded, his eyes popping under the strain.

"You mean that you're looking for him?" Diane challenged.

Colonel Singh tossed his hands in the air in frustration, sat on the railing, and wearily replied, "I am looking for anything or anyone who can help me solve this crime. The pressure is coming from so many people in so many places: the English government, my government, the military—and I am in the middle, always in the middle. And the woman, Ute, is the only one who knows the truth, and she still tells me a different story each time. Now I'm forced to wonder if she did it, if she killed Peter."

Sam and Diane and Buddhananda were all stunned by the Colonel's outrageous conclusion.

Sam said, "I don't believe it."

Diane said, "I can't believe it."

Buddhananda said, "I don't want to believe it."

The Colonel shrugged, apologized for the interruption, and said goodbye.

"It's not true," Sam reiterated after Colonel Singh disappeared from view. "But it's the easy way out for him to believe it's true."

Buddhananda said, "Knowing India as I do, this crime will never be solved because the best way out of anything is money, and I would imagine that someone has already paid the price to hide the truth."

31

It was a long and arduous flight from Kathmandu to New York, with many stops between continents, and many conflicting thoughts and feelings. Shunya had been away from home for more than three years, and he could not stop wondering whether he was returning a better person, a better friend, a better son, a better father. His daughter, Grace, was eight years old now, and had spent nearly half of her short life away from her father who posed more of a concept to her than a reality. Shunya wondered if she would still love him? Would she understand? Would she remember him?

Shunya had always been more afraid of facing her than facing prison. He was thinking about her as he passed through New York customs without incident; indeed, his lawyer had been right. He caught a cab to a friend's apartment near Kings Highway in Brooklyn, where he planned to stay until he returned to India.

*　　*　　*

"Expectation is the seed of disillusionment. It presumes the future is based on past experience and leaves no room for the dynamic of self discovery," the Doctor said.

These were great words from a great man that did not mean much to Max. He was sitting on the floor directly in front of the Doctor, who was addressing the nightly gathering in his living room. Though Max's position in the group had changed, moving from the back of the room to the front, he had not drawn close to anyone.

"Doesn't living, just being alive, imply expectation?" Clark questioned. He was a notable new arrival, Ivy League all the way down to his penny loafers and the person Max was least inclined to like. "Because you live, you expect to live. And when we go to sleep, we expect to wake up."

The Doctor nodded, then turned his attention to Clark's girl-friend, Linda, a tall, pretty brunette sitting beside him. "Because you are in love with Clark today, does it mean you will be in love with Clark tomorrow?"

Linda looked at Clark and smiled before returning her attention to the Doctor. "Probably, but not definitely. Because he might change or I might change."

The Doctor looked at Clark before posing the next question to Max. "Which means?"

"She's probably better off without him," Max cracked.

Several people in the room laughed, but Clark was not amused. He was humiliated and left the room in anger.

The Doctor was likewise upset and dismissed everyone from the room—except Max.

"And now you can tell me why you have embarrassed this young man?" the Doctor began.

"Because I don" like him," Max declared.

"Because he has had an easier life than you?"

"I didn't fly here on a 747 and stay at the Imperial Hotel in New Delhi."

"Are you saying that Clark must suffer as you have suffered to be your equal?"

"I suppose, something like that."

"Then I suggest you kiss the feet of every beggar and leper in India, and pick your next fight with someone you perceive as your equal." Max looked down at the floor and sighed. The

Doctor continued pressing his point without mercy. "If I am not mistaken, I believe it was your Native American Indians who were inclined to measure their self worth against the strength of their enemies. Enlightenment does not preclude curiosity about the world." The Doctor reached for a copy of the *Teachings of Don Juan* before continuing. I am reading this now.". "You are familiar with this book?"

"I read it awhile ago."

"And what do you think?"

"Don Juan sounds pretty good, but his student, the Castaneda guy who wrote the book, is a total idiot."

"Why do you say that?"

"Because he is shown a lot about life by his teacher, and he doesn't believe his own eyes."

"And you do?"

*   *   *

Shunya spent his first two days in New York visiting with friends and reorienting himself to the reality of having so many riches and choices at his fingertips. Most of all, Shunya was overwhelmed by the omnipresent variety of good food. He gained four pounds during those first two days in the city.

On the third day he went to Greenwich Village to claim the rugs that were in dispute. Shunya had spoken with Rich Tom's sister, Carol, upon arriving in New York; she thought the rugs belonged to her.

It was a cold and stark autumn day when Shunya boarded the F train to Manhattan. Carol lived in a luxury high-rise overlooking Washington Square Park.

"You say these rugs belong to you?" Carol began, after an awkward exchange of greetings and some small talk in the living room.

"One of them," Shunya said. He went on to explain where he had purchased the rugs in Kathmandu. "I bought the three of them—two for you, as Tom said, and one for me to give to my wife, Cheryl, my ex-wife."

Shunya's account made sense to Carol, except for one important detail. "If one rug does belong to you, then why did Tom send them all to me?"

"I sent them, knowing they would be waiting for me—at least one of them. He was supposed to call and tell you all this."

"Except Tom hasn't called me in months!"

Shunya looked down at the loaded green Tibetan rug on her living room floor and sighed, "I should have known better."

Exasperated, Carol finally smiled and said, "I think I understand. Tom is not an easy person to know. And dealing with him is never easy."

Though delicate, the situation was not altogether unpleasant. Among other things, Carol was a pretty good looking woman—somewhere in her late twenties, Shunya guessed, tall and thin with straight, black hair and smart, brown eyes.

"And now I suppose that you're going to tell me this green rug is yours because it's my favorite."

"I suppose," Shunya sighed, eying the rug loaded with hash oil and the promise of bigger things.

Though challenging, Carol was not offensive. In an effort to ease the tension, she invited Shunya to have a cup of tea, and was duly fascinated with his life in the East.

Shunya was flattered but not deterred, his eyes alternately drifting between her bright, brown eyes and the green rug which meant so much more to him. He was about to lean over and roll the rug up when Carol upped the ante.

"What about the money?" she challenged.

"For what?"

"For the rug."

"You mean you want to sell them back to me?"

Carol placed her hands on her curvaceous hips and shot him a devilish smile before replying, "I may be a bit naive, but I'm not stupid. My brother doesn't do anything without getting something for himself. I don't really need to know what's going on here, but I could always use the money."

Which Shunya still found hard to believe. The apartment itself had to be worth a few hundred thousand dollars. The living room was filled with a remarkable collection of antiques, fine art and mahogany furniture. In any event, Shunya didn't have enough money on him to pay for the rugs.

Returning her smile, he posed an alternative to money. "Would you accept a gift?"

"I guess that would depend," Carol coyly replied. She liked Shunya.

"I take the green rug, and I take you out to dinner on Saturday night."

Following a ritual exchange of phone numbers and flirtatious smiles, Shunya marched out of her apartment with his green Tibetan prayer rug worth eight thousand dollars.

*   *   *

Shunya's father lived in Pelham Parkway, across the street from the New York Botanical Gardens, less than six blocks from Fast Freddy Fein. Fast Freddy was a linguist, with a Ph.D. from N.Y.U., and he was fluent in eight languages. He was also the man who smuggled guns to Castro in Cuba with Delhi Dave. Now teaching Arabic at Fordham University, he augmented his modest income with an occasional hash deal, and he was highly recommended to Shunya by Delhi Dave.

With that ringing endorsement from a borderline sociopath, Shunya knocked on Fast Freddy's door with enough drugs to put them both away for five years.

With the ease of drawing another breath, Fast Freddy welcomed Shunya into his home. "Any friend of Dave is a friend of mine," he declared. "Because no one in their right mind would dare to cross our mutual mad friend, Delhi Dave."

Fast Freddy was a short and balding Jewish man with an engaging smile. Quite likeable, Shunya thought, as he unrolled the rug of fortune. The oil, wrapped in plastic and molded around the edges of the rug, was easily displaced with the artful use of a seam ripper.

Sampling a drop on his tongue, Freddy said, "Pretty sweet, intense but not rancid." Upon smoking it he added, "Very smooth and fresh. This is great shit."

Both were quite stoned after smoking several drops of oil, and the conversation tended to ramble until the deal was concluded without a hitch. Fast Freddy paid $15,700 in cash for two kilos of hash oil.

*   *   *

Near six o'clock in the evening, his pockets full of money, Shunya felt as if he had been blessed as walked down the block to his father's building. Taking the elevator up to the fourth floor, Shunya began to measure himself against his father's expectations, and was uneasy with the result. He had accomplished nothing his father could relate to. If not an NBA. player, Shunya could have been a college coach. At the very least, he could have finished college and stayed home and stayed married. But he didn't, and his father didn't know how to relate to him.

Following the untimely death of Shunya's mother when he was in junior high school, Shunya and his father drifted apart—each suffering their loss in their own private way. Theirs was not an affectionate relationship. It was polite, but times were changing and absence did make the heart grow fonder.

When Shunya extended his hand, his father ignored it and embraced him.

*   *   *

His pockets still full of money, his arms filled with presents, Shunya took another taxi to Sheepshead Bay early the following evening. Now measuring himself against Cheryl's expectations as he climbed the stairs of her brownstone, Shunya came up short again: He wasn't a good husband; he could have stayed married; he could have tried harder—if only for the sake of their child. He was still berating himself when Cheryl opened the door and embraced him.

A Sicilian with wavy brown hair, soft olive skin and large, riveting brown eyes, she was even prettier than Shunya remembered. And she looked more like a woman, less like a girl; he rightly imagined that raising Grace alone had a great deal to do with Cheryl's maturity.

As planned, Grace was already asleep, both thinking that they needed some time to bond with each other before Shunya was reunited with his daughter.

"I know it's been hard on you," Shunya said over coffee in the kitchen.

"It's life, William," Cheryl sighed; she would never call him Shunya. "But I've had a lot of time to adjust. I've been so busy that I don't have the energy to be angry with you anymore—and Grace still needs you. She misses you so much."

As the night wore on, they compared the trajectory of their lives and realized that their marriage would have never lasted. Though the attraction persisted, their values had evolved along different paths. A high school teacher, Cheryl flourished in a secure environment and Shunya thrived on chaos.

They talked until eleven, much too late in the evening to wake Grace. When Shunya stood to leave, with a promise to return in the morning, Cheryl invited him to spend the night on the living room couch.

*   *   *

The following morning Shunya awoke from a dreamless sleep into a state of grace. His daughter was standing over him with her mother at her side.

"Is that really you, Daddy?" Grace began, thoroughly intrigued by Shunya's long, red beard.

"If it's not Santa Claus, it must be me," Shunya said.

"You mean you really are my daddy?"

"You don't remember?"

It was an awkward, if not painful moment. Both Shunya and Grace looked to Cheryl for help.

"Of course we remember Daddy," Cheryl declared. "He came to visit last night, when you were sleeping—and he does look like the pictures he sends us, doesn't he?"

Grace hesitated and then ran into her room.

Shunya was crestfallen.

"It's been awhile and she might need some time to adjust," Cheryl said before Grace returned to the living room with a picture of her daddy wearing a beard that she kept by her bed.

"It is you! It is you!" she exclaimed.

When Shunya sat up on the couch and opened his arms, they were filled with Grace.

32

Shunya spent three more weeks in New York before returning to Kathmandu. Each time he visited his daughter he brought her another present: gold and silver bangles, turquoise and coral earrings, long, silk scarves, and an ivory Tibetan mala, which was Grace's favorite. She wore it day and night; it meant so much to her.

He also spent a great deal of time with Carol. She had opened her heart and home to him after their first date. In small increments, during a variety of conversations, Shunya discovered that Carol really didn't think too highly of her richer brother Tom.

"Who cost me a small fortune," she bitterly declared. "Because I trusted him. It was an investment he talked me into, and I lost a lot of money. As much money as he made, he never explained himself to me; he never offered to share his good fortune with me. Now I only have the apartment, my antiques and a small art collection. And I have to look for a job."

At other times, she spoke admiringly of Tom, who was the youngest of five brothers and sisters.

Shunya listened carefully, expressed sympathy for her plight, but drew no conclusions. After all, he owed a great deal of his good fortune to Tom. Between visits to his daughter and evenings with Carol, he spent a lot of time walking around the city, window shopping and eating, and sitting on a bench in Washington Square Park watching the world go by. He was very happy and most flattered by one event in particular.

It was a warm, clear and sunny Saturday morning. Shunya had just purchased two Sony tape recorders in anticipation of executing his next drug deal, when he passed a renowned schoolyard on Sixth Avenue in the West Village.

He was standing outside the fence watching a pickup game involving several high school all-stars and some local college talent, when he fell into conversation with a basketball coach from Long Island University. One court-side observation led to another until the coach asked Shunya how he knew so much about the game.

"Because I played," Shunya said, smiling brightly. "I'm Willie Rennet."

The coach said, "You were the best high school point guard I've ever seen." Taking a closer, second look at the former all-star, he asked Shunya what had happened to him.

Shunya stroked his long, red beard and sighed, "I guess I fouled out."

*   *   *

The following morning, after having breakfast with Carol in a local bistro, Shunya headed back to Brooklyn to hang out with some old friends. He was waiting for the train when a Hasidic rabbi passed in front of him, and he was reminded of his conversation with the old lama, who compared Shunya's life to the plight of the Jewish people.

"When you will know yourself as the spirit, and not as the place you seek, you will know who you really are," the old lama had said.

No matter how many times Shunya thought about it, he could not fathom the teaching. The words turned over in his mind for the entire train ride to Sheepshead Bay, where he spent the day with his daughter, mostly shopping and running errands, and helping her with homework. Before dinner, Shunya took her down to the bay to watch the fishing boats dock.

The sun setting and the new moon rising, father and daughter held hands as they walked and talked along the water.

"Do they have an ocean in India?" Grace began.

"Two, I think. One on each side of the country, like we have the Atlantic Ocean and the Pacific Ocean. India has the Indian Ocean on one side and the Arabian Sea on the other."

"You mean Arabians like *Ali Baba and the Forty Thieves* and *Sinbad, the Sailor?*"

"Like them and not like them. India has all kinds of people, like the Tibetans who live way up in the Himalaya Mountains. They look like American Indians, but they wear very funny hats sometimes." Shunya reached into his ever-present, colorful jhola and pulled out a bright red triangular Tibetan hat with ear flaps that stuck out like wings. "Like this," Shunya said, placing the small hat on her head.

When Grace laughed and said, "I feel like an air-o-plane." Shunya told her to close her eyes and pretend she was flying over the Himalayas, "Over the mountains covered with snow, over all the people, and over all the rainbows."

As Grace flew across the world with her imagination, Shunya marveled at the wonder of Grace, the red Tibetan hat covering her thick and curly black hair. She looked like her mother with her perfectly smooth olive complexion, her long, black eyelashes and dark eyebrows, but she had her father's imagination.

Opening her eyes, Grace continued, "Are those Tibetan people really like us?"

"Pretty much. But they wear different clothes."

"Are the little girls pretty?"

"Very pretty, but not as pretty as you."

"Really, Daddy?"

"Really."

"Did you kiss them?"

"No."

"Why?"

"Because I saved all of my kisses for you."

When Grace leaned forward, Shunya kissed his daughter on her forehead and felt somehow completed.

"Mommy said you went to school there and learned things there."

"Some things."

"What things?"

"The most important thing of all," Shunya said, looking into Grace's wide eyes.

"What's so important?"

"Home," Shunya said. "Because home is where your heart is, and my heart has always been here with you."

*   *   *

It was a cold and windy night in Almora when the change came. Diane woke after midnight—with menstrual cramps, she thought, but there was no evidence of a period. She was on her way out of the bathroom, holding a kerosene lamp, when she glimpsed her reflection in the mirror and was stunned by its strangeness; she could hardly recognize herself.

She raised the lamp higher and lower, leaned forward and back, then turned sideways; when she moved the lantern around her face, it began to change, to evolve and devolve. She became an angel with short, curly hair, then a beast with long, dark hair and huge flaring nostrils; then she became an alien with a long face and translucent skin; then she heard a baby crying and calling out to her.

Disturbed, Diane returned to bed and woke late the following morning, feeling ghastly, thinking she'd had a bad dream. She stumbled onto the porch and was rubbing her stomach when Sam returned from the bazaar.

"You don't look so good," he began.

"I don't feel too good."

A sudden gust of wind nearly knocked her off her feet; winter was rapidly approaching.

When Sam reached out to steady her, they looked into each other's eyes and realized it was time to leave Almora. Apart from the change in weather, neither had fully recovered from the shock of Peter's death; neither felt entirely secure on the ridge—making sure the doors and windows were locked down every night—and all of their friends had already left Almora , including Big Jane and Gary, and Ute.

A week later, they were on their way to Delhi, riding a third class sleeper across the northern plains. Sam was reading an article in *The Times of India*. Diane was looking out the window at the waxing moon, rubbing her stomach—still feeling queasy, now thinking that she had a mild dysentery infection—when Sam cried out, "My God, you're not going to believe this!"

Diane closed her eyes as Sam read aloud: "'A French couple was apprehended at the New Delhi airport yesterday morning in a terribly misguided attempt to smuggle several pounds of opium in the body of their deceased child. The baby, who doctors believe was only six months old, had been gutted, its insides then replaced with the opium in an attempt to smuggle the illicit cache through airport customs. The couple, who has said that their baby died of natural causes, is being held for murder pending an investigation.'"

Diane was nauseated. "It's so hard to believe," she agonized.

"It boggles the mind," Sam said.

"It tears at the heart," Diane added, twirling her ruby earring.

33

The war in Viet Nam continued to rage and a lot of people were afraid of much bigger wars looming on the horizon. The end of the millennium was in sight, and fear of the future rivaled the inability to exact change in the present. From this perilous gap, emerged the likes of the Doctor, Puri Baba, Kenchi Baba, Sayadaw, the old lama, and thousands more who offered a path to salvation. But no two paths were alike, and not every teacher could be trusted.

The good rivaling the bad, distinctions were hard to make. Faith was sorely tested, and Max suffered the consequences. By the end of October, many of Max's friends had arrived in Sonepat: Mani and Narayan from Benares, White Mike and Bill from Nainital. James arrived with his new French girlfriend, Martine, the good-looking redhead he had met in Nainital.

The scene around the Doctor had swelled to twenty-three young Westerners, and many of the Doctor's neighbors were offended by their presence. Sonepat was a working-class town that ascribed to middle class values, values that these young foreigners had apparently rejected. Consequently, the Doctor's medical practice suffered, and he was victimized by increasingly scandalous rumors: harboring a throng of over-sexed and drug-induced misfits.

Money was also tight, and space at the Doctor's house was at a premium. The scene was threatening to implode when Rich Tom arrived in the nick of time to save the day. It was his timely and generous donation that provided for a rented house to accommodate the overflow.

"In exchange for your best efforts to help me with my headaches," Rich Tom told the Doctor.

"It's a good situation for us, and I promised Tom that I would do my best to help him," the Doctor told Max over a cup of chai in his office one evening.

"I didn't know we were for sale," Max snidely replied. He didn't like Rich Tom very much, even though Tom was referred to the Doctor by Shunya.

"Considering how much Tom has helped us, he could have asked much more of us," the Doctor countered.

"Which is true," Max told James over breakfast the following morning. They were sitting in the chai shop at the edge of town that overlooked the somber gray chemical plant, already bellowing clouds of noxious black smoke into the blue sky. "But I still don't like the idea of having to like someone or cater to someone because I have to. It's like feeling the pressure to swallow the company line on wisdom."

"Except nobody's asking you to swallow anything, least of all the Doctor. He's not telling you that you have to like Tom, or Clark, or any of those other wusses, for that matter. He's just telling you that the scene is expanding, and in doing so, it needs to be accommodating. Other people do have other needs. He's not asking you to like it or dislike it; he is asking for your understanding—which is awfully flattering."

Max was about to reply when he saw the Doctor walking along the street with Linda, Clark's girlfriend.

"She ain't bad," James noted, his attention easily swayed by a pretty face.

"But not as good-looking as Martine," Max said.

James' smile quickly faded when he saw Rich Tom walking behind the Doctor with Martine. "Fuck does she want with him?"

"His money, maybe."

"Except she's not for sale," James sneered, gripping the edge of the table.

As Max knew, James was no one to trifle with. He had a reputation as a street fighter in high school. "You can't exactly punch him in the mouth if you did find out that he was coming on to her. I mean we are in India taking teachings from a master in an effort to better ourselves."

James drew a deep breath and sighed, "I suppose not, but..."

Max studied Tom's profile as he turned a distant corner and said, "You know, I'm sure I've seen that guy before—maybe it's his profile or his gate, it's so familiar to me—but I just can't place it."

*   *   *

As usual, Delhi was crowded with young people going East and West at the end of October. It was a great time to party, and Max and James began to frequent Connaught Circus under the guise of shopping for the scene in Sonepat. They were on their way into the city, for the third time in as many days, when they chanced to meet Rich Tom at the Sonepat train station. Out of courtesy, Max asked Tom to join them.

Out of gratitude, Rich Tom invited them to lunch at Berry's, which was among the best restaurants in the city. By the end of the meal, Max had a better feeling about Tom; James didn't. He didn't like the attention Tom continued to lavish on his girlfriend in Sonepat.

James was quietly seething and Max was smiling when they exited the restaurant and ran into Shunya, who had returned from New York that morning.

The atmosphere was celebratory, and all headed across the Circus for ice cream. Max sat with James and Tom sat with Shunya, who was pleased by their success and bewildered by Tom's behavior.

"First of all, your sister doesn't know me from Adam," Shunya told Rich Tom. "Then she makes me pay for my own rug. And she didn't receive a word from you until two days ago. You said you would call and tell her I was coming."

Tom said, "I was afraid someone might be listening in so I mailed a letter the same day from the AMEX office we sent the rugs. They said it would get to New York at about the same time. I'm sorry. I really am."

Shunya accepted Rich Tom's apology before telling him about his affair with Carol.

Rich Tom was surprised, and Shunya began to wonder if he wasn't offended by the relationship. Each time he tried to talk about his experience with Carol, Tom deflected the subject matter until he declared that he was returning to Sonepat, where he needed to nurse a worsening headache.

So the boys returned without Tom to the Palace Heights Hotel, where they ran into Sam and Diane talking to Delhi Dave and Carl Kent on the second floor patio.

Following another rush of greetings and introductions, Max approached Carl and said, "I know you, don't I?"

Carl hesitated, then studied Max's face for an extended moment and smiled. "In the end we all took it in the ass."

"Kabul!" Max exclaimed. "I stayed with you and Howard at the Ansari Guest House,"

"You remember those two other guys, the guys we played cards with?" Carl asked.

Max remembered. "Dean and Dennis, right?"

Carl pulled Max aside and continued, "They weren't right guys at all. They were cops."

Carl was about to explain when Shunya cried out for help. Opening the door to his room, he caught two French junkies in the act of stealing his two Sony recorders that he purchased in New York—one man was handing a recorder to another, who was straddling the window. They had apparently climbed the two-story back wall and come in through the window.

On cue, the boys came running to his aid. Shunya grabbed the guy in the room; James grabbed the guy in the window.

"Now what?" Shunya said, turning to Delhi Dave.

Delhi Dave walked to the window, waved James off, and pushed that guy out of the window. The second guy jumped under a threat of death, both sustaining a variety of painful injuries upon landing in the alleyway.

"That's what," Delhi Dave said, before leaving everyone else in the room to debate the ethics of this behavior.

"The fall could have killed them," Diane said, looking out the window and watching them limp away.

"As if it really matters?" James said.

"To God, maybe," Shunya said.

"As if He's watching," Sam concluded.

End of debate. The room filled with music and hash while Max and Carl returned to the veranda to resume their conversation.

"You heard about David?" Max began.

"Diane just told me. I remembered her from Kabul also. Fucking world is getting so small you can choke on it," Carl said.

Max was surprised by Carl's cynical point of view; Max remembered a much happier man.

"I was happy until we got caught in the squeeze by our own stupid fucking greed," Carl explained. "Howard and I couldn't return to the States if we wanted to because of those explosive revolutionary crimes we committed against the government, and we were desperately in need of money—and everyone knew it. So we had Mohammed's family on one side, which seemed to include every fucking person in the country, and we had the CIA, in the form of Dean and Dennis, on the other side.

"All we wanted to do was smoke some good shit and make some money. But they had other ideas. It was a setup from the beginning. The Russians are leaning against the Afghanis, and the Americans don't like it. So the CIA decides to use us to front for them, to run guns into the Khyber Pass. If we don't do what they say, we go back to the States, and straight to jail for twenty years."

"But you're here now."

"Doing business with Delhi Dave, while Dean and Dennis keep their eyes on Howard in Kabul. And if I don't get back there soon, they'll take it out on him and come looking for me."

Max was mesmerized by Carl's story. When he began to wonder why Carl was being so candid with him, Carl answered his thoughts.

"The truth is, Max, I don't know if I'll ever get back to America.—and I don't want to go to jail if I do. I just want you to know that if I die, it's because they found a way to kill me."

If you ain't dead already, Max thought before saying goodbye.

*   *   *

It was another beautiful autumn evening in New Delhi: sixty-five degrees, light breeze, and a full moon rising over the city. Max was having such a good time with his friends that he decided to spend the night in Delhi. Near midnight, he wound up talking to Diane as they walked around Connaught Circus.

Max began, telling her about Peter's death and his subsequent escape from Almora. "And I came to India thinking I was looking for God," he ironically concluded.

"And I thought I could find myself in a relationship with Sam," Diane said. "But it's not that easy, because I'm a slow learner. I still have more of a problem with myself than I do with him. I take a step forward; I take a step back. I try to stay focused, then I look for distractions, and I wind up blaming him for my own shortcomings. Even if he isn't the most affectionate guy I ever met, he might be the best guy for me. I thought we'd be spending the winter in Benares or Bodh Gaya; now he's talking about Goa, telling me how beautiful it is, but I don't know if that scene would be so good for me."

Max smiled and said, "Meanwhile you look good."

Diane turned and looked into his wide eyes. "You really think so?"

Max said, "Yes." Her hair was much longer and curlier than he remembered; her eyes seemed even bigger and bluer, and she had kept her weight down.

"I just wish I felt a little better. I still have these cramps that started last week in Almora," Diane said, rubbing her stomach. "And I get really irritable sometimes."

"Sounds like you're pregnant to me," Max surmised.

"I thought so too, at first, but I haven't had a period in a year, ever since I left Greece with David—Jane too. In fact, most of the women I've met here don't have their periods—it must be because of the foods or the climate or something—so I hardly think I am pregnant."

Diane flashed a flirtatious smile, placed her arm within his and continued, "It's good to see you, Max—even better to go for a walk with a handsome man on a beautiful evening."

"You mean you miss me?"

"I do sometimes. The truth is that I felt a little strange when I returned to Almora and you were gone. And I felt really bad about you and Maya. Did you ever see her again?"

"No, and I haven't even heard about her, who she's with, what she's doing—which is just as well."

"You mean it still hurts?"

"A lot sometimes, and it's still hard to understand why. I never liked her as much as I liked you, but . . . she got to me in a certain way."

"Or maybe it was your inability to get to her that bothers you."

"Could be. I've thought about that. In the meantime, I've got other things on my mind—like the scene over at the Doctor's. It's changing and maybe I'm changing. I've also been thinking about going to Goa, just walking on the beach eating mangos and getting away from all the India stuff for awhile. You know it was a Portuguese colony, and it's still Christian there, more like the Mediterranean country."

They continued to walk and talk about Goa until Shunya pulled up in a taxi and invited them to party at the Imperial Hotel.

"Everyone's already there," he said. "Including Sam!"

*   *   *

The Imperial was a three star hotel which offered all the comforts of home, including a fully appointed disco featuring a long, dark bar, a parquet wooden dance floor, a surprisingly good selection of music, and an inversion of cultures—the Westerners wearing kurtas, pajami and lungis, adorned with colorful bangles and beads, the Indians dressed in slacks, sport coats, and dresses, wearing an assortment of gold watches and jewelry. And everyone was having a great time drinking and smoking hash.

The dance floor was filled with people doing different dances to the same music. Hair flying, breasts bobbing, butts shaking, a cloud of sweet blue smoke clung to the ceiling. More than an hour passed until Shunya decided to spike their experience with a few tabs of acid that he got from a well-dressed, fat Sikh businessman, who was hanging around the bar—very strange indeed.

"Where did you get this?" Shunya asked him, breaking the tabs into small pieces for his friends.

"From someone like you," the Sikh replied, swallowing a whole tab.

Max was standing next Shunya, sipping a martini, when Maya walked into the room wearing a blue silk dress that accentuated every curve of her long and sensuous figure. She also looked more beautiful than Max remembered, and it was too painful to look at her in the company of another man. She had arrived with Erik, the German sadhu.

Max finished his drink and was thinking that he should leave when Maya walked up to him.

"Hello, Max," she began, smiling and running a hand through her long, black hair.

"Goodbye to you," Max coldly replied, wishing he had already left.

"You mean we're not friends?"

"If we were friends, Maya, we would still be lovers."

"Is that what you want?"

It was a loaded question, which Max did not deflect. He was in a weak position and captivated by her beauty. He wanted to be flattering, but he continued defensively.

"I would have you the way I want you, but not the way you are."

"Which is?"

"Self-serving."

Maya became so enraged that she made a fist. Max was trembling inside, he was so unsure of himself, and decided to retreat.

"Sometimes self-serving," he stumbled.

"And the other times?"

Max looked into her glaring green eyes and fought back tears. "I was in love."

Maya relented, relaxed her fist and smiled warmly. "And I was in love with you."

Max was surprised and encouraged, but pressed on sarcastically, "So that's why you ran away, because you were so in love?"

"No, Max. That's why you pushed me away, because you weren't comfortable with your own feelings, and you made me uncomfortable with my feelings. You're the one who sabotaged the relationship, Max. Not me."

Now Max was stunned, he had so many different thoughts and feelings vying for expression. The music was so loud and he was getting so high that he couldn't focus. "Not here," he said. "Outside. We can talk better outside."

Maya said, "No, I can't."

When Max asked why, Maya widened her smile and crushed him. "Because I am still with Erik, and I was always more in love with him in Almora."

34

Max left the bar in tears, and the partying reached epic proportions with the introduction of an ounce of cocaine—everyone moving faster, becoming louder, and turning wilder. Inhibitions were lost, clothes were shed: the men dancing bare-chested, the women stripping down to flimsy halter tops and hiking their dresses, beads of sweat dripping down their lithe, gyrating bodies.

Near one in the morning, Shunya was leaning against the bar, about to order another drink, when Maya leapt onto the bar and began to dance. The crowd was clapping and shouting for more of her, for all of her, for Maya to take off her clothes, when management finally stopped the music and turned up the lights; the night was apparently over. The crowd was staggering out the door when the fat Sikh stood on the chair and invited all of them to his house.

Sam was inclined to go back to the hotel, but his friends talked him into a taxi that took them to a stately Tudor mansion, located in the heart of the finest New Delhi suburb.

Opening the front door, the Sikh said, "My house is your house. And everything that is mine is yours."

"Can you believe this?" Shunya asked Sam.

Sam said, "I still can't even believe that you talked me into this."

Within thirty minutes, the party turned into a debauchery, the revelers swilling scotch out of a bottle, shooting cocaine and heroin, eating opium, smoking hash and dancing naked in the living room.

Sam was telling Diane and Shunya that the scene was getting out of hand; he was suggesting that they should leave, when Shunya noticed a silver-haired old man who appeared at the top of the grand staircase in a bathrobe.

"What? What is? What is??" the old man shouted, his body trembling with rage and bewilderment.

"'Fuck is with you?" someone shouted back.

Shunya knew something was amiss and went looking for the fat Sikh and returned with bad news. "He's gone," Shunya told his friends.

"Who's gone?" Diane asked, her eyes at half mast following another toke of hash.

"The Sikh. I can't find the guy anywhere."

"Then it is time for us to leave," Sam said, getting to his feet. He was reaching for Diane's hand when the police came.

*   *   *

"Turns out the old man was a cabinet minister, and the fat Sikh set us up for a laugh and split the scene," Shunya told Max the following morning. "It was classic, totally insane. Everyone's so fucked up on drugs, climbing out the windows and running through the street in the middle of the night looking for places to hide in other people's backyards."

"Anyone get caught?"

"No, but a lot of people left a lot of their clothes in this guy's living room."

Max had to laugh no matter how much he hurt. No matter how hard he tried, he couldn't stop thinking about Maya.

*   *   *

Delhi Dave and Carl did not discuss their business with Max and Shunya. To be sure, it was a dirty business involving desperate men profiting from the despair of others, and no one could imagine how it would impact all their lives.

In any event, everyone left Delhi on the same day: Carl returned to Afghanistan, and Delhi Dave headed to Bombay with Sam and Diane, who had decided to spend the winter in Goa. Shunya and Rich Tom went to Kathmandu to open *The Eclipse*.

Shunya invited Max and James to come along, but James wanted to spend more time with the Doctor and Martine. Max was tempted to join Shunya, but he feared jeopardizing his Indian visa. He also thought that he needed the Doctor's help to diffuse his feeling about Maya.

"I could have hurt her more than she hurt me. I could have said things to her, about her life, about her motherhood, about her son, but I didn't," Max told the Doctor. They were sitting in his office in Sonepat.

"And why not?"

"Because it wouldn't change anything, because she's already dead inside."

The Doctor nodded. "Perhaps in the process of denying her pain, she has also denied her life."

"But she dances so well. Just watching her is like a celebration of life."

"Perhaps, but she is not conscious of it. It passes through her, from the soul to the body, without awareness. History is filled with accounts of great men and women, great artists, who do great things who are not necessarily great people. Maya can celebrate life and never really know its meaning or appreciate its value. And you can continue to do better with yourself and never be a better man."

"You mean I was wrong to confront her?"

"I mean you were foolish, if only because you couldn't win, let alone help. By your own admission, you saw the end at the beginning when you met her. Usage will always beget more usage, no matter how lofty our intentions may be."

Once again, Max had been humbled by his own misjudgment. "I just wish I understood how someone I knew for a few weeks could hurt me so much."

The Doctor shrugged. "Some things we cannot know, and time is not always a measure of cause and effect. There may have been other times and other lives."

"You mean karma?"

"I mean the knowing may not be as important as the healing, nothing more."

Which was easier said than done. As time passed, the Doctor and James became increasingly concerned for Max's welfare.

"Maybe because I also got the sounds in my head again," Max told James over a cup of chai one morning. They were sitting outside a familiar chai shop near the Doctor's house. "It happened once before—on my way to Almora with Shunya, out of nowhere, after I had an audience with Kenchi Baba—when Shunya asked me why I was in India—and I couldn't answer him.

"All of a sudden, I felt like my reason for being was over and I got these high frequency sounds in my head—I think they call it tinnitus. Then it went away after a while and I started to feel better about myself. Then you guys showed up with the Doctor and I felt that I was back on the quest—until I met Maya.

Max looked up at the blue sky as if he were looking for a clue before continuing, "The Doctor said the sounds are a sign of psychic transformation, but I'm not becoming anything but crazy."

"Then you can just stay here and keep watching yourself until you can feel comfortable with yourself again, or maybe you should take another Sayadaw course."

"I thought about that. But I'm also starting to think that all the constant seeking and pressing to understand things is what's really hurting me—as if I reached my limit a while ago. The other strange thing is that I seem to see other things and people very clearly—aside from Maya, of course—and my mind is somehow recording everything I experience.

"But I get really freaked out sometimes when the experience of observation becomes disassociating. That's when I get really scared—like I'm watching what's happening to myself and everyone else and *I'm* not there, *I* am not present, and I have this thought that comes into my head and it says 'remember this'—like even right now as we're talking. For what reason, I don't have a clue."

"What does the Doctor say about all this?"

"He says that I should just observe the observer, but the whole process is freaking me out because I don't want to see anymore. I just want to live; I just want to forget and move on."

"Then maybe you should return to America."

"I would except I like it here more than I would like it there—still! I mean I'm in India, the most amazing place in the world, and I don't want to return a failure."

"Because you didn't find God or enter Nirvana? You have got to be kidding me and yourself, Max, to have come here with those expectations."

Max forced a painful smile, sipped his chai and sighed, "I'm not that crazy yet—as if I don't know that this journey to the East is a metaphor? As if God only lives in India? That's not it, James. It's more like I came here to find myself, to learn about myself, and I'm getting lost in the process. And I don't want to return a loser. I mean how many at bats do you think we get? How many times do we get to journey to the East as a young man?"

35

Sam and Diane planned on spending four days in Bombay. Diane needed a visa extension before heading to Goa, and thought she had a deal worked out with a greedy magistrate. When it bogged down, she realized that it could take weeks to renegotiate. Given the circumstances, Sam thought it best to continue on to Goa alone.

"Because it's too expensive for two people to stay here," Sam said. They were sitting in the back of a cab, on their way back to the infamous Rex Hotel. "And I could be renting a house for us on the beach in the meantime. I'll leave a letter for you at the post office in Calangute, and tell you where I am."

Sam went to Goa, and Diane went back to her old ways: shopping, dining out, dancing, and getting high. The simple truth was that despite her resolve to change her life, and all those hours she spent meditating, Diane liked partying: she loved that wild night out in Delhi, she liked looking pretty and garnering the attention.

"The way I see it, I earned a vacation from my higher instincts," she told Laura, her new fast friend that she met at the hotel.

It was late in the afternoon. The two had been up partying the night before. Now sitting on the edge of the bed in her seedy Rex

Hotel room, Diane was trying to tell Laura that she had no regrets—despite puking her guts out for the past half-hour.

"What do you have to regret, that you're gorgeous and you want to enjoy it?" Laura said, echoing Diane's sentiments.

Laura wasn't very pretty by comparison: tall and thin with natty brown hair, dull brown eyes, hollow cheeks and a raspy voice; she was only twenty-eight, but looked like she was pushing forty, and associating with Diane made her feel pretty.

"I have no regrets, actually, except for this persistent nausea. I should take something for it."

Laura conjured a wicked, little smile and declared, "Opium."

Diane said, "I'll try anything. I'll be ready in minutes."

Laura said, "I'll get a cab." Laura was often in a hurry to get high. She was a junkie.

The Bombay traffic was horrendous at five o'clock: few working traffic lights, no one to direct traffic, and a lot of people, cars, trucks, and buses and bicycles competing for the right-of-way as the women conversed in the back of the cab.

"I was married for three years," Laura said. "It was the 'guy next door' type of thing. We both grew up in Brooklyn, in Bay Ridge. It was an Italian thing. We were both Sicilian, and I really loved him a lot. But I couldn't deal with his job, and he couldn't deal with me."

"What did he do?"

"He was a mafia guy. He shot people and I shot dope—until he went to jail and I left the country."

Diane was oddly moved. The mafia thing was colorful. The mention of dope reminded her of own dead husband. She was thinking about David when their taxi arrived at the edge of the infamous red light district, also known as The Cages.

"You can get anything here," Laura said, paying the taxi driver.

"Things you can get, but the people are even cheaper," the driver said, before speeding off.

Which was unfortunately true. A grown man could sodomize a ten-year old boy or girl for fifty cents. The narrow skein of streets and alleyways were crowded with johns, pushers, pimps, and thieves. The Cages were aptly named for the chicken wire that separated the shops and stalls from the impoverished streets. The girls and boys locked inside lived like animals.

Diane and Laura posed an odd sight in this sorry side of a life that was without hope or shame. Though she had been there many times before, Laura was nonetheless revolted by the sight and smell of the place. Diane was privately intrigued by the perversity: the shadows begetting darker feelings and impulses, beguiling her senses and bludgeoning her instincts as she followed Laura down a dark and forbidding alleyway.

The opium den was sequestered at the back of the alley, behind several taller buildings. The walls covered with soot, the red metal door lined with rust, it looked like the gateway to hell.

Once inside, Diane found a little bit of heaven in a pipe dream. The floor was covered with an odd variety of worn and frayed oriental carpets. The furnishings included a colorful array of oversized pillows, sofas and couches, servicing two dozen people in various states of euphoric narcosis; a lazy cloud of blue smoke clung to the walls and ceiling.

There were no clearly defined parameters, no points of reference, and no windows. Space was curved and time was suspended. Dreams begot dreams in a never-ending soft, three-dimensional spiral for two days and nights—until Diane got sick of herself.

"I have to go," she finally agonized, waking from a terrible dream. She imagined that she was back in Calcutta looking for David. "I have to find David."

"He's dead, you said," Laura stumbled, her eyes half open.

"I have to find myself, I have to leave. . . .I have to. . . .I have to," she said, trying to raise herself off an overstuffed, red couch.

Laura was no help; she was too stoned to move.

"Help. . . .I need help," Diane said, before falling onto the carpet.

She was waving her arms in the air and mumbling to herself when Hong Kong Rosie, a beautiful Eurasian, came to her aid. A friend to Laura, Rosie had just entered the den when she saw the problem and helped Diane into a taxi.

Back at the hotel, Diane slept for eighteen hours. She woke in a daze, dehydrated, cursing herself, and unaware that she had been high for two full days. She was trying to reconstruct events when Laura came by to check up on her.

"Are you okay?" Laura began, sitting on the side of Diane's bed.

"Not as good as you," Diane said, gazing at Laura, who looked remarkably well.

Laura smiled. "I've had a lot more practice than you."

"Don't tell me practice makes perfect."

"I'm a junkie, Diane. I'm not a yogi."

Diane had to laugh. She was about to reply when Hong Kong Rosie entered the room. Black silk skirt, green silk blouse, raven black hair, huge almond eyes, her wrists full of gold and silver bangles, her earrings filled with diamonds and emeralds, Rosie was the most exotic woman Diane had ever seen.

"Do I know you?" Diane began.

"She saved you," Laura declared.

"From myself," Diane muttered, realizing that she was wearing the same dress. "I guess I should thank you."

"No thanks for me. How come I haven't seen you before? You have been here long?"

The question prompted Diane's memory. "Too long it seems, waiting to get a visa. I was supposed to get a visa. What day is it today anyway?"

Laura said, "Thursday."

Diane said, "Shit!"

"What is shit?" Rosie asked.

"My life," Diane agonized. "I had an appointment this morning to extend my visa and I fucked up. I really fucked up." Diane leaned forward and held her head in her hands.

"How much cost for the visa?" Rosie asked.

"I think it was seventy-five dollars for three months."

Rosie said, "You give me one hundred dollars and I give you six months."

"You know someone?"

"Myself," Rosie said, reaching into her bag and producing a rubber stamp. "It is, how you say, a perfect copy of real thing. I have it made in Thailand last year."

When Diane produced her passport, Rosie stamped it. When Diane stumbled across the room looking for her money, she discovered it was missing.

"I was robbed," she cried out.

Rosie said that she would be willing to accept Diane's favorite blue silk dress as payment—and the deal was done.

"I feel so dirty inside," Diane told Laura, following Rosie's departure. "So fucking stupid."

"Because you lost your money?" Laura asked.

"Because I lost my way again," Diane sighed.

The following morning Diane borrowed money from Laura and boarded a rotting old steamer to Goa. It was a twenty-four-hour journey to Panjim. Though cabins were available, Diane paid to sleep on the deck.

The sun beating down on her bare shoulders, the wind whipping through her hair, she was standing at the back of the boat looking across the water, when the motion of the sea made her sick. Doubled over from cramps, she cried out in pain, fearing the worst.

*   *   *

Shunya had never felt better and was convinced that he was moving in a totally positive and virtuous cosmic flow. *The Eclipse* turned out better than he expected. The long, curved bar was honed and polished to shiny perfection. The tables and chairs were level, and Paul the Poet had installed a small dance floor.

As night fell and the full moon rose over the Kathmandu Valley, *The Eclipse* opened for business. Shunya worked the door, Paul worked the bar, and Rich Tom clung to the shadows. He wouldn't dance and hardly spoke. By eight o'clock, *The Eclipse* was packed to the walls with patrons from all over the world.

*   *   *

Max thought it was time to leave Sonepat. Altogether, he had spent nearly four weeks there following his crushing experience with Maya, and he was increasingly uncomfortable with the situation. In spite of the Doctor's efforts to help him, Max did not wholly trust him.

"I love the guy," he told James over another cup of chai at their favorite chai shop." And I believe that he might be the wisest guy I ever met, but there's something else—how the whole scene around him is continuing to evolve, the kind of people that keep showing up, like Clark and Rich Tom—now there's forty of them, and I can hardly relate to any of them. And I've got to listen to the same watered-down, schlock teachings every night, with all those sounds in my head—nothing's changed and nothing's better for me, which is making me feel even worse and more disassociated . . . And now they're all talking about raising money, and bringing the Doctor to America, and spreading the word about silent mind; I mean, who gives a fuck?"

"You should, Max, but you don't because you're just so fucking cynical. Because things aren't good for you, they have to be hard for everyone else. You mean everyone has to come to India to take teachings? As if you're not going to return to America one day and want to share your experiences with other people."

Max sipped his chai, drew a deep breath and sighed, "I don't know what I mean. I just know that I'm not comfortable with myself, and because of that I'm really scared—even if I don't show it—and I don't really feel connected to anyone or anything.

James finished his chai and tossed his hands in the air in frustration. "And what, Max? Nothing and no one is ever good enough for you, including Diane. And she was one of the most beautiful women I've ever seen—and she's got a lot of heart."

"Not so much when I met her."

"Yeah, well, she's got it now, and you've got nothing! The Doctor might be the wisest person we ever met, and if he's not wise enough for you, you can wind up with less than nothing! Is that what you want?"

Max wasn't sure. He returned to the Doctor's house in silence, in time to hear a discourse on the nature of the guru/disciple relationship.

"If you want to understand the disciples, you may look at the guru. If you want to understand the guru, you may look at the disciples. Altogether, they are nearly perfect reflections of one another."

Max studied the disciples sitting at the Doctor's feet, then looked to the Doctor and realized it was time to go.

"I just don't fit," he told the Doctor later that night. "Not here, not now."

The Doctor shook his head and sighed. It was an old story already. "Of course, you know that this discomfort you have with us is merely a reflection of the difficulty you are having with yourself?"

Max agreed, but he was terribly impatient. "Because I'm worse off now than I was before I came here, and I can't just hang around here looking at who I am until I become someone else."

"And why not?" the Doctor challenged. "Until you can learn to embrace the worst of what you see in yourself, you will never see the best of yourself. You have already crossed half the world only to discover that the pain of who you are bears no relationship to the place you are in."

"You mean I'm not supposed to go anywhere ever again?"

"Perhaps. It was the great resolve of the mighty Gautama Buddha who, upon witnessing the discomfort of his own being, resolved to sit under the Bodhi tree until he saw the greater and deeper truth of himself. It was also something that happened to me. The pain became so great in my life that it was reflected everywhere to me, until I learned to embrace it. It is a catharsis of being, which comes in its own due time to all beings, at different stages of their lives. To you, it has come when you are still a very young man. To others, it does not come until they are much older, when they experience the loss of a loved one, or when they are faced with their own deaths. Most people shrink from the challenge, or do not recognize the tremendous opportunity for transformation it represents."

"You mean people like me?"

"I mean that the opportunity is here and now with us. We will love you as you are, and in turn you may learn to love yourself."

It was a gracious offer, but Max declined. Within its magnitude, he perceived an all-too-familiar and cautionary threat that was endemic to most teachers and teachings: we know the truth and if you do not accept our version of it, bad things will happen to you.

So Max left for Rajasthan the following morning. "To Jodhpur, the end of the line, at the edge of the desert, to see if I can find myself on my own," Max said.

James wished him well, and he looked forward to seeing Max in Goa for Christmas.

Max made no promises; he was so lost, he couldn't see that far ahead himself.

The train echoed his emptiness, the rhythmic, unerring, unending click-clack, marking time that was without meaning to Max. Hours passed without significance. Between meals, he read a cheap novel about love and the lust for power in corporate America.

At night he rode the steps at the back of the car, watching the farmland recede in the distance, and watching the coconut palms and the mango trees sway in the breeze. His nostrils filling with the spiraling locomotive smoke, his mind melded with that unerring and unending click-clack mantra, alternately irritating him and easing the pain that defined a life that he could not understand.

*   *   *

The opening bash at *The Eclipse* that began with a bang ended with a fatal whimper. It was nearly 3 a.m. when the party began to peter out, and Shunya found Dutch Peter dead in the back yard. He was a novice, having arrived in Kathmandu at the beginning of the week, but he was treated like an old friend: free food and drink, and as much hash as he could smoke. Being tall, blond and handsome, he attracted the attention of several women. As the night wore on and on, Shunya was introduced to him on two different occasions by two different women.

"The next thing I know, the guy turns up dead," Shunya told the Kathmandu police as dawn spread across the Valley.

Though true, Shunya had to spend the entire day in jail, negotiating a price for his freedom, and promising to pay the cost of Dutch Peter's cremation.

"A total of five thousand rupees," he told Rich Tom, following his release from jail.

The cause of death was officially listed as "unknown." But Shunya knew better; he had found a syringe lying beside Dutch Peter's body.

Nevertheless, and true to his word, Shunya spent the next day buying the wood, procuring the incense, and enlisting the services of several Tibetan lamas to sanctify the cremation. It was a sad scene that unfolded under an ever-darkening afternoon sky. The lamas chanting, flames leaping, the body burning, joints popping and bones breaking, Shunya pondered the significance of the young stranger's demise.

As promised, Shunya gathered Peter's ashes in a brass urn, which he would deliver to a Dutch liaison. He was holding the urn in his hands, about to enter a waiting taxi, imagining the pain of Peter's parents upon receiving the remains of their dreams in a can, when he saw the old lama walking down the dry river bed with his young disciple.

Shunya handed the urn to Tom before running after them.

"*Tashi delek*," Shunya began, pressing his palms together, bowing low to master and disciple as he caught his breath.

Lama and disciple returned his greeting.

"My master wants to know what you are doing here?" the disciple asked, interpreting for the lama.

Shunya looked back at the taxi and sighed, "Burning a body. I hardly knew the guy. I just met him, but I felt responsible because he died in my place."

"You mean that you should have died instead of him?" the old lama challenged.

That was not what Shunya meant, and the twist on his words caught him by surprise. He was fumbling for a reply when master and disciple pressed their palms together and bowed to his confusion before leaving.

36

It was a miscarriage. Diane was seven weeks pregnant and didn't know it, didn't want to know it, and could no longer deny it when it ended in a surge of blood and protein inside a filthy bathroom on a dirty old boat—first thinking it was a hemorrhage, then realizing it was her own child that had called out to her in the dark depths of the night in Almora.

The shock turned to fear, comprehension, then turned to guilt. As a result, Diane spent the night on deck alone, crouched between pylons in a dark corner of the stern, far from the crowd. She couldn't look at another passenger, let alone speak with them. She was so ashamed of herself, wiping tears from her eyes throughout the night, and mourning until the first light of dawn, thinking it was the use of drugs in Bombay that had killed her baby.

The old steamer arrived in Panjim at sunrise. As the boat drew closer to shore, Diane was struck by the expanse of white sandy beaches and palm trees. The water sparkling in the intense sunlight as the boat neared the dock, she was reminded of Africa, of a scene from *Mogombo*; everything was so lush and green.

She was enchanted, she was relieved, and she was still weak from the spent emotion. She left the boat thinking she should see a doctor, but decided to grab a taxi to find Sam. Under the circumstances, she figured that love might be the best medicine.

The drive through Panjim was beautiful. The stone and brick and stucco buildings were covered with vines, the cobblestone and brick streets were worn to a sheen. Diane was amazed at the number of potted flowers that decorated the window sills, and she was surprised by the women wearing so many different colorful sun dresses. In many ways, Panjim reminded her of a sleepy old town in the Mediterranean.

The Goan people spoke Portuguese and traced their ancestry back to colonial times when the Portuguese empire rooted itself in East Africa, and stretched across the Arabian Sea to Goa. A territory of India since 1961, Goa retained its unique historical mélange, combining the cultures of Europe, Africa, and India, creating a people with multiracial characteristics. Predominantly Catholic, many Goans still ascribed to primeval rituals associated with their African heritage.

Diane saw several colorful traces of these practices during her taxi ride to Mopsa. The stucco and brick houses and churches were enveloped in tall palms, their trunks painted many different colors, bearing an array of odd symbols and animal skulls that were nailed to the gray bark.

"To keep away the bad things and welcome the good things," her driver explained as they passed a grove of Mango trees thriving on the edge of a banana plantation.

Bananas, papayas, dates, coconuts, pistachios, wildflowers: Goa was far more beautiful and exotic than Diane had expected. The scent in the air was intoxicating. She was nearly asleep in the back of the taxi when it arrived in Calangute Beach. Exhausted, she went to the post office to retrieve the letter from Sam, who had promised to tell her where he was staying. Finding no letter, Diane sank to her knees and burst into tears.

*   *   *

Shunya's chance meeting with the old lama left him in a daze, trying to reason a karmic connection between his life and the dead young man. Near midnight, he phoned Carol in New York.

"I have good news and bad news," he began. He told her about Dutch Peter before telling her he was coming back to New York within a month.

Carol was ecstatic; after all, she had fallen in love with Shunya.

Shunya wasn't in love, but was enchanted, thinking he could live with Carol and divide his time between India and New York. In fact, the longer he spoke to Carol, the less he thought about Peter and the challenge posed by the old lama.

"I miss you," Carol said.

Shunya said, "But not for long. I'll see you soon."

Hanging up the phone, Shunya headed for *The Eclipse* beneath a darkening sky. The valley would be covered with frost by morning.

Entering *The Eclipse*, he found Rich Tom and Patrick drinking beer and playing chess across the bar. Apart from them, *The Eclipse* was empty. In the kitchen, he found his two new Sony recorders that he had purchased in New York, both encased in Samsonite, 18 inches wide, 14 inches long, more than 3 inches deep, weighing less than ten pounds. Once gutted, Shunya imagined that they could each hold five pounds of hash oil. He could make as much as forty-thousand dollars if he succeeded in bringing them through customs alone, which was the plan.

Returning to the bar, he sat beside Tom and asked who was winning.

Tom said, "He appears to have the edge, but I have the better strategy."

Patrick smiled and took Tom's rook with a pawn. "If you say so, mate." Looking at Shunya, he continued, "In the meantime, I need to know your plans so I can make my plans for the winter."

"Another month around here, then six weeks in New York—maybe more. It's hard to say right now."

"What's so hard?" Rich Tom asked. He was upset. Shunya assumed it was a result of losing the rook.

"So you're going to stay with your ex?" Patrick casually asked.

"Here and there. . . We actually got along pretty well, but she has a life of her own now and I'm not sure it would be good for my daughter, so I'll probably stay in the city with Carol most of the time."

Shunya could not read the negative reaction on Tom's face. There was only one light on in the bar. Shunya was about to get up and check stock behind the bar when Patrick moved a bishop across the board and checked Tom's king.

Tom glanced at the board before issuing a warning. "Are you sure you want to do that?"

"Why not?" Patrick asked.

Tom locked eyes with Shunya and tersely replied, "Because you expose your queen, and you shouldn't put the most important woman in your life in jeopardy without just cause."

Shunya caught the inference and threw it back in Rich Tom's face. "Fuck is that supposed to mean?"

Tom returned his attention to the chess board. He was contemplating his next move when Patrick resigned. "Under extreme duress," he said before leaving Tom and Shunya alone.

"You want another beer?" Shunya said, hoping to reduce the tension. Rich Tom winced and declined the offer. "You okay?" Shunya pressed.

"It' a headache, that's all."

Shunya studied the man before responding. "If you don't want me seeing your sister, you should say so."

Tom winced again and agonized, "That's not it."

Shunya reflected on all the possibilities until he picked the least likely. "You mean the drugs?"

Rich Tom nodded and winced again, before rubbing his forehead.

Shunya was stunned. "It was your idea to send the Tibetan rugs to your sister's house in the first place."

"A bad idea," Rich Tom agonized, the pain so great that he gritted his teeth and squeezed his eyes shut in an attempt to stifle a scream. "I didn't realize the risk—especially this time around."

Shunya had seen Tom with a migraine headache before, but none as bad as this. "Is there anything I can do? Anything I can get you?"

Tom raised his head slowly and drew a deep, unsteady breath and exhaled, "Another life."

*   *   *

Diane took a room in a small guesthouse on Calangute Beach, and spent the next three days convalescing and cursing Sam, who she still could not find. On the fourth day she decided to look for him at Anjuna Beach. She woke before dawn and traversed the sand, walking north along the water. The south end of Calangute Beach was so far away that Diane could barely see it.

It was another perfectly beautiful morning in Goa: the sun rising, the palm trees at the back of the beach swaying gently in the tropical breeze. The waves were rippling at Diane's feet when an old fishing schooner emerged from the bend: twelve bare-chested men worked in unison to beach the old boat, as their women and children scurried across the sand with woven baskets in hand.

Diane sat and watched as the men unfolded the huge net on the sand and divided the catch. The good stuff went to market with the women; the five deadly sea snakes, and two hammerhead sharks, and the one stingray were left to die in the sun.

Enchanted by the culture and the exotic scenery, Diane eventually crossed the shallow Baga River, a slowly moving estuary that emptied into the Arabian Sea, then climbed an overgrown lava flow which descended into Anjuna beach.

For some, the road ended in Kathmandu; for others, it ended in Goa. Going east or west, one of these two places often posed the end of a rainbow—where dreams came true and nightmares came calling. Many people were sick and exhausted upon their arrival in Goa, having lost their health or their youth along the way. Naked and bewildered, they often turned to Three-Finger Louie for help and guidance.

As always, Louie spent his summers in Kathmandu and his winters at Anjuna Beach. As needed, he fed the hungry, nursed the sick, and served as a general point of reference for the mindless and listless, and the manifestly clueless.

Diane spent the entire day wandering around Anjuna Beach before she finally turned to Louie for help. "I can't find Sam," she told Louie, arriving on his porch at dusk.

The porch, a cracked, concrete slab located in the heart of a lush coconut grove, served a house with no roof, no windows, and crumbling walls. As always, Louie was a gracious host and inquired into Diane's general welfare before addressing her problem.

"Which Sam is it that you are looking for?" he asked, stroking his goatee. His wavy, brown hair slicked back behind his ears, he looked more like a fifties beatnik than a sixties radical.

"How many Sam's are there in Anjuna?" Diane challenged.

Louie smiled and said, "There's Sad Sam from America; he never smiles. Then there's Sadhu Sam with the dreadlocks from Miami, and there's Spanish Sam from Spain, and Sudden Sam."

"I don't think my man Sam goes by any other name. He has a crew cut, dark hair, not very tall, and he doesn't look like anyone special. He's just this guy from Canada."

Louie looked over Diane's shoulder. "Like that guy?"

Diane followed Louie's eyes, and saw Sam walking arm-in-arm through the palm trees with another, younger woman.

*   *   *

Try as he did, Shunya never resolved the dispute with Rich Tom over his sister. Tom said it was because of the drugs, but Shunya sensed that it was something else. Despite the resentful undercurrent, their friendship persisted until Thanksgiving when each went their separate ways. Rich Tom went to Bodh Gaya to take a Vipasanna meditation course to quell the pain in his head; though helpful, the Doctor's teachings were not curative.

Shunya went to Sonepat to visit with the Doctor before returning to New York, thinking he needed to ground himself in those teachings before risking his freedom.

"Are you sure you really want to go through with this?" James asked, upon greeting him in Sonepat.

"It's not a question of want," Shunya said. "It's fate—because I have the ability to do this, and the willingness, I believe I should do it. I can help many people with the money, and I can get to work on building that school for esoteric research and help even more."

James understood, even if many other people wouldn't: using drug money to further a spiritual quest. It was a generational thing, after all.

The Doctor also understood—he had no moral complaint about the use of drugs—but he wasn't encouraging. He had surmised the nature of Shunya's business by inference, and spoke with Shunya about it after dinner, after he had ingested a thousand micrograms of LSD out of curiosity.

Shunya said, "You don't seem high." He was sitting across the desk from the Doctor in the study.

The Doctor said, "I am not high, because I am not the pill. I experience the hallucinations, and I experience an expansion. It is very interesting, but not revealing. I also think that the use of this drug can be dangerous, because the transition between the ordinary to the extraordinary happens too quickly—so fast that it could be devastating to a weak mind and break the will. It can approximate various stages of Samadhi, but it will never take you beyond the kundalini experience, which is still a projection of your own mind. Truth is not a projection; it is a perception of things as they are. Projection governs the world of things; perception is a highly refined state of awareness of these things. You can spend your life amassing wealth and power, or you can devote your life to serving the truth. There are no shortcuts, Shunya, and an awakened soul cannot serve two masters."

*   *   *

Roni was only eighteen years old. Her long, blond hair cascaded over her bare shoulders, her slim waist was accented by a bejeweled silver belt, and she wore a black silk lingotti between her long, thin legs. From a distance, she looked like a primeval seductress.

"That's Sudden Sam," Louie said.

"Suddenly an asshole," Diane snapped. She could hardly believe her angry blue eyes.

Sam had just passed the porch he heard her familiar voice. When he turned to Louie's porch and saw Diane, he smiled brightly and ran to embrace her.

"It's about time!" he exclaimed.

"I'm sure it is," she shot back, looking past Sam at Roni.

Sam laughed and called Roni over to meet her. As Roni came closer, she posed less of a threat to Diane. Her hair was terribly unkempt, as if it hadn't been washed in a month. Her tanned skin was dry and cracking, and crow's feet were beginning to form around the edges of her dull brown eyes. When she was introduced to Diane, she sounded like she had just walked out of a Brooklyn schoolyard.

"I hope you don't mind me bein' wit 'im for a while. We been friends an' he's been really been good for me," Roni said.

Diane managed a smile. "Not too good, I hope?"

Roni shook her head. "No, no, not good like that. It ain't like he's my boyfriend or nothin'."

Diane turned to Sam and continued, "That still doesn't explain why you didn't leave a letter for me telling me where you are. I've been looking for you for the last three days."

Sam declared, "I did leave a letter for you in Mopsa!"

"You said Calangute."

Which was true, but she was too tired to argue the point.

"Are you sick?" Sam pressed, looking into Diane's sad, blue eyes.

"Just sad."

37

There was no form of authority on Anjuna Beach: no police, no local government, no rules, no restrictions, and no sanctions. Life was perfectly free, and the beach was perfectly beautiful: the emerald green sea shinning in the mid-day sun, the tall palm trees shading the houses and wildflowers, the temperature hovering in the eighties between sunrise and sunset. The nights were cooled by a steady sea breeze.

Sam and Diane were sitting on the beach at dusk, a few stars twinkling above them, the waning moon rising behind them. There was still a trace of purple on the horizon, marking the end of a very long and tiresome day for Diane, and also marking the beginning of another phase in their relationship.

"As beautiful as this place is, I'm not sure it's the right place for me," Diane said.

Sam said, "Perfectly beautiful, but perfection is a hard thing to live up to. So if you're not feeling good about yourself here, you need to take drugs to pick up the slack. If you are feeling good, there is a tendency to intensify or extend the experience—which is why I wanted us to come here, to intensify our life experience and test our limitations. Goa is life on the edge of extremes, not where you meditate and observe as much as it is a place to test what you've learned."

"Except that I failed myself before I ever got here. My god, Sam, I didn't even want to admit to myself that I was pregnant—which is worse than ignorance. It was sinful, killing my own baby, our baby," Diane agonized. When she burst into tears, Sam held her in his arms and sheltered her from the sea breeze—the waves crashing against the shore. "I used so many drugs," she sobbed. "I was so bad, so stupid. . . . I should have known. I had that dream in Almora . . . and I heard a baby crying inside of me, my baby, our baby, and I had morning sickness."

Sam said, "There are junkie mothers who used more drugs than you ever dreamed of using, and they had healthy children. I find it hard to believe that you were responsible for the miscarriage. I also think the dream you had in Almora was most revealing, that there was a problem with the baby, that it was a soul who couldn't be born into this life under the best of circumstances."

"Do you really believe that?" Diane asked, looking up into Sam's soft brown eyes.

"With all my heart," he said, stroking her hair.

*   *   *

Meanwhile, Shunya crossed the world against the advice of wiser men, looking very cool, making small talk with passengers and flight attendants. The plane, a brand-new 747, stopped first in Abu Dhabi and was surrounded by soldiers, then in Lebanon, where it was surrounded by many more soldiers—all looking to thwart a terrorist attack.

*   *   *

Whether out of tradition or necessity, Three-Finger Louie posed the nearest thing to an authority figure on Anjuna Beach. Forty-two years old, he was among the oldest people there, and he had been in India the longest. He had arrived in 1963, running for his life, following a harrowing debacle in France.

Before living in Europe, Louie lived in Detroit, where he was married to a stripper and played the stand-up bass with his renowned three fingers, then in New York, where he hustled gray-market goods on the street. Tall, lanky and dark, he had a prominent hooked nose, which denoted his Armenian descent.

Louie was a good-looking guy, in an ethnic sort of way, and charismatic; and the legend of his remarkable life preceded him.

On this beach freak scene where so many people felt so special, Three-Finger Louie was royalty—if only because he had endured the most for the longest amount of time. He was the king of the road, his porch functioning as his court, where everyone on Anjuna Beach eventually came calling in friendship, in trouble, in passing, or out of curiosity—where Louie woke each morning at the crack of dawn, and tuned into a morning raga on his ever-present shortwave radio, and made mudras with his long and lanky arms.

Dancing with his hands with such effortless grace, Diane was often mesmerized by his talent. She lived with Sam in the house next door to Louie's porch and often woke on her front porch at dawn in between a dozen other men and women who shared their house. No one wanted to sleep inside, it was so beautiful in Goa.

Diane wanted to live alone, but Sam convinced her otherwise. "Like I said before, I would rather live in the middle of things than on the edge of everything. And like the Doctor said, you can only really know yourself in relationship to others—which is why I think living with other people is the right thing to do, because it's the hardest thing for us to do."

Diane reluctantly agreed, and adjusted to their lifestyle after several weeks. To begin with, she saw a western-trained doctor in Panjim and discovered that she was in good health; there was no apparent damage to her uterus, and no reason why she couldn't have another baby. She also spent a lot of time alone on the beach, walking the two-mile length of Anjuna Beach alone almost every morning and processing the emotional trauma of the miscarriage.

She bathed after the walk and took breakfast with Sam in one of several restaurants that were snuggled between the palms. The closest, Joe Bananas, was right behind their house, but the food wasn't very good, the old wooden tables were warped, and the junkies who frequented the place looking for a cheap meal were not a pleasant sight. So Sam and Diane often dined at Mrs. Rodriquez's restaurant, which was a five-minute walk from their house.

The chores came after breakfast: fetching water from a nearby well, sweeping the porch, washing clothes, shopping in Mopsa, or a taking a long walk to the smaller market in Calangute. It was during one of those long walks to Calangute with Sam that Diane learned how he got his nickname, Sudden Sam.

"In Kathmandu two years ago. I guess I moved pretty slow compared to most people and the name stuck—but only in Kathmandu."

Lunch on Anjuna Beach was a push. It was too hot to eat very much. Most people took a nap, or read a book, or played chess or scrabble, or smoked a chillum, or exchanged idle gossip. Secrets were hardly kept by all these naked people who cherished their freedom.

Despite the enormity of Goa's international reputation—which was almost entirely derived from the scene on Anjuna Beach—the beach population at the height of its holiday peak did not exceed three hundred people. Anjuna Beach was essentially a very small, transient community that thrived on its uniqueness. Idle gossip begot rumors, and the rumors begot stories that turn into legend, and the names were often changed to enhance the legend and denote the players, like Sudden Sam.

Dinner was the highlight of each and every day, when parties were given and restaurants were crowded, when the men combed their hair and the women wore sheer silk, and when idle gossip reached its maddening peak. The nearer to Christmas, the bigger the crowd.

More than anything, Diane had hoped to be alone with Sam. She needed the time and attention to process the pain. But privacy was at a premium. With each passing day, more friends arrived on their porch from all over India. Some stayed only a few weeks, like Bill Velititsky—to everyone's delight—while others like James and Martine, and White Mike and Rich Tom, and Laura spent most of the winter.

*   *   *

Shunya's plane landed in New York at 6:09 p.m., on a crystal clear winter night. The good weather heightened his spirits; it seemed a good omen. He was tense, but not frightened though he was facing twenty years in jail if he were caught. The terminal was crowded, everyone moving so fast that it was hard to focus, which was exactly what Shunya hoped for. He fit right in the holiday mix as he passed through the crowd, his arms overflowing with colorful baggage from the East, and two Sony tape recorders.

He had recently shaved his head and had combed his long, red beard to a perfect point. His clothes handmade from raw silk, Shunya gave the impression of a man of substantial means. He could have been an artist, a film maker, or a painter; he decided on being a photographer. He had two expensive Nikon cameras, which he had borrowed from a friend in Nepal, tucked in one of his Bhutanese bags. And he continued to smile and make small talk with fellow passengers as he waited his turn at customs.

But he had a passport with numerous entry and exit visas that would cause inquiry. He was telling himself that he should have applied for a new passport in New Delhi, when his turn came. His palms sweating, his heart racing, his head throbbing, his hands trembling, Shunya managed to smile at the customs man as he presented his papers.

The man, thumbing through Shunya's passport, said, "You get around a bit, don't you?"

Shunya looked the man in the eyes and widened his smile. "The nature of the beast, I guess."

"Which is?"

"Photography mostly, and journalism."

"Interesting life."

"If you can stomach it," Shunya sighed, rubbing his abdomen and alluding to various bouts of dysentery.

The man nodded and asked Shunya to open his bags, which were purposely filled with colorful, silk prayer scarves, Tibetan malas, coral and turquoise earrings and necklaces, a variety of silver bangles and bracelets.

"Mostly gifts for my wife and daughter," Shunya said, attaching a story to several items, telling the man where he bought the scarves, and where he found an old lama's skull.

The man, looking and feeling for a weakness, found nothing suspicious and finally asked Shunya if he had anything to declare.

Shunya, looking down at all the jewelry and clothes and his two Nikon cameras, began to unfold a large set of Tibetan Tonka paintings. "These maybe, but I don't think . . ."

The man passed on the Tonkas and pointed to the Sony recorder cases.

Shunya pushed his bags out of the way before sliding the recorders forward.

The man inspected the closed cases while Shunya fumbled to produce two sales receipts, indicating that the recorders were bought in Manhattan during his last visit to New York.

The man ignored the receipts, opened the first recorder case and said, "You must really like your music."

"I do, because it does remind me of home," Shunya said. His heart racing so fast he thought it was going to explode. His head throbbing, his body trembling, Shunya continued to smile and casually babble. "It's got a great sound. I taped all this stuff when I was here the last time. I mean I can just sit around and listen for hours. And I got this converter. I can listen to music almost anywhere, in Europe, or in India, and it'll be great on safari in Africa."

"Is that why you have two?" The man said, closing the top of the first recorder.

Shunya said, "No," before the man opened the second case for his inspection.

Much to his surprise, the guts of the second recorder were missing. Only the casing remained and it was filled with dozens of cassettes and reel-to-reel tapes.

Shunya smiled so wide that the muscles in his face began to ache. "I told you, I like my music."

The man said, "I can see that."

This was the apex, the dreaded moment of truth, when Shunya's freedom hung in the balance of another man's perception: If the man removed all of the tapes and picked up the empty case, he might feel the added weight in the lining and look further into the matter, and have Shunya detained.

Shunya fought to maintain his composure as the man picked up one of the cassettes and said, "You like Sinatra?"

"At night, when it's raining, in any hotel room, in any place in the world," Shunya said.

The man was middle-aged and pleasantly surprised. He closed the case and told Shunya, "You may go."

Shunya re-packed his belongings, quietly thanking the powers watching over him, thinking that he had beaten the odds and bested the wise.

38

The nearer to Christmas, the more concerned James became for Max's welfare. "Not a word from him, or about him, since he left for Rajasthan, and he wasn't in very good shape when he left Sonepat."

Diane shrugged. She was too wrapped up in her own life to worry about Max. "For all we know, he could also be taking a series of Sayadaw courses. Besides, he knows where we are; he knows how to find us."

Both topless, they were talking in the back bedroom of their house on Anjuna Beach, where they stored their belongings. James was sitting on the tile floor. Diane was standing in front of a broken mirror taped to the cinder block wall, applying her makeup and donning her jewelry. It was early evening, and she was getting ready for a big dinner party.

"But I understand your concern. I also think about Jane. We were such good friends, and I've written about a dozen letters to her in Benares, and Bodh Gaya, and Bincer, and she never writes back, which is unlike her. I know she has a boyfriend, but . . ."

Diane backed away from the mirror, looked sideways at her reflection, and asked James if she looked good in her white cotton mini-skirt, made from a shawl that she wrapped around her shapely butt.

James said, "You look great."

"Do you think I should go topless? It seems a bit tacky to sit down at a dinner table with my boobs hanging out."

James said, "Then wear the halter top, you can always remove it."

"You're coming, aren't you?" she asked James.

"I wasn't really invited."

Diane wet her fingertips with saliva and used them to twirl a curl on her forehead. "Martine was."

"I know. She's going with Rich Tom."

Diane turned to James and met his eyes. "And that' okay with you?" She knew it wasn't.

"If that's what she really wants. She can have the big prick and his money," James spat, reaching across the broken tile floor for a pack of bidis. Their house wasn't very nice—which was another reason why everyone lived on the long, front porch. The clay tile roof leaked in several places and the plaster was peeling off the cinder block walls and ceilings. James lit a bidi and exhaled, "Sam going?"

"Not this time." Diane slipped the halter top over her head and stepped further back from the mirror to appraise her appearance.

"It's not tight enough," she said. "It makes me look heavy, as if I'm trying to hide something."

"On Anjuna Beach? As if everyone at that party hasn't already seen everything you have?"

Diane threw her hands in the air and sighed, "What's a girl to do?"

"Stay home, read a good book, meditate, find yourself," James wistfully replied.

Diane twirled her ever-present ruby earring and said, "Maybe I should wear a little red, a necklace or something."

Unable to find the coral necklace in her bags, she reached into Sam's bag and found the unexpected. "What the hell is this?" she exclaimed, showing the waxy black little ball to James.

"Looks like opium to me," James said.

It was opium. She was staring at the small ball of dope when Laura entered the room with Roni, who was too stoned to stand on her own. James helped Laura lay Roni across a makeshift bed of soft luggage.

"Drugs?" Diane asked.

"And men," Laura added. "We went to Calangute yesterday and this really cute English guy, John, shows up at the market and starts telling Roni that she's the most beautiful woman he's ever seen. And she's buying into it, of course, thinking this guy might be different from the last hundred guys she had.

"Then this guy starts telling her how he's a doctor and she believes him! And she goes back to his place. I don't see her again until this morning when I go back to the market, and she's walking around in a total daze, looking for me, thinking it's still yesterday! Then she shows me this note that says, *'Get well soon'* and it's signed, *'Doctor Doom.'* She said the guy stuck the note inside of her."

*   *   *

Shunya woke to a snowy winter morning in Manhattan. He was reading a newspaper at the kitchen table in Carol's apartment, waiting for Fast Freddy to return his call from a payphone in the Bronx.

"You look worried," Carol said, serving him a three-cheese omelet.

Shunya looked at the phone resting on a corner table and sighed, "Not worried, anxious. I was also thinking that I should get a hotel room for a few days."

"Why would you want to do that?" she asked, unaware of the nature of Shunya's business—which he hoped to conclude by the end of the day.

"Because I promised your brother that I would look out for you."

"As if you're not?"

"I suppose, but . . . I think it might be best. We'll see."

Carol tossed her hair back and laughed; she looked ravishing in a black nightgown. "I think I know what's best," she seductively replied, leaning forward to kiss him.

Shunya was about to reach for her shoulders when the phone finally rang. It was Freddy calling to tell him, "We can't all make it to the game today, but Tuesday looks good," meaning that Freddy needed more time to raise the money.

"Looks like a hotel room after all, and maybe a trip to Brooklyn to see my daughter," Shunya told Carol.

"And a lot of me in between," Carol said, sitting on his lap.

*   *   *

Laura and Roni had grown up in similar blue collar neighborhoods in New York, and had come from similarly ethnic families: Roni was Jewish, Laura, Italian. They had met on the beach on Mykonos last summer, where Laura talked Roni into going to India.

"To get high and have a good time, but I didn't think she was gonna wind up hurting herself so much," Laura told Diane the following morning over a cup of coffee at Joe Bananas. "At the rate she's going, she's gonna wind up dead one day."

"Sounds like my husband to me," Diane sighed. "He was another one who never knew when to stop."

"And we do, right?"

"We can only hope," Diane said, finishing her coffee, wondering if she wanted to spend the rest of the winter in Goa.

She had a great time at the party the previous night, dancing to Motown and The Rolling Stones, drinking beer, smoking hash and snorting cocaine. But she woke up with a hangover, thinking that she might like to take another Sayadaw course. She also thought she would enjoy spending more time alone with Sam. When she asked him about the opium she found in his bags, he said he kept it to take for a bad stomach.

Then she thought about Max. She did miss him and regretted marginalizing him in her conversation with James.

She was nearing her porch when she overheard a conversation taking place on Louie's porch between him and two reporters on assignment for *Life Magazine*, both dressed in chinos and sport shirts. They had come to Anjuna Beach to do a feature on Three-Finger Louie's life, but Louie wouldn't cooperate.

"Not even for five thousand dollars?" one bewildered reporter challenged.

"Not for a million," Louie said. "Not until you pay everyone else on the beach, if you want me to talk to you about my relationship to them."

The other reporter left the porch to speak with Diane. "You know him?" he began.

Diane said, "Well enough to know that he won't sell us short."

Turning away from the reporter, she stepped onto her own porch and found Rich Tom and James engaged in a grudge game of chess. Martine was sitting between them, apparently savoring the contest, pitting the blue collar guy from the Bronx against the preppie young man from old family money.

Diane stood behind Martine while Rich Tom made his move and said, "I think your queen's in check."

James saw the obvious; he looked at Martine, then smiled at Rich Tom before proclaiming, "Checkmate!"

Tom said, "You mean you resign?"

"I mean you lose."

"You didn't move yet."

James said, "If you like," but he didn't move one inch.

Tom returned his attention to the board, and studied it intently until he realized that he made the wrong move at the wrong time. He was so caught up in catching James' queen that he had left his king unattended. His defeat was a moot point among players of reasonable caliber. "I guess I underestimated you," Rich Tom grudgingly admitted.

James reached for Martine's hand and said, "And if you ever try and fuck with my girl friend again, I'm gonna fuck you in places you never dreamed of."

Rich Tom was shaken. Martine was stunned. Bill and White Mike were entertained.

Diane was exacerbated by the negative energy and decided to take a long walk to Calangute Market.

Climbing up and then down the backside of the overgrown lava flow, Diane walked carefully between the sharp rocks and thorny underbrush. Too many cuts led to staff infections in Goa.

Crossing lazy and picturesque Baga River at high tide, she held her clothes and jhola over her head. Nearing the other side, which was the beginning of Baga Beach, she noticed a shark fin zigzagging at the mouth of the river. Most likely a Hammerhead, she thought as she tied her red cotton lungi around her neck. With no reports of shark attacks in Goa, Diane had no fear.

Now walking carefully to avoid the dirty needles, syringes, and broken morphine vials, that denoted this infamous little stretch of sand, she began to reflect upon the increasing shallowness of her life: wearing makeup and jewelry and sexy clothes, going to parties and getting high, engaging in idle gossip. Diane had made a lot of new friends, but she still considered Max her best friend.

She was nearing the south end of Calangute Beach, wondering what Max would think of her, when she saw him sitting in the sand next to another man, in the shade of a broken down fishing boat. Both were deeply tanned and apparently disinterested in her.

The stranger was frying a stinking piece of fish over an open fire while Max sat quietly, staring out across the sea.

"Max!" Diane called out, as she walked toward him.

Max kept looking ahead, across the sea, as if Diane weren't there.

"Max, Max, it's me, Diane," she excitedly repeated, as she drew closer to him.

When Max finally looked up to her, he blinked before he returned his attention to the sea.

39

"I'm telling you, he hardly recognized me! He acted as if he didn't even know me!" Diane told Sam and James, after returning to Anjuna.

Both found it hard to believe. She found them sitting on the beach watching the sunset. On cosmic cue, three seagulls flew across the face of the reddening sun as it descended the western horizon and touched the sea. All remained silent in deference to the momentous beauty.

"It's not like we don't believe you. It's more like we don't want to believe you," James eventually said. Her account of Max gone mad was deeply disturbing.

"It was harder to see than believe," Diane said, fighting back tears. "It was so pathetic, it was heartbreaking . . . And this guy he was with looked more dead than alive. And he had this really strange look in his eyes . . . And when I got close enough to look into Max's eyes, it was like there was nobody there, like they were totally vacant.

"Then he asked me if I wanted a piece of fish that this weird guy was cooking . . . It was all so strange and so sad, I couldn't even answer him. I just walked away before I began to cry."

*   *   *

At the first light of dawn, Sam and James headed over to Calangute Beach to find Max.

"No fucking way he doesn't know me," James said, as they crossed the Baga River.

Sam said, "That may be, but if he didn't know Diane it's because he didn't want to know, maybe because it hurts too much, and we should respect his limitations until we understand them. We should try and meet him where he is as opposed to where we want him to be."

It was good counsel, though James had trouble accepting it. He had known Max since childhood and was convinced he could reach him, no matter what the obstacles.

Max didn't see a problem, didn't want to think. He had been living on Calangute Beach for three weeks, and he had found a measure of security in the daily routine. He woke at dawn, took a long walk on the beach, and returned home to the rotting old boat for breakfast. As usual his buddy, Shiva had something cooking on the stove, something he had found dead in the sand, or something he had stolen from somebody else's backyard.

On this morning, Shiva had found three freshly laid eggs, an overripe papaya, a small coconut, and some kind of small scaly fish. By nature, Shiva was a scavenger who lived off the dead and discarded.

It was not long after sunrise, after Max's breakfast, when Sam and James emerged from a small patch of fog on the beach and saw Max sitting in the shade of the rotting old boat, looking out across the sea. Shiva was down by the shore cleaning dishes.

"Yo, Max!" James called out as he approached his dear old friend.

Sam followed, keeping one sharp eye on Shiva.

Max looked up to James and winced before returning his attention to the sea.

James sank to his knees and got right to the heart of the matter. "It hurts that much?" he inquired, speaking very softly with great care.

Max nodded and said, "I still got those sounds in my head."

James was about to reply when Sam placed a hand on his arm and squeezed it. Shiva had finished his chore and was approaching. The closer he came, the more uncomfortable they became.

Tall, bald, ghastly thin, covered with tattoos, Shiva's brown eyes bulged out of his head like a gargoyle. The guy was so ugly; he was scary as the devil, but James would not betray a weakness.

"We're friends," James began, standing and extending his hand to Shiva.

Shiva unsheathed a razor-sharp bayonet and stammered, "I am Shiva, the l-l-lord of destruction!"

Sam noted a trace of spittle dripping from one corner of Shiva's mouth and backed away.

James grabbed a handful of sand and spat, "You don't scare me, motherfucker."

Shiva tightened the grip on his knife and sprang ahead; James threw the sand at his eyes.

Shiva ducked, missing most of it, then dropped to his knees and lunged further forward.

                    *   *   *

"He" totally fucking insane is what he is," James told Louie, returning to Anjuna Beach with Sam later in the morning.

Sam was quick to agree. "If it weren't for Max, we'd both be dead. Max grabbed Shiva's arm which gave us time to run."

Diane said, "But that's a good sign, isn't it? Max protected you, and he was talking to James."

Louie stroked his goatee and pondered the question for a few moments before answering. "A very good sign, I would say. And I think you all have a pretty clear understanding of the situation. Your friend Max probably did disconnect when the pain of his life became too great. But he's still aware of it because he talked about it, the sounds in his head. And it's this awareness of the pain that still keeps him in touch with reality; it also saved your lives. This Shiva guy is another story. He is less aware of his suffering. When he perceives a threat he becomes his pain, and relieves it by inflicting it upon others."

"I still can't imagine how they found each other," Diane said.

"Because misery loves company," Louie said. "And the only way to change it is to embrace it, embrace them."

James said, "Be kind of hard to get close to that Shiva guy."

"Time will tell. In the meantime, it's probably best to back off and see if your friend Max can't find his way back to you."

Diane drew a deep breath and sighed, "From what I've seen, I think that's asking an awful lot of him."

"On the contrary, from what you've told me, it seems like he's come a long way already. He knew you were in Goa."

*   *   *

Shunya had no way of knowing what happened to Max, and he was greatly frustrated by the continued bad weather in New York, which wreaked havoc with his timing. More than eighteen inches of snow fell in two days, followed by a bone-chilling cold spell. Public transportation was a mess. Local traffic through the Boroughs was thwarted by four-foot drifts.

Fast Freddy Fein called at the height of the storm on Tuesday and said, "I guess you could say that the game was canceled, but I'm thinking we could reschedule for the weekend."

Owing to the bad weather and pressure from Carol, Shunya never checked into a hotel, and he didn't see his daughter. In fact, he didn't even call her.

"Because I can't afford to disillusion her by making an appointment I can't keep, regardless the reason. I think I've disappointed her enough for one life already," Shunya told Carol.

Carol understood. She had grown up with disappointment. "My father was always away on business or something," she explained.

Shunya said, "It must have been hard on Tom, too?"

Carol said, "Everything is hard on Tom. Nothing's ever really right for him. He has so much trouble accepting things, and people for that matter, as they really are."

"That's probably why his head hurts so much. I've often thought he tries too hard to understand things, to reason things, and he hurts himself in the process."

"And others," Carol sighed. "I told you about the money. And when I confronted him about it, he claimed to have a really bad migraine and nothing was ever resolved. He went away on business and left me holding a half-empty bag."

"What kind of business?"

"He never said, but I think its part of the reason why he went to India."

*   *   *

The disparity in Diane's life persisted: being in India while being in Goa, which wasn't like being in India at all, being high and happy after being in great pain; and seeking a greater meaning to her life than finding the perfect necklace to match her ruby earrings to wear to the next best beach party; having dinner with two junkies, one gangster, and one lady-killer while her friend Max was dying to himself.

The backyard at *Gregory's* restaurant was filled with candle-lit tables, and crowded with wealthy young patrons—including Hong Kong Rosie and Delhi Dave, both of whom had recently arrived in Anjuna for Christmas.

Rosie had invited Diane, Laura and Roni to *Gregory's* as her guests. "Anything you want tonight, and I will pay for it. I make so much money," she kept saying. Her wrists jangled with a flashy collection of exotic gold and silver bangles. Her ruby and emerald necklace sparkled in the candlelight.

Diane was dining on grilled langoustine when Delhi Dave walked in, and Rosie invited him to join them.

"Tonight I pay for everything, even for you," she gushed.

"Makes me wonder how much it cost the other guy," Delhi Dave cracked.

Rosie carved a sardonic smile. "His life," she said. "I make him pay for his life."

Delhi Dave said, "Yeah, well, I don't mind sittin' wit' you, but I'll pay for my own life."

As the drinks flowed, the conversation grew more animated, until the infamous Doctor Doom entered the restaurant. He was the despicable young man who left a note between Roni's legs.

"Hey, Doc, over here!" Delhi Dave called out.

Roni was shaken. Laura was incensed. "You know that bastard?" she demanded.

"Oh, yeah, I met 'im in Bombay. We were staying at the same guest house, at the Soona Mahal. And we did a little 'O' together in the dens an' shit. An' when I got too fucked up, he got me better."

"You mean the guy's really a doctor?" Laura pressed.

Doctor Doom overheard the question and met the challenge. "Dr. John Lister at your service—Harvard Medical—but I lost interest."

"But you had me, you little fucker," Roni snapped.

The doctor smiled. "Yes, and I did leave my calling card, if I remember correctly."

"Fucking bastard," Laura sneered.

When the doctor widened his sarcastic smile, Roni began to cry.

"A little touchy, aren't we?" the Doctor said.

He was the most self-serving, cold-hearted bastard these women had ever seen, and not easily dismissed. He was looking for a chair when Delhi Dave stood up for Roni, if only because she couldn't defend herself.

"We are touched," Delhi Dave spat. "An' if you don't wipe that stupid fuckin' smile off your face, an' get the fuck out of here right now, I'm gonna fuck you up!"

Doctor Doom was no match for Delhi Dave and left in a hurry. All the girls lauded Delhi Dave's heroics—except Rosie. She had noted the gold Rolex on his wrist and was sorry to see it go.

*   *   *

Sam had also been invited to the dinner at *Gregory's* but declined the offer, choosing instead to spend the evening on the beach. It was another beautiful night in Goa. The stars twinkled above, the palm trees swayed on the breeze, and the ocean rushed the shore as Sam walked the length of the beach. He was nearing the south end when he saw Max sitting on a rock.

"Can I sit?" Sam began, following a cautious approach, looking around the beach for any sign of Shiva.

Max said, "Okay."

They sat together for almost twenty minutes in silence, watching the ebb and flow of the Arabian Sea beneath a glittering sky.

"You must think I'm really crazy, don't you?" Max began.

"Not that crazy, because you're aware of it."

"Today I'm aware of it. Not every day. I did know who Diane was, but I didn't want to know."

"It hurts that much?"

Max winced and sighed, "Sometimes. It began with Maya when she left., and I still don't know why it hurt so much. I didn't even like her that much. I liked Diane a lot more. I loved Diane in my own way, but it was this little thing with Maya that finally broke my back. It was the last straw, the last painful thing I could handle. I can only assume that it must have connected to something deeper inside of me that I've been carrying around for a long time—but I still can't figure out what that is. It's not like I was abused as a child or anything like that. In fact, I had a good childhood. I had great parents.

"Anyway, I became really insecure and frightened when Maya left. Then I got weirded out from Peter's murder, and I started losing touch with things and people. It all just added up, and I became so embarrassed that I couldn't bear to look at anyone any more, least of all myself. I was never really comfortable at the Doctor's house.

"So I went as far away from myself as I could, to Jodhpur in Rajasthan, to the desert, thinking I could take a vacation from myself, but I got lost along the way. It was sort of like taking a walk in the woods, and everything's really beautiful until it gets dark all of a sudden, and you can't find your way home—and all the beasts come out at night and you get scared. But I was okay at first. I wound up going to Pushkar Mela, the camel festival, and hung out with all these tribals in their tents. When they left Pushkar, I went with one of the tribes; I traveled with them, just going from place to place for a month—hanging out with them in the desert—and I started feeling okay about myself, living really primitive, and they were really nice to me.

"Then one morning I woke up really late—I was drinking a lot of this funky beer with them the night before—and I wake up and all these people are gone, and all my things are gone with them. They ripped me off for everything I had except my passport, and they left me in the middle of nowhere in the middle of the fucking desert—like the dumb white schmuck I really was, thinking I could be like them in an effort to forget myself.

"Then I began walking around from village to village talking to myself, I was so angry, telling myself I didn't deserve better—then I started stealing food and whatever else I needed. It got to be this survival thing, and my fear turned to anger at everyone and everything in this whole fucking world. Then I thought about killing people all the time, every person I ever knew who ever hurt me, because knowing them seemed to hurt me so much, as if they were part of some kind of cosmic conspiracy to punish me for a crime I didn't commit. Then I wondered if I was guilty of something, and that's when I really must have lost it, when I tried to find out what was wrong with me, what I had done wrong."

"Is that when you met Shiva?"

"Just about. I eventually got on this bus and I wound up sitting next to him, which was really strange. We were probably the only two white guys within five hundred miles. Anyway, the bus gets held up by dacoits ten minutes after I get on. They come on the bus, and they start taking a couple of rupees road tax from everyone. One of these guys is casually carrying a shotgun, and when this guy puts out his hand to take money from us, Shiva pulls his bayonet and puts it to the guy's neck. When the guy looks into Shiva's eyes he begins to shake—even with the gun in his hand. And he runs off the bus, and me and Shiva became friends.

"We wound up going to Bombay together, doing all kinds of weird shit, stealing, living like animals on the street. But we never talked very much, and he didn't like anybody talking to us; he still doesn't. The poor guy is in more pain than anyone could possibly imagine, probably because he caused so much pain. His real name is Jack. He grew up in Texas and he wound up in Vietnam. He told me that he killed a lot of people, innocent people, all kinds of people, and I think the guilt finally got to him, and he ran away from the military."

"Do you still think about killing people?"

"Sometimes, when the hurting turns to anger, because the anger feels better than the fear. I can't function with the fear, but I can do okay with the anger. I can draw strength from anger. I can walk around and feed myself and defend myself. And if I can't do it, Shiva does it for me. But I guess I came to Goa knowing that I couldn't keep living like that, especially with him; I feel so bad for him. I guess I was hoping that somebody I know would show up. But I couldn't reach you. I was actually even more fucked up than I thought. I was so embarrassed when I saw Diane, and when I saw you and James. But when I saw that James was willing to risk his life to save my life, I realized that I had come to the right place. It connected with me; he connected with me at that moment. But it still hurts so much sometimes, and I still don't know what it is."

Sam was about to reply when Max began to cry, and Sam held him in his arms.

40

Enlightenment was not a game. Barring attainment, it did not necessarily reward a good showing. It was a process of unfolding, which often turned into an unraveling, requiring the need for guides and gurus, inviting an array of charlatans, and the wisdom to make the distinction.

Max was lucky; he had good friends to turn to who didn't require faith in their teachings or loyalty to a cause. He spent Christmas at Anjuna Beach leaning on them for support. By New Years, he had apparently returned to himself—spending less time with Shiva, who he had visited on several occasions with food and clothes.

"I think he's beginning to hold my good fortune against me," Max told Diane during one of their long morning walks on the beach. "He wouldn't accept food from me the last time I saw him."

"What do you talk about?"

"Not much, but we never talked much. And if we did, it was during meals. I've asked him to come here to meet my friends, especially Louie, who might be very helpful. He's heard about Louie, which is really interesting."

"Why so?"

"Because he never acknowledges anyone else. But when I mentioned Louie's name, he said that he heard about him in Nepal."

"What did he hear?"

"That he helps people. The problem is that Shiva doesn't think he needs help, and I think it's because if he admits that he needs it, he has to revisit the pain of his life, which is extraordinary by any measure—raping, killing, torturing people for the fun of it. His only saving grace was his conscience, which eventually got the better of him and forced him out of Vietnam. He has nightmares. A lot of nights he wakes up babbling, just rambling on and on until he falls back to sleep."

As the blood-orange setting sun neared the horizon, Diane pointed at three birds flying across the face of it. "I can't tell you how many times I've seen this scene before, the birds flying in front of the sun as it sets. And it's almost always three birds, maybe even the same three birds. It's really strange, which adds even more to the beauty of this place. On the other hand, I'm beginning to think this place is evil; there are so many evil people here, really broken people who don't want to be fixed.

"What's worse is that I like a lot of them, and every time I complain to Sam about it, about leaving, I also think I want to stay because I like it here so much. And Sam keeps telling me that our experience here provides a good balance for our experience in Almora—or Bodh Gaya for that matter. He says it's a good testing ground for the reality of any teaching, applying it to all the self-indulgent insanity around here. He has no conflict about being here whatsoever."

"Neither do I, Diane, because coming here might have saved my life," Max said, before stopping to pick up a small green and red sea rock and examine it.

"I'm amazed at how quickly you recovered; what's it been, two weeks since I first saw you?"

"I guess it is really strange because it all seems so natural to me, being here with you now, as if none of that stuff happened to me in Rajasthan. I hardly even think about it."

"What about Maya?"

Max flung the rock back into the sea and sighed, "I do think about her, but not so much anymore. She's more like a distant memory now. I mean it still hurts sometimes, thinking about her, but I guess I lost enough of my mind to be helpful in some ass-backwards way; the memory of losing you also hurts."

"You mean you still love me?" Diane asked, looking into his eyes.

Max reached for her hand and said, "Of course."

Diane kissed him on the lips and said, "I love you, too."

Max asked, "Is this okay?"

"Okay with me," Diane said, leading him into a grove of palm trees on the less populated north end of the beach.

"What about Sam?" he asked.

"Sam's still my man, but I want more of you just one more time."

So they lay side by side beneath the swaying palms, kissing and cuddling, often looking into one another's eyes, but they never made love in deference to Sam.

They returned to their house an hour later holding hands.

"Looks like you two had a pretty good time," Sam said, standing to greet them.

Max said, "I guess you could say that I got a kiss and you still have the rest of her."

Sam wasn't surprised and he wasn't threatened. He had just asked Max to join Diane and him for dinner when Roni ran up to Louie's porch and told a frightening story, nervously running her hand through her tangled hair as tears streamed down her cheeks.

"I was partying on my porch, me an' these two other guys, an' then they leave, an' I'm supposed to watch the house, an' I'm really wasted, so I fall asleep on the porch. Next thing I know it's getting dark an' this guy's standin' over me—just standin' there with his body covered with paint an' ashes. He's like really skinny an' bald an' I'm thinkin' he's like from hell or somethin'. Then I think that I'm dreamin, I was so fucked up. Then I ask 'im who he was an' what he wants from me, an' he says, 'Death,' an' I guess I just started screaming an' he ran away."

"But he never did anything to you? He never touched you?" Louie asked.

"No, but I don't understand who this guy is—I was so scared—an' what he was doin' there wit' me."

"Probably looking for me," Max said.

*   *   *

On the day of the deal, after having spent a wonderful and loving week with Carol, after all the bad weather had passed, Shunya woke on a Tuesday morning, thinking that success begot success: he had passed through customs without a hitch, so he would conclude his deal with Fast Freddy Fein without a problem. The sun was out, and the ice and snow were beginning to melt. All he had to do was make love to Carol, have breakfast, get dressed, get a taxi to the Bronx, and get the deal done.

"By noon," Shunya told Carol before leaving. "By one o'clock we should be sitting in Cafe des Artistes having a very expensive lunch, if you like."

Carol could hardly wait; she was so in love with Shunya. She had concluded that Shunya was involved in some kind of a major drug deal, and she wasn't concerned—as long as it wasn't hard drugs. After all, she smoked pot and hash. It was a sign of the times, and Shunya believed that he was engaged in something necessary and revolutionary. His heart was in the right place; he did intend to share his good fortune with the world.

The cab ride to the Bronx took more than an hour, much of the snow turning to slush and pools of water which slowed traffic. It was a beautiful day nonetheless, and Shunya continued to think the best of everything as his cab crawled up the West Side Highway to the Cross Bronx Expressway. It wasn't until Shunya's taxi turned onto the Bronx River Parkway that he began to reflect upon the prospects for failure, and the cautionary words of the old lama and the Doctor.

The closer to the Bronx, the less certain Shunya was of success. Was something really wrong? Or was he experiencing the norm, the usual apprehension before consummation? He had never closed a deal as big as this.

Shunya exited the taxi, recorders in hand, looked up and down the block and across the street into the park , and was pleased by the normal flow of traffic and people.

Fast Freddy lived on the fourth floor, in a one-bedroom apartment that overlooked the park. Shunya was walking through the lobby, recorder cases in hand, when he began to think about his father, who he planned to visit later in the week. Then he thought of his daughter. He was imagining how they would both benefit from his success, when he knocked on Freddy's door.

Freddy opened it almost immediately, as if he had been standing right behind it. "I was looking out the window. I saw your taxi pull up," Freddy explained.

"After an exchange of pleasantries, Shunya followed him into the kitchen, asking for a pliers and a screwdriver as he opened the first recorder case.

"I have a class to teach over at Hunter College this afternoon," Freddy said, handing him the tools. "A taste will be enough. I can tell by a taste."

Shunya did most of the work himself, carefully removing the oil from the lining of the first case without puncturing the plastic. Upon finishing, Shunya caught Freddy looking out the window, the sun reflecting off Freddy's balding head.

"Pretty nice out there, huh?" Shunya asked.

"What's nice?" Fast Freddy challenged. He was tense.

"The weather."

"Yeah . . . Sure, great," Freddy stumbled.

He seemed preoccupied, and Shunya was finally concerned. "You have the money, don't you?"

"Oh, yeah, yeah, the money really wasn't a problem. I had to get several people to go in on this with me. It was only a matter of collection because of the weather."

Shunya had no reason to doubt him. After all, he had no problems with him before, and Freddy was a good friend of Delhi Dave.

"Terrible weather," Shunya nervously said. The nearer to the pay-off, the greater the anticipation.

"What weather?"

"The bad weather?"

"You mean the snow?"

Of course Shunya was referring to the snow, which was still on the ground and reflecting the sunlight. It was an odd conversation he was having with this very intelligent guy.

"But it is kind of pretty," Shunya began again, after disemboweling the second case with relative ease.

"What?"

"The snow."

"You mean outside?"

"Where else?" Now Shunya began to notice small beads of sweat gathering at the front of Fast Freddy's head. "You're sure you're okay?"

Fast Freddy looked out the window, drew a deep breath and sighed, "This is a pretty big deal for me—even for me. It's a lot of money."

Shunya was surprised. After all, Fast Freddy had run guns to Castro with Delhi Dave, which was not a small-time affair, and far more risky than this proposition. Something was amiss, Shunya thought, but he couldn't imagine what. Then again, this was the biggest deal Shunya had ever done; he wasn't sure if he was projecting his own fear onto the situation.

When he squeezed a drop of oil out of the plastic, Fast Freddy scooped it up on his forefinger and placed it against his tongue.

"Tastes great to me. It's even stronger than the last batch. Are the other bags are the same?"

Shunya said, "Yes."

Freddy nodded and weighed each bag on the triple beam. Afterward, he lit a pipe. "Just a couple of tokes," he said. "Like I said, I do have a class this afternoon."

Shunya welcomed the abrupt change in Freddy's unfocused and stressful demeanor, and he was delighted with the price. Shunya was prepared to go as little as $3,650 a pound; he was pleasantly surprised when Fast Freddy offered to match the original price, $3,925 per, for the whole ten pounds.

Stoned, Shunya had to count the money twice before stuffing it into an expensive leather bag that he had purchased for the express purpose of securing the deal.

He left Fast Freddy's apartment looking forward to his next appointment with destiny, at his own school for esoteric studies in Nepal. He was a very high and happy young man, and so preoccupied with his own success that he forgot to press the first floor button in the elevator; consequently, he wound up taking it to the basement with a Sears serviceman wheeling a refrigerator.

Once in the basement, Shunya followed the refrigerator out of the elevator door, out the side of the building and onto the street in front of the serviceman's truck.

Of course, Shunya had no idea how lucky he was until he called Carol from a phone booth on the avenue.

"Dear God!" Carol exclaimed upon hearing his voice. "Are you okay?"

Shunya said, "Better than okay, I'm rich!"

"You're also in a lot of trouble," Carol heatedly explained. "I just got a call from Freddy Fein. He was calling from his neighbor's phone and he said that he set you up, that he was arrested a while ago and the cops used him. They were sitting in a car in front of his house, waiting for you to come out, and you somehow got away. He was watching from his window, and he felt so bad about it that he called me to warn you.

"The police must be looking for you as we speak," she continued, sobbing. "The phone in Freddy's apartment was tapped, and everything you said and did in his apartment was recorded. Freddy said you have to leave New York in a hurry, and he hoped that you wouldn't mention this call if you were caught because he did try to do the right thing after all."

Shunya was shocked and shaken to the marrow of his being, and he could not find the right things to say to mollify Carol. She continued to cry as he spoke. "You have to try and pull yourself together. You have to listen to me. If the police speak to you, you have to play dumb. You can say that I did stay at your house, but

you can't say that you saw those Sony recorder cases. You have
to protect yourself. You have to plead innocent to everything, as
if you never knew anything."

"But I know you," Carol sobbed. "And I love you so much."

"I love you, too, Carol, but love won't help," Shunya sighed,
turning away from a prowling police car.

41

Shunya remained in the phone booth for ten minutes, pretending to make calls, until a taxi stopped at the corner in front of him. He entered the taxi as the previous fare exited on the other side, only seconds before the ominous, unmarked Ford turned the same corner.

"Where to, mister?" the cabby asked.

Shunya said, "Philadelphia."

*   *   *

A small crowd had gathered around Roni on Louie's porch, asking her questions, when Delhi Dave walked by.

He looked at Max, then at the girls on Louie's porch and said, "It's no wonder you're so fucked up in the head, tryin' to figure out what happened to you, while you got all this pussy waitin' around ready to clear your mind."

"I beg your pardon," Laura said. She was sitting between Roni and Hong Kong Rosie.

"You see? They're beggin' for it."

Some people laughed, some didn't. Delhi Dave was about to leave when Rich Tom asked him if he had heard from Shunya.

"No, but me an' Fast Freddy's been pretty tight for a long time, so you got no reason to worry. Meanwhile, you know I'm getting a piece this time for connecting you guys wit' 'im."

Tom shrugged and said, "You can get a piece from Shunya's end."

"Fuck do I care which end," Delhi Dave said.

"Have you heard from Shunya?" Tom asked James.

James said, "No, but if I hear you coming onto Martine one more time, you're going to hear from me, prick."

"I keep telling you that we're friends," Tom said. "That's all, nothing more."

"But you're not my friend, because you keep taking her out to dinner, and buying her things in Mopsa that I can't afford, which is showing me up."

"But it's not my intention. Besides, no one is telling her to say yes all the time."

James turned to Max and said, "What would you do with a prick like this?"

Max shrugged and said, "Not much."

Delhi Dave said, "I'd punch 'im in the fuckin' mouth."

Without hesitation, James sprang forward and punched Rich Tom in the mouth, knocking him onto his back, out cold.

The crowd was momentarily stunned, then deeply concerned for Tom's welfare. They were hovering over him as Shiva snuck up behind Three-Finger Louie and put a gun to his head.

*   *   *

It was a long and pensive ride to Philadelphia. Shunya hardly spoke to the driver, who observed Shunya and his discomfort through the rearview mirror: constantly changing positions in his seat, looking out the back window, wiping sweat from his shaved head, often clutching his expensive leather bag.

The driver had seen it all before; given the length of the fare, he knew Shunya was in trouble.

"You didn't kill anybody, did you?" he nervously asked, crossing the George Washington Bridge.

"Myself," Shunya sighed. "Only myself."

The driver was appeased and remained quiet for much of the drive into the heart of Philadelphia. As planned, Shunya shaved his beard in a restaurant bathroom, and proceeded to the airport in another taxi, his weary eyes darting from face to face, from shadow to shadow, looking for trouble, clutching his bag until he boarded a plane to San Francisco under an assumed name without a passport, which he had left in Carol's apartment.

He bought a pair of slacks and a sport shirt in the airport, purchased a ticket to Calcutta under another assumed name, and boarded that plane without a passport, let alone a visa. His heart aching, his mind spinning as he recalled the admonishments of the old lama and the Doctor, he drank a lot of brandy in a fruitless attempt to kill the pain.

The flight, stopping in Tokyo and Bangkok, seemed endless— but not pointless. Shunya did have a lot of money on him, enough to bribe a customs official in Calcutta, and more than enough to live on for several years. He also imagined that he could purchase another passport in India, maybe even meet his ex-wife and daughter in Europe for vacation. He didn't think he would ever see Carol again, and he prayed that she would be okay.

The further away from America, the more warped his perspective. Guilt turned to rage and vindictiveness about enemies real and imagined. Although Fast Freddy had saved Shunya, he had planned on hurting him, despite the high recommendation from Delhi Dave. Then there was the question of Rich Tom's other "business" interests in India.

The rage and drink and guilt eventually combined to drive Shunya to the brink of a breakdown. He was sweating profusely, shaking in his seat, almost wishing that the plane would crash and put him out his misery when it took off for Calcutta. Assuming he survived the journey, Shunya needed a plan: an explanation for all his money, and for traveling without papers.

He was on his way to the bathroom to clean up, midway through the four-hour flight, when he exchanged smiles with an attractive young woman and despair forced another fateful decision upon him. She was in her mid-twenties, Shunya guessed, with short brown hair and soft, brown eyes, dressed in colorful silks and wearing a pair of blood-red coral earrings. She had boarded the plane in Bangkok and was sitting alone by the window. She was approachable, Shunya thought, and he was running out of time and options.

Returning from the bathroom, still trembling inside and clutching his bag, always clutching his bag, Shunya took the aisle seat and asked the woman if she minded.

Much to his relief, she removed her earphones and smiled and said, "I can always use another friend."

So Shunya placed the money bag in the empty seat between them and stumbled, "I'm Shunya, really. I mean . . ."

She giggled and said, "And I'm really stoned."

Shunya said, "Me too."

"I'm Grace," she said, extending her hand "Saying Grace, actually. You know, like saying grace before dinner? My full name is Saying Grace, the whole enchilada."

Shunya was surprised that the woman shared the same name as his daughter. The coincidence was encouraging, and conversation flowed effortlessly between them for more than an hour. As it turned out, this was Saying Grace's second trip to India.

"I got so sick the first time that I had to leave," she explained. "So I went back to California, to Mt. Tam in Marin County. But I kept dreaming about India, so I put a few things together, made some bucks, and here I am again."

'Things' meaning deals, Shunya surmised. After all, the only difference between her business and his was degree, and Mt. Tamalpais was a renowned location for spiritual retreats. When Grace claimed to be a deeply spiritual being, Shunya told her about his plans to build a school for esoteric studies, and a plan was hatched: Grace would take the bulk of his money through customs for a generous fee, while he worked a deal to enter India.

*   *   *

Three-Finger Louie had seen it all before: the guilt, the rage, the insanity, and he'd had a gun pointed at his head before.

Turning to look up into Shiva's eyes, Louie saw the same pain, and heard the same threats.

"I came to kill you," Shiva said, without stumbling over one syllable.

"Why me?"

"Because you are the enemy."

Cocking the trigger as Rich Tom regained consciousness, Shiva began to stutter," W-Where d-did you want it? In your head or y-y-your-your heart?"

It was a mind-numbing choice, but Louie didn't display an iota of fear. He puffed on his bidi, looked directly into Shiva's wild eyes and softly replied, "In my hands, where it'll be safe."

Shiva began to tremble; the gun began to shake.

The watching crowd was aghast, not knowing whether Shiva would fire or fold.

When Louie extended his arms, Shiva began to shake violently, convulsively. When he tried to scream, the pain stuck in his throat. It was a terrifying sight, the raging pain fighting the pent-up guilt, until Shiva burst into tears and fell forward into Louie's arms.

*   *   *

The arrangement was simple. Saying Grace would stuff more than thirty-thousand dollars into her bra and panties and the lining of her jacket. She would pass through customs and take a first-class room at the Sheraton Hotel in Calcutta. Shunya would meet her in the lobby at 6:00 p.m. to retrieve his money. Assuming he was successful, Saying Grace would get three thousand dollars for her efforts. If he wasn't, she would deliver the money to his friends in India. Accordingly, Saying Grace would be paid more money for her greater efforts.

Landing in Calcutta at sunrise, Shunya felt surprisingly good about his plan—if only because he had no other choice. "See you at six," he said, parting from an embrace on the plane.

She kissed him on the lips and said, "I can't wait."

Shunya was surprised. In the process of recruiting Grace for business, he had apparently won a little bit of her heart.

Confident, and steeled by two shots of Cognac, Shunya approached the first official in uniform he saw and said, "Take me to the man in charge."

The man being yet another Colonel Singh, Shunya had to wait an hour and a half before seeing him in his office.

"I understand that you are having a problem," the Colonel began, twirling his thick, black mustache.

"Yes," Shunya declared, upon introducing himself under another assumed name. "And I am certain that you can help me."

"We will see," the Colonel said, seemingly impressed with Shunya's appearance.

Dressed in black slacks, a blue shirt, and an expensive, white cashmere sweater, Shunya looked like a successful young business man.

The Colonel's office, though located inside a major airport terminal, reminded Shunya of a regional Indian police office. It was relatively small and poorly lit, with threadbare wooden furnishings and yellowing legal files piled high to the ceiling. The Colonel posed a striking contrast to the surroundings. He was a tall man, wearing a traditional red turban and a perfectly tailored uniform. His dark, brown eyes were sharp as a tack. He looked smart and Shunya got right to the point.

"I lost my passport," he began.

"On the plane?"

"Possibly, but I think I might have lost it in San Francisco, even before I got on the plane."

"You still have your plane ticket?"

Shunya produced his ticket and continued to talk while the Colonel examined it. "I was running late to catch the plane; I was in such a hurry."

"You also in so much of a hurry that you also forgot your luggage?" the Colonel challenged. There were no luggage claim tickets attached to Shunya's plane ticket.

Shunya was momentarily shaken; he had forgotten about the lack of luggage and began to stumble, "Well . . . I, uh, suppose you could say that. But I, uh . . . I usually travel pretty light, especially on business."

"And what is the nature of your business in my country?"

"I am planning on building a school for esoteric studies in Bodh Gaya."

"You have been in my country before?"

"Several times, and I've studied in many different places with many teachers."

"You have also attended the university in your country?"

"I played basketball for my school."

Their cat-and-mouse conversation flowed effortlessly for almost twenty minutes, each participant looking for an opening to unveil the truth. But the Colonel had a lot more patience than Shunya. Ultimately, it was Shunya's problem and Shunya's play to make. He waited until the Colonel ordered chai for both of them before inquiring into the Colonel's personal life.

"You, uh, have some children of your own at the university?" Shunya inquired.

"At the moment, I have two daughters who are in college and another that will be entering soon."

"It must be very costly."

Colonel Singh sipped his chai and sighed, "The dowry is costing more each year."

This was the opening that Shunya was waiting for. Without hesitation, Shunya reached into his bag and produced five thousand dollars.

The Colonel feigned surprise and studied the money on his desk as Shunya continued. "This is my contribution to the welfare of your children. It is my gift to you for helping me solve my problem."

A thoroughly honorable man might have refused the bribe and repatriated Shunya to the U.S. for prosecution. A greedier man might have pressed Shunya for more money, which was another reason why Shunya gave the bulk of his money to Saying

Grace. In turn, the wealthy young white sahib might have asked to see his superior and consummated a better deal with that man.

A practical man like Colonel Singh, with practical needs, took what was offered and did what was asked. Within one hour Shunya had a one month visa to enter India.

"Which should provide you with enough time to apply for a new passport at your embassy here in Calcutta," the Colonel said.

Once again, Shunya had apparently beaten the odds, having no idea how much it had really cost him.

42

Goa wasn't really evil. It was simply beautiful and totally free. Despite the lack of authority, and all the temptations, and all the drugs, the vast majority of people on Anjuna Beach fared well that winter. Max found himself, Shiva was learning to live with himself with Louie's help, and Roni had managed to survive all the men she had been with, and all the drugs she had taken.

Maya eventually showed up on the beach, but Max never saw her. Small though the community was, it remained cliquish, and Max didn't go to many parties. James eventually lost Martine to Rich Tom; though hurt, James realized that holding onto her was hardly worth the effort. And Sam and Diane continued to draw closer in spite of their differences.

As Louie said, "This is the place where children become adults, where you have perfect beauty, and perfect freedom to do what you want and to become who you want. The people who've made it this far—especially the ones who came overland—have paid their dues. They're the cream of the crop; they're most worthy of transformation, which is why this place is very special. It tests you in ways other places couldn't."

More than six weeks passed in relative harmony, until the winter scene on Anjuna Beach began to draw to a close. Some people went home, many more headed north to the Kumbh Mela in Haridwar.

Rich Tom was first to leave with Martine to Delhi, hoping he would find Shunya there. He had made several unsuccessful attempts to phone his sister from Panjim, and had become increasingly concerned for Shunya's welfare. Diane left with Laura the following week for a tour of South India. Max, Sam, James, and White Mike were among the last to leave, and as luck would have it, Max finally ran into Maya on the boat to Bombay.

It was dusk on the Arabian Sea. Nearly everyone on the boat had been watching the sunset. Max was lingering on the starboard railing when he turned and saw Maya walking toward him with Hong Kong Rosie and Doctor Doom.

He was shocked, and was trembling inside as she drew nearer—then relieved when she entered a bathroom into a bathroom. He wanted to walk away; he also thought it was wiser to confront the issue. Then he thought about his life and his journey to the East, how it had begun with so much promise, and how it had taken so much out of him.

Despite all the progress he had made, at twenty-four years of age the quest that had taken Max across half the world and into the depths of his soul was over. It had ended somewhere in the darkness of the dancer that was Maya Nightingale, he realized. She didn't really break his heart; she stole his youth, and that's what hurt so much. She was simply the last straw.

Tears were gathering in his eyes when Maya opened the bathroom door. Now Max hoped she would walk away from him, but she walked toward him.

"I'm sorry," she began, looking up into his surprised, wide eyes.

When Max looked down into her sad, green eyes, he saw a tear gather in one corner and roll down her cheek.

"Me, too," he softly replied, catching the tear on his fingertip and clearing it from her face before continuing. "I will always be sorry."

*   *   *

There was no way Shunya was going to apply for a new passport at the American Embassy in Calcutta. He rightly assumed that his name had made the watch list; he was, indeed, a wanted man in need of somebody else's identity to maintain his freedom. He needed a passport, preferably Commonwealth, which did not require a visa for India. But business came first.

More than anything, he needed the money, so he spent all day and night looking for Saying Grace in the Sheraton Hotel lobby. First thinking that she might have registered under an assumed name, then thinking she had been detained at the airport, it wasn't until the crack of dawn that he realized she had ripped off his dreams.

43

Haridwar was a holy old town created from one drop of heavenly milk, spilled in the heat of an apocalyptic Hindu mythological battle. Just south of Rishikesh and straddling the banks of the mighty Mother Ganges, it was one of four holy places in India that hosted the Kumbh Mela, the biggest party on Earth—more than fifty million people, speaking ten thousand dialects, praying to a thousand different gods and goddesses, gathering every twelve years since the dawn of man to celebrate the realization of the human soul.

The temples were filled to capacity, the bathing ghats overflowed with piety. The streets were jammed to the walls with a mind-boggling collection of humanity—from albino white to charcoal black, from sallow yellow to Indian red, from fat and filthy rich to ghastly skinny and painfully poor, from seven-foot giants to three-foot dwarfs. The Mother Ganges River, giver of Hindu life, flowed effortlessly by them all, reflecting the sun, rebirthing the faith, anointing the holy, absolving the guilty, healing the sick, seeding the infertile, promising salvation to the dying.

This incredible multitude pushing, shoving, shouting and chanting, the air filling with music, incense, body odor, waste gases, and the smoke from thousands of duni fires, and camp fires, and coal burning stoves; the speakers affixed to the temple walls blaring sacred verse and the promise of a better life in the next life as the reality of this life challenged. The Kumbh Mela was so big, so crowded, so complex, so implausible, so chaotic, so mighty and magical, that it boggled and bedazzled the already manic minds of Max and his dear friends, many of whom had arrived in Haridwar on the eve of the March new moon.

Mani and Narayan had secured a very large tent inside a big ashram beside the Ganges River, for the use of their friends. Arriving in Haridwar a week late following her tour of South India, Diane found them huddled around a huge duni fire at the back of the tent. As the new moon ascended the evening sky, she told them about her descent into darkness and perplexity.

"Everything started out really well when we left Goa, and Laura went cold turkey. No dope at all, nothing—at least that's what she said. So we headed to Cochin from Goa, and everything was absolutely gorgeous, so green and lush. There were all these beautiful lakes and rivers and canals; it was like being in the jungle. Then we get to Cochin, and it turns out to be the oldest Jewish settlement in the world outside of Israel. And they have people there with names like Schwartz and Cohen, and they have bagels and knishes to eat, and real Jewish doctors, and dentists, and lawyers, with these really overbearing Jewish mothers."

Everyone laughed and began passing a chillum. The fire burning brighter, the flames growing taller, the cinders crackled and ascended into the night as Diane continued.

"So we wound up spending three days there flirting with a couple of lame Jewish guys, getting our cavities filled, and eating bagels and knishes. Then we decide to go to the Sayadaw course. When we get to Madras, we find out there's no Sayadaw course, and that the beggars are on strike!"

Diane passed on the chillum when it came her turn. She looked up and down the Ganges River, at the hundreds of duni fires burning into the night, then up at the sky, watching the cinders merge with the glittering stars. It is a magical night; she wished she had another story to tell and continued sadly.

"The whole city was shut down. It's getting really hot, and I was thinking we should start heading north anyway, maybe stop up in the Nilgiri Mountains for a while and then come here. Then

Laura starts telling me about this huge deal that she has going with Rosie, and if we go back to Bombay, and it pays off, we can fly to Delhi and take a limo up here to Haridwar.

"So now I'm starting to think that Laura's been getting high on the sly, because she never got sick—not even one day—and she never complained, and she was a major junkie. Anyway, I decided to go back to Bombay with her because it's getting so hot, and she insists on paying for a room in the Soona Mahal Guest House, one of those fancy old brownstones in front of the bay, down the block from the Rex. And I was kind of happy with it because it was air conditioned—that is, until Rosie showed up. Turns out she was staying in the same place, upstairs with Dr. Doom no less!

"As much as I don't like him, I wound up going out to dinner with him and Rosie and Laura because it was so hot and there was nothing else to do. Then I ran into Delhi Dave as we were leaving the restaurant, and he took me aside and asked me what I was doing with these fucking people. Then he told me to watch my money and my ass because Rosie and the Doc can't be trusted, and I was thinking to myself, *I've got to get away from these people*, and so I decided I'd leave for Delhi the next day—no matter what."

Diane's story was interrupted by the arrival of two sadhus, friends of Mani and Narayan, who came by to share a chillum. While introductions were being made in Hindi and English, Diane studied her friends, her eyes moving from person to person, their faces glowing in the ever-heightening duni flames. They all looked so organic, so tribal—some with very long hair and beards, others with shaved heads and painted faces.

Narayan and Mani sat in lotus positions looking like great yogis from a storied and distant past. Even Bill Viletitski looked good in the firelight. Diane was so focused, and so wrapped up in her story that she never realized she was the only woman present.

When Mani introduced Diane to the sadhus, he said, "She is one of us."

Both pressed their palms together and bowed to the lady of the moment. Diane waited until they were seated before delivering the deadly punch line to her story. "So Laura was really upset about me leaving the restaurant, but she stayed out all night. And when she came back in the morning, she told me Dr. Doom was dead!"

The reaction around the duni fire is was an equal even mix of surprise and stoicism. Nobody liked the guy, and everybody figured he was probably better off dead. Nevertheless, curiosity persisted and all wanted to know how he died.

Diane explained. "At first it looked like an overdose. But when the police realized that Rosie had disappeared with everything he had—his money, his gold Rolex watch, his passport— they said it was murder! So I wound up staying in Bombay with Laura, who was all freaked out. Then the Chief of Police showed up and told me that Dr. Doom was poisoned, and how Rosie's done it before. He says he figures that she's killed at least four people in Bombay, but he has no actual proof of anything, because all the witnesses are dead.

"So Laura was getting more freaked out because the Chief thought that she might have been working with Rosie. He knew they were friends, and that Laura's a junkie. All of a sudden I was in the middle of this whole fucking mess, and I wanted out in a hurry—Laura, too—and we decided that we were leaving Bombay that night, no matter what the Chief thought. We waited until dark. We were both packed and ready to leave when the phone rang.

Diane drew a deep breath, and looked up at the sky again before continuing. "Laura answered it and told me that she'd be right back. She walked out of the room in her bare feet; her hair was still wet. She said she was going down to the lobby. She left all her money and her passport behind, and she never returned. So I'm completely freaked out, and I spent a week in Bombay looking for her everywhere, including the opium dens, and nobody had seen her. I finally told the Police Chief she's missing, and he can't find a trace of her!"

"What about the desk clerk? Didn't he see Laura leaving the hotel with anyone?" White Mike asked.

"He says that he didn't see anything."

All assumed that Laura was dead, and that Hong Kong Rosie was somehow responsible. But what was even more remarkable was that while so many of their friends had died, everyone simply took it in stride.

*   *   *

The following morning, Sam directed Diane to a small temple he had found, far from the maddening crowd. Enveloped by a thicket of tall trees, the vast majority of worshipers had already come and gone after the sunrise. Sam left within a few minutes to run some errands.

Diane sat on a flat rock at the bottom of the bathing ghat beside the river and meditated for an hour. Then she chanted to Lord Shiva before bathing in her clothes, her lungi tied around the back of her neck. She was immersed in the water when she recalled her attempt to drown herself in that same river in Benares upon arriving in India. She thought about Peter, who had saved her from herself, and her husband, David, who had lost his soul to drugs. Then she began to pray for Laura, hoping that she managed to meet a better fate than Dr. Doom.

After bathing, Diane returned to the steps and thought about Sam. He was a good man, probably the best man she had ever known. Finally, she thought about her miscarriage. She was tearful, watching several children playing in the shallow water, when Max arrived.

"Are you okay?" he began, stroking her hair.

"What's left of me," she sighed.

"You're starting to sound like me."

Diane wiped the tears away from her eyes and forced a smile. "I guess that's always been a problem we shared; in so many ways, we're more alike than different because we're never really happy with ourselves, because we can't seem to find ourselves without losing ourselves in the process. We're just not the sort of people who can get ahead of themselves, Max. We're lucky if we just break even in this life. And I think it's because we don't define ourselves on the basis of how much we have. We still define ourselves on the basis of how much we lose."

It was a somber and reflective moment, both watching their lives flowing by, the children playing on the steps of an adjacent ghat, the holy men chanting, the water reflecting the sky reflecting their thoughts.

Several minutes passed before Diane began again. "How did you find me here?"

"Sam told me."

Diane leaned forward and looked up into Max's dull brown eyes before continuing, "Your eyes are a little cloudy, yellow, actually. Are you feeling okay?"

Max shook his head and sighed, "Just when I'm starting to feel a little better about myself, a lot better."

"You mean you feel sick?" Diane asked.

"And tired. So tired that I can hardly stay awake. As much as I've been sleeping lately, its not enough." Max feared he had hepatitis, but he wouldn't mention the disease aloud for fear of confirming the diagnosis.

Diane understood and switched subjects. "What about Maya? Sam was telling me this morning that you ran into her."

Max looked across the river and explained. "I met her on the boat coming up from Goa, and we talked a bit. She actually said that she was sorry. Then I started to think about it, and I finally realized that she wasn't so much different from me after all. She had simply disconnected from her pain in the same way I did, because she couldn't handle it. In fact, in many ways, she was a step ahead of me when I ran into her."

"How can you say that?"

Max drew an uneven breath, and exhaled, "Easily, because she found the courage to apologize."

44

Virtually every sadhu belonged to a sect, and every sect was represented by an akhara at the Kumbh Mela, where many of the sadhus gathered around a duni fire every night to perform sacred rituals, telling magical stories that celebrated their past and present lives on many different planes and places in the universe.

As a rule, these gatherings were closed to the public; even curious men of great wealth and power were often barred from attending. Few white people, regardless of position or persuasion, had ever attended one of these sacred meetings. But Mani and Narayan were held in unusually high regard by many of these holy men; consequently, allowances were made, rules were bent, and dispensations were occasionally granted.

The disappearance of Laura continued to prey on Diane's conscience; bewilderment turned to guilt, and Diane often thought that she should have never left Bombay until she discovered the truth.

"Because not knowing if she is dead or alive is like not caring about her at all," she told Sam.

They were talking quietly inside the big tent. It was late in the evening. Diane had trouble sleeping and turned to Sam for consolation.

Sam was sympathetic, but not agreeable. "Living and not knowing why we live is the point to life," Sam said. "Some things that happen just can't be explained. It's a part of the growth process, getting older and moving on with the information we do have, and living with the chasm of not knowing. It is also the beginning of faith. You may never see Laura again and never know why, and you may learn more about yourself by accepting the truth than fighting it."

Diane said, "It's not about me, Sam, it's about Laura, because looking for her is an act of love for her no matter what it does for me. And by giving up the search so soon, it feels like giving up the love, and from what I've seen, too many people give up on each other too easily."

Sam tried to console her, but Diane was adamant; she even thought about returning to Bombay, and eventually left the tent for a breath of fresh air. Though nearing the beginning of the hot season, the evenings were still cool and refreshing. The sky was clear and the stars were shining brightly. Diane had intended to meditate, but sank to her knees instead and raised her hands to the heavens, asking God what had happened to Laura.

Mani was sitting in the grass beneath an old Banyan tree. He overheard her cry and spoke to her frustration. "I don't know the answers, but I know a couple of people who might, if you will come with me."

Diane always held Mani in high regard, and she left the tent with him to meet darker men with greater powers, hoping to assuage her discomfort. They had planned on taking a tonga across town to the akhara, but none were available, so they navigated a crushing path between the many millions of people camped out in the grass, on the sidewalks, and in the streets.

Turning a corner, their ears were filled with the music of many classical ragas competing with Hindi film scores for attention—the juxtaposition of pop culture and traditional values reflecting the changing times and adding to the cacophony.

Crossing the street, they passed a rich Brahmin discarding half eaten fruits from a pillow-laden stretcher, creating conflict among the beggars who fought one another for the ripened scraps. They saw the sighted leading the blind, the legless feeding the armless—a kindness begetting a kindness. An advantage was taken whenever possible: the enormous crowd was filled with charlatans, hustlers and thieves who rivaled the high priests, great gurus, and renowned swamis for a percentage of the take.

Diane was particularly intrigued by the dozens of naked Naga Babas weaving their way through the maddening throng, their bodies covered with holy ash.

"It's just so hard for me to imagine, having their penises broken in homage to Shiva, then spending the rest of their lives wandering aimlessly and begging for food in the name of their God," Diane said.

"Great despair begets greater sacrifice to a greater God," Mani said, before entering a small park and witnessing something especially bizarre: a man jamming an ice pick into his arms, allowing his blood to spout like a geyser in an effort to garner money from the gawking passersby.

"This is something even I have never seen," Mani added.

And yet, despite all the discord, and the magnitude of the crowd, there was an undeniable ease to the ebb and flow of events at this Kumbh Mela. Diane was thinking how lucky she was to be at the Kumbh Mela, when they finally arrived at the entrance to a very old akhara, set atop a small hill overlooking the Ganges. The crumbling walls were covered with vines and wildflowers, and the entrance was guarded by a tall Gurka warrior.

"One man, a Brahmin priest who I met in Benares, keeps an ancient old book with him. If your name is inside this book—or Laura's name—he can tell you about your past incarnations. Another man who is blind can see the future very clearly sometimes. And I think that between these two men, you can find out what has happened to your friend Laura," Mani told Diane before entering the ashram alone.

Diane waited outside, looking down at the river reflecting the firelight along the banks, then up to the heavens, until Mani returned to escort her inside the akhara.

There were many tall trees in the courtyard and several small duni fires burning near the center, encircled by dozens of naked sadhus, their faces aglow in the dancing flames, and all looking very strange and other worldly to Diane: chanting, meditating, passing a chillum and telling stories of past incarnations and astral projections—none of whom paid any interest to Diane, the only woman in the akhara, and the only white person aside from Mani.

She followed Mani to a small tent in a far corner of the ashram, her eyes darting from duni fire to duni fire, from strange face to stranger faces smeared with holy ash and painted with mythological images that confounded Diane.

Mani sensed her growing discomfort and took her by the arm as they neared the entrance to the small tent. "Be as you are and not as you think you should be, and you will belong here," he said.

She was about to question Mani when two men emerged from the small tent, one a stout, middle-aged man with a round face and beady brown eyes, wearing a dhoti and long white kurta. He was the akhara manager, and was apparently unhappy with Diane's presence. Looking down at her, he shook his head and walked away into the night, grumbling to himself.

The second man was much taller and thinner, and far more severe. He was a sadhu, the head of the sect, whose dreadlocks reached down to his knees; his bare chest was covered with holy ash and colorful paint. His wild and intent black eyes looked right through Diane, as if she weren't there.

Diane stepped forward, met his gaze and said, "What's your problem?"

The sadhu backed up, looked deeply into her eyes, then looked to Mani and said, "It is good."

The small tent was dimly lit by a small kerosene lamp that hung on a center bamboo pole. There were three men inside sitting on the bare ground. The oldest, a fat Brahmin priest, sat in a far corner, his frail right arm resting on a very old and thick book.

"It is a book of karma I told you about," Mani reiterated. "It is a list of past incarnations, and if your name—or Laura's—appears in the book, the old man can read your past lives and interpret your present and future tendencies."

Though hard for Diane to believe, she pronounced her name and Laura's name loudly and clearly. The old man, who interpreted the tonal quality of the given names, looked through the book and found no point of reference..

Turning his attention to the second, younger man, Mani continued to explain and translate to Diane. "He is a blind man who can see the future. The man sitting beside him is his translator."

The blind man was terribly thin with a scar-pocked, flat face and an oddly shaped, bald and bony head. He acted strangely, his arms flailing as he babbled in a high-pitched voice, often spitting as he spoke, the saliva dribbling out of the corners of his mouth and down his chin. His translator was dressed in white, and was not distinctive.

"This is just too weird, even for me," Diane said.

Just then, the blind man raised three fingers and spat on them, the overspray hitting Diane in her face.

"Disgusting," Diane added, wiping the spittle from her cheek. She turned to leave when the blind man began to babble again.

"He says that there was a woman inside of you, crying inside, dying to be free of birth because the soul was not ready."

"I had a miscarriage," Diane stumbled, stunned by the apparent reference to her lost child.

"He also says that the other woman, your friend, Laura was also crying to be free, but that she has lost her life beneath the water and will never rise again."

"You mean she drowned?"

"She was killed by three different people or forces, or a combination of negative people and forces. She was born to this death in the way you were born to live for another life."

"What life?"

"A hard life that you will love more than your own."

"Does that mean I'll have another child?"

"He doesn't say, but he does say that not all souls are reborn as a whole in themselves. He says that a great many souls, who are not well defined, vibrate at the same intensity; they are often joined to one another after death and are born again together and occupy one body for good and for evil."

Diane twirled her ruby earring and said, "I'm not sure I understand."

"Then you must have the faith until you are able to understand. All souls have purpose, and all purpose is divine."

Diane was about to ask another question when the blind man frantically waved his hands and began to spit, indicating that the interview was over.

Outside the tent, Diane asked Mani if he believed the blind man.

Mani said, "Yes, he speaks for God."

"How can you say that? He doesn't even look sane let alone divine."

Mani explained, "He is not entirely sane by our standards; he is a mast, a man who has realized God a long time ago, but his intellect was not refined enough or evolved enough to accommodate the experience of God on this plane. Instead of becoming wise, he became disconnected, maybe even insane from our point of view in this reality. Although his body is with us, he primarily exists on another, higher plane, and what we see and hear is not what he is seeing and hearing. He is hardly aware of himself as a functioning human being.

"The other man is his servant who serves as a link for him to this plane. They have been together for so long that many people believe that they make for one thoroughly enlightened being. Whether you know it or not, Diane, whether you believe it or not, you were just in the presence of a man who has touched the mind of God."

Diane looked up to the heavens and sighed, "I find it so hard to believe."

Mani smiled and said, "Then you must keep searching."

*   *   *

Max left the Kumbh Mela a few days later; he was so sick and tired. He had indeed contracted hepatitis and needed to convalesce. He thought about going to a hospital in Delhi, but wound up in Sonepat with the Doctor.

"Feeling no better in some ways than I was when I left here five months ago, and the sounds in my head aren't so bad. I guess I just learned to live with it," Max concluded after narrating his descent into hell in Rajasthan.

The Doctor said, "Misjudgment is not a crime, and accepting things we cannot change or understand is a sign of wisdom and maturity."

"But the embarrassment is hard to live with, losing control of myself like that. It's strange how I can hardly remember most of the things that happened to me in Rajasthan. I don't even remember being crazy, but I do have a profound sense of shame sometimes—like now, having to come here when I'm sick feels shameful, as if I failed myself somehow by getting sick on top of everything else. And just when I started to feel better about myself."

"Better or worse is not the question here, Max. The point is seeing or not seeing. You went to the edge of your ability and fell off; there can be no shame in trying. Even if it was an ill-advised effort, it was an effort nonetheless. It was an expenditure of an enormous amount of energy, and in doing so you may have inadvertently saved the life of your friend, Shiva. There can be no shame in this, in the body telling the mind that it needs to take rest."

So Max spent the next two weeks sharing a rented bungalow with fifteen other students he hardly knew. He ate well, took a handful of vitamins each day, and slept a lot. At the beginning of the third week, he began to frequent the Doctor's house and attend the evening talks. Grateful though Max was for all the support he received, he was not pleased with the direction of the teaching—which was even less challenging than he had remembered. He was also resentful of Clark, who was now in charge of a movement to incorporate the Doctor's teaching.

Max didn't know about the rising tide against young Westerners in Sonepat that had swelled into a series of violent reprisals during the winter. Two students had been assaulted in the marketplace; another knocked off a bicycle, and the Doctor's house had been pelted by rotten fruit and eggs on several occasions.

"In an effort to defend ourselves and gain legitimacy in the larger community, we are forced to organize," the Doctor explained over a cup of chai in his study one morning. "Among other things, it is the result of cohabitation in the bungalow. Five of our students are women, and rumors have been circulating in town about the practice of unsavory sex acts. In an effort to deflect this behavior, we have agreed to formalize the teaching and rent a second house for our women students."

Max understood, but he also remembered how the Doctor railed against organization. "You said that if we organize this teaching, we will kill it.'"

"I still believe that, but we are doing this to suit others, not ourselves."

"What about the teaching? Does that continue to be diluted in an effort to cater to the limitations of others?"

"We meet people where they are, Max, and not where we would like them to be. As I had said in Almora, I was learning to be a teacher in the way you were learning to be students."

"Meanwhile, I have to sit around and listen to this stuff every night?"

"No, your attendance is not required, but if you had been paying attention to the teaching in the first place, you may not have lost your mind in the process of finding yourself."

"Meaning I have to settle for second place?"

"Higher or lower is not the issue, Max. Clark has become a great help to us because of his understanding of things as they are. While he may lack your courage to face the edge of himself, he has the good sense to recognize his limitations and function accordingly. Then again, your legend precedes you. It was in your house where this teaching took root; it was your unorthodox lifestyle has won the interest of so many other students."

Which was true. Many of these new students had heard a great deal about Max and his friends, and were duly impressed with their existential lifestyles.

"So you think I should be talking to them?"

"And why not? There is no doubt that much of what I've learned has been derived from many of the mistakes I have made. There is a place here for you, Max, to learn what is necessary for yourself, and to teach others what you have learned."

Max was pleased. He was about to stand and shake the Doctor's hand when Linda, Clark's girlfriend, came in to refill their cups of chai. It was at that moment, when Max saw them exchange a warm glance, that he sensed something amiss.

"Clark knows about this?" Max challenged after she left the room.

"About what?"

"You and her," Max declared, nodding at the door.

The Doctor was momentarily stunned, then forthcoming. "He knows," the Doctor sighed.

"And your wife?"

"She also knows."

"And everyone else in the town must know, because your wife must have told them, but you were just trying to tell me that it's everyone else's fault that you're having so many problems in the community."

"Perhaps, but it's not because I intentionally misled anyone; it is because this relationship is so new, and flourished so suddenly in the midst of these all difficulties, and we're all in a process of adjusting—especially Clark."

"Who's still running around town trying to legitimize you, while you're undermining him."

"What would you have him do?"

"Punch you in the fucking mouth, if he was any kind of man I could respect."

45

The Fonseca Hotel was a renovated three-story brownstone located in a plush New Delhi suburb. Surrounded by taller trees, it was a favorite respite for high-end dope dealers, wanton celebrities, and international businessmen looking for a little walk on the wild side. It was a great place to party, but Max was still convalescing, and Shunya was too tense.

They met in Delhi following Max's return from Sonepat and Shunya's timely arrival from Bodh Gaya. Both were staying with Rich Tom, who had rented a suite of rooms in the Fonseca following his lonely arrival in Delhi. Martine had left him in Rajasthan, within a week of their exit from Goa.

"She even told me that she loved me before we left Goa," Tom agonized, wincing from the pain in his head and fighting back tears as he explained. It was early evening, and Tom was sitting between Max and Shunya on their private patio in the Fonseca.

"I believed her. I wanted to believe her, but . . . We, uh, spent a few days in Bombay eating in all the good restaurants and shopping—she loves clothes. We even stayed at the Taj Hotel. Then we took off for Udaipur, and she became withdrawn. I kept asking if there was something wrong, and she kept saying no. A week later, I went out to get papayas; when I came back and she was gone. She left me a note, telling me how much she liked me, but how we don't fit together in some ways. She said that she needed some time alone to think."

"Do you know where she went?" Shunya asked.

"Not exactly, but she did say something about taking a Sayadaw course somewhere. But I think she went to the Mela, back to your friend James," Tom said, rubbing both temples with his hands and blinking back the pain in his head.

It was hard for Max to feel sorry for the guy who had slept with his best friend's girl, but Tom had provided a much needed room for him in the suite. So Max placed an arm around Tom's sulking shoulders and patronized him, telling him that Martine had most likely taken the Sayadaw meditation course. "I didn't see her in Haridwar or in Sonepat," Max said.

Shunya followed Max's lead and added, "I don't know anyone who's seen her in Delhi, and she would have had to pass through here to get to either place."

Tom was momentarily placated, but thoroughly debilitated by a migraine when he finally retired to his room.

"Poor bastard," Max said, looking over the railing at the branches of a tree swaying in the warm breeze. "He's got everything, but nothing to make him happy."

"I suppose," Shunya said, "But my problem is not feeling bad for him—it's understanding him. Carol told me that he came to India on business. When I mentioned it to him, he told me that he came here to get away from business. Then there was all the nonsense about the rugs and my involvement with his sister during my first trip to New York. Meanwhile, he warned me about getting her involved with all this, and I feel really bad about that."

"You mean she's in trouble?"

Shunya said, "No, not from what I gather. She just got scared, and brokenhearted. I guess I loved her after all, but I can't look back. I've got to look ahead. I've got to get a passport—preferably a Commonwealth passport, this way I won't have to deal with the visa thing anymore—and I've got to get out of Delhi. What about you?"

Max drew a deep breath and sighed. "I've got to get well, and I won't go back to the Doctor's place."

"I understand your reluctance, but we all make mistakes, Max," Shunya replied, attempting to equate his criminal mischief with the Doctor's moral indiscretion. "The Doctor never said he was perfect. He said that he was still on the path toward self-realization, and he found a tool—silent mind. He never claimed to be celibate, and he never recommended it to others, as I recall."

"In other words, it's okay with you that he takes some other guy's girlfriend, even if the guy is a dumb prick? Then he hides his little faux pas behind the guise of other Western women on the scene, who are supposedly provoking all this reactive behavior in the town. Meanwhile, he's mostly responsible, because apart from being a spiritual teacher, he's a medical doctor with a high community profile, and now he's in the process of incorporating the whole damn thing to lend it credibility—using Clark as his front man, no less."

"I have to admit, it sounds a bit dicey, but you can't fault the Doctor if Clark's an idiot."

"But I expected so much more from the Doctor. Even if he didn't say he was enlightened, he implied it. He implied living by a high moral standard, and by doing so, he filled us with high expectations."

"He also said that expectation is the seed of disillusionment."

"So he sets us up for the fall. When we take the plunge, he calls it the practice of wisdom, and we're supposed to buy into it."

"Obviously you're not buying it, Max, or else you wouldn't have left the scene. And the only thing I'm buying is a passport—tomorrow if I can."

*   *   *

The following morning Shunya headed to Connaught Circus, his heart still breaking, his mind filling with guilt, still punishing himself for placing Carol in jeopardy, and for running out on his daughter, knowing he would never see his money or Saying Grace again.

Leaving the taxi in a surly mood, he descended a long staircase to a small but crowded indoor bazaar, filled with wares and foodstuffs that fronted for trade on the black market. He'd heard about a fat Sikh who was selling a New Zealand passport for a thousand dollars, which was more than twice the going rate, but Shunya was desperate.

He spent an hour weaving between stalls and wares and merchants looking for the fat man; the more people he spoke to, the more frustrated and paranoid he became. He was on his way out of the mall, thinking he had already over-exposed himself, when he locked eyes with a bald-headed Jesus freak, who assailed him with the promise of salvation.

"Fuck are you talking about? You look half dead already!" Shunya barked.

"Halfway to s-salvation," the Jesus freak stuttered, shoving a copy of *The Watchtower* in Shunya's face.

Shunya was incensed. He smacked the paper aside, thinking this guy was a harmless idiot, when Delhi Dave came to his rescue. Fortunately for Shunya, Delhi Dave had recognized him in the crowd and realized the danger.

"Everything okay here?" Delhi Dave began, placing a protective hand on Shunya's shoulder.

The freak stuttered, "He-he-he . . ."

"He's very sorry," Delhi Dave replied, taking Shunya by the arm and leading him out of the bazaar to safety.

"Fuck was that all about?" Shunya challenged.

"Shiva!" Delhi Dave exclaimed.

Shunya remembered what he had heard about Shiva from Max and shuddered. "He's a killer, isn't he?" Shunya said, as they stood in the shade of a concrete overhang. It was already nearing a hundred degrees at nine o'clock in the morning.

"He's a fuckin' lunatic, tellin' people that he's found redemption in Christ 'n shit after he left Goa, but I been seeing 'im around Delhi a lot lately, an' I don't see Christ in his eyes. Fuckin' believe it, he scares me, too. Meanwhile I gotta apologize for Fast

Freddy settin' you up like that. He must've been facin' some really hard time to do somethin' like that, but at least he did the right thing when he had the chance."

Shunya could hardly argue the point, which he had already written off to bad karma. "I guess I must've been paying off some past debt; I just didn't see it coming even though I did have forewarning. I didn't want to see it, and now I'm just trying to understand it before I go blind to my entire life and lose everything for no reason I can understand."

Delhi Dave said, "You're startin' to sound like Max, who had the balls to lose his mind to begin wit' an' the strength it took to recover it. Problem is that he might be in the process of losing his mind all over again—goin' back to that Doctor guy an' shit. I heard all about it already, an' I seen it a million fuckin' times, all those spineless fuckin' wimps who come here lookin' for a God who ain't lookin' for them, an' they wind up losing themselves in some wimp-shit guru's life an' take no responsibility for their own lives 'cause they ain't worthy of the God they're lookin' for.

"It ain't like they're like this fuckin' whacko Shiva guy who's comin' off the real battlefield of life, who's suffered somethin' more than his own neurotic self-indulgence, who's committed some real crazy criminal shit an' needs to be redeemed for real, or die tryin' in the process, the way he risked his life in the war. Crazy as this fucker is, in my mind, he's at least worthy of God. I mean most've these kids ain't got that much to give up to begin wit' apart from some cushy bullshit life in America. So what kind of stupid fuckin' guru are they goin' to find anyway? What kinda God?

"But you got more brains and balls than that because you're willin' to take greater risks, an' you deserve better than you're givin' yourself credit for. So maybe if you stop lookin' for yourself in all the wrong places, you won't go blind to yourself. An' don't ever forget that Christ took two-a-those wretched fuckin' scum thieves up to heaven wit 'im, an' those two fuckin' guys weren't lookin' for nothin' but a few dollars extra an' maybe a little pussy on the side."

Shunya had to smile. Despite its rather unique criminal twist, he was nonetheless impressed and elevated by Delhi Dave's analysis of becoming. In fact, it was the first time Shunya felt good about himself in months. "But I am running out of time and places to go, and I'm not sure I can ever go home again."

"Bullshit!" Delhi Dave declared. "Home ain't no place. It's a perception of bein' true to yourself no matter how fucked up you are. I seen that in jail. It's what you want, what you dream about, that takes you away from home, which don't mean you shouldn't dream. It means you shouldn't confuse what you get wit' what you want."

"Right now I want a passport," Shunya said.

"You'll get that. I can see to that. I'll find that fat fuckin' Sikh. I mean I owe you for settin' you up wit' Fast Freddy. It's the least I can do. But you still gotta have a place to go."

"I'm thinkin' Dharamsala."

"An' I'm thinkin' you're insane . . . . fuckin' Dharamsala? In the mountains where the Dalai Lama lives, wit' two hundred cops watchin' his holy ass while you're runnin' around on someone else's papers? Fuck that an' go to Kashmir where everyone's on the take. Meanwhile you can get back into business wit' my man Mohammed up in Phalgam. I told you about 'im, an' you can be livin' in the middle of fuckin' nowhere in the most beautiful place in the world wit' him an' the other Mohammeds watchin' your ass until things mellow out down here. Meanwhile, I'm goin' to see this Kalib guy in the Khyber Pass an'. . . "

Shunya raised his hand and stopped Delhi Dave in mid-sentence. "The less I know, the less they can find out if and when the squeeze comes."

*   *   *

It took the entire day for the two of them to locate the fat Sikh, who asked fourteen hundred dollars for the much-coveted New Zealand passport, the picture bearing a striking resemblance to Shunya: crew cut brown hair, scraggly beard, same color eyes, and similar facial structure. At a glance, Shunya could easily pass for the owner the passport, Neil Benjamin Cottles, in this chaotic third-world country. So he wound up paying eleven hundred dollars after spending another two hours haggling over the price; he had also decided to go to Kashmir.

Returning to the Fonseca by sunset, Shunya had just emerged from a much anticipated shower when Sam and Diane walked into the room, having returned from the Kumbh Mela the day before, after finding messages for them at Amex. After an exchange of warm greetings and a couple of beers, Shunya and Sam retired to the patio; Max and Diane remained in the air-conditioned living room; Tom returned to his room.

"You look so much better," Diane told Max, caressing his face. They were sitting opposite each another on the carpeted floor.

"But I still need a lot of rest; I get tired so easily. But you look great!"

Her blue eyes sparkling, her shiny, chestnut hair reaching down to her shoulders, Diane was altogether radiant. "Because I think I'm going to have another baby." Max listened carefully as Diane went on to characterize her experience with Mani and the Mast in Haridwar. "I just think it's a matter of time and I feel really good about it. Meanwhile, I finally heard from Jane. It turns out she became pregnant in Bincer and went back to America with Gary, which I think was a good idea. So Sam and I decided to see as much of India as possible before we leave the country, assuming I become pregnant. I don't think I want to risk having a baby here. We're leaving for Kashmir tomorrow."

Max was genuinely happy for her, if not a little envious. *It could have been my baby*, he thought.

Diane read the sadness in his eyes and ran her fingers through his hair; she felt so sorry for him. As much as he had progressed with himself, Max still had such a long way to go. "What about you? Where're you going to spend the summer?"

"I don't know yet. I just want to get better and feel better about myself. In the meantime, I guess I'll just tag along with Shunya, who's also talking about going to Kashmir."

"Then maybe we'll all go together," Diane said, before telling him that Martine had shown up at the Kumbh Mela looking for James. "But he wasn't having anything to do with her. He went back to the Doctor's house looking for you; he thinks you're still in Sonepat."

While Max went on to profile his experience with the Doctor, Sam and Shunya found a great deal of trouble.

"It has been awhile since we sat like this, my dear old friend" Shunya sighed, sitting beside him, both looking over the railing as they spoke.

Sam lit a bidi and exhaled, "And nothing's changed, after all the energy you expended, after all the places you've been."

"You mean I'm still at the beginning, right?"

"There's no place like home."

Shunya was stunned by Sam's choice of words. "What made you say that?"

Sam was about to reply when he looked through the branches of a tall tree at a smaller hotel across the street.

"Something bad," Sam said. "But don't turn around."

Had Shunya looked, he would have seen two men standing in front of an open window, watching them through binoculars.

46

Two days later, Shunya and his friends left for Kashmir. Sam and Diane left early in the morning, taking most of their luggage with them, and buying all of their plane tickets at the airport. Shunya and Max followed several hours later, taking a taxi to Connaught Circus, carrying nothing with them, acting as if they were going shopping, then changing taxis twice until they arrived at the airport. Rich Tom stayed behind, telling them he had a headache, and promising to join them within a week with the remainder of their baggage.

The four arrived in Srinagar late in the afternoon, rented rooms for the night on a boat on Dahl Lake, then took a bus to Phalgam early the next morning; they arrived before sunset, convinced they had outwitted prying eyes, and dumbstruck by the sheer beauty of the place.

Shunya awoke at dawn the following morning. The mountains towering above him, the rising sun turned the snow caps to gold as he followed a map drawn by Delhi Dave to Mohammed's house, first walking through a dewy meadow, then crossing a small bridge over fast moving stream until he arrived at the edge of a thick forest—so dense that the foliage blocked out the sun.

Shunya was thinking that it would be a great place to hide when he emerged into a clearing and arrived at the house, a two-story white-washed bungalow, badly in need of another paint job and a new roof.

Shunya expected something better from Delhi Dave's business partner. After all, Mohammed's uncle was a high-ranking magistrate in Srinagar. He began to think that he had made a mistake coming to Phalgam when Mohammed appeared at the door, holding a pair of powerful binoculars.

"You are Shunya, yes?" Mohammed asked, looking over Shunya's shoulders.

Shunya smiled and sighed, "I was."

Mohammed's smile revealed a mouthful of crooked teeth. He was tall and thin, about thirty-five years old, with sunken black eyes, short black hair and a warm smile.

Shunya entered the house thinking the guy couldn't afford a dentist, and was struck by the high quality décor: floors covered with expensive Persian rugs; heavy chairs and tables made of mahogany. The contrast between the interior and exterior of the house served as an apt metaphor for life in Phalgam: nothing and no one were as they appeared.

"I have been waiting so long to meet you," Mohammed said, guiding him into the living room.

Shunya was surprised to find an entire wall unit dedicated to hi-tech electronics, from powerful radio transmitters and receivers to radar scanners and one very expensive stereo.

"I love American jazz, especially this Gershwin fellow," Mohammed said, reaching for a vinyl album. "Please sit," he added, gesturing toward a magnificent, teakwood coffee table at the center of the room.

Shunya sat cross-legged in front of the table as *Rhapsody in Blue* emanated from two tall Bose speakers. Mohammed sat opposite him. Shunya was about to pose a question when a young boy entered the room with an ornate silver tray bearing one steaming coffee pot, two Chinese porcelain coffee cups and an assortment of pastries and bagels.

"You will please enjoy something," Mohammed said.

"Looks like you were expecting me," Shunya noted.

"But of course," Mohammed said, widening his smile. "I received a telegram from Dave, and I had the boy watching for your arrival in town. He is Yoseph, the son of a second cousin.

Yoseph smiled and bowed out of the room. He was about ten years old, Shunya guessed, with dull, brown eyes, a shock of brown hair and freckles.

"So, now you can tell me what the problem is from your perspective," Mohammed said.

"No money and too many prying eyes. I think we were being watched in Delhi."

"This is not Delhi. My eyes are what counts in this town. You have papers?"

"We got them in Delhi," Shunya said, showing him his New Zealand passport.

"A very good likeness," Mohammed said, handing the passport back to Shunya. "I cannot see a problem for you here, though I am surprised you came with so many friends."

"They can leave if necessary."

"No, no. I said I was surprised. I am not unhappy."

"They're all friends of Dave."

Mohammed smiled. "This too makes me very happy, because as we speak I have an idea to place you all in a house that is very special, and not very far from here."

Shunya was pleased. He was also impressed with Mohammed's command of the English language.

"I attended university in London for three years," Mohammed explained. "It was a special program sponsored by the Delhi government for nefarious reasons, I believe, thinking if some of us Kashmiris are educated in the West, we will somehow become more sympathetic to colonialism and imperialism, and that we will be easier to reason with."

Shunya looked directly into Mohammed's bright, brown eyes before segueing to the point of their meeting. "For the right price, of course."

"A very reasonable price where you are concerned, I can assure you. But in the meantime I must caution you to never forget that you are living in a very small, occupied country that is bordering five other countries—Russia, China, India, Pakistan and Afghanistan—who are not as friendly to us as they pretend. While all have expressed sympathy to our cause for freedom from India, they are inclined to use it to suit their own ever-changing political agendas. This town has many ears, Shunya, that are attached to many people who are not as they seem."

"Including me," Shunya said.

"That may be, but your papers are in order, and I am in control—and there is no reason to foresee a problem. In fact, I am looking forward to a very wonderful summer together. But you will have to remain in your hotel until I can negotiate a house for you and your friends."

*   *   *

It was a small hotel perched on a cliff, the back windows overlooking the Lidder River two hundred feet below. The fast and cold mountain water ricocheted off the canyon walls creating wonderful white noise, making it easy to sleep.

The days passed slowly. There wasn't much to do in Phalgram. The daylight was shortened by the tall mountains overshadowing the town, and the weather was quite changeable: warm when the sun came out, cool and rainy when the clouds rolled in.

The fifth morning in Phalgam was particularly cold and dreary. Sam and Diane missed breakfast with the boys and decided to remain in bed; it was so warm and cuddly under the covers. They were talking about mutual friends when Diane finally broached the subject of having another child.

"If it wants to be born, it will be born," Sam said.

Diane said, "That's hardly positive."

"It's reality, being in this moment."

"And never planning for the next?"

"This summer in Kashmir, the next winter in Goa. What other plan do we need?"

"I thought we agreed that it would be better if we had the child in America."

"I don't disagree, if we're having a child."

"You mean you're not sure you want a child?"

"I mean that I'll take what comes."

"That's not very positive, or even romantic for that matter. In fact, I don't think you want me to have a child."

"Right now I just want to have fun," Sam said, kissing her neck and stroking her thigh.

"Then go fuck yourself," Diane snapped before leaving the bed.

Sam reached for a bidi on the night table as Diane reached for her clothes. She left the room several minutes later, and ran down the hallway past Max and Shunya without saying a word.

"What the hell was that?" Max asked.

Shunya said, "Love, I guess."

Diane was so angry that she hardly noticed the sun peeking through the clouds as she crossed the meadow. She really wanted a baby, and she was convinced that Sam didn't; it was that simple and that infuriating—especially when she thought about the baby they had lost. She crossed the small wooden bridge and began to follow one of two paths, one leading to Mohammed's house, the other, which she took, leading to another bigger house further upstream.

The clouds breaking, the sun shining brightly, Diane was stunned by the beauty of the two-story log cabin, which reminded her of a sky lodge in Vermont. She peeked through several ground floor windows, saw the wicker furniture but no evidence of personal belongings; the house was apparently empty. On a lark, she lay down in a hammock strung between the porch and a thin tree and recalled her conversation with Sam, now thinking that she might have over-reacted.

The sun felt so good on her face that she drifted asleep. She awoke twenty minutes later when a cloud passed in front of the sun, and decided to return to the hotel to apologize to Sam. Retracing her steps, she followed the path along the stream until she tripped over a wet rock and ran into Steven, a total stranger.

"Slippery, isn't it?" he began, helping her to her feet.

"No more than some people I know," Diane cracked.

Diane looked up into his bright blue eyes and realized how handsome he was. Tall and thin with short blond hair, together with his blue jeans and flannel shirt, he looked like he had stepped out of an L.L. Bean catalogue. Though hardly her type, Diane appreciated his attention.

"I came here to do a little hiking and climbing with some buddies of mine from Afghanistan," he explained.

"Afghanistan?" she repeated, looking down at his lizard skin cowboy boots. Diane was surprised. Steven looked and talked as if he had only recently arrived in the strange and mysterious East; he was also the first Westerner she had seen in Phalgam.

"Geological survey," he explained. "And yourself?"

"Myself, I survey myself. I meditate and I observe, and try to assimilate my observations."

"And you find that profitable?" Steven said, widening his smile.

"My boyfriend says it's an investment in our future."

The smile faded and stymied Steven's advance. "With pleasure, I hope. He's obviously a lucky man."

Diane smiled and said goodbye, struck by the oddness of their chance meeting.

47

It was a forty-minute walk back to the hotel. Diane was nearing the entrance when she was caught in a cloudburst. Her arms wrapped across her chest, she was trembling from the coldness of the rain when she passed Max's room. The door was open; yet another Colonel Singh, in the seemingly never-ending line of Colonel Singhs, was standing at the center of the room talking to Max, Shunya and Sam.

Diane figured it was trouble and was about to scurry out of the way when Sam saw her at the door and beckoned her inside.

"This is Diane," Sam told the Colonel.

He was a slight man, relatively short and thin, in his mid-fifties with graying hair and a very thick white mustache; it was the mustache that lent him an aura of distinction and authority. His khaki shirt and pants were perfectly pressed.

Her wet brown hair was slicked back behind her ears, and her wet, black cotton dress was clinging to the curvature of her body. "Is there a problem?" Diane began, running her fingers through her hair, thoroughly unaware of her sultry appearance.

"No, no, not at all," the Colonel said with a smile. "I am only here to do my job, to check on everyone's papers. We do not get so many foreigners here as you might think—few who are staying more than a few days."

"We told the Colonel that we have been looking to rent a house for the summer," Shunya added.

"And if you find it, it appears that you will have much to do for all these men," the Colonel said.

Diane thought the Colonel was referring to household duties, until she caught a telling gleam of perversity in Colonel Singh's eyes. The sexual inference was unmistakable and infuriating. "If you'll excuse me," she tersely replied before storming out of the room.

*   *   *

Shunya went looking for Mohammed following the Colonel's departure. "Everything seemed to go well with him—he didn't appear to find a problem with my passport—but I thought I should speak to you to make sure that his visit wasn't out of the ordinary," Shunya said, arriving at Mohammed's house between cloud bursts. They were sitting on Mohammed's front porch having coffee. Yoseph was sitting at the far end.

"No problem whatsoever," Mohammed declared. "It is true that he is doing his job, especially if you are planning to stay here for some time. And maybe he is looking to protect himself, as I am always looking to protect myself."

"From what?"

"From what I cannot see," Mohammed said, looking through his binoculars. Setting them aside, he continued, "It is a way of life here—nothing more, I can assure you."

"I still don't understand where I fit in."

"With me, and the Colonel is watching out for his interests."

"You mean that he's your enemy?"

Mohammed laughed. "He is my partner in many things, and his interest in you is purely financial, to see how he can profit from your relationship to me. He is also here to see if you are posing a threat to his profits."

"How can that be?"

Mohammed looked into Shunya's intense, blue eyes and smiled.

Shunya blinked and nodded his head. He had posed a very stupid question—as if Mohammed would betray a family confidence to a stranger—and apologized for his naiveté. "It was my stress talking, not my brain," Shunya added.

Mohammed nodded and smiled. "No matter what is said you should not worry. You will please believe me if I tell you everything is good. For two thousand everything will be better, and everything will be included."

"Rupees?"

"Dollars. We are only dealing in dollars here, and in gold."

The unexpectedly high price took Shunya by surprise and begged further inquiry. "Assuming there is a problem, I can understand the price. But no one here knows anything about my situation but you." Shunya pressed.

"For two thousand no one will want to know, and you will never have a problem. You will live in a beautiful house for six months, and you will become happy and healthy in the mountain air. You will please come with me and the boy and I will show you."

Shunya followed Mohammed and Yoseph out of the house into a light rain. Together, they walked through the evergreen forest to the log cabin that Diane liked so much.

"As I have said, all is included—the house and the boy, who will serve you as well he serves me. I am having my jeep returned from the shop in Srinagar next week, which will also be at your disposal. There is much to see here, and you will find much to do in the mountains; you will not even think about the money. In time, I am sure we will find a way to make much more money together."

After walking through the cabin, which was filled with fine wicker furniture, grand fireplaces and picture perfect windows, Shunya reconsidered. "I guess it is a pretty good price to pay to call this home."

"And you may pay me as you please, something now or everything, or nothing until you can afford it," Mohammed added.

Shunya gave him five hundred dollars on the spot and returned to the hotel, singing to himself in the rain.

*   *   *

The following day, Shunya moved into the house with his friends, and all were delighted.

"My dream house," Diane called it.

Within a week, the novelty of living together in such a big and beautiful house became routine. Each morning, at the crack of dawn, Yoseph delivered fresh curd and milk at the back door. After breakfast, each engaged in the daily chores: fetching water, stacking firewood, cleaning the house and shopping in town.

The afternoons passed slowly. Sam spent most of his time on the front porch watching the clouds go by. Shunya often sat next to him, thinking about his daughter and Carol, sometimes punishing himself, sometimes forgiving himself. He also thought about Rich Tom. He was long overdue with the remainder of their belongings.

Max spent most of his days lying in the hammock convalescing. "From the disease that never ends," he often said. No matter how much rest he got, it was never enough.

Diane spent much of her time hiking around the north end of the valley. She felt so good about herself that she was often reminded of Almora, where she first began to feel good. She also thought that Kashmir might be a healthy and auspicious place to conceive a child among dear friends. But she wouldn't tell that to Sam; she'd rather surprise him.

The evenings were also reminiscent of their lives in Almora. Preparations for dinner began at four in the afternoon: cleaning the rice and dahl, washing and slicing the vegetables and kneading the dough for chapatis. The chef duties rotated on the basis of desire and acumen. Diane was particularly good at baking casseroles. Max made a great spaghetti sauce. Sam liked to stir fry vegetables; Shunya often made the chai and the desserts.

After dinner, the four sat around the living room fireplace telling stories, playing chess or reading.

Within two weeks, Max got used to watching Diane walk into the bedroom with Sam. "Because I already saw you together in

Goa, but mostly because I know how much you love me and the knowing doesn't hurt," he told Diane.

At the end of their third week in the house, they invited Mohammed to dinner and opened a bottle of wine to celebrate their homecoming. He was quite delighted and entertaining. It was after his third glass of wine that he finally admitted that he was a spy—to no one's great surprise. He would not say whose side he was on, but everyone assumed that Mohammed worked all sides for a profit.

*   *   *

At the end of the month, the boys went into town to shop for the heavier stuff. Max was shouldering a bag of potatoes and Sam was carrying a bag of charcoal, when they met Shunya at the entrance to the small bazaar. He was supposed to meet them with a can of kerosene, but showed up holding only a letter.

"I was expecting something from Dave; I also thought that maybe I'd hear something from Tom, when I discovered a letter from Carol! Tom must've told her where I was."

"Which doesn't explain his absence," Max said.

"On the contrary. She says she's coming to India next week and staying at the Fonseca, which was why Tom is still is Delhi—waiting for her."

"You mean she's coming here?" Max asked.

"Eventually, with Tom I would imagine."

Max and Sam were dumbfounded; they found it hard to believe. Then again, they were happy for Shunya.

"Looks like it might be a great summer after all," Shunya said, smiling all the way home.

He was talking about buying a bigger bed for his room when they emerged from the forest and saw Diane entertaining a stranger on the front porch.

"This is Steven," Diane said, upon their arrival.

Steven stood to meet them and the boys introduced themselves. "I met Diane a couple of weeks ago," Steven explained, still standing after he had shaken their hands.

Max forced a friendly smile before taking his bag of potatoes into the house.

"You mean you live here?" Sam inquired.

"No, not at all. I spend most of my time in Afghanistan."

"He's a geologist. He does surveys," Diane added.

"Of what?" Shunya challenged. He wasn't comfortable with this preppy looking guy, wearing blue jeans and a wool sweater, who just happened to walk by.

Steven smiled. "The Afghani government hired my company to look for mineral deposits. I heard so much about this place I figured I'd come here on vacation and do some hiking and climbing."

"In those?" Shunya asked, looking down at his feet.

Steven looked down at his lizard skin cowboy boots and laughed. "Not today. My gear's in town, at the hotel."

"You mean you're a climber?"

"I've done my share. And yourself?"

"The best I ever did was Amarnath with ten thousand other people."

"You mean the pilgrimage. I heard about that. It sounds great."

When Shunya began to describe his August trek to Amarnath to see the iced Shiva Lingam, Sam went into the house with his bundle of groceries and found Max leaning against the kitchen wall.

"You don't look so good," Sam said. "Are you sick?"

"Sick of this fucking life," Max spat. "That fucking bastard."

"Who?"

"Steven."

"You know him?"

"From Afghanistan, in Kabul. And he ain't Steven. He's CIA."

48

"Are you sure it's the same guy you knew in Kabul?" Sam asked.

"Absolutely," Max declared. "It's been a long time, almost two years since I was in Afghanistan, but I spent three weeks in Kabul, in the Ansari Guest House, with that cocksucker Steven, who I knew as Dennis, and Dean, his partner. Those are the guys that handle that guy Carl, who was in Delhi last fall at the Palace Heights doing business with Delhi Dave and his friend Howard. But that's not the worst of it."

*   *   *

Max waited until Steven left before he returned to the porch with Sam to deliver the final crushing blow. "I stayed in Kabul with these guys, Carl and Howard, and Dean and Dennis. It's also when I met David—and Rich Tom! He was sharing a room with David when I got there; he didn't stay very long, and he looked kind of scruffy compared to everyone else, depressed really. He was growing his beard, I think. I knew he looked familiar the first time I saw him in Sonepat. I was telling James, but I just couldn't remember. His beard's so thick now, it really makes a big difference in recognizing him. But I'm almost positive it was Rich Tom, and he knew Dean and Dennis. He had to know them."

Shunya was crestfallen, thinking Tom worked for the CIA, but it made no sense: After all, Tom introduced him to his own sister, and they used his sister's address to smuggle drugs into America to make a profit from a business that Tom didn't need. Then again, Carol old Shunya that Tom went to India for business reasons. *What kind of business?* Shunya kept asking himself until Diane lent more credibility to Max's story.

"I don't think I told anyone, but I met that Steven guy before, about a month ago, when I was out walking along the river. I didn't think anything of it; I just thought it was an innocuous thing. But he said that he was here on vacation back then, which was a month ago! I was asking him about that when you all showed up."

"What'd he say?" Shunya asked.

"He said that I had a good memory; then he started coming onto me again, telling me how pretty I was."

"And you fell for that shit?" Sam challenged.

"I wasn't falling, Sam. I was flirting, trying to get more information out of him before you returned. I knew that him showing up on this porch when I was alone—a month later no less—was no coincidence."

Shunya's bewilderment turned to rage and paranoia as he tried to reason his plight. "Somehow all these people and events are connected. Someone's been after me from the beginning. I just have to figure out who and why before they can get their hands on me."

"First thing you have to do is to get the fuck out of here in a hurry," Max said. "Then you can worry about all the causes and effects."

Shunya agreed, but it was too late in the day to leave Phalgam. At the very least, he had to spend the night in the house; he also felt that he had to talk to Mohammed. He went into the house to get an umbrella; Colonel Singh emerged from the woods moments later, heightening the drama.

"I am here passing by only to say hello," the Colonel began, twirling his thick, white mustache, flashing a dubious smile.

Nobody believed him.

"Perhaps you will have a cup of chai with us," Diane said, acting as cool and relaxed as possible.

"Please," Max added, following her lead.

"No. No. I am fine as I am. But I am wondering where your other friend is."

"You mean Neil!" Sam exclaimed, loudly enough for Shunya to hear, he hoped. "I think he went to get water."

"Perhaps, if you are saying so, but it is not Neil Cottles I am wondering about; it is William Rennet. Where is William Rennet?"

Max looked at Sam and Diane, shrugged and asked, "You know anyone by that name?"

Sam said, "Never heard of him."

Diane asked, "Who's he supposed to be?"

"Neil Cottles," Colonel Singh declared. "Neil Cottles, William Rennet, the same person."

"That's news to me," Max said.

"You have known him long?" the Colonel asked.

"Who?"

"Neil Cottles."

Max shrugged again, looked at his friends and said, "About a year I guess, maybe more."

"Since you are living in Almora?" Colonel Singh pressed.

"What's Almora got to do with any if this?" Max asked, fighting to maintain his composure.

"You will see. You will all see," Colonel Singh said, before turning back into the woods.

*   *   *

Shunya overheard everything from inside the house and was completely devastated. "I'm not sure I could leave here if I wanted to," he agonized, sitting back in a wicker chair in front of the living room fireplace, rubbing his temples.

"What about me?" Max asked, sitting opposite Shunya. "How would he know about Almora? Why would he even want to know where I was last year?"

"And if he knows about you, he has to know that we were there," Sam said.

"But we never did anything wrong," Diane said.

"This isn't about right or wrong," Shunya said. "It's about bad karma, and how we're all connected to it by one event, or one person, and the only one I can think of that is connected to everyone involved in some way is Delhi Dave."

"Can't be," Max said.

Sam agreed. "There's no way he's giving you up."

"I can't imagine, but I have to. And I have to speak to Mohammed before we do anything."

"You think that he gave you up?" Diane asked.

"The only way to know is to ask," Shunya said. He was about to grab an umbrella and head over to Mohammed's house when Yoseph entered the back door with a written note from Mohammed to Shunya. It read: *You and Max will please come to my house with the boy after dark. Follow him through the woods without lights. He will know the way. And please do not worry so much.*

Max was surprised and shaken by his inclusion in the invitation. "Fuck do they want from me?" he asked Yoseph.

Yoseph shrugged and said nothing; he sat on the porch until dark while Shunya and his friends worried themselves sick, trying to reason their plight for the umpteenth time: It was Tom; it was Delhi Dave; it was Mohammed; it was all them; it was two of them; it was none of them; it was bad luck. They were driving each other insane with conspiracy theories, until the day crept into night, and they became afraid of the dark. They heard noises outside the house, familiar sounds in the wild that took on whole new meanings in their shaken minds.

While Shunya paced, Max and Diane trembled. Sam was the only one who appeared to maintain his equilibrium. When no one was looking, he had reached for a piece of opium, hidden in his bag, and ate it, as he often did in an effort to save face and steady his nerves.

"He's been eating opium since Goa," Diane told Max over a cup of chai in the kitchen. Sam was sitting in the living room. "I found it in his bag one day when I was looking for jewelry. James was there, and I made light of it. In fact, I never told anyone, but I found more of it in his things from time to time. When I finally asked him about it, he insisted that it was because he had a chronically bad stomach."

"And you believed him?"

"I wanted to believe him."

"And now?"

"I believe what I see. Getting high is getting high—every junkie has a reason."

Max was saddened, but not shocked. "You know I love the guy. He's been a great friend to me when I needed him most, but I always thought his equanimity was a façade, wisdom under the guise of not feeling much of anything very deeply."

Diane was roiling in disillusionment when Yoseph finally appeared at the door and said that it was time to go. Shunya and Max hugged their friends, grabbed two umbrellas and followed Yoseph into the night.

It was a short but harrowing walk through the woods to Mohammed's house, so dark that Max and Shunya held hands as they followed Yoseph. Both were surprised to find several cars parked in front of the house, and a Miles Davis tune playing on Mohammed's stereo.

"Sounds like a party to me," Max said, hearing laughter emanating from the house.

"Or the beginning of a wake," Shunya surmised.

Once inside the house, they followed Yoseph into the living room and found Mohammed pouring a drink for Colonel Singh. Steven was sitting on the Persian rug, holding a bottle of beer.

"You never mentioned your problem in Almora," Mohammed began, pointing at Max.

"Smuggling is one thing, killing is another," Colonel Singh noted.

"Which is something the American government will not condone," Steven added.

"You can't believe that! None of you can believe that I killed Peter. I hardly knew him or his wife. I just tried to help because no one else would."

"Maybe yes, maybe no, but we have no proof one way or another," Colonel Singh said. "So the case remains open, and you remain suspect."

"You mean this is all about me?" Max asked incredulously.

Steven said, "No, you're not worth that much."

"As if you're worth more than two shits, Steven—assuming that's you're real name."

"As if you might lose your delicate little mind again trying to figure any of this out my old friend, Max."

"Bastard," Max shot back, stunned by the amount of information they had on him.

"Please, please, let us all try and be civil," Mohammed said, crossing the room and gesturing for Max and Shunya to sit on the carpet opposite Steven. "There is no need for animosity here. We have a problem, and we are here to find a profitable solution."

"We have Max Rild, who is a suspect in a murder," Colonel Singh reiterated. "And we have William Rennet, who is wanted for drug dealing in America, and who is traveling under a false identity."

Shunya nodded and sighed, "I still don't know how you figured the passport thing out."

"The walls, they have ears, even in the black market in Delhi, where life is cheap," Colonel Singh explained.

Shunya was momentarily relieved upon realizing that Delhi Dave hadn't betrayed him; it was the fat Sikh after all. "What about Tom?"

Mohammed and the Colonel looked at Steven who said, "Tom is not the issue here, and neither is your friend Max, who does not suit our purpose."

"Which is?"

"You going to work for me on behalf of your country."

"Doing what?"

"Whatever it takes."

"For the right price," Colonel Singh added. "You will pay me one hundred thousand."

"Dollars!?" Shunya exclaimed.

The Colonel smiled and twisted his thick, white mustache. "If you like, but I will accept rupees, ek lak!"

Shunya looked at Mohammed, who nodded.

"That's about ten thousand dollars give or take," Shunya said.

"Then you will give and I will take, because that is the price of freedom. There is the one murder in Almora, and someone must pay me to answer for it, and I am finding out there was a second death in Nepal, in Kathmandu."

"You mean at *The Eclipse*, in my place? That wasn't murder."

"Perhaps not, but if you are owning the place, you are owning the death no matter what you will call it. That is also why I am having so much trouble believing you, because such things seem to follow you—bad things—and you have to pay. It is karma, no more and no less."

Shunya looked at Max, then down at the carpet, filled with contempt for this man and hatred for his own life. "And I came here to find God."

"The wrong God, it would seem," Colonel Singh surmised.

Shunya looked at Mohammed again, pleading with his tearful eyes for help.

"There is nothing more I can do here," Mohammed said.

In fact, Shunya would have been arrested if it weren't for Mohammed, who had worked out a deal with Steven and Colonel Singh before Shunya arrived.

"You will pay me from the money you will make working for your government," Colonel Singh said.

Ratting on people, Shunya thought. He felt so sick that he wanted to vomit.

*   *   *

It was a rotten deal, but Shunya was forced to accept it: work for Steven so he could pay off Colonel Singh in an effort to secure his freedom and the safety of his friends. In the meantime, four of Colonel Singh's heavily armed men followed Shunya through the woods, every sullen step of the way, breaking another piece of Shunya's heart. It hurt so much he wanted to scream and run out of the woods, out of his mind, and out of his body into another life.

Back in the house, Shunya spent the remainder of the night sitting around the fireplace with his friends, lamenting his choices and cursing his fate. "I really didn't want that much for myself. I never did. No matter how much money I made, I intended to share it with others. I didn't deserve this; none of you deserved this."

No one discussed the morality of the drug business, because no one had a problem with it. The problem was with the power structure that Shunya failed to deceive.

"I can't believe they beat me," he reiterated throughout the night. "I always thought I was better than that, better than them."

In the end, they all shared Shunya's sentiment.

Max said, "I can't believe they didn't even think enough of me to threaten me with punishment—even if it was for a crime I didn't commit. And I tried so hard to do my best to do the right thing, but my best wasn't good enough."

"As if my efforts were?" Diane rhetorically asked. After all, she had traded in a junkie husband for a junkie boyfriend and lost a child along the way.

Sam said little, and spent much of the night nodding out in his chair.

At the first light of dawn, when the world trembled in the balance of the dark and the light, Shunya arrived at a noble decision: he would not accept the deal, and he would go to prison in Kashmir. "Because I've hurt too many people already, beginning with my daughter, who I may never see again, and because I won't hurt anyone else by working for them. I guess I can live with being fool, but I can't live with the idea of becoming a rat."

His friends were saddened, but not surprised; and although they knew that Shunya's refusal to accept the deal could have an adverse affect on all of them, they still supported his decision. Max could be arrested on suspicion of murder; Sam and Diane could be arrested for aiding and abetting two fugitives. At the very least, they would all be beaten, and Diane would most likely be raped.

Colonel Singh was already counting his money when he arrived at the front door at sunrise with eight heavily armed men, and was enraged by Shunya's decision.

"No deal, no compassion," he spat before turning away and barking orders to his men.

While they surrounded the house, Max and his friends sat around the fireplace holding hands, fearing the worst.

When Colonel Singh ordered his men forward, the whole damned thing, and all their dreams, went up in smoke.

Reunion

Diane was working in her vintage clothing store on Canal Street when the first plane hit the World Trade Center. She lived in Brooklyn, where she raised her daughter, Anjuna. Despite all her reservations, she married Sam and had his child.

Shunya's plane had just landed at LaGuardia when the second plane crashed into the South Tower. He'd been living in San Rafael for twenty years, and drove a limousine in San Francisco to support his family. He married Carol following his return to America and had a son, Govinda. His daughter, Grace, lived in Manhattan.

Max was still at home in Denver, packing for his trip to New York, when he got the horrific news. Max had no children. He had lived in five different cities since he returned from India and never married. He eventually settled in Colorado where he painted houses for a living; he had also written several novels in his spare time.

All were shaken and a pall was cast over their long awaited reunion in Manhattan. The three had spoken on the phone throughout the years, but they had not seen each other in more than twenty-five years—since they returned from India.

*   *   *

Diane was pondering the odd timing of their reunion as she climbed out of the subway at Chambers Street and walked down Broadway toward Fulton. It was a clear and crisp October evening, the waxing moon ascending the night sky, shedding light on the darker impulses of the city. More than three weeks had passed since the collapse of the Twin Towers, and the city was slowly returning to normal. The traffic was brisk, creating an odd melody in the minds of the many people who thrived on the urban beat. It was hard to believe that so many had died; the stench that emanated from Ground Zero was a grim reminder.

As she neared the tragic site, Diane began to think that this might not be the best place to reunite with old friends. She was about to cover her nose with a tissue when she was taken by a grander instinct. Diane wouldn't give in to the terror, no matter how bad it smelled. He would rather vomit than submit, and tossed the tissue into a trash bin.

Shunya was likewise inclined to cover his nose as he neared Ground Zero, and was also moved by a greater design on life. In a wanton act of defiance, he drew a deep breath and inhaled the tragedy. Shunya had no fear of pain or death. He remained irrepressible in spite of his ailments, which included a bad heart and a seizure disorder.

Max was too wrapped up in himself to make a fine gesture. He had taken two Xanax before he found the courage to step on a plane to New York, and another pill before he boarded a train to the city. He held a handkerchief over his nose as he passed the store windows and brick walls covered with hundreds of wilting photos of lives lost.

Turning a corner at Ground Zero, he found Shunya and Diane locked in a friendly embrace.

"Got a cold?" Shunya cracked, referring to the handkerchief.

"I got life, and I guess I should be happy for that much," Max said, discarding the handkerchief as he looked over the pile of devastation.

It was an eerie sight: the smoke rising from the massive wreckage of lives and steel and concrete, the night turned incandescent white by the power of huge array of spotlights trained on the heartbreak and the dirty business at hand. .

"I guess I've seen enough," Diane finally said, her eyes filling with tears as she parted from an embrace with Max.

"Too much," Shunya somberly added.

"I just can't believe the smell," Max said. "Doesn't it bother you people?"

Diane said, "I want it to bother me."

Max took two more steps before he was reminded of the spirit that joined them.

*   *   *

It was a short walk uptown to an elegant Indian restaurant on Spring Street. Their collars turned up to a stiffening autumn breeze, Diane walked between Max and Shunya and was warmed by their presence.

"It was never this cold in India," Diane said.

"Not that I can remember," Max added.

"Except in Nepal around Christmas, when I opened *The Eclipse*," Shunya said. Max and Diane had forgotten *The Eclipse*. Neither had ever seen it.

"I guess we were too busy looking at ourselves," Diane said.

"And blinding ourselves to the larger picture," Shunya added.

"Until it came crashing down on us in Kashmir," Max concluded.

The house was sprayed with bullets and tear gas. No one was wounded in the attack, but all were subsequently beaten. As feared, Diane was molested, and Shunya was jailed in Srinagar for a year—until Delhi Dave bailed him out.

It was a distant memory now, weathered by the shortfall of their lives. Diane hated the old clothing business, Max was tired of painting houses, and it pained Shunya to drive a limousine. "It's just too hard on my back," he said. He also had a ruptured disc.

Diane drew a deep, cold breath and exhaled. "Hard to believe."

Max said, "What?"

"Us."

They thought they were special. They never anticipated living ordinary lives: working simple jobs, paying mortgages, putting their kids through school.

"I couldn't even imagine mediocrity," Max said, arriving at the restaurant.

Shunya looked down at his sizable pot belly and sighed. He had been sickly for years. He wore a Yankee baseball cap to hide his thinning, gray hair.

Max looked better than Diane expected: still thin, dark and handsome, his thick, black hair graying around the temples. But Max didn't feel as good as he looked. He was lonely and frustrated with his writing.

Diane felt better than she looked. She had gained twenty pounds during the past five years, despite hauling heavy bails of old clothes into her store to make it a success.

"It just takes so much money to live," Diane said. "I can never make enough, especially now that my daughter moved back in with me while she's looking for a teaching job."

"It is hard," Shunya added. "If it's not the money, it's something else. Now it's Govinda and his obsession with war. He's been stationed at Virginia Beach waiting for orders to move out. He can't wait to go to Afghanistan and kill people."

Govinda was a staunch patriot, a Navy aviator who flew Cobra helicopters.

"Not having children makes it hard for me to imagine, the pain and the fear of it," Max said.

"Then again, you do have a good imagination," Shunya said as they entered the restaurant. It was crowded, and the spicy aromas were reminiscent of their journey.

"Do either of you ever think about going back to India?" Diane asked, following the hostess to their table.

Shunya said, "All the time."

Max was about reply when they arrived at their table and were greeted by the children.

Dinner

Grace was thirty-six-years-old, Anjuna twenty-six; Govinda was twenty-five.

Max was stunned. He hadn't seen Anjuna and Govinda since they were babies, and Grace since she was eleven. Shunya and Diane had arranged for their children to come to the restaurant to surprise Max.

"So you're Max," Govinda began, smiling brightly. He was a good looking young man with a military crew cut and brilliant, brown eyes.

When Max stood to shake his hand, Govinda embraced him, then Anjuna. They had heard about Max their entire lives.

Grace remembered him. "You came to my house in Brooklyn. You had long, black hair, and you talked to me about my father."

"And I remember you as a little girl," Max said. Grace had grown into a beautiful woman, tall and thin with curly, brown hair.

Anjuna was petite and curvaceous by comparison, with the same large blue eyes as her mother and long, straight, blonde hair. She kissed Max on the cheek before parting from their embrace. Max couldn't stop smiling, feeling as if he were reuniting with his own long lost children.

They children sat on either side of Max, answering all of his perfunctory questions: Where were they living? What were they planning to do with their lives, and why?

"Are you sure you don't have children?" Anjuna eventually asked.

Max said, "Pretty sure, why?"

"Because you sound like a parent," Anjuna replied, smiling. "My mother asks me the same questions every day."

Govinda said, "My father asks me twice a day."

"It seems that a lot of old people have this incessant need to repeat themselves," Grace added, making everyone laugh. "As far as I know, none of you had any idea of what you were going to be doing with your lives when you were our age."

"I guess we thought we'd find God and have Him figure it out for us," Max cracked.

"And the rest of us thought we would never grow up, thinking we'd most likely die from a nuclear holocaust, so we didn't make very many plans. We didn't see much of a future," Diane said.

"As if things are any better now?" Govinda bemoaned.

"Maybe not, but just because we were shortsighted doesn't mean you have to be. You could learn from our mistakes, our own myopia, and plan for the future," Diane said.

"But we *are* making plans, and we're not so pessimistic," Anjuna emphatically replied. "We're all planning on a career: I'm going to be a teacher, Govinda is already a pilot, and Grace is working on Broadway. We *are* different than you. It's just your overbearing interest in our lives that is so annoying."

"Better to be loved too much than too little," Max concluded.

"She is beautiful though, isn't she?" Diane gushed, running her hand through Anjuna's hair.

Anjuna rolled her big, blue eyes and shot back, "You have to stop!" Turning to Max, she continued, "My mother says you're a science fiction writer; maybe you could write a book on how an overbearing mother drove her child into another dimension to escape her."

When the laughter subsided, Grace asked Max about his writing. "I'm just curious to know why you chose to write science fiction?"

"Probably because it was the most difficult thing for me to do," Max explained. "I always liked reading sci-fi, but I had no science background at all, so the writing forced me to do a lot of research—which was fun. I also thought it might pose an easier way to express some of my ideas when they're projected into the future. And you, how did you choose the stage?"

"It seems more like it chose me. I had the voice, I grew up singing around the house, and I guess that the acting was a natural extension of the singing—the desire to project myself. But it's so competitive, and I'm getting older so I took a job off-stage with a producer. I still go on casting calls from time to time, and I do get some work. I'm also thinking about going back to school for a masters degree in teaching."

"Sounds good to me," Max said. Turning to Anjuna, he continued, "Do you know what you would like to teach?"

"Maybe English Lit in a good private school, but I've also been thinking I'd like to travel first."

"To India?"

"To see my Dad, to ask him why he never wanted to see me," Anjuna sadly replied. Sam never left India.

"Alone, you mean want to go alone?" Diane asked.

Anjuna shrugged and rolled her big blue eyes. "I'm twenty-six years old, Mom, older than you were when you went to India."

"To find myself," Diane tersely replied. "As if finding your father is worth the effort? You know that he never helped; he never gave me a dime to help raise you. He never responded to the letters I wrote, when I told him that I needed some financial help. He never even wrote you."

"And you don't want to know why?" Anjuna pressed.

"As if it would change anything," Diane shot back, the subject matter filling her with so much dread.

"For me it could," Anjuna replied, her voice quavering, her eyes filling with tears.

Diane shook her head and looked to her friends for support.

Max remained silent, fearing he would say the wrong thing. He always liked Sam, but didn't respect him, and he wasn't sure if Sam would be responsive to Anjuna after all these years.

Shunya liked Sam more than Max did and was inclined to be encouraging. Turning to Anjuna, he said, "Despite all of his shortcomings, I know he loves you. I can't imagine Sam not willing to embrace his own daughter in India."

Grace locked eyes with Shunya and declared, "I can," and a long and deeply felt pain was revisited. Despite of all of her years in therapy, Grace had not forgotten the disappearance of her own father from her life when she was seven years old.

Shunya was surprised and terribly hurt. He had been under the impression that his daughter had forgiven him, and he was loath to express his disappointment—in a restaurant no less. He remained a fiercely private man and averted Grace's eyes, pretending to miss the heart-wrenching inference.

Diane saw his discomfort and abruptly changed the subject. "I still can't believe how naïve we were," she said, looking at Max. "Do you remember seeing me inside that little dessert place in Bombay after the Sayadaw course?"

Max nodded. "Dipty's. I remember some Anglo-Asian guy came in, really aggressive, asking me about you."

"He was Charles Sobhraj, as I later discovered."

"The serial killer?"

"Serpentine, the guy they wrote the book about."

"We were so close to death so many times, and it is amazing how often we didn't see it or even acknowledge it," Max said.

"Among other things, it was a state of mind," Shunya added. "A sign of the times, traveling without much money, without visas sometimes, without much fear."

"Talk about naïveté, I actually hitched a ride across Afghanistan in the middle of the night," Max said, before dinner was finally served.

*   *   *

"Your generation had it *really* good," Govinda declared after taking several bites of his food. "Apart from all the freedom you had to travel, student loans were cheap, and there were so many jobs back then."

"We also had a war," Max said.

"That you didn't fight," Govinda said.

"Because I didn't want to," Max said.

"Because you convinced the draft board that you were insane—my father told me," Govinda said.

Max shrugged and savored a spoonful of dahl before responding. "I did what I had to do, which was a lot better than dying for something I didn't believe in."

"And you're proud of that?" Govinda challenged.

"Not entirely, not in retrospect. If I had the balls back then, I might have stood up to the draft board and told them to go hell with their shit-fucking war and suffer the consequences. But I didn't realize any of this until I was in India, when heard about a kid I knew in my old neighborhood who got the Congressional Medal of Honor by jumping on a hand grenade and saving other people's lives. I never forgot it, and no matter how I look at it, an act of self sacrifice is a much higher calling than a lifetime of seeking self awareness."

Govinda smiled and said, "At least you're honest about it, which is more than I can say about most of your generation."

"Meaning what?" Shunya shot back, still roiling from the quiet pain that his daughter had exacted.

"Meaning selfishness, Dad, which has to be the best way to describe your generation. I mean even now, thirty years later, you people can't stop talking about yourselves, and searching yourselves, and remaking yourselves so you can look and act young. But you're not. And you keep complaining that you don't have enough when you've already had everything—and you keep on trying to impress us with your values, which are no longer relevant."

"What values?" Shunya challenged.

"Political values for one thing, like telling me that I have to be a Democrat when I want to be a Republican; like telling me not to join the Navy and go to war because you wouldn't go to war for this country because you don't trust the government; or how you're always telling me how much this country sucks when I think it doesn't."

"So you want to go war and die to prove me wrong?" Shunya snapped.

"Not hardly," Govinda declared. "Because my life or death in combat, if it comes to that, is not about you, Dad, it's about me, my life, my choices and my beliefs that my country needs me to defend your right to be self indulgent!"

They were talking so loudly that their voices caromed off the restaurant walls and into the kitchen, bringing two waiters back into the near-empty dining room to check on the commotion.

Diane lowered her voice and said, "I hardly think this is the time or place to argue the point of our lives."

"Because you say so?" Anjuna challenged.

Diane looked at Grace and asked, "What do you think?"

"That Anjuna and Govinda are mostly right, that your generation has a habit of exaggerating its own importance, which has the effect of diminishing our own efforts," Grace concluded.

"I never looked at it like that," Diane said, now wondering if the children were right.

"Me either," Shunya added.

"Helluva reunion this is turning out to be," Max sighed.

Govinda drew a long breath and exhaled, "It's not what I expected. I should've known better and I think I need to apologize to all of you."

"For what, Govinda? For life as you see it?" Max rhetorically asked. "As far as I'm concerned, you don't owe anyone an apology. You have every right to express your opinion—at this table especially."

"Even if it means killing people for what I believe in?"

Max had no answers, and the evening drew to a close on that solemn note: like it or not, this kid was going to war and loving it.

Second Reunion

More than four years passed until Max, Shunya and Diane met again at the same Indian restaurant in New York. They had spent a lot of time talking to one another on the phone in the interim, and Max had kept in touch with their children. He drew closest to Govinda, who called him each Christmas from Afghanistan, where he served two tours of combat duty.

"It's good to see you again, actually great to see you," Max said to Govinda, parting from a welcoming embrace.

It was a beautiful spring night in New York City, near sixty degrees with a gentle breeze rolling down Spring Street. Max met Govinda in front of the restaurant; they were the first to arrive for dinner.

Govinda said, "It's even better for me to see you."

"It was that rough?"

Govinda nodded. "Very intense, unlike anything I imagined. But it's amazing what a person can get used to—even war."

Max said, "I can't imagine." Max leaned on a parking meter; Govinda leaned on a parked car. "You look good," Max added.

"Not bad, I guess, considering." Govinda was still tall, dark and handsome, still wearing a military buzz cut.

Max was about to reply when his cell phone rang; it was Diane telling him that she and Anjuna were stuck in mid-town traffic.

You're not going back again, are you?" Max asked, closing his phone.

"I am, most likely."

"And that's okay with you?'

"If that's where my orders take me," Govinda said, looking up at the sky; Max looked over his shoulder at the passing traffic. "Have you had any luck selling your books?" Govinda asked.

Max said, "No," before asking Govinda if he was still a Republican.

Govinda said, "As if it matters. The Republicans love the wars—as long they don't have to send their own children to fight them—and the Democrats talk a lot and do little about anything that really matters. In the meantime, I found myself flying combat missions between bouts of ineptitude and wishful thinking. Overall, I think reinstituting a draft— with no exemptions—would be the best thing to test the mettle of this country. Then we could see where everyone really stands. In any event, you were right about the government, Max: it can't be trusted. I mean from what I understand, we did have bin Laden in our sights in Tora Bora and we let him go."

"And you're still willing to fight?"

"For my buddies, I am; for the ideal, and for the people who're oppressed."

Max was impressed with Govinda's dedication to service in the face of so much disillusionment. He had no doubt that this was a deep thinking young man who had begun to question the meaning of his own life.

Max exhibited a playful, little smile. "Ever think about going to India to ruminate over all of it?"

Govinda returned his smile and for the first time since they met, Max saw his brown eyes sparkle. "Thought about it and did it, four months ago—I took a ten day Sayadaw meditation course in Rajasthan."

Max was stunned. "Your father never told me."

"That's because I never told him, or anyone else. I just didn't want to answer to anyone, because I have no answers, because I'm still searching for a perspective."

"On life?"

"On war, on the reality of taking another life. The meditation was really difficult for me. I couldn't sit still at all for the first two days. I was getting ready to leave the course on the third day when one of the aides arranged a private audience for me with Sayadaw. That was the difference. I spent a half-hour with him— it seemed like two hours. It was like my mind came to rest for the first time in my life, and I could see some things clearly—like how I became a Republican, because my father was Democrat."

"That's quite the rebellion," Max cracked.

"It suited me for the past ten years or so, and it did screw with my dad pretty well, so it was effective. Anyway, the war thing really played with my mind during the meditations, which was why I had trouble sitting. Sayadaw told me something that I hardly expected to hear from him: how an act of violence may be unavoidable in some circumstances, and that it wasn't the act, but the state of mind a person is in when he is engaged in the act that was even more important."

"Which is?"

"Remorse. He told me that there can be no pride in the taking another life, and no joy taken in victory."

"Sounds a bit like the *Bhagavad-Gita*."

"Sayadaw told me to read it."

"And?"

Govinda was contemplating his answer when Shunya and Grace showed up at the restaurant; the rush of greetings overwhelmed the serious thrust of their conversation.

*   *   *

Max was astounded. The boy had grown into a very serious and complicated young man, whose quest for the meaning of life was far more pressing than Max's ever was, and far different. Govinda was a warrior. Max was a seeker, an intellectual by comparison, who could only imagine the burden on Govinda's life: to kill or be killed, to end the journey of another soul or lose his in the blood-letting process.

Concerned though he was for Govinda's welfare, he put it out of his mind when Shunya showed up with Grace.

"You still look good," Grace said, parting from their embrace.

Max ran his hands through his silver hair, looked down at his modest paunch and said, "For my age I do, I guess. But you look great."

Grace found it hard to believe. She was nearing forty; she married two years ago, and recently had a baby girl who was at home in Brooklyn with her father.

"I put on some weight and my hair is a lot shorter," she said.

"Which suits your eyes. They look even bigger and brighter than I remember," Max noted.

Shunya smiled at Max and said, "You always knew what to say to a woman."

Max shrugged and said, "Problem was that I never understood what they were saying to me."

Entering the restaurant together, they were seated at a round table in a quiet corner. Once again, the aromas brought back a rush of memories from Max and Shunya's youth in India.

"I never asked, but I always wondered if you still had those sounds in your head," Shunya said to Max.

"Never left. I just learned to live with it. Meditation helps."

Shunya nodded, "It all helps, but you would have thought from all we learned from all those teachers that we could have been even more helpful to ourselves and others. I've been thinking about that a lot lately."

Max said, "I've never stopped thinking about it. In fact, I finally began to write about it, about us: what we learned, what we gained, what we lost, who we've become."

Grace smiled. "Nice people, I think."

"Except we wanted more, and now I think that we're just leaning to live with less."

"Which is another sign of old age," Govinda cracked.

Max and Shunya exchanged knowing smiles. Turning back to Grace, Max continued, "Your Dad tells me that you're about to become a teacher."

"A music and art therapist actually. I'll be teaching kids how to use their creative ability to connect with deeper emotional issues and express them as a healing process. "

Shunya looked at both of his children and smiled. He was quite proud of them and was feeling much better about himself. Despite all the medication he was taking, his health had improved a great deal during the past few years and he had benefited from a timely inheritance. "It's hard to believe I lived long enough to see this much. Even harder to believe I was ever young with a head full of red hair."

"Not this again," Grace groaned. "Can't anyone of your generation ever grow old gracefully?"

Max said, "No, not if we can help it. Even the illusion of being young sounds good to us."

"And you still haven't married?"

"No, but I might have found a good prospect this time, a rich and pretty woman from Santa Fe, with no interest in becoming self-aware, so we don't have to compete."

Everyone laughed; they were still laughing when Diane and Anjuna arrived.

Diane had lost twelve pounds and looked great.

Anjuna didn't look very well at all: much too skinny and pallid. She was a recovering alcoholic who recently finished her second stint in rehab.

"I just got out two weeks ago," she said, when Max asked how she was doing. "And I can only say that I'm doing really well today."

Shunya raised his water glass and declared, "One day at a time!"

Everyone raised their glasses and echoed his sentiment.

"And you all need to know that it wasn't because of my dad that I got into so much trouble with myself," Anjuna declared.

Everyone looked at each other and nodded, even if they didn't agree with Anjuna's assessment. After all, she did go to India with Diane to confront Sam. They found him living in Goa, in a big house near the beach. When she asked him why he had deserted her, he admitted to being weak and afraid. When she cried, he embraced her.

"He gave me twenty thousand dollars, and told me that he would give me more if I needed it."

Which would never be enough, Diane thought, but she wisely kept her thoughts to herself. They all did, because they believed that discretion was better than honesty in this instance. Anjuna was so fragile; her brilliant blue eyes had dimmed to a flicker.

When Max reached for Diane's hand under the table, she suppressed a tear. They had spent the night together after their last reunion dinner, and it did reaffirm their friendship.

Shunya said, "I suppose we have to be grateful for whatever we get."

"You mean settling for less?" Govinda challenged.

"Sometimes, many times, it seems, as we get older."

"What about those of us who are still young?" Govinda pressed.

All looked to Shunya for the fateful answer. Now sixty, with a few strands of long and wavy white hair swept back behind his ears, his ever growing Buddha paunch pressing against the edge of the table, he looked like a wise man, like the guru he was meant to be.

"I can't tell you what's good for you, Govinda, because the times have changed and being young now is not like being young then. The parallels between looking for God in the sixties and fighting the present challenges are hard to make."

Govinda was surprised by his father's answer. "You mean you believe in the war?"

"Not in Iraq, never in Iraq. Then again, I do believe that we are locked in a deadly struggle against a terror that is real, which is magnified by the people in power in our own country who prey on our fear under the guise of patriotism. Afghanistan is a threat, because of its proximity to Pakistan and all those nuclear weapons. And our own government poses a larger threat, if only because of its proximity to great wealth and poor leadership. I have no doubt that we could win the war against terror and lose our freedom in the process."

"Then you do support the war effort in Afghanistan?"

"I mean that I support you, Govinda, as a kindred spirit who has chosen his own path through this world to the Almighty. I believe in you, I respect you, and I admire the courage of your convictions. Whether I agree or not is hardly the point anymore, because you're old enough to pick your own fights against your own enemies, and I'm old enough and grateful enough to sit back and pray for the best."

All fell silent, and dinner was served under a spell of great wisdom and understanding, generated by a father who was petrified by the prospect of losing his only son on the battlefield of life.

Conclusions

This dinner went well despite the pressing issues of Anjuna's rehab and Govinda's likely return to Afghanistan. Toward the end of evening, when the children began to talk amongst themselves, Max, Shunya and Diane exchanged information about their mutual friends.

Delhi Dave was serving fifteen years in a Florida prison on an old manslaughter charge. He was apprehended in New York within a week of his return to America. Though incarcerated, he put his time to good use. A candidate for a Ph.D. in history, his thesis was entitled, "The Criminal as Revolutionary."

Sadhu Mani had returned to Europe and assumed the role of a renaissance man: Sanskrit scholar, yoga teacher, Aryuvedic doctor.

Narayan remained in India. He became president of his own akhara and a revered guru.

White Mike had returned to Almora, eventually moving into Swami Buddhananda's cottage above Snowview and inheriting the legacy: he was a crank in training.

Three-Finger Louie never broke stride. He continued to spend his summers in Nepal and his winters in Goa, lending compassion and wisdom as needed, serving as an unwavering point of reference to the march of time and people, until he died in Goa in 2010.

James became a social worker in California, defending the honor of the needy against the arrogance of the wealthy.

Maya Nightingale married two more times and became a renowned California artist. Her admirers pointed to her bold strokes and uncanny use of color; her detractors claimed she was all form and no substance.

Big Jane had two children with Gary before becoming a professor of anthropology at the University of California. Her doctoral thesis was entitled "The Evolution of the Female in Religious Experience."

Diane said, "I heard Bill married a Hollywood movie star."

"Probably another nut job," Max replied.

"That may be," Shunya said. "But the man earned what he got. Despite our measure of him, he also made the journey to the East; and he also risked his life to discover the truth about himself."

All agreed before turning their attention to the subject of Doctor Chandra, who had died in 1982. Only forty-eight years old, he had a heart attack while traveling through Europe, discoursing on the virtue of silent mind.

"He was a great man," Shunya said, eyeing another gulab jaman; he had already eaten three.

"A truly wise man," Max said, swallowing a spoonful of rice pudding. "But not completely integrated."

"Because he didn't meet up with your expectations?" Shunya challenged.

"Because he didn't meet up to his own promises," Max shot back.

A familiar philosophical debate was about to be entered into until Diane nipped it in the bud, declaring, "He's been dead so long. What does it matter now?"

In fact, all the great gurus they had known had died—Kenchi Baba, Puri Baba, the old lama—and none of their successors held any particular interest for them.

Max said, "I don't think people should have gurus when they get older."

"How old?" Shunya pressed.

"Old enough to know better," Diane replied. She agreed with Max. "The parent is the guru, for better or worse. And your own pain is still your best teacher. Seeking guidance I can understand—on a timely or measured basis or in the throes of a life crisis—but not blind devotion to anyone outside of your own family. At some point you must take responsibility for who you are and what you have created."

"You mean Max can't have a guru, and we can because we have children and he doesn't?" Shunya asked.

"I mean at some point in life you have to look at what you have created—whether it's children, or books, or a job, or a house—and say: *this is mine, this is who I am, this is what I believe, this is how I live and love. This is how I suffer. This is how I die.* And you become the guru, the witness to your own becoming—for better or worse—and you take responsibility for your own actions. If you don't know the difference between what's right and what's wrong by the time you're fifty years old—who and what's good and bad—and how to suffer your own shortcomings and everyone else's, you don't need a guru; you don't even need a lobotomy, because you're already an idiot."

Max laughed, raised his beer glass to the ceiling, and offered a toast. "The guru is dead. Long live the guru!"

Shunya could hardly press the point any longer; it was so well defined by Diane and delivered with such passion. "To the guru of our own becoming," he added.

*   *   *

Rich Tom's part in all the madness and mayhem was never revealed. When confronted about his likely CIA affiliation, Rich Tom vehemently denied it: he did stay at the Ansari Guest House in Kabul, he did know Dean and Dennis, he even admitted to sharing a room with David Appel. But he wouldn't tell anyone why he had lied about it. Over time, Shunya was forced to think better of him in deference to Carol. After all, Tom did loan them the money to buy a house in San Rafael. Still rich, he had become a successful author and self-help guru.

The table had just been cleared when Carol finally arrived. She was a handsome woman. Still tall and thin with long, straight silver hair. But her good looks belied her insecurities. She was highly self-conscious, and not very comfortable in a roomful of strangers. She hardly knew Max and Diane, having met them only in passing following their return from India nearly thirty years ago. She had never met Anjuna, and she had an awkward relationship with Grace, who grew up thinking that Carol had taken her father away from her.

"I just had to come to meet you all," she awkwardly reiterated after a lengthy exchange of greetings. She had planned on meeting Shunya and Govinda at another location after dinner.

"You can still have dessert," Max said. "It's not too late."

Carol managed a nervous smile and said, "No, no, I don't want to interrupt."

She looked across the table at Govinda and widened her smile, then looked down the table at Grace, hoping her smile would be returned.

Grace left her seat, walked behind Carol's chair, wrapped her arms around her shoulders and said, "It's not an interruption, Carol, it's our pleasure." She knew that Carol was a mother who had come to New York to see her son off to war.

It was magnanimous gesture. In fact, Carol was a mess. Always fearing for her son's life, she had taken many pills and required a great deal of therapy over the past few years. Facing Govinda's third tour of duty, she could hardly sleep, let alone eat.

Max looked at Govinda and said, "Maybe you'll get lucky and your orders will be changed."

Govinda said, "It's not a matter of luck, Max, it's my job. Besides, I received my orders yesterday. I'm going back in two weeks."

Despite all the ensuing hopeful and animated talk, the night eventually ended on a somber note.

End

It was a sunny fall day in Northern California. Max and Shunya and Diane were sitting beside the Pacific Ocean on Stinson Beach. They had just returned from Govinda's cremation. As Shunya had feared, Govinda was killed in action in Afghanistan. Anjuna and Grace decided to remain behind at Shunya's house in San Rafael with Carol, who was inconsolable.

Shunya was holding a letter from Govinda in his hands. "It's the last thing he wrote. We found it on his laptop when the Navy returned his things to us."

Shunya read the letter aloud, fighting back tears:

Dear Mom and Dad,

I decided to write this because I think I would have a hard time talking to you about a lot of this stuff, and make you worry too much. I feel okay most of the time, but sometimes I feel really tired, exhausted actually. I'm in the middle of my third tour of duty here, and I don't like it very much because it's the same thing all the time, two steps forward and two steps back. It's getting harder and harder to see the progress here. The summer's coming again, and the place starts to smell like a toilet in a lot of places, especially the bigger towns. It can get really hot in the helicopter. Bad as that is, I can't imagine what it's like on the ground wearing all that field gear. It's just so hard on the infantry, and really dangerous, walking around the streets.

I guess things are almost easy for me compared to those guys. All I do is fly, press buttons, hit targets, and return to base. It's a bit more intense than that sometimes, but that's the gist of it. Overall, the Afghanis seem like nice people, like a lot of other people in the world that don't want to be at war with anyone, but I think they're getting tired of the fight. Almost everyone has a family member or a friend that was killed or wounded by this war, and, like I said, nothing REALLY changes.

The boredom's another thing. I spend too much time sitting around watching TV, working out, playing video games, and trying to avoid all the gung-ho stuff I hear from the new guys. Sometimes I think that's the worst of it, going into action for three hours, then spending all that down time pretending I'm in America. The contrast can be so weird, extreme actually—at least for me it is.

The truth is that I can't wait to leave here and move on with my life outside the military. It seems I've gone from one bad relationship to another ever since I've been in the military, and I have to wonder whether the problem's with me is not being grounded—literally. Be nice to settle down somewhere with someone. The truth is also that I'm becoming afraid, because I'm not so interested in what I'm doing anymore, and it's really easy to lose focus, and get hurt on the job.

It is just a job for me now, not a duty to my country, and I do get paid well for it. But the more the more I have, the more afraid I am of making a mistake and losing it all. I'm actually becoming afraid of dying, which is why you'll never really read this letter because it would freak you both out. It freaks me out to write it, because I'm also afraid that by writing about it I might make it real.

I even spoke to Sayadaw about it at the last meditation course. I took in Bodh Gaya. It's also hard to believe how much I've come to like India, all the craziness and stuff

that Dad always talks about with Max and Diane. The
more I think about it, the more I wonder if I wouldn't
have been happier as a kid growing up in the sixties just
wandering around for awhile and not worrying so much. I
think that I'm beginning to worry too much, which is also
why I'm writing this.

As always, Sayadaw told me to relax and observe and
maintain the practice so I can be mindful on the job. I've
been reading the Bhagavad-Gita again and other books
like that, and I remembered meeting this wealthy Brahmin
after the Sayadaw course in Bodh Gaya. I told him that I
was a pilot in the American Navy and he smiled and said,
"Kshatriya." I didn't pay much attention to it until recently. I didn't understand it. Have to go now.

I just spent two hours having dinner with some buddies, and a few Congressmen who started pontificating
about democracy, telling us how noble we are putting our
butts on the line for the great cause that they wouldn't let
their own sons and daughters fight for. I just don't feel
noble. The truth is, a lot of the older guys think about
going home all the time. Hard to believe that I'm 31 and
I've been at war for 6 years—not all the time, but it seems
like forever when I remember telling you how much I
wanted to kill people. I guess that I was really young and
dumb.

Maybe I'm old enough now to have perspective on
things, especially on life, how precious it is, how one guy
gets killed or hurt and the guy next to him doesn't. It
poses so many questions, but I do feel a lot better about
myself when I look for the answers, like when I take the
time to internalize all this stuff, and meditate on the idea
of taking a life or losing my own life in the process. I also
think that we should have more respect for our enemies,
even if we don't like them, if only because they're willing
to fight and die for what they believe in—like the Ameri-

can Indians did. Even they worshipped some of their enemies.

Anyway, this kind of stuff has been on my mind lately, like becoming Kshatriya, a noble warrior of the spirit, and fighting to recognize a higher calling than my country right or wrong. I also started to think a lot about the process or becoming self-realized as a soldier—if it's at all possible, like Arjuna on the battlefield in the Bhagavad-Gita talking to Lord Krishna.

As if God's going to appear before me and sit me down for a talk in my Cobra? Anyway, when I looked up Kshatriya, I came up with a couple of interesting things, how Kshatriyas will only attack if they are attacked first, which is hardly the stuff of this war.

I just don't see the nobility in it anymore, and I guess I do have to find it within myself.

It's two days later and I just reread this thing, and I freaked myself out by reading it because it sounds like I'm saying goodbye in some way, maybe to my lower self, I hope. Now I'm thinking that the money isn't so important. I already saved enough money for awhile, and maybe I'll just kick around a bit, and go back to India when my tour is up, and visit all the places that Dad always talked about with Max and Diane. Or come back to New York again, to that Indian restaurant for another dinner and talk about all this stuff to everyone.

I guess I am getting older when I start thinking about Max and Diane as friends, and I'm not so pissed off at my parents any more. But the strangest thoughts I've have to be about re-upping which is really surprising to me to because I can't wait to get out most of the time. When I began this letter a few days go, it was all I was thinking about. Now I think that maybe that it wouldn't be so bad to be stationed somewhere else, in the States somewhere, and train younger guys to fly, and maybe I can even talk some of them into re-examining their own lives, becoming warriors of the spirit instead of dumb cogs in the wheel of, 'Yes sir, my country right or wrong', or simply stupid.

I also read the Art Of War the other day, which was really interesting and amazing to me that so many people so long ago thought so much about war, about trying to take it to a higher plane. I mean, having no wars would be really nice, but there are some really bad people out there, and someone's got to fight them. It's just a matter of trying to keep it all in perspective, to cherish your own life and even the lives you're taking—until you get to the point that you become so conscious that you can't do it anymore, and you transcend good and bad and merge with God.

The simple truth is that I don't want to do it anymore. and maybe I shouldn't want to teach others how to do it. Obviously, I'm more than a little conflicted about the whole thing, the military, the war, my place in all of it.

It's almost a week later, and I've been on two more missions, and I'm even more conflicted over so many things, staying in the military or leaving, having money and not having so much, finding God or myself in the process, or just wanting to settle down in a relationship.

Something else happened too. I had this incredible dream last night, like nothing I ever had in my life before. It was so strange and so beautiful. I was flying a helicopter. It was at night. It was really dark out, and I remember telling myself that I needed a flashlight or something. Then I started looking on the dashboard for a way to turn on the headlights—as if I were driving a car.

I was on a secret mission of some kind, and I reminded myself that I have to keep a low profile and fly by radar. But there was no radar screen, and I was afraid that I was going to crash into the side of a mountain. I was flying alone, no co-pilot or anything, and there were no other helicopters in the formation.

I was going to turn back—it was getting so dark—when all of a sudden I came under attack, all these lights, these missiles were coming at me from the ground. I was about to take evasive action when they passed right by me, dozens of them. Then I realized that they were tracer bullets, hundreds of them flying by me up into the sky.

It was beautiful actually, and all of a sudden I realized that I couldn't be killed, so I sort of leaned back in my chair and watched the bullets, all different colors flying by me up into the sky and turning into stars! It was amazing. Then I heard this buzzing sound, and I became really confused, really scared. I remember wanting to go home, and the strangest thing happened. I saw this woman. I was looking up at the sky—it was pitch black—and I saw this incredibly beautiful women. She had black hair, and she was smiling at me, coming closer to me.

She was smiling and she had these really big black eyes. I remember flying higher to get a better look, and she gesturing to me, spreading her arms. But it was her eyes. I was captivated by her eyes, and they got bigger and bigger.

All of a sudden I was face to face with her in the sky, looking into her eyes, and my body exploded into sensation. Then I fell through her eyes, and I merged with her somehow. For one moment, we were like one person, one soul, and there was this big golden halo around us, and I knew what it was like to be in love, really in love. Then I began to fall toward the ground.

There was a big fire, and I felt like I was burning, like the whole world was burning, and I got really scared again. When I looked up in the sky to find the woman, I heard a voice—her voice, I think—and she said, 'Don't worry, our Father will come for us soon.' And all I could think about was going to Bodh Gaya and sitting beneath the Bodhi Tree. I began to imagine I was sitting there in the sunken garden; the whole sky was turning to gold, like a halo. It changed me in a way I can't explain, and I can't stop thinking about it. Duty calls. Talk to you again later.

"He went into action again somewhere in Southern Afghanistan," Shunya explained. "He was killed fighting the Taliban just a few hours after writing the last entry, and now we're thinking about taking his ashes to India, to Bodh Gaya, because of the dream."

"Amazing," Diane said, weeping as she spoke. "He was truly blessed by the intensity of his own becoming, his desire to transcend himself."

Max nodded and echoed her sentiment. "He died in the process of finding himself on the battlefield of his own life."

"It's nice to hear, but it's hard to accept that he had to go fight this god-damned war and lose his life to find his soul," Shunya agonized, tears now falling from his eyes as successive waves broke and rippled into the shore. "It's just so hard for me to believe that Govinda's gone, that he's never coming back to us, never seeing the sky again or the sun or the ocean, never having another chance at anything and. . . ."

Shunya's voice trailed off in pain, and the three were joined as one to the heart-wrenching silence.

Hereafter

Three months later, Max and Diane accompanied Shunya to India, to Bodh Gaya, where they spread Govinda's ashes around the Bodhi tree at sunset.

"It's the least I could do for him," Shunya said before leaving the sunken garden with a heavy heart.

No matter how hard he tried, nothing could mollify his pain. The past few months had been so hard on Carol and him that it was destroying their marriage. She was so grief-stricken that she couldn't make the journey to India.

"I just wish I could find a way to believe in God again, and accept Govinda's passing on faith," Shunya added, his eyes filling with tears as he looked back at the Bodhi-tree. "I try, God knows I try, and I want to believe that Govinda's soul has already moved on to another life, into the arms of another loving family. I want to believe that. I tell Carol that, but . . ."

Shunya's voice trailed off in pain; Max and Diane placed their arms around his shoulders. It was a familiar ritual that always helped and never healed.

"Maybe you should come with us and see if the process of revisiting the past can't be of help somehow," Max said. He and Diane were planning a trip to Almora and Rajasthan.

"If I felt better about myself I would, but I don't. I don't feel worthy of joy."

"Where will you go?" Diane pressed.

"Home if I can, home to my heart."

Max and Diane feared he might take his own life, but Shunya assured them that he would not. "I still have a daughter and a wife. I just have to find a place in my heart for my son that's without grief, a place where I know that he is at peace, and I have to do this alone."

Begrudgingly, Max and Diane left Bodh Gaya the following morning, bickering in the back of a taxi over who was going to get the window seat on the train to Delhi.

"I get the window because I bought the tickets," Max declared.

"With your rich girlfriend's money," Diane snapped.

In the end, some things never changed.

*   *   *

It was a long walk up the one hundred and eight steps to the wheel of life atop Swayambhunath, each step denoting a path to the God that Shunya prayed to, yet never answered. Of all the experiences in his life, the timely meetings with the old lama were the most precious and indelible, so special that he never mentioned them to anyone.

It was a dark night. The faint light of the waning moon was hardly visible. The valley below was dotted with the light from many kerosene lamps and small clusters of light bulbs. Mount Everest, still visible in the faintest light, soared above the northeastern horizon. The cool mountain air would have been invigorating if Shunya weren't so infirm, clutching at his chest and gasping for breath after every few steps, jeered at by monkeys each time he sat on a step to take rest.

He knew he could have a heart attack, but he was driven by instinct and despair, hoping that his effort would be rewarded with some kind of insight or vision that would heighten his understanding or stem the pain of his loss, something he could share with Carol upon his return to America.

It took an hour and a half for him to reach the top of Swayambhunath. His heart was beating so fast when he arrived at the temple that he thought it would explode. He also lacked the strength to turn the huge Tibetan prayer wheel, and spent another half hour trying to catch his breath, breathing rhythmically and deeply until he finally entered the temple.

As always, Shunya pressed his palms together and bowed to the magnificent gilded Buddha at the center of the room. The light of a thousand butter lamps flickered in his eyes. When he sank to his knees and looked up, the wrathful deities painted on the ceiling began to swirl in his eyes.

He was losing consciousness when a bony, old hand gripped his shoulder.

Shunya thought it was the old lama and mustered the strength to remain conscious and said, "I thought you died. You must have died."

The lama smiled. He was a slight man, in his seventies, Shunya guessed, with a shaved head. But he did look as old as old as Shunya remembered.

"I don't understand," Shunya added.

The lama sank to his knees, wrapped his burgundy robe across his chest and explained, "My master died many years ago. I am Tensing, the disciple, and you are not well it seems. I was told you were in here, and that you may be in need of some help."

Shunya nodded and clutched his chest. "It's my heart; it's breaking from the loss of my son."

The disciple studied Shunya's face before closing his eyes for a moment. Opening them, he smiled brightly and exclaimed, "I remember you now as a young man! I was told to remember. I was told to help you if you returned, and I am here for you now as my master wanted."

Shunya tried to speak, but was stymied by a rush of emotion and began to weep.

The disciple said, "It is always this pain that is taking us home to our heart. It is the beginning of life to cry out for it, and the end of life to cry over it."

"If I could only accept the pain; but I can't because I can't understand it, and I'm afraid my son's soul won't come to rest until I make peace with myself."

The disciple nodded. "I am afraid that it is not for us to understand the cycle of birth and death. It is for us to find the path to end the suffering by surrendering the mind to the heart and embracing this pain."

"I can't," Shunya sobbed. "I just can't."

The disciple said, "If you can dream you can, if you are not afraid to dream. If you can find the courage to enter the dream and slay the dragon that has become your fear of life and death, you can be free of this great pain."

The disciple looked up, and Shunya followed his eyes to a fire-breathing dragon painted on the ceiling.

"If you can help me," Shunya said.

"If you will trust me," the disciple said. "If you can close your eyes and see this pain."

Shunya closed his eyes, gasped for breath, and looked into his heart beating too fast and irregularly. He was afraid that he was going to die when he heard the prayer wheel spinning outside the temple, and was reminded of the sound of a helicopter: *my son's helicopter*, he thought.

He saw it flying through his mind against a brilliant blue sky and smiled to himself thinking Govinda was still alive—until he saw the enemy missile find its mark. Horrified, Shunya watched the helicopter crash and burn on the desert floor, at the edge of a nondescript town. His mind screamed *NO!* as he ran to save his son from the flames.

But the heat was too great and the flames were too high; then he heard the sound of gunfire and bullets whizzing by his head. Now fearing for his own life, Shunya was about to turn and run when he was seized by the greater power of love. He plunged headlong into the fiery wreckage, burning alive in his mind, and searched for Govinda.

Shunya was crying out in pain—wandering blindly through the flames—when he found the broken body of his son, and was joined to his soul as it ascended heaven into the heart of God.

For whoever holds something truly dear—be it God, a dream, or another human being—they hold the world.

Glossary

akhara: an organization of different sects of sadhus or Hindu ascetics.

akashic record: psychic record of human history.

asana: a body position typically associated with the practice of yoga.

atman: soul.

Avatar: embodied manifestation of God.

Bhagavad-Gita: foremost Hindu spiritual text. Excerpt from ancient epic poem, *The Mahabharat*. Dialogue between Lord Krishna and Arjuna on the battlefield of Life wherein various processes of

self-realization are revealed.

bhajan: religious songs.

bidi: Indian cigarette.

bhi: brother.

bhakti: devotional form of worship. A path of yoga. Dualistic relationship (guru-disciple, God-devotee) culminating in unity through surrender to divine will.

bodhisattva: Buddhist sage who defers enlightenment until all beings are enlightened.

Brahma: creator of universe. First person of Hindu trilogy.

Buzkashi: national game of horsemanship in Afghanistan.

burka: an all-enveloping cloak worn by some Muslim women.

chador: a veil and or shawl worn by Muslim and Hindu women held together with there hands. A loose robe often worn by Muslim women that covers the body from head to toe.

chakra(s): seven centers of psychic energy in subtle body.

Chapendas: horsemen of the buzkashi game.

chillum: small clay cone pipe generally used in smoking hemp or hashish.

chota: small.

chowkidar: watchman, caretaker.

dacoit: member of a gang or robber band in India.

darshan: blessing often given by guru upon seeing him.

Dharmapada: virtue, righteousness. Verses of righteousness as spoken by Lord Buddha. Foot of the Dharma.

Dharma: law, righteousness. Virtuous law of life as disclosed by Lord Buddha.

dharamsala: two-story rectangular building with an inner courtyard.

dhoti: unstitched cloth (usually white) worn by men. Wrapped around lower torso and passed between legs.

duni: small open fire maintained by sadhus in honor of the gods.

Durga: Hindu goddess of fire; austerity.

ek lak: 100,000 rupees.

Ganesh: elephant-headed God of success. Son of Lord Shiva and Parvati.

ghat: steps leading down to river's edge

ji: mister.

jhola: purse, handbag.

Hanuman: monkey god. Embodiment of devotion, servant to Lord Rama.

Hinayana: the more orthodox, conservative school of Buddhism.

I Ching: ancient Chinese oracle. Book of wisdom.

Kali: consort of Lord Shiva. Dark principled goddess. Aspect denoting destruction (of ignorance).

karma: action. Automatic reciprocal action. "One sows what one reaps." To be bound by.

Kit-na bhaji: What time is it?

Krishna: incarnation of second aspect of Hindu trinity (Vishnu). Embodiment of love.

Kriya: system of yoga encompassing various modes of purification (bodily).

Kshatriya: "Royal caste." Warrior class in ancient Hindu social structure. Noble warriors of the spirit.

Kumbh (kumbha): large, great, grand.

Kundalini: psychic energy force located at base of spine often characterized by image of coiled serpent. Form of yoga wherein this serpent force is activated and rises up the spinal column opening up various chakras in its ascent to crown of head.

Lakshmi: goddess of wealth and beauty.

lila: divine game, play of life.

lingotti: length of cotton tied between legs to make and underwear garment.

lota: brass cup.

lungi: three yards of unstitched cloth worn by men—similar to a sarong.

mala: holy necklace, similar to rosary.

mandala: a circular design emanating from a center point. Artistic representation of subtle energy force(s). Can be used in visual meditation to apprehend the wholeness that lies beneath the differentiations in life.

Mahatma: highly evolved soul. Spiritual father. Respectful term for saintly person.

mantra: a single syllable or combination thereof discovered and developed in ancient times. When repeated can activate psychic body and bring about inner harmony. Passive yoga.

maya: illusion. Veils of deception enveloping causal planes.

mela: religious festival.

memsahib: A form of respectful address for a European woman in colonial India.

mudra: symbolic gesture of hands and/or body representative of various subtle energy states.

Murti: image. Idol of deity.

Naga Baba: sadhu or wandering monk, generally found naked.

namaskar: respectful Indian greeting.

namaste: common Indian greeting.

netti, netti: not this, not this. Hindu concept defining "negative" progression of consciousness, trying one path to awareness, then another in the quest for knowledge.

nirvakalpa: highest state of consciousness in the yogic path wherein an individual soul absolutely merges with universal soul.

pashmina: very fine texture of wool derived from the Iver mountain goat.

pajami: baggy white cotton pants with draw string; Yoga pants.

puja: ritual of worship.

Rama: embodiment of righteousness. Avatar of Vishnu, husband of Sita.

Ramayana: epic religious poem characterizing the life of Lord Rama, and other members of the Hindu pantheon of gods and goddesses.

rishi: sage or wise man.

sahib: A form of respectful address for a European man in colonial India.

sadhana: spiritual "work." Striving for god realization.

sadhu: Hindu ascetic; wandering monk.

samadhi: state of super consciousness.

samsara: world of desire and disillusionment.

sari: five yards of un-stitched cloth worn by women.

satsang: communion; gathering of those who share in truthfulness.

shakti: energy. Female (receptive) energy.

shakti-pat: initiatory supercharged energy transferred from guru to disciple.

Shiva: third aspect of Hindu trinity. Destroyer of the universe. Destroyer of illusion.

Shivaratri: night of Lord Shiva. Festival in celebra-tion of his birth occurring during the dark moon phase in the month of February.

siddha: one who has accomplished an evolved state of consciousness through practice of yoga. One with great power.

Glossary

siddhi: talents, projections or powers a yogi attains with practice of yoga.

Stupa: Buddhist commemorative monument.

Swami: master. Title of reverence.

Tantra: union of opposites (male and female). Yoga path of realization that can include utilization of sexual act as vehicle toward higher consciousness.

tantric: used in story as colloquial expression denoting or hinting at possible esoteric meaning behind common daily (sensuous) act.

tapas: austerity(s). Purification by fire.

tashi delek: traditional Tibetan greeting.

tonga: horse-drawn carriage.

tonka: religious Tibetan painting.

Trimurti: Hindu trinity composed of Brahma-Vishnu-Shiva.

Vedas: ancient spiritual writings (philosophy) upon which Hindu religion is based.

Vishnu: second aspect of Hindu Trimurti. The preserver. Sustainer of life.

Yeti: alleged half man, half beast alive in Himalayas.

yoga: union, practice of culminating in spiritual union.